VEIL OF CIVILITY

a Black Shuck thriller

IAN GRAHAM

KIRKGRIM
BOOKS

www.iangrahamthrillers.com

VEIL OF CIVILITY: A BLACK SHUCK THRILLER

Copyright © 2013 by Ian Matthew Graham

Published by:
Kirkgrim Books
P.O. Box 511
Cloverdale, VA 24077

Published in the United States of America

Cover design by Jane Dixon-Smith (www.jdsmith-design.co.uk)

Author Photo by Colin Graham

To Kinley, whose birth provided the inspiration
to make this project a reality and whose little life
continues to inspire me every day

PROLOGUE I

Eight Years Ago – Late September 2004
United States – Mexican Border
Near Yuma, Arizona

Juan Izek Ramirez unscrewed the cap on the two liter thermos and splashed warm water onto his face, washing away a thick layer of dirt. He took a quick sip before handing the bottle to his son, Ignacio, who did the same before turning with his father to face the twelve men behind them.

"Señores, we are almost there," Juan said. "Now is when we must be the most careful. If you need water or a brief rest now is the time. Once we cross, we will not be able to stop until we meet your friends."

As soon as he'd seen these men, Juan's gut feeling had been to run; something about them scared him. In the end his common sense had won out over his fear. Had he followed his gut, he'd have had to explain to the men who'd hired him why he'd run, then face the punishment, which was not a pleasant thought since he was certain they were members of one of the many cartels active in the area. Instead, he'd decided to fulfill the terms of his employment and guide the men fourteen miles across the Goldwater Bombing Range to State Route 195, just south of Yuma, Arizona. There someone would be waiting to take them on into the city, at which point Juan hoped he'd never see them again.

His announcement was met with several throaty groans.

They'd been walking for three hours, two hours east and one hour north, and now stood one hundred yards from the Mexican border with the United States of America, a trampled chain-link fence the only evidence that they were about to enter another country. With a little less than half the journey done, the men already looked ragged from the morning heat; they lowered themselves slowly to the dirt and opened canteens.

The twelve men had left La Choya shortly after one o'clock in the morning and traveled north in a two car caravan for three hours, then in the minute town of Las Adelitas, Juan and his son had been waiting, as instructed. Their job should have been simple. They'd been hired to guide the men across the U.S. border on foot and avoid law enforcement patrols at all costs; something Juan had been doing for nearly two decades. What should have been easy money had turned into anything but as soon as he'd laid eyes on the twelve. Their pale complexions, dark features and thick accents told him that he wasn't dealing with other Mexicans or South Americans, as he was accustomed, but an ethnicity that he was unfamiliar with, one he had not yet seen crossing into the States.

He avoided eye contact while quickly surveying the faces in front of him. Each was red from the sun that had been blazing down for just over an hour and beads of sweat rolled off their foreheads. They'd been overdressed for the journey and he'd had to tell them to leave behind much of what they'd brought. Dressed like American tourists and carrying large backpacks, they'd been a guaranteed giveaway to law enforcement. After getting them new clothes from his house they looked much better. In white T-shirts, torn blue jeans and plaid button-down shirts, most of which had been shed and tied around their waists, they looked more like the migrant crop pickers Juan would claim they were if approached. He could tell they were uncomfortable in the heat and it was taking its toll on them, but they looked healthy, no signs of heatstroke. Based on the guttural-sounding language they spoke to each other he thought they were some kind of Europeans, perhaps Slovakians or Romanians, but he wasn't sure. All he knew for sure was that they were accustomed to a much colder climate, and it showed.

"Let us go now, señores. We must not keep your friends waiting."

"Why must we leave so quickly?" a heavily accented voice asked. Juan wasn't sure which of the men had spoken, but the hostility in the voice made him feel cold in spite of the glaring sun.

"Señores, if we want to make it to our destination we must avoid being seen. We must move as quickly as possible."

Begrudgingly the twelve men got to their feet. In single file, they followed Juan and Ignacio over the battered fence and into the desert beyond. Juan had chosen to use the edge of the Goldwater Bombing Range, an expansive property owned by the U.S. Military and used for munitions testing, to cross north to the highway. As long as they were on the range they would not have to worry about the Border Patrol that had largely succeeded in closing Arizona's border. The U.S. military was responsible for the range and seldom patrolled it.

Once over the border, the men walked at a quick pace across the desert. Juan kept a close eye on the horizon to their left. While they didn't have to worry about running directly into any border guards, they did have to worry about being seen from a distance. Scanning, his hand shading his eyes, Juan saw nothing that alarmed him; only rocky sand broken up by occasional sagebrush or cactus.

Allowing himself to fall back towards the rear of the group, Juan let his sixteen-year-old son take the lead. At the back of the group the youngest looking of the twelve walked briskly to stay in step with the others. Although he knew better than to ask questions, Juan was curious about where they were from and this man seemed the most approachable. His face and arms were unscarred, the borrowed clothes hung loose from his thin frame and the intensity that seemed to radiate from the other eleven was absent.

"Señor, you are okay? The journey is not too much?" Juan asked quietly.

The young man regarded him coldly for a moment, looking him up and down, his eyes moving rapidly as if he was searching for something. For a moment Juan thought he'd made a mistake. Perhaps the man was older and more experienced than he'd thought.

"I am fine," the young man finally responded. "How much further?"

"We will be at the edge of the road in a little less than three hours. It is not hot where you are from?"

"No. In the Caucasus it is colder, and the sun...I have never felt it like this."

"It is because of the sand, señor. The sun reflects off of it and makes it feel even hotter. Where is this place you speak of?"

"The Republic of Ichkeria is in the southern part of what westerners call Russia, but it once belonged to its own people, to us, and if Allah wills, it will soon belong to us again," the man said, holding up the index finger on his right hand.

"Enough!" boomed a voice from up ahead. The entire group stopped moving and Juan looked forward. All of the men stared at him.

"Your job is to take us where we want to go. Not to ask questions!" a tall man with a long scar down the left side of his face yelled as he stalked towards Juan.

"I am sorry, señor. I meant no disrespect," Juan said, his eyes lowered to the sand. He gripped his hands together to keep them from shaking as the man stared down at him. Juan could feel his hot breath on his forehead.

"From now on you walk, not talk!" the man yelled, then turned his attention towards the young man who Juan had been speaking with.

"*Nasil bu kadar aptal olabilir!*" *How could you be so stupid,* he screamed and back-handed the young man, nearly knocking him to the ground. Tugging him along by the collar, he pushed him forward before turning again to stare at Juan. "*Kafkasya'da size olu olacakti,*" *You would be dead in the Caucasus,* he hissed as he gently pushed Juan forward. Juan could feel the man's eyes on him, all the way to the head of the group.

"Let us keep going then, señores," Juan said, his voice quivering. He didn't know what the man had said, but he knew it was a threat and that these were the type of men that would carry it out. He turned and started walking, mouthing a prayer as he trudged through the sand.

Nearly three hours later Juan clasped his hand on Ignacio's shoulder as the edge of a road came into view. "State Route 195," he said, pointing. Soon he'd be rid of these awful men.

The road before them turned sharply north and waiting in the bend was a battered passenger van, its paint scratched and chipped away. Juan and Ignacio kept a careful eye on their surroundings as they approached. When they were within fifty yards of the van they stopped.

"Here is where we leave you, señores," Juan said. "Your ride is waiting."

Eleven of the men brushed past him without a word, but the tall man with the scar stopped. Juan held his breath as the man stared. Two men emerged from the van and opened the side doors as the party approached. Within seconds the eleven men were inside and hidden by deeply tinted windows.

"What are you waiting for?" one of the men next to the van yelled. He spoke the same language as the scarred man and though Juan could not understand what was being said, the message was obvious: "We need to leave now!"

The scarred man continued to stare without a word. Juan crossed himself and the man scoffed. "You would be dead in the Caucasus," he spat as he walked away, turning briefly to kick sand at them.

Juan watched intently as the man arrived at the van, slapped shoulders with the two drivers and disappeared into the vehicle. Moments later the van pulled onto the highway, its rear wheels churning sand and dust as it crossed from the coarse earth to the smoothly paved road. As it drove north and faded into the distance, Juan turned and looked at his son, whose face was ashen.

Speaking their native Spanish and crossing himself again, he said, "Let us pray for the souls of the Americans those men have come to kill."

"Yes," Ignacio responded. "Let us also ask God to forgive us for showing them the way."

PROLOGUE II

Two Weeks Ago
Ognenny Ostrov Prison – 650 miles north of Moscow
Lake Novozero – Vologda Oblast, Russia

Deputy Director Antonin Turov waited impatiently as the small motorboat edged ashore, its outboard motor tilted up due to the shallow water at the edge of the island. The two Federal Penitentiary Service sergeants in the boat with him pushed hard against the stony lake floor with wooden oars, trying their best to ensure their superior would not get wet as he exited. The craft grounded and Turov stepped off without a word, leaving the two subordinates with the boat as he strutted up a gravel pathway with his hands behind his back. His breath evaporated in frozen puffs as a light snow fell, dusting the top of his fur hat.

Stopping in front of a twelve foot high chain-link gate topped with spiraled razor wire, he looked up at a thick waterproof canvas covering that concealed the clustered buildings beyond. Only a few tall spires could be seen above the fencing that surrounded the compound. A uniformed guard stood at either side of the gate, Kalashnikov rifles held at the ready across their chests.

Fire Island, Turov thought with an amused smile as he waited for the guards to approach. The name was due to some religious fanatic who claimed to have seen a pillar of fire strike the island over five hundred years ago. At the hands of the sheep, who flocked anytime someone claimed to see an apparition or some other supposed sign from God, the island had quickly become home to a monastery. Monks had existed there for centuries until 1917 when the Bolsheviks had captured it and converted it to a prison to hold their enemies. It had remained a prison ever since and, in Turov's opinion, a prison was a much more fitting use of its nearly impenetrable medieval architecture.

"*Kto tam?*" one of the guards barked in Russian as the two approached. *Who's there?*

"*Zam nachalnika* Antonin Turov," the director responded sharply, "*pozvol'te mne proiti!*" *Deputy Director Antonin Turov, let me through!*

The guards took in the uniformed man in front of them and snapped to attention before responding, "Yes, sir!"

"Open the gate," one of the guards yelled up to the watchtowers positioned on either side of the entrance.

A buzzing alarm filled the air as pneumatic gears ground and the gate began to separate in the middle. Turov stepped inside the compound and was met by two more guards who had been sitting inside a tiny shack beside one of the watchtowers. A thick plume of white smoke poured from the shack's tin chimney and the air smelled of burning wood.

"I am Lieutenant Rostislav Kutzow. How may we help you, comrade deputy director?" the commanding guard announced as he approached and stood at attention. Behind Turov, the gate screeched closed.

Turov drew his thick frame up and squared his shoulders. "Take me to the warden."

"Yes, sir," the lieutenant said, saluting before he turned and marched toward the grouping of non-descript two story buildings, painted white to camouflage them against the surrounding area. All evidence of the facility's former pious use had been erased by nearly one hundred years spent housing the motherland's worst criminals. Traitors, defectors, spies and Nazis had all been imprisoned here and most had died within these walls, their remains buried in shallow graves on neighboring islands. Since the last years of the twentieth century the facility, referred to in Russian as *pyatak*, had housed only those prisoners whose crimes had earned them a death sentence.

Once someone was committed to Fire Island they did not leave, not even after their sentence had been carried out. Instead of their remains being returned to relatives, their bodies were burned in an incinerator along with the facility's trash. But that would change tonight. For the price of one million euros, Antonin Turov, one of six Deputy Directors of Russia's Federal Penitentiary Service, had arranged for a prisoner to exit the facility and disappear into the wilderness beyond.

As the lieutenant ahead of him unhooked a set of keys from his belt and approached a heavy metal door, the sound of it being unlocked from within surprised him. Moments later a stern looking man in a neatly pressed uniform emerged. The lieutenant snapped to attention and saluted without a word, staying completely still as the man looked him up and down before moving his gaze to Turov. A knowing look crossed his face and he gave the director a curt nod. He was the prison's warden and his assistance had only cost twenty five thousand euros.

"Colonel Vitaly Kupchenko, I presume?" Turov asked.

"Get lost," the warden barked at the lieutenant, who was on the move before his superior's breath had evaporated in the frigid air. "Yes. I am he," he said to Turov, before he turned back towards the metal door and disappeared inside.

Turov decided to let the warden's lack of proper recognition of his superior slide for the moment and followed him into the prison.

Once he was inside the warden slammed the door shut and locked it. Water ran from Turov's eyes immediately as the smell overwhelmed him. A mixture of what he could only imagine was feces, urine and human decay assaulted his nostrils. He removed his fur hat and held it to his face to avoid being sick, the smell of his sweaty head preferable to the stench of the prison. The warden seemed unfazed. He walked ahead of Turov and led him deeper into the prison.

The floor was unfinished wood and creaked bitterly as the two heavy-set men passed over it. The walls were constructed of a rough plaster, painted green on the bottom half and white on the top, although it had obviously been many years since it had been properly maintained. In many places bare wood was visible, the plaster chipped away. Turov imagined the bare spots could easily have been caused by the heads of inmates being struck against the wall; brutality was commonplace throughout the Russian prison system, especially this far from Moscow's oversight.

"I must admit, comrade director, that I had second thoughts when you told me who it was that you wanted. I cannot imagine anyone having a use for this animal," the warden said, as they passed through another metal door, the slam as the warden closed it behind them echoing along the empty corridor.

"I have no use for him. Most likely he will be hunted like wild game, but that is not your concern."

"Yes, sir," the warden replied and handed Turov a thin olive green folder.

From there they walked in silence, twisting and turning through the prison corridors. On either side of them were white metal doors that marked the entrances to cells. Each door had a three inch by six inch slot through which prisoners would put their hands to be handcuffed, all now closed for the night. Occasionally they passed a larger open room where bored guards sat watching fuzzy television sets no bigger than Turov's open palm. The guards all stood suddenly and saluted as they passed.

After descending a switchback of a staircase that led into the facility's basement and walking another one hundred yards Turov could feel the heat from the incinerator, hear the constant roar coming from the end of the corridor. The warden approached a white door, unlocked the hand slide and barked an order. "Get up, filth! You have an appointment!"

Seconds later a pair of hands appeared through the slide and the warden removed a set of handcuffs from his belt, ratcheting them around the man's wrists before unlocking the heavy door and pulling it open. From the darkness within the cell a skinny man with a dark complexion emerged. He appeared to be hairless and was wearing a black and gray striped jumpsuit and matching hat that sat atop his bald head. Looking him up and down, Turov was surprised that someone would pay so much for his freedom, but his instructions had been clear. The mysterious, disembodied voice he had come to know as Levent Kahraman wanted the Chechen child killer, Ruslan Baktayev.

Turov couldn't imagine why anyone would want such a man. The only assurance he had asked for was that whatever Kahraman's purpose was, it would be fulfilled far from the borders of Mother Russia. Kahraman had agreed, the money had been real and the deposit untraceable, so it was Baktayev that Kahraman would get.

Unwinding the string that bound the olive green folder, Turov opened it. Inside was a dossier and a mug shot. He ignored the dossier and looked closely at the photo and then at Baktayev. It was hard to believe he was looking at the same man. Eight years inside the living hell that was Fire Island had a tendency to change a man. Although Baktayev did not appear to have ever been a heavy man, there were marked differences in his face; his skin was sallow and his eyes sunken, obvious signs of malnourishment. His clothes hung from his body like rags from a scarecrow. The warden pushed the man's chin up revealing the words *Cut Here* tattooed across his throat in Russian. This was the man Turov was looking for. He gave the warden a curt nod signifying his approval.

"Assume the position," the warden ordered.

Baktayev turned his back and bent over in silence.

The warden grabbed his handcuffed wrists and pushed them upwards into the air, holding him in a stress position. Pushing the prisoner forward in the same position all the way up the stairs, the warden made his way back to the door they had first entered, Turov following closely behind. Just before reaching the exit, the warden pushed Baktayev into a side room containing only a plain government issue desk, a telephone and two metal folding chairs. The warden shoved Baktayev into one of the chairs where he sat looking up at the two Russian officers, his eyes burning with hatred.

"So tonight I meet Allah?" he asked, his voice almost joyful.

The warden spat at the prisoner. "The only afterlife you will meet, you filth, is the angry souls of the fathers whose children you murdered."

Baktayev smiled as the spittle ran down his face, the toothy grin revealing a set of black teeth.

Turov walked behind the desk and picked up the telephone. Pressing several numbers, he waited for an answer. Baktayev and the warden listened as someone picked up on the other end and a voice gave instructions. After a few brief exchanges, Turov hung up and nodded at the warden who walked over to a tiny closet door, opened it and removed a small black package. "Get in," he said to Baktayev as he unrolled the package on the floor, revealing it to be a body bag. He pulled a knife from his uniform and made three small cuts near the head of the bag. "Get in, now."

Minutes later Turov and the warden emerged from the prison with two guards following them, the body bag being carried between them. They walked through the deepening snow to the front gates, which the warden ordered them to open. None of the guards even looked up as they passed; their orders were obvious. At Turov's boat, the body bag was carried aboard by the two sergeants who'd arrived with him and placed at the very front, where all three pairs of eyes could be on it as they made their way back across the lake.

Lastly, Turov withdrew a white envelope from the breast pocket of his crisp uniform and handed it to the warden, who opened it, peered inside and nodded before turning to walk back to the prison without a word. "*Soblyudaite subordinatsiyu!*" *Follow the chain of command!* Turov ordered, not letting the warden's disrespect slide this time. The warden froze in place, turned on his heel and saluted, a terrified look on his face. Turov flashed a sideways smile and scoffed as he boarded the vessel. Had the warden really thought their business arrangement made them equals? He'd find out soon just how wrong he was.

CHAPTER ONE

Present Day
9:28 p.m. Eastern Time – Thursday
Verndale Drive
Roanoke, Virginia

The sound of his own footfalls and the occasional whish of a vehicle passing over the wet pavement were the only sounds Declan McIver heard as he jogged through the old neighborhoods of Northeast Roanoke. Constructed in the 1960s and 70s, the streets were lined with one story brick ranches and split foyer homes on postage stamp lots, most featuring well-manicured lawns. The occasional work truck sat dormant along the curb in front of its owner's house and once in a while a dog barked from behind a fence as he passed by. The dense clouds threatened rain and the crescent moon was visible only with the occasional break in the gloom. Silver birch trees lining the main road rustled slightly in the early spring breeze and the air smelled of damp hydrocarbons from the well-traveled asphalt.

At just shy of six feet tall, with dirty blonde hair, icy blue eyes and a closely trimmed beard sporting flecks of grey, Declan was a common sight to anyone who lived nearby. Although he purposely varied his routine, anyone who paid attention would recognize him as a regular that jogged through the flower-named streets, whether he chose to do it in the pre-dawn hours or shortly after nightfall, as he had tonight. He was in top physical shape for a man of forty-one years and his rugged but handsome looks fit in nicely in the working middle class area.

His daily run was more than exercise; the five or six miles a day served as an escape, a time when he could work through the trials and tribulations of his life as a successful business owner. His company, DCM Properties, was his dream come true, but it was not without its headaches. Under the DCM banner, he'd been buying, fixing and selling distressed commercial properties for a decade and had become moderately wealthy doing so.

Making a mental note of everything he passed and turning his head slightly to look back in the direction he'd come, Declan cleared his former six o'clock position as he turned right, making sure he wasn't being followed. To all but the most trained observers, his seemingly paranoid technique wouldn't be noticeable. He had good reason for being cautious; sixteen years on the hit list of a half-dozen terrorist organizations dictated certain behavioral differences from the average person.

At the bottom of a steep street he glanced right and left before crossing over the main road into the park adjacent to the neighborhood. The loose gravel of the park's walkway shifted, making a soft crunching sound as his New Balance sneakers rolled from heel to toe over and again as he pushed himself along, breathing heavily as he neared the end of his route. Looping through the pathways of the wooded grounds, he stopped as he felt his cell phone vibrate in the pocket of his gray sweat pants. Annoyed at the interruption, he fished for the Samsung smartphone and looked at the display as it lit up with the calling number. As his eyes focused in the glare of the bright LED he read the number from left to right, not recognizing it. His mind searched for an answer as he looked at the 202 area code indicating the caller was from Washington D.C. Trying without success to slow down his breathing, he answered. "Hello," he said, his Irish accent evident in his enunciation.

"I hope I haven't caught you at a bad time, old friend."

"Just out for a run," Declan said, searching the voices in his memory for the identity of the caller. The voice was deep and obviously foreign, but its English was academically perfect. He didn't have to think very long. The voice belonged to Abe Kafni, his former boss and a man he had seldom spoken with in the last decade since leaving his employ in 2002.

Dr. Abaddon Kafni, as he was known to most people, was a popular author, teacher and pundit of subjects ranging from the War on Terror to the crises throughout the Middle East. His most recent book had debuted at the number one position on the New York Times bestseller list for adult non-fiction and had remained for a record-setting thirteen weeks. Known only to a select few was the fact that Kafni was also a former operative for Mossad, Israel's national intelligence agency.

"It's been a while," Declan said, surprised. "What can I do for you?"

"How about telling me how you've been for a start? As you said, it's been a while."

"Great, Abe. The market has been a bit of a bear the last few years, but I'm a careful investor, so no cause for alarm here. But you didn't really call for an update on Mid-Atlantic real estate sales, did you?"

"No," the Israeli said with a chuckle. "I was hoping you would have time to meet with an old friend on short notice."

"Of course," Declan said. "My wife and I have plans to attend your speech tomorrow night."

Kafni had recently accepted an honorary position with the conservative, pro-Israel Liberty University in Lynchburg, Virginia, an hour's drive from where Declan lived in Roanoke. The speech he was referring to was the keynote address at the newly constructed C.H. Barton Center for International Relations and Politics, home of the university's newest Graduate and Post-Graduate programs.

"Yes, I saw your name on the guest list and was glad. I was hoping we could have a meal together afterwards, certainly there's a decent steakhouse somewhere in Lynchburg."

"I'm sure we can find something. I'll let Constance know, she's excited about meeting you."

"As I am her, she must be an extraordinary woman to put up with you."

Declan chuckled. "Aye, I'm sure her and Zeva could swap some war stories. Perhaps Zeva can give her a few pointers."

Kafni laughed. "Touché, my friend, touché."

Kafni had had a long career as an intelligence agent and had certainly deserved to retire with his wife, Zeva, and their children in peace at the conclusion of his services to the state of Israel, but instead he'd chosen to take up another cause. Kafni's passion had always been academia and politics so he'd moved to America to become an author and public speaker. Their contact had been rare in the ten years since the terrorist attacks of September the 11th, when Kafni had seen his profession become far more controversial. His unyielding support for the state of Israel and for the war on terrorism, coupled with his unapologetic style, had won him no shortage of enemies. In the last fifteen years there had been six attempts on his life, all from radical Islamists keen on claiming the head of one of Israel's chief lightning rods. As a member of Kafni's all-too-necessary security detail for several years before leaving to start his own company and begin a new life, Declan had been responsible for thwarting three of the assassination attempts himself.

"So I'll see you tomorrow night?" Declan asked rhetorically.

"I'll look forward to it. I will send a car for you at six," Kafni said.

"That won't be necessary. I prefer to drive myself."

"Spoken like a true security-minded professional. Very well then, I will have Levi meet you at the front door. And thank you, my friend, you know I wouldn't call if it wasn't important."

"Of course," Declan responded, taken off guard by Kafni's suddenly solemn tone. "Is there something else going on? What aren't you telling me?"

"I will see you tomorrow." The line went silent as Kafni hung up.

Ending the call, Declan returned the phone to his pocket. He stood looking through the trees, unable to shake a sense of foreboding. Abaddon Kafni wasn't the type of man to be troubled by trivial things. In his world something of concern could be anything from Iranian nuclear weapons aimed at Israel to Russian submarines off the coast of Florida. Although he had exited the stage of international espionage years earlier, Kafni's influential status and many friends had kept him well-informed.

Returning to his jog at a full run to elevate his heart rate, Declan exited the gravel path and ran across a concrete bridge spanning an ankle deep creek that connected the neighborhood to a two acre spread of mostly wooded land. On the opposite side of the lane from the park a half-mile strip of pavement that served as his driveway stretched along behind two moss-covered stone columns, each supporting a rusted wrought iron gate. Jogging from column to column like a pacing wolf, Declan waited as the gates swung open with a metallic screech.

Rain-drenched leaves from the maple trees above squished under his feet as he made the final push towards his house. Slowing to a stop and pulling his sweat soaked T-shirt off as he broke the tree line into the small clearing where his home stood; he placed his hands on his knees, bending over to catch his breath. With Kafni's voice still echoing in his head, he stood looking down on his bare arms, thoughts of the past haunting him as he took note of the many scars.

A large chunk of skin on the back of his left hand was permanently scarred following an accident with the chemical component of a letter bomb. His left forearm had suffered a four inch gash when a piece of flying glass had hit him when a building he had been entering was blown up by an IED, an attack that he had only barely escaped, and his left shoulder bore a round burn mark from a flaming piece of timber broken loose from the same building as he'd tried unsuccessfully to free a friend from the rubble.

Still breathing heavily, wiping his brow with his T-shirt, he looked at his right arm. It had only one scar, but it was the deepest of all of them in his mind. It sat just below his elbow on the underside of his forearm and symbolized a former life he'd like to have forgotten. The three claw-like markings had been tattooed onto his arm during his days as the lead operator of the Provisional Irish Republican Army's secret weapon, an elite terror unit codenamed Black Shuck.

CHAPTER TWO

A baying sound filled the humid night and jarred Declan's thoughts back to the present. He bent down with a broad smile as a flabby, floppy-eared guard approached his position. "Hello, old girl," he said, stroking the beagle on both sides of its face as it lapped its tongue over his hands. "Out for a bit of nighttime gallivanting, are we?" The pooch responded by happily padding its front feet up and down and wiggling its rear end. Declan stood and looked up towards the two story cedar-sided house that stood in the clearing atop a rounded hill, a forked driveway stretching around it.

Belmont Knoll, as the property had been named by its previous owner, had originally been constructed in 1898 by the Belmont family, who had immigrated from Ireland in the 1880s during the railroad boom that marked the beginning of the Roanoke area's industrial development. The original stone cottage that had stood overlooking the better part of the property and the driveway leading into it had burned to the ground in the 1930s. All that remained was an immense stone chimney that provided the cornerstone for the current house, which Declan had custom built and lived in for a decade. Dim lights from the living room told him his wife was still awake and likely waiting for him to return. With a slight bounce in his step he patted his leg as a signal for the beagle to follow him as he moved up the right side of the drive to the home's wrap around porch. Peering through the windows as he walked around the porch towards the door, he could see his wife sitting alone, a tissue in one hand and a pregnancy test in the other.

Even without seeing the results of the test he knew they'd failed again as he arrived at the door.

At five foot six inches with her auburn hair spilling loosely over her shoulders, Constance McIver got up from the leather sofa and padded barefoot across the carpeted living room as Declan walked through the front door. Pressing her slender frame against his, she kissed him softly and said, "I missed you."

"Oh, you did?" Declan said, returning her kiss. They'd been married for eight years, but had until just recently put their careers ahead of starting a family. Last summer they'd decided it was time. The previous eight months had been marked with several disappointments. Tears gathered in her green eyes as she embraced him tightly.

"Hey, it's grand, it's grand," he said reassuringly, and he wiped away a tear that slid down her cheek with his thumb. He knew what she was thinking. At thirty-five years old, Constance was beginning to fear that she'd waited too long to have a child.

Constance laughed and wiped away more tears as their beagle pushed its way stubbornly between their legs and waded into the house.

"Shelby, I swear," Constance said, as the dog bounded onto the leather sofa and peered over the back of it at them with an open-mouthed expression that could only be interpreted as a smile. "You're a mess, dog."

Declan chuckled as he closed the front door. "I got a call while I was out," he said, as he walked over to the chestnut armoire that stood along the wall between the kitchen and living room. He took out a metal thermos and twisted off the cap.

As he took a sip Constance said, "Oh? Who from?"

Declan breathed heavily as he poured the concoction from the thermos into his mouth. The liquid was a special combination of vitamins mixed with soda water; it tasted horrible. "Ugh," he said as he finished and wiped his mouth on his forearm.

Constance laughed. "Well, you're the one that drinks it."

"It's supposed to be good for you," he said, returning the thermos to the armoire.

"Nothing that smells and tastes that bad can possibly be good for you. Now who called? Quit keeping me in suspense," she said, playfully pushing him.

"Kafni," he answered, in a matter of fact way.

She looked at him for a moment waiting for him to say he was joking. To her, Abaddon Kafni was a current events celebrity that graced the television screen on news and opinion programs, seemingly on a nightly basis. Although she knew her husband had once worked for him, she also knew that it was long ago and that the two hadn't been in contact for many years.

"Seriously," he said. "He saw our names on the guest list. He's having one of his aides meet us at the door tomorrow night to guide us around."

She smiled and her mood seemed to stay chipper, which was the effect he'd hoped the news would have. He was trying to steer her away from the failed pregnancy test and to cheer her up. His decision to attend the event the next night was an effort on his part to slowly begin spoon feeding her bits of the past he'd so carefully hidden for so long. She knew nothing of his past life in Northern Ireland. He wasn't sure exactly why he hadn't told her the truth. Beginning their relationship with a lie wasn't something he was proud of and his dishonesty on the subject nagged him. He supposed that when they'd met he had wanted her to think of him as the man he was instead of the man he had been. Was his past really all that different from someone who'd gone to Vietnam or Desert Storm and seen the horrors of war, he reasoned? Many of them had chosen not to speak of their experiences either.

"Your evening begins at six, Mrs. McIver," he said with a wry smile. "While Dr. Kafni probably won't have a lot of time at the gala itself, he's asked to meet us for dinner afterwards. I told him we'd try to find time in our busy schedule."

"Really?" she said, acting as if she was impressed. "I didn't know you were a man of such connections. Can I touch you?" She held out her index finger and reached towards him, grinning like a star struck teen.

He shook his head and laughed. "Why yes, you can."

Gently, he cupped her face and kissed her. Wiping her eyes with her hands, she returned the kiss with passion. She laughed and pretended to protest as he picked her up off her feet and carried her down the hallway towards their bedroom.

"I just thought of something we can do," he said, kicking the door shut with his foot as they entered.

"Oh you did, did you?" she asked.

"Aye, I did."

CHAPTER THREE

The brakes of the decaying Crown Victoria ground against the rotors as the taxi cab pulled to a stop at the corner of Ralls Avenue and Van Deman Street in an industrial area just southwest of the city of Dundalk, one of the first suburbs inside what was known as the inner ring of Baltimore. Anzor Kasparov knew he was taking a great risk coming in broad daylight. Dressed in an open flannel shirt over a faded blue tee, and jeans with a hole in one knee, he hoped he looked the part of someone who belonged in and around the manufacturing district at this hour of the morning.

"You want me to wait?" the cabbie asked as he turned to look over his shoulder. "The cost is twenty dollars."

"No," Kasparov said pulling a Baltimore Orioles cap further down over his brow in hopes of keeping the man from getting too good a look at him.

"Okay. The fare is fifty-five."

Kasparov tossed three crumpled twenty dollar bills into the front passenger seat as he opened the door and exited. His hands in his pockets, he walked south on Ralls Avenue for twenty yards, as the cab drove away and disappeared from view, then he turned and headed back to the corner, this time going north onto Van Deman Street. He walked for two blocks until he reached a building with a rusted sign above the door reading *Broughman's Welding Service.* He surveyed the vicinity and looked over the odd collection of junk beside the building as he took his wallet out and removed a key.

Opening the blue metal door, he walked into what had once been the front office of someone's business. Now mildewed boxes sat collecting dust and the air smelled of rotting cardboard. He closed the door behind him and locked it. He could hear the sound of a power tool running in the larger part of the building behind the office and walked that way.

Inside what he imagined had once been some type of machine room a lone man lay on his back underneath a tattered panel van. The van had been driven onto a pair of mobile ramps for easier access and two red toolboxes sat open on either side of the mechanic. Undoubtedly the van was how their mysterious benefactor planned for them to get around without attracting attention. From such a humble veil, the surveillance, the collection of intelligence, and finally the selection of a target could be accomplished, and there was little chance that anyone would notice. After the target was selected their benefactor would make sure any necessary documents were supplied without hesitation. Blueprints, fire escape routes, mechanical, electrical and plumbing maps, whatever was needed. The plan was brilliant and Kasparov thanked Allah as he approached the mechanic.

As if the man could sense someone's presence, in one fluid motion he pushed himself out from underneath the car, removed the welding mask that had shielded his face and reached into the coat he was wearing as if he were going to pull a gun.

Kasparov removed the baseball cap and stared down into the face of Ruslan Baktayev. The frail, skeletal appearance of the man nearly brought tears to his eyes. What had the Russians done to him? Where there had once been dark hair and a thick beard, there was now only pallid flesh with the beginnings of dark stubble. Where there had once been muscles chiseled by the Caucasian winters, there was now a malnourished prisoner. He looked deep into Baktayev's eyes and gloried at the defiant look that stared back at him. Despite even the cruelest treatment the enemy could muster, his friend, his brother in arms, had lost none of his fire. Kasparov opened his arms wide as Baktayev came to his feet, the Chechen's full height of six feet bearing down over the smaller and more robust Armenian.

"Abu, Abu," Kasparov said, using Baktayev's chosen Islamic name, Abu Tabak, as the two embraced and each clapped their hands loudly against the other's back. "It has been too long. Tell me it's true? Tell me it is all true and we will finally deliver the sword of Allah deep into the hearts of the infidels?" A look of sheer elation spread across Kasparov's face as the two drew apart after their embrace.

"It is all true, Anzor, it is all true."

"Glory be to Allah, Allahu-akbar!" Kasparov shouted throwing his arms in the air triumphantly. "I have prayed so diligently for this time to come. Ten years, Abu, ten years it's been since we set out on this journey, but Allah has finally delivered us!"

"That he has, little brother," Baktayev breathed, "and soon he will deliver up the head of my enemy and I will wash myself in his blood." Baktayev clenched his fists as if he could barely contain the hatred within him. As his knuckles turned white, he continued; "Soon the killer of my brothers, the hated Jewish pig, Abaddon Kafni, will be dead and Allah's vengeance will be mine."

Kasparov nodded his approval. "He can do it, this Sheikh Kahraman, he has arranged it all? He has arranged for the killers of Vadim and Deni to be brought to you?"

"Only Kafni, he was the father of the operations against my brothers. His agents may have been the ones doing the shooting, but Kafni made it happen."

Kasparov continued to nod. "Then glory be to Allah, we shall taste his blood."

The shrill sound of a ringing phone echoed through the hollow chamber of the garage and interrupted the reunion. Baktayev moved towards a workbench littered with tools and watched as a greasy telephone receiver vibrated against its base with each ring. After three rings the phone lay dormant. Seconds later the shrill sound came again and after two rings, Baktayev picked it up and said, "Broughman's."

A disembodied voice on the other end responded, "Is this

the big blue welding service?"

"No," Baktayev responded sharply. "It is the big red welding service."

"Very well then," the electronic voice responded. With their code words spoken correctly, Levent Kahraman continued. "Everything is set. You are to deliver your products to the president's home tonight. Simon and Peter will be waiting for you."

"Very good, I appreciate your business," Baktayev responded. He hung up the telephone with a satisfied smile knowing that the term "president's home" was code for a mansion near the former retreat of U.S. President Thomas Jefferson and that Simon and Peter were code for Kafni and his chief of security, Levi Levitt. He turned back to Kasparov who looked at him with a question in his eyes.

"Let everyone else know. Abaddon Kafni dies tonight."

Kasparov nodded, replaced the Orioles cap on his head, and turned to exit the building.

CHAPTER FOUR

3:16 p.m. Eastern Time – Friday
Eastbound on Route 460
Lynchburg, Virginia

The late afternoon sun glinted off the passenger side mirror and Declan squinted as he looked left and right over the edges of the four lane highway. Driving east on route 460 heading into Lynchburg, the sprawling campus of Liberty University had just come into view. Covering both sides of the highway, the campus was seemingly in a constant state of construction to keep up with the rapid growth of the student body. In the distance to the right a brand new building stood connected to the main campus by a long parking lot and a string of modern dormitories. The C.H. Barton Center for International Relations and Politics was designed to look like a larger scale model of Thomas Jefferson's Poplar Forest retreat, located a few miles southwest of Lynchburg. In a few hours Declan and Constance would be attending the center's grand opening, along with about three hundred other guests.

"Seriously, I don't see why you put up with this guy," Constance said, from the driver's seat of her late model Nissan Z sports car.

"He's not that bad," Declan said, with a small laugh. She was referring to Brendan Regan, an employee of DCM Properties and a man Declan had known for nearly fifteen years. To say that Regan was a bit abrasive was an understatement and

Declan did at times wonder why he put up with some of the man's antics. In the end, he supposed it came down to feeling sorry for him.

"Not that bad? He's completely obnoxious and he causes more problems than anyone else working for you. Not to mention every time I'm around him all he does is stare at my breasts. Ugh."

"I do a healthy amount of staring at your breasts, too."

"Yeah, yeah," she said, backhanding him on the shoulder playfully and trying to hide a grin.

"Ow," he said, pretending that it hurt. "They were bouncing up and down last night, you know? It was quite entertaining."

"Stop it!" she said, turning bright red and covering an ear to ear grin with her hand.

Declan smiled broadly and laughed. Teasing her was almost the best part of being married.

"Left exit here to 501," he said, waving his hand across the gearshift to signal left.

"I know which way left is," she responded sarcastically.

"Just making sure, you are a Republican."

She signaled left and slowly glided over into the turn lane. "How far is it from here?"

"Not far. Go up Candler's Mountain Road then take a quick left onto Edgewood Avenue."

A few minutes later Constance pulled the sports car to a stop in front of a yellow brick ranch with a faded brown roof and broken out windows. Two utility body work trucks sat parked in the yard, the red and blue logo of DCM Properties ablaze against the vehicles' white paint. In the driveway sat a Ford Escape with a "City of Lynchburg" seal on its door, a grey logo at the bottom clearly identifying the vehicle as a hybrid. While most of the road was residential, the area's rapid development meant that businesses were starting to take over the first block of the Edgewood Avenue and that put this particular property under the purview of Declan's company.

"Right, then, let's go and see what Regan's gotten us into this time," Declan said, opening the passenger side door and stepping out.

"Yes. Let's," Constance said through clenched teeth.

They walked across the small patch of grass that made up the home's front yard and as they arrived at the door a tall black man dressed in white overalls appeared from inside.

"Hey, boss," said Poindexter Perry.

"Dex," Declan said, as he stepped up onto the covered front porch.

The sound of a raised voice with a Boston accent erupted from behind Perry. "I told him to take it easy this time," Perry said in his deep baritone voice.

"Why don't you have a look around the place with Dex while I go and straighten this out? The back rooms could use a woman's touch," Declan said to Constance.

"How do you do, Ma'am?" Dex said, tipping the edge of his white painters cap.

"Fine, Dex. Thanks for asking. How are Sherri and the girls?" Declan heard her say with a smile in her voice as he stepped away towards the basement stairwell.

Inside, the house looked like it was two different properties. To the left of the basement stairwell, which marked the center of the house, the one story ranch's bedrooms, bathroom and floors had been completely remodeled with new carpet, paint, tile and fixtures. To the right of the steps, where the kitchen and living area were located, were bare wooden subfloors, exposed support beams and loose drywall, covered with a thick layer of settled construction dust. Like all of the properties DCM worked with, this one had been bought out of foreclosure and they were now in the process of remodeling it into commercial office space so that it could be leased out.

"Hey, listen to me," a loud voice said from in the basement. "Hear the words that are coming out of my mouth. I'm not replacing an entire electrical panel because of a little bit of rust. There's no water in here. Do you see any water?"

Declan shook his head and descended the basement stairs. The aged wood creaked underneath his weight and the two men standing in the unfinished room looked up as he reached the bottom. Standing in front of an open electrical panel in the musty smelling room was Brendan Regan, an overweight man with a clumsy cluster of blonde hair, a beer gut hanging over his belt and a lopsided expression that gave him the look of a fat kid in an ice cream shop faced with an impossible number of choices. Regan's six foot frame towered over the building inspector in front of him, a stout man in a blue denim shirt with receding gray hair and a bushy mustache.

"Hi, I'm Declan McIver. I'm the principal for DCM Properties," Declan said, extending his right hand toward the inspector.

"Howard Terry, Mr. McIver. Lynchburg City Planning and Zoning," the man said, as they shook hands. "Your subordinate here was just telling me you have no plans to replace the electric in this house, but I'm afraid the city is going to require an update before we can issue a certificate of occupancy."

"I haven't had a chance to look at it yet. We just started this project a few weeks ago. What are we dealing with?"

"Well, this desk jockey here says the whole thing has to come out because it's rusted," Regan said. "But the only rust I see is the quarter-sized spot there. Here, I'll scratch it off."

"Easy, Brendan," Declan said. "We're all professionals here."

"Professionals, my big ass; he's a hack."

"That's enough. Mr. Terry's with the city and if we're going to be successful in expanding our business to Lynchburg we need to listen to what he has to say. Why don't you wait upstairs while we finish up down here?"

"Fine, you want to kiss his ass, you kiss his ass," Regan said, as he pushed his way between Declan and the inspector and headed for the steps mumbling, "Stupid desk riding bureaucrat."

Declan watched the inspector as Regan climbed the steps, the man's eyes followed him with a disapproving glare.

Declan flashed a smile as the inspector looked back at him. "I've raised him since he was thirty," he said, with a short chuckle as he bent down to take a closer look at the electrical panel. Pulling a multi-tool out of his back pocket, he opened it and produced a Phillips head screwdriver. After loosening four screws, he pulled the face off the junction box at the bottom of the panel. Rust colored water slopped out of the bottom of the box and spilled onto the floor.

"There's your problem, Mr. Terry, ground water," Declan said, pulling out a fistful of hastily taped wiring. "We'll install a new watertight conduit and a NEMA-4 junction box. Think that'll get us a C.O.?"

Terry nodded. "Yeah, that'll do."

"Thank you, sir," Declan said, as he stood and shook hands with the inspector again. "Let me give you one of my cards. My cell number is on there if you run into anymore issues."

Terry took the card and withdrew one of his own from his pocket. "I'll be by for a final inspection when you're done remodeling," he said, handing his card over.

Declan nodded and followed the building inspector up the basement steps. As the man left the house and closed the front door behind him, Declan turned and looked into the kitchen. Constance sat uncomfortably on an upturned five gallon bucket, with Regan and Dex standing nearby, Regan grinning ear to ear as he attempted to position himself at just the right angle to get a view down her shirt. Declan grinned as she flashed Regan an annoyed look and pulled her jacket closed.

"You about ready, then?" Declan asked.

Constance jumped to her feet and said, "Yes, very much so."

"Dex, good work man," Declan said, as he opened the door for his wife. "I'll be round Monday to help you secure the back deck. Regan, try not to bring the entire city council down on us in the meantime, will you?"

Regan grumbled a response as Declan closed the door.

"You're fired," Constance mouthed inaudibly from outside the house.

Declan flashed a smile. "He works cheap," he said, as he put his arm around her and led her back to the car. "Let's get to the hotel and get checked in."

CHAPTER FIVE

6:02 p.m. Eastern Time – Friday
C.H. Barton Center – Liberty University
Lynchburg, Virginia

By six o'clock a light rain had begun to fall. Arriving at the campus, Declan followed the directions of the orange-vested parking attendants and pulled into a spot just big enough for his wife's sports car. They'd chosen to drive her car rather than his truck for that exact reason. College campuses weren't known for spacious parking and the crowd expected for the night's event would exacerbate the problem.

Opening the door and exiting the vehicle, he looked south along Candler's Mountain Road. He could tell security was tight, just as he had expected it would be. White SUVs with flashing LED lights blocked entrances and men in navy blue security uniforms stood at the edges of every sidewalk, .40 caliber Glock sidearms visible on their hips. Opening the door for his wife, he waited as she stepped out of the car.

In the distance the indignant shouts of a group of protestors could be heard from a sidewalk just beyond the Campus limits, but in full view of the arriving guests. Some things haven't changed, thought Declan. Like many others who vocally supported America and Israel from their platforms as authors and speakers, Abaddon Kafni was a target of constant protests. Signs reading *Free Palestine* and *Occupation Is A Crime* were waved defiantly in the air as chants of "Stop Israeli aggression!"

were shouted loudly at anyone who came within fifty yards of the group. The people taking part in the protest were likely the same ones who would protest the appearance of war veterans, members of a Republican administration and conservative personalities, all of whom frequently appeared at the university's many venues.

"Does Kafni always travel with this much security?" Constance asked, as they wormed their way between parked cars towards the path leading to the front entrance.

"No, I don't think so," Declan answered. "At least he never used to. There are a lot of other guests tonight in addition to Kafni; senators, congressmen, probably some ambassadors as well. No one wants to miss a photo-op."

"Always the pessimist," she said, rolling her big green eyes towards him and grabbing his hand.

"I prefer the term 'realist' when it comes to politicians," he said, pulling her closer as they walked.

Ahead of them the newly constructed C.H. Barton Center for International Relations and Politics stood separated from the main campus by the four lanes of Route 460. Nestled into the side of Liberty Mountain, underneath the university's gigantic hillside logo, the building was an impressive sight. The Barton Center, as it would likely be nicknamed by the students and faculty, was as ambitious an architectural project as the university had attempted to date. Not known for shying away from a challenge, the university had designed the building to look like a larger scale version of a retreat once owned by Thomas Jefferson, the third President of the United States.

Octagonal in shape, the Barton Center was three stories high, with two floor-to-ceiling windows on each level of the eight sides. Like Jefferson's former plantation, Poplar Forest, the building was capped at both the front and rear entrances by a white gabled portico supported by four marble columns. A one story rectangular hall jutted off the east side in the same position as the servant's quarters at the original property. At the base of a set of steps extending from the front portico, a circular hedge surrounded a mock carriage court paved with cobblestones. Wrought iron benches were positioned every ten feet in a wide circle. In the center of the court stood an imposing bronze statue of Thomas Jefferson, holding a feather pen and a copy of the Declaration of Independence. He looked down on everyone who approached the building, his soft but knowledgeable gaze conveying the seriousness of the task he had undertaken two hundred and thirty six years earlier.

Walking through the carriage court to the base of the steps, Declan and Constance entered a tent that had been set up as a covered valet. Several limousines were unloading their tuxedo-clad occupants, who strode into the entrance as if they were late for an important meeting.

"See what I mean?" Declan asked wryly as they approached the security team at the front door and one such tuxedo-clad man strode past the security without a second look.

"Name, please?" a guard seated at a gray card table announced.

"Declan and Constance Mc—"

"I said *name*, not *names*. Unless she's mute, she can speak for herself in a moment."

"I see the manners haven't improved much over the years," Declan grumbled, before repeating his name loud and clear. "Declan McIver."

The guard made a tick mark with his pen and motioned towards two other guards standing at the base of the steps. "Remove your coat and stand with your arms and legs open wide, sir," one of the guards said as Declan approached.

Declan took off his coat, as instructed, and handed it to a guard who patted it down and searched through the pockets. Meanwhile, as he stood spread-eagled, the second guard ran a metal detector over his body. As he endured the security screening, he took note of his surroundings. Inside the tent, in addition to the guard checking the list of names and the two currently dealing with Declan, there were several young men in black raincoats guiding cars into and out of the tent, and holding doors for the occupants as they exited their vehicles and entered the building. A white Ford Crown Victoria sedan sat parked at an angle behind the card table with a full set of clear LED emergency lights on its roof and bright red lettering down the side of the vehicle reading *security*.

"Good to go, sir," the guard with the metal detector said

as he moved onto Constance, who had successfully stated her name and was next in line. Declan stood waiting for his coat, but the guard handed it to a woman in a black raincoat instead. She wrote a number on a ticket and tore it in half, placing the first half on a hanger along with the coat.

"Don't lose my coat," Declan said to her, as she handed him the stub. "I like that coat."

The woman flashed him a quick smile then took Constance's coat from the guard as Declan was joined by his wife. "C'mon," she said. "Quit giving them a hard time."

"What?" he asked, as she took him by the arm and led him up the stairs. "I like my coat."

Ahead of them at the building's front entrance, two more guards stood on either side of a set of open oak doors. A short man in a tweed three piece suit stood next to them and he smiled and extended his hand as the McIvers approached.

"It's good to see you, Declan," he said, in a Semitic accent. "Sorry about all of that."

Gripping the man's hand, Declan said, "I guess I should've taken Abe up on that car," as he watched an older gentleman step out of the back of a Lincoln Town Car and stride past the security. "It's good to see you too, Levi. This is my wife, Constance."

"Hi," Constance said, smiling as Levi took her hand and kissed it.

"I'd say something in French," Levi said, "but my memory fails me at the moment."

Constance laughed shyly.

"Constance, this is Levi Levitt, Dr. Abaddon Kafni's chief of security."

"And personal assistant and errand boy and everything else these days," Levitt said with a laugh. "I sometimes think I'm getting too old for this stuff."

"I bet the traveling schedule is horrendous," said Constance.

"Oy, you have no idea. If it weren't for e-mail, I wouldn't even remember my mailing address. Now, if you both want to follow me, I'll walk you through the room to Dr. Kafni. He's quite excited that you've decided to attend."

Levitt turned and walked through the double doors past the guards. He was a small man in height but made up for it in a sturdiness that communicated the idea that he was not a man to fool with. Declan knew that somewhere beneath the professor-like tweed suit, bushy gray beard and thick rimmed glasses lay the instincts and training of a former Mossad agent, much like his employer, Dr. Kafni.

Declan's road to friendship with him had been rocky. Levitt had been injured during an attempt on Kafni's life by a group of vengeful gunmen and it had been Declan who intervened to save the lives of both Kafni and his family.

Aware of Declan's past in the IRA, Levitt had regarded him with more than a little suspicion. despite Kafni's assurances to the contrary and insistence that Declan was the perfect candidate for their fledgling security team. It had taken three years and another assassination attempt before Levitt had let down his guard and began to trust him. Seeing Levitt again tonight, Declan still heard a flicker of the old mistrust present in the man's voice. Taking Constance's hand, he moved slowly after Levitt into the crowded room beyond.

The first floor of the Barton Center had been completely emptied of whatever fixtures would be present when it went into use as part of the university's new graduate programs. Blue velvet security rope ran around the entire room and was held up at six foot intervals by bronze-colored stanchions. Behind the rope, on the eight surrounding walls, hung artwork featuring scenes from Thomas Jefferson's tenure as Minster of France and Secretary of State. At intervals across the dark mahogany floor were approximately twenty-five round dinner tables, each draped in dark blue cloth and with enough room to seat twelve guests.

The murmur in the room was deafening. Like a crescendo of mating grasshoppers, four and five person groups of politicians, aides, journalists, and those hoping to become such, clamored for attention. Right away, Declan recognized several of the guests from interviews on various news programs and mailers that had flooded his postal box during the last election. With the agonizing speed of a snail caught in molasses they moved between the tables towards a stage decorated with the flags of various nations. In the center was a stately podium bearing the university's seal, ready for the evening's speakers to begin.

"Osman and Nazari are making the rounds through the building. They'll be joining us later," Levitt said, referring to the other two bodyguards whom Declan had worked closely with during his time with Kafni.

"Grand," said Declan, as they neared the stage.

"This will be your table here," Levitt said, as he indicated a table with a tent card reading *six*.

"Right up front, I can deal with that," said Declan.

"Dr. Kafni wanted to make sure you had the best seats in the house," said Levitt, as he motioned them forward. "You'll be seated with Dr. Coulson, the Barton Center's dean, and Chancellor Falwell, once he arrives. But for now, let me show you to where Dr. Kafni is."

Declan and Constance followed as Levitt led them past the last row of tables to the side of the stage, on either side of which a blue velvet curtain had been hung from the ceiling to create a backstage area. Levitt pulled back the curtain and held it open as Declan and Constance entered.

Standing in the center of the space were two men, both dressed in suits. Declan immediately recognized Dr. Abaddon Kafni, known to anyone who had the honor of calling him friend as "Abe", but had no idea who the second man was.

Dressed in a black and gray pinstriped suit that seemed to hang off his lanky appendages, and with a broad brow, a face that closely followed the contours of the skull beneath his flesh, and large ears that seemed to sit just a little lower than normal, Kafni looked the part of educated pundit. He smiled broadly as he saw Levitt returning, followed closely by Declan.

"I found him harassing the security," Levitt announced with a grin as he stopped mid-way between the curtain and the two men.

"My friend, I'm glad you could come," said Kafni, in perfect but accented English. He extended his hand as the McIvers walked past Levitt.

Grabbing Kafni's hand firmly, Declan said, "Well, I've never been one to disappoint."

"No, you haven't. You, my friend, have always been very

consistent, and that is something of value." Kafni turned back towards the man he'd been standing with. "This is Dr. Michael Coulson. He is the dean of the new programs here at Liberty and a man I'll be working closely with as we attempt to win the hearts and minds of this nation's youth. Michael, this is Declan McIver, a close friend, and his wife, Constance."

"Hi. How are you?" Declan asked, as his right hand left Kafni's and moved towards the hand of the tall, dark haired man. With a lined face and a bell-shaped nose that stood atop a bushy mustache, rather like a five and dime disguise, Coulson fit the academic persona perfectly. His well-tailored suit swished as he extended his hand; it was as if the polyester dreaded the movement for fear of a wrinkle.

"Let me guess, East Belfast?" he said, shaking Declan's hand, a toothy smile giving him the air of a politician or used car salesman.

"Galway, actually; close though."

"Oh well. What can I say…I never was any good at telling the difference in the accents, even after seven years at Queen's," Coulson said, referencing time he had apparently spent studying or teaching at Queen's University in Belfast. Declan didn't care enough to ask which.

"No, you did well. I'm surprised you picked up on it at all. It's been a long time." Declan knew it was more likely that Coulson had picked up on his name rather than his accent. With the "Mc" prefix it was obviously British as opposed to the more Irish sounding names that often began with an "O". East Belfast was home to the majority British Protestant population of Northern Ireland's largest city and Coulson apparently knew that much.

Conscious that the past held events that neither of them cared to discuss at any length with Coulson, Kafni clasped his hands together loudly and said, "So, this is your wife? She's more beautiful than you described, Declan, you should be ashamed."

Constance blushed as Kafni took her hand lightly. "Hi, Dr. Kafni, it's a pleasure to meet you."

"Abe, please call me Abe. I'm delighted to meet you."

Constance smiled and said, "Okay, Abe then."

"Did your husband ever tell you about the time he saved my life?"

"No, he didn't," Constance said, rolling her eyes towards Declan. "That must be quite a story."

"It is and I can't wait to tell you about it. I'm looking forward to catching up with both of you after my speech. Would you mind terribly if I took a moment to talk with your husband in the last few minutes before I am to go on stage?"

"Not at all," Constance said smiling.

"I'll escort the lady back to our table," Coulson said, as he guided her out.

Declan watched as they left and the curtain closed behind them. "Is the news that bad?" he said, when they were out of earshot.

"No," Kafni said, with a wave of his hand. "I didn't know how much you'd told her and I don't want to scare her. I know very well how families handle the kind of events we've been involved in."

Declan nodded. "Yeah, I suppose you do. How are Zeva and the kids?"

"Great. They are great. David just finished his last year of law school and is setting up his own practice near our home in Maryland. He's hoping to work alongside the American Center for Law and Justice. Hanah graduated at Virginia Tech this past spring and is starting veterinary school there this week," Kafni said, referencing the eldest of his five children. David and Hanah were the two Declan had had the most interaction with during his time helping with the family's security. The other three, two sons and a daughter, were much younger and still in grade school.

"Do you remember the name 'Baktayev'?" Kafni continued.

"Kind of hard to forget," Declan answered.

The Baktayevs had been two Chechen brothers that Kafni had run afoul of during his last assignment as an agent of Mossad. Having killed one of them during a botched weapons trade in which Mossad had been trying to capture an Iranian terror leader, the younger of the two brothers had sought revenge on Kafni when he'd immigrated to America a year and a half later. Through an incredible set of circumstances, Declan had been in just the right place to learn of the plot and had decided to intervene, since Kafni had done him a similar favor a few years earlier in Ireland. It could be safely said that without each other, neither of them would be alive.

"I thought they were both dead, but I'm getting the feeling you're about to tell me that's not the case."

"The two older brothers, Vadim and Deni, are dead, yes. You killed Deni yourself. But there is a third, a Ruslan Baktayev. I found out about him when I received a threat from him. As is the usual protocol, with the help of my contacts, we kept a close eye on him. After the second Chechen war broke out he lost interest and the matter died. He's been held in a Russian prison since the end of the Beslan School Hostage Crisis in 2004."

"He was involved in Beslan?"

"Oh yes, one of the architects of it, in fact."

"So if he's in prison, what makes him such a concern all of a sudden?"

"Two weeks ago he left the prison and hasn't been seen since."

Declan grimaced. "Corruption in the ranks again, huh?"

"Oh, I'm sure," Kafni said, raising his eyebrows. "As you well know, the Russian military is ceaselessly corrupt, and Moscow is being Moscow and telling bold faced lies, as usual. They are saying Baktayev died in a fight with another prisoner and that his body was incinerated, but Mossad had a *sayanim* in the prison, a sympathizer if you will, so we have it on good authority that he's anything but dead."

"And you think he's going to come after you?"

"Oh, I have no idea," Kafni said, with a shrug. "My family and I are well protected. I'm telling you this because this man has a personal vendetta against me and probably against you, too. Although you acted on my behalf, you were responsible for Deni Baktayev's death. I thought you should know so that you can take the appropriate measures to protect yourself and your wife. I am certain that if he could get into the U.S. he would try and kill me, and possibly you, too, if he knows who you are."

"That's a really big 'if', Abe. It's far more likely that this guy's running and hiding right now. He's probably holed up in some derelict tent city in the Caucasus hoping he doesn't freeze to death."

"Normally I'd agree, but it's the manner of his escape that bothers me the most. He just left the prison and Moscow is denying it completely. Even with the notoriously corrupt system in Russia, do you realize the influence and money it would take to pull this off? Somebody wanted him out of there for a reason."

"Did he have any contacts with enough resources to get him out?"

"The Chechens have received a lot of aid from terror networks like Al Qaeda over the years, but to my knowledge Baktayev himself has no connections wealthy enough to pull off such a feat. They were in contact with an Iranian financier named Sa'adi Nouri in the mid-nineties, but Nouri is dead. He has been for over a decade and his network did not survive him." Kafni ran a hand through his hair. "Look, it's anyone's guess as to what that reason is and it probably doesn't have anything to do with us, but I thought you should know all the same."

Declan nodded. "Thanks."

Kafni looked down at his watch and clapped Declan on the shoulder. "It's almost time for my speech. I'll see you afterwards. We'll talk about old times and good friends, and leave all of this in the past where it belongs."

Declan nodded, smiled and turned to walk out, hoping as he made his way back towards the settling crowd that Ruslan Baktayev and whatever bloody intentions he had did, in fact, remain buried in the past.

CHAPTER SIX

"What was that about?" Constance whispered, as Declan took a seat next to her in the now darkened room. She was seated with Michael Coulson, a woman that was apparently his wife, and two other couples. In addition to Declan's empty seat, there were four others. Declan recognized one of the men as the sitting congressman from his congressional district. He nodded to him politely before leaning towards Constance and giving her a quick kiss on the cheek. "Nothing," he said, "just a newsflash on an old friend of the family."

"I bet," she said dryly, as she raised her eyebrows.

Declan smiled. "Would I lie?"

Constance answered with a quick smile of her own, though it was obvious that she was less than convinced.

"Congressman Mark Alley," the man seated next to Constance said, as he stretched out a hand toward Declan. He was younger than most politicians, with a shock of blonde hair, an angular face and a cordial smile.

Declan gripped his hand firmly and said, "Hi. How are you? Declan McIver."

"Let me take you around the table," Alley said. "This is my wife, Sherry; these two fine people here are George and Sharon Barton; Ambassador Barton's son and daughter-in-law, Dr. Michael Coulson and his wife Elizabeth; and our table mates that have yet to arrive are Senator David Kemiss and his wife Mary Ellen; and Chancellor Jerry Falwell Jr. and his wife Becki."

Upon hearing everyone's names and titles, Declan felt

sorely out of place. What did an Irish immigrant and real estate developer say to a table full of people from a much higher social status than his? *Hi, I'm a voter?*

Michael Coulson glanced nervously at his watch.

"Something wrong, Dr. Coulson?" the congressman asked.

"Chancellor Falwell should be here by now. He's supposed to speak briefly and then introduce Dr. Kafni," Coulson said in a hushed voice as he leaned forward so that only those seated at the table with him could hear.

"Well, perhaps you should call him?" suggested the congressman.

Coulson nodded and stood up. He walked to the right of the stage and disappeared behind the curtain.

Declan looked around as hushed whispers rippled around the darkened room, an obvious feeling of uncertainty washing over the seated guests.

Moments later Coulson reappeared on the stage from behind the curtain, buttoning his suit coat as he walked to the podium. Clearing his throat and adjusting the microphone, he looked out over the gathered crowd.

"Ladies and gentlemen, welcome," he said. "At this time Chancellor Falwell had planned to talk with you briefly about the building you are in and its mission here at Liberty University and abroad. However, I have just received word that the Chancellor's mother has fallen and been taken to the hospital, so he will be unable to attend tonight. We'll all certainly be praying that all is well with Mrs. Falwell and I'll keep you updated throughout the evening.

"Now, you'll have to forgive me for the ad-libbed nature of my remarks, but I'm going to attempt to take you briefly around the building and then I will introduce our keynote speaker."

The audience applauded politely and Coulson took a sip of water from a cup underneath the podium.

"Now, as you all know," he began, "you are in the C.H. Barton Center for International Relations and Politics. The center was named after Dr. Charles Henry Barton, who until his passing two years ago was a beloved professor of our undergraduate international relations program here at Liberty. He was also a good friend of Jerry Falwell Sr. and one of the key advisors in the founding of the university in 1972. In addition to his post as professor here, he also served our country as Ambassador to both France and Germany during the Ronald Reagan and George H.W. Bush administrations respectively."

Coulson took another sip of water and nervously wiped his forehead with a handkerchief.

"If you'll indulge me further I'll tell you briefly about this building and its academic mission. The building has obviously been constructed to look like a replica of Thomas Jefferson's Poplar Forest, which of course is located only a few miles from here. As one of America's founders, one of its first foreign diplomats, and because of Jefferson's connection to this area, Chancellor Falwell and the board of directors thought it an appropriate design."

Coulson laughed slightly before continuing, "And if you promise not to tell anyone I told you, I suspect it was also because we here at Liberty, in the spirit of our founder, are just not capable of thinking small when it comes to such projects."

The audience laughed heartily and Declan glanced over at his wife. She seemed to be enjoying herself and that's what he had hoped to accomplish by coming. His idea of a good time certainly wasn't sitting in a crowded room with people he had little or nothing in common with, while wearing a suit, but if he was going to begin opening up to Constance about his past then Abaddon Kafni was a good place to start, and the gala was the perfect opportunity to meet him.

As the laughter died down and the harried conversations of the guests ceased, Coulson continued speaking. "The floor you are currently sitting on will be used as a small library and will house reference materials about countries throughout the world, including maps, photos, written and spoken examples of their native languages, details of any conflicts they have been involved in, and many other items useful to a government student at the graduate level.

"The second floor contains ten state of the art classrooms where those students will be taught, and the third floor, a set of spacious offices where the professors of the program, Dr. Kafni, and I, will reside. That is the conclusion of my remarks. I'd like to thank you for attending and for your gracious support."

The audience applauded briefly and Coulson beamed at them, looking relieved. Clearing his throat once again, he continued.

"Our keynote speaker tonight is a man who needs no introduction. Since moving to America from Israel in the mid-nineties he has been a constant presence on the stage of international politics. His books *The Coming Storm*, *The War We All Must Fight* and *Lest We Forget* have reached the top of bestseller lists all over the world. He regularly appears as a commentator on news programs with such hosts as Bret Baier, Piers Morgan and Sean Hannity. I'd like you all to give a warm welcome and a huge round of applause to my colleague, Dr. Abaddon Kafni!"

The entire room stood and applauded thunderously as Kafni stepped from behind the blue velvet curtain at stage right. He stopped briefly, taking in the audience with an affable wave before striding quickly to the podium where he removed a set of folded papers from his coat pocket and flattened them out in front of him.

"Hi, good evening," he said, with another wave and a shy smile. "It's great to be with you tonight."

The audience continued clapping as Coulson shook hands warmly with Kafni and exited the stage. Kafni stood beaming for a moment as the applause died away and people sat back down.

"Good evening," he said again, in his accented English. "As you may have guessed, I am Dr. Abaddon Kafni."

The audience laughed.

"It is very wonderful to be here at Liberty University tonight. I am so very excited to be joining the faculty here and to have a chance to help shape the minds of tomorrow's political leaders. Students from Liberty have gone on to become some of the brightest and best in their chosen professions, professions that include, but are not limited to, filmmakers, comic book writers, comedians, authors, world famous musicians and, of course, journalists and television reporters, whom I see regularly."

The audience chuckled again.

"In America, we are at an important turning point, the point where we must decide whether we will hold to the ideals of our founding. The ideas of limited government, free market capital—"

The blast was deafening. It boomed from the front of the building and the entire structure shuddered under the pressure. For a split second everyone froze, then a wall of heat followed by a wave of debris washed through the room and the screaming began. Declan leapt from his seat as burning pieces of drywall hit him from behind. Pulling Constance with him, he dived underneath the table as the stage lights went out and plunged the room into darkness. Holding Constance tight beneath him, Declan shielded her with his own body as the table was overturned in the chaos and people fell over them.

As quickly as it had erupted into turmoil, the room suddenly fell silent. His ears affected by the blast, Declan was barely aware of the hushed whispers and moans of the injured. People began calling out for their companions, needing to check if they were safe. As Declan's eyes adjusted to the new light, an eerie reddish hue cast by the wall of flames where the front entrance of the Barton Center had been, people began to realize what had happened and terrified screams rang out.

"Are you okay?" he shouted to Constance over the din.

Constance stood up slowly, looking shell-shocked, and nodded. Her eyes went wide as she turned and saw the devastation behind them. Declan pulled her close and shielded her from the sight of the mangled bodies that the force of the blast had thrown forward from their seats further back in the room.

Declan quickly looked her over and saw no signs of injury. "We have to get out of here," he said, turning her around by the shoulders and pushing her towards the stage. As he started to move, a hand grabbed at his ankle.

"Help me," said a shaky voice. "Help me!"

Declan turned to see Mark Alley on the floor at his feet, a deep gash over his right eye bleeding profusely and blinding him. Declan reached down and pulled Alley to his feet, wiping the blood away from his face with the sleeve of his coat. Alley blinked and looked around. Three others arrived beside him, clearly shaken and disoriented. Declan looked at the faces of Michael Coulson and the two wives. Coulson held his left arm and grimaced painfully. The women appeared uninjured.

"We have to get out of here. Guide your husband," Declan said to Sherry Alley, who obeyed and gripped her husband's arm as he struggled to wipe his eyes clear of blood again. Declan gripped Constance by the shoulders once more. Moving around her, he took her hand and began to pull her behind him as he moved towards the stage. Cries for help came from all around, but Declan pushed forward, stepping over tables and chairs. He had to get the few people with him out before he had any chance of saving others. Remembering the emergency exit in the backstage space behind the curtain, he turned left when he reached the stage. The blue velvet curtain was covered in gray concrete dust, but had not fallen.

"Arghhhhh!"

Declan snapped his head to the left as a man came running towards the curtain, his clothing on fire. Pulling his suit coat off hastily, Declan jumped at the man, tackling him to the floor and patting out the flames. Standing upright again and leaving his coat on the injured man, he rejoined his group, which had stopped moving in his absence. He held the curtain open as he guided the three women and one man through. Several people had already made their way to the emergency exit, which stood open. Declan surveyed the chaos. Like crabs in a bucket, people grabbed at each other as they tried to reach the clogged exit, with the result not many people were getting out.

"Get out of the way," Declan said, pushing a man aside who'd grabbed a woman in front of him and was trying to pull her away from the door so he could get through. Keeping hold of his wife's hand, he shoved his way towards the front of the crowd and pushed her out of the door. Then he turned and with his arms opened wide, blocked the exit and yelled, "Whoa, stop!"

A few faces at the front of the melee looked up at him. "Alright," he said. "You, go!" He grabbed a man and pushed him out the door. "Go!" he said to another woman standing nearby and shoved her out. Repeating the process several times, the room slowly began to clear and people moved in an orderly fashion out of the exit and into the small parking lot beyond.

Suddenly the curtain to the stage was ripped aside and Levi Levitt appeared with Abaddon Kafni at his side. Kafni was being held up by his security man and it was clear that his leg had been injured. As Levitt moved forward and neared the door, Declan took hold of Kafni on the other side, helping to hold him up.

Cool night air and drops of rain attacked Declan's face as he moved through the doorway, holding Kafni. The parking lot behind what would be the servants' quarters of the original Poplar Forest was about as long and narrow as the east wing of the building itself. Clearly intended to hold only the cars of the faculty that worked in the building, it was empty of vehicles with the exception of a black GMC Suburban that Declan recognized instantly as the armored SUV Kafni had received from the Israeli government after the first attempt on his life. Blue-suited security personnel appeared from around the side of the building and began helping injured guests as they poured out of the emergency exit.

"Move, move!" Declan yelled to people who were leaning against the side of the SUV. Levitt let go of Kafni and reached into his pocket, unlocking the doors of the vehicle. A man standing near the SUV opened the rear door and held it as Declan helped Kafni inside. Closing the door, he turned to Levitt and said, "Get him someplace safe. Where are you staying? I'll meet you there!"

Levitt nodded and jumped in the driver's seat. "The Briton-Adams mansion on Cottonwood Road," he said, as the SUVs brake lights blazed brightly in the darkness and the vehicle roared to life. "There are three guards. I'll tell them you're coming."

"Aye, I know the place. We're driving a white convertible!" Declan said, as he slammed the door closed.

Slowly Levitt drove forward, sounding the vehicle's electric horn and being careful not to hit any of the people who had escaped the building. Declan watched as the taillights of the SUV faded down a one lane road that ran behind the building towards Liberty Mountain, an uneasy feeling settling over him as he turned to look for his wife.

Constance was seated against the building holding a sobbing woman whose arm had been burned. Sirens filled the air in the distance. "We have to go," Declan said to his wife. "We need to make sure Kafni is safe."

Constance spoke to the woman gently. "It'll be okay," she said, as tears gathered in her eyes. A man in a navy blue security uniform stepped over and took the woman.

Declan reached out and grabbed Constance's hand, pulling her behind him as he began to walk towards the side of the building. Digging her heels into the soft ground at the corner of the building, she stopped.

"Where are we going?" she demanded. "Why are we leaving?"

Declan couldn't explain it, but something inside him told him that whoever was behind what had just happened wasn't finished yet. Bells ringing through his mind like a sudden thunderstorm told him that Kafni had been the target.

"Because Abe's still in danger!" he said.

Constance relented and struggled to keep up as he moved briskly around the side of the east wing. As they rounded the building and the parking lot came into view, Declan looked to his left. A twisted metal frame engulfed in flames was all that was left of the white Ford Crown Victoria that had been parked near the security canopy at the front steps of the building. His mind raced as they headed towards their car. Having more than just a passing knowledge of bombs, and particularly car bombs, from his years in the IRA, Declan knew that the device had to have been inside the vehicle. This was an inside job.

The low lying clouds were awash with red and blue flashes from the LEDs on the emergency vehicles that were arriving as Declan turned over the ignition in the sports car, the six cylinder engine purring to life. He shifted furiously through the gears and piloted the convertible out of the lot and onto the small state road that ran alongside the Barton Center. As the orange glow from the burning building faded into the distance, Constance put her head in her hands and began to cry. Declan had no idea what to say to her. As the headlights chased away the darkness in front of them, he couldn't escape the feeling that two worlds that had been separated by a decade of peace had just collided violently.

CHAPTER SEVEN

Being hired by Sweat Security to operate the gate and man the tiny sunroom that had been erected to temporarily serve as a guard house for the Briton-Adams mansion was the best Chris Evans could hope for after losing his job at the White Rock Intermet Foundry. The last three years had been marked by long periods of unemployment after the plant he'd worked in for twenty-two years had closed; in the current slow economy, a forty-eight-year-old father of three without a college education wasn't exactly at the top of the hiring list.

Putting his feet up on the particle board desk, Chris spread a copy of the *Lynchburg News & Advance* open in front of him as he leaned back in the black leather office chair that had been borrowed from the mansion's study. The chair creaked under his two hundred and fifty pound frame. Working a toothpick through his teeth with his tongue, he looked over the inside front page of the paper. A full page spread with pictures of the newly completed construction at Liberty University and the guests expected to attend that night's gala unveiling kept his attention for a moment before he moved on to the sports page.

His experience as an MP with the Marine Corp Reserve and his lack of a criminal record meant he'd met the base qualifications for the job and had been hired as part of the three man team that was providing the security for the mansion while

Abaddon Kafni was staying at the property.

The Briton-Adams mansion was a three story brick plantation house that had been constructed in the late nineteen-thirties by a wealthy industrialist named Morgan Adams on a high knoll two hundred yards off Cottontown Road in the northeastern part of Bedford County, Virginia. After his death, the house had been sold to pay off his debts and had been bought by the Briton family, who owned it presently.

The Britons were a family from the British West Indies who had played a key role in the development of the area and had owned a large portion of the land that now made up the neighborhoods surrounding their home. As wealthy developers, they had helped in the founding of Liberty University and continued to donate large sums to its projects. Since they spent much of their time traveling, they'd offered their home to the university's latest lightning rod professor, Abaddon Kafni, while he took up his new post and set about finding a permanent residence for his family in the area.

In the eyes of Chris Evans, the Britons were old money suburbanites who didn't have to worry about a slow economy or the closing of a factory. In all probability, they were the kind of people who closed factories and sent the jobs overseas to a country with far lower wages and living standards than the United States.

But it was an easy gig, he reasoned with himself, as he took a drink of coffee. Kafni had his own three man security detail to take care of everything inside the house. The only thing Evans and the other two hired guards had to do was keep a watch over the perimeter of the property and call the police if they noticed anything out of the ordinary. Two weeks on daylight and two weeks on nights was a bit rough, but it was an income and he'd been guaranteed several months of employment while Kafni stayed at the mansion. If Sweat Security's contract was renewed once Kafni moved to a more permanent residence in the area, he'd been assured that he would be a shoo-in for continued employment.

Closing the paper and fighting a yawn, he removed his feet from the desk and sat up just as the headlights of a vehicle coming up the road attracted his attention. Standing and leaning out of the door, he looked east on Cottontown Road as a dark colored truck rounded a bend from the south. Immediately he was struck by the speed the vehicle was traveling, but was prepared to write it off as another crazy teenager with a lead foot until the vehicle began to slow down. As it got closer, Evans recognized it as one of the two black GMC SUVs that Abaddon Kafni and his security team drove. He stepped out of the guard shack with his hand on the radio clipped to his belt. The SUV made a right turn, the driver's side window descending into the door frame as the vehicle came to a stop.

"Open the gate!" someone inside the SUV yelled.

Evans squinted into the darkness and saw the face of Levi Levitt, Kafni's no-nonsense assistant, staring back at him. He ran back to the guard house and hit the button to open the gates.

"There's a white sports car coming in, too. Lock the place down behind us and don't let anyone else through until the police arrive!" Levitt yelled, as he floored the accelerator and the SUV roared up the long straight driveway towards the house. Evans watched the taillights vanish into the mansion's detached garage, then reached for the radio on his belt to alert the other two guards positioned along the north and west sides of the property. Suddenly another set of headlights washed over the guardhouse from the west and a dark red Chevy Suburban made a left hand turn into the drive and accelerated through the gates.

"Hey! You can't go in there!" Evans shouted as he ran out onto the paved drive, radio in hand. He turned as he heard another vehicle approaching. A second dark red Suburban screeched to a halt in front of him, the headlights preventing him from seeing who was inside.

Evans heard the driver's door open, followed by brisk footsteps, then a short man with dark receding hair and a thick beard stood in front of him. He regarded Evans coolly for a moment before raising a suppressed pistol.

"What? No!" exclaimed Evans, frozen to the spot.

"Excuse us," the man said, as he fired three times and stepped away towards the guard shack.

Evans felt the rounds enter his chest as the radio slid from his grasp. He stood still for a moment trying to draw breath, then fell to the wet pavement, still struggling to breathe. The sound of the gate beginning to close and the driver's door of the SUV being shut were the last sounds he heard as he clawed his way towards the guard shack and died, lying in the grass beside the one lane driveway he'd been hired to watch.

CHAPTER EIGHT

7:04 p.m. Eastern Time – Friday
Cottonwood Road
Forest, Virginia

Declan shifted furiously through the gears as he turned right and accelerated onto Cottonwood Road. They flew past the two shopping centers that occupied the corner of Cottonwood and the highway and over a concrete bridge spanning railroad tracks, then large brick homes came into view. Rounding a leftward bend, Declan finally saw the house he was looking for.

Sitting on top of a high knoll on the right side of the road, the Briton-Adams mansion was a well-known local landmark.

"What's that sound?" Declan asked, looking towards the floor.

"It's my phone," said Constance, hearing the tiny beep. Her mascara had run while she was crying and smudged around her eyes. She dabbed at them with a tissue as she said, "That's the sound it makes when it's passing in and out of service."

She leaned over and pulled the Samsung smartphone from her purse, tapping on the display to light up the screen. "See?" she said holding it up. "No signal."

"This close to Lynchburg? That's odd."

"The tower changes over in Bedford, remember? There's never a signal here for a few miles."

"Yeah, but that's twenty miles down the road," Declan said,

reaching for his own phone before realizing it had been in the jacket he'd left inside the Barton Center.

The convertible whined as Declan downshifted and swung into the driveway. He stopped at the closed gates. Pushing the automatic down button, he waited as the driver's window descended with a low hum.

"Where are the guards?" Declan said as he looked around. "Levi said there were three guards at the property."

Constance looked around. "I don't see anyone. Are you sure there's supposed to be someone here?"

Declan didn't answer. Outside of the Barton Center he'd been unable to escape the feeling that Kafni was still in danger. While he couldn't be sure that Kafni had been the target, his instincts told him that was the case. Was it an old skill that had been reawakened by seeing his old friends? He'd learned to trust his feelings in his two decades in the field and if something didn't feel right, he'd learned the hard way that it probably wasn't right. Even though there had been several representatives of the United States government inside the building, none of them had carried the notoriety of the event's keynote speaker. Nor had any of them been the target of six previous assassination attempts or the subject of a handful of *fatwas* calling for their deaths.

Opening the door, he stepped out onto the wet pavement and looked three hundred and sixty degrees around the car. The first thing that drew his attention was a set of muddy tire tracks ten feet away. On closer examination it was obvious that the tracks had been made recently as a vehicle had turned left into the property at high speed and had cut a corner, tearing up the wet grass. Could the vehicle have been the SUV driven by Levi Levitt? From his knowledge of the area, Declan doubted it. While it was possible Levitt had taken a less direct route through one of the neighborhoods south of the property, Declan thought it was highly unlikely. The routes through the neighborhoods were full of turns and Levitt had only been in town for a few days. The risk of getting lost, especially at night, would have been far too great.

He walked towards the guard house. Inside an opened newspaper and a cup of coffee sat on a cheap particle board desk, but no guard was present. He turned and walked out. As his eyes swept the area, he saw a black boot lying on the ground in the high grass near one of the brick columns that supported the gate. Rushing over, he knelt beside a heavy set man with brown curly hair, wearing the same type of navy blue uniform as the security at the Barton Center. He reached down and felt for a pulse with his index and middle fingers, although it was obvious from the man's glassy stare and the entry wounds on his chest that he was deceased. The man's skin was warm to the touch, a sign that he had only recently met his end.

Declan ran back to the driver's side of his car and opened the door. "Do you have a cell signal yet?" he said to his wife, who looked at him wide-eyed from the passenger seat.

"No," she said thumbing the device's screen, "nothing."

"I need you to drive down the road until you get a signal and call the police."

"Declan, what's happened?"

"Tell them to come to the Briton-Adams mansion immediately," he said, ignoring her question. "Tell them the guard's been killed."

Her response seemed to catch in her throat as she watched him reach under the driver's seat. With the sound of tearing Velcro he removed a leather pouch and opened it to reveal the black grip of a Glock pistol. Withdrawing the gun, he released the magazine and checked it before reinserting it into the grip and chambering a round.

"What are you doing?" Constance asked, as her eyes darted between her husband and the gun in his hand.

"I'm going to find Abe. Get going and don't come back until I call you and tell you it's safe."

He slid the pistol into his pocket and pulled off the neck tie he'd been wearing, before jogging towards the gate. He jumped and gripped the top of the gate. Pulling himself up and swinging his legs over, he heard his wife shift her sports car into reverse and exit the driveway. Landing on the wet pavement beyond the gate, he pulled the pistol from his pocket and ran towards the well-lit house on the hill two hundred yards ahead of him.

CHAPTER NINE

Reaching the top of the knoll, Declan entered a cluster of dogwood trees that occupied a teardrop shaped yard formed as the driveway forked left and right, meeting at the front door of the mansion fifty yards ahead of him. Nickel sized drops of rain fell from the trees above, soaking his light blue dress shirt as he dodged through the yard using the trees for sporadic cover. Arriving at the edge of the yard, he concealed himself behind the broad trunk of a tree and leaned around in search of anyone outside of the house.

The Briton-Adams mansion was well lit with small spotlights spaced evenly at three feet intervals down the brick walkway that led to the front door, and further apart across the front of the entire house. The brightness of the area surrounding the house made the darkness beyond it seem all the darker. This, Declan thought, seemed to be a contradiction in terms of security. The red and brown brick surface of the house rose to three stories before the steep, architecturally tiled roof disappeared above the reach of the spotlights. The flat front of the house featured six high windows on each level and an expensive looking set of double doors, which served as the entrance to an interior that was surely just as attractive as the exterior.

Declan surveyed each of the windows, looking for any signs that the house was occupied, but only the faintest hint of a dim light near the front door gave any sign that anyone lived there. Taking a last look at each of the windows, he crossed the driveway to the front door, pressing his back against it when he got there. Leaning to the left, he craned his neck so that he could see through the floor to ceiling windows on either side of the entrance. Inside the home was dark with the exception of a small light ablaze in the luxurious foyer. An LED on an alarm keypad across from the door flashed red every few seconds, indicating the security system was armed. Each of the four rooms off the foyer was dark and all the signs pointed to the conclusion that no one had entered the home recently.

Even with the house dark, Declan knew there had to be someone about. Whose vehicle had made the tire tracks he'd found near the gate? Who had killed the guard? It was one of the security company's vehicles that had exploded outside of the Barton Center. Had the guards been part of the attack? If so, then it was possible that Levitt had put the guard down himself as he and Kafni entered the property.

Declan raised the pistol in front of him as he moved to the left towards the side of the house, speeding up as he passed each of the three first floor windows on that side of the front door. Rolling out around the corner of the house, he again found no one and he continued to move cautiously towards a darkened Florida room that jutted off the northeast side of the house. The room beyond the floor to ceiling windows was populated with wicker sunroom furniture, but otherwise empty.

Seen through the Florida room's windows to the north, a vehicle caught Declan's attention. Sticking out from around the front of what appeared to be a garage was the tail end of a dark red SUV. Declan moved around the room onto a section of pavement that ran off the main driveway and made his way towards the garage, taking momentary cover behind several tall shrubs as he approached.

Like the house, the garage was made of brick and was large enough for a minimum of three full sized cars. With no windows or doors on the side, Declan placed his back against the outer wall and slid towards the front, where the dark red SUV protruded into the driveway. The SUV Kafni drove was black, so the vehicle wasn't his. As he got closer, Declan could hear a hissing sound as water from the vehicle's undercarriage dripped on the hot exhaust manifold, a sure sign that the SUV hadn't been parked there for long.

Rounding out into a full view of the garage doors, Declan

noticed the driver's side door of the red SUV had been left open, along with the window. Yellow light from the open garage stabbed the darkness and glared off the sleek paint of the vehicle. Making a quarter turn into the garage, he saw the black GMC Suburban that Levitt and Kafni had left the Barton Center in. Suddenly his fears were realized as his eyes rested on a small pool of blood near the base of the Suburban's front door. It was obvious to him now what had happened. Whoever had been driving the red SUV had followed Kafni's vehicle through the gates before the guard could close them and had ambushed Levitt and Kafni as they'd exited the vehicle. Clearing the rest of the garage, Declan rushed over to the driver's side of Kafni's vehicle and looked inside. Small spots of blood flecked the inside of the driver's compartment but it was clear from the small amounts that the gunshot had not been an exit wound. From the location of the blood, it appeared to have been Levitt who'd been shot, but where were he and Kafni now? Declan looked over the smooth concrete floor leading out of the garage. Amid the dirt and dark oil stains that littered the floor were a few more drops of crimson blood leading around the vehicle and to the left, out of the garage. Aiming his gun in front of him, he followed the trail outside.

"Hey!" a voice shouted from outside as he momentarily cleared the garage; he ducked back inside. Two suppressed gunshots erupted, one tearing into the hood of the dark red SUV and the other glancing off the garage's brick exterior. Declan pressed his back against the inside wall and listened, his pistol at the ready.

"What did you see?" an obviously foreign voice asked.

"There's someone in the garage with a gun. A guy in a blue shirt," another voice answered, this one rough and gravelly.

Declan thought he detected the presence of Slavic accents. He listened as the sound of shoes against the pavement indicated the men were moving, trying to get a view of him. Hidden in a corner between the garage door and the outer wall he waited, knowing the men would have to cross into his line of fire to see him. Having caught only the quickest glimpse of them before he'd ducked away he was pretty sure there were only two of them, but he couldn't be certain. The men began speaking quickly in hushed whispers using a foreign language, then suddenly one of them bolted forward, firing into the garage. The back window of Kafni's SUV shattered and Declan rounded out of his hiding spot to return fire. Squeezing the trigger three times in rapid succession the report of the weapon echoed loudly in the hollow building.

The running gunman dove for cover behind the passenger side of the dark red SUV and Declan's rounds passed over him. Suddenly, Declan caught sight of someone approaching from the edge of the garage. He moved left a millisecond too late and the broad end of a shovel slammed down on his extended arms and again in quick succession to the right side of his face as the first strike drove him downwards.

Falling backwards from the second upward impact of the shovel, Declan held tight to his gun as his back slammed hard against the concrete, knocking the wind out of him. His attacker stepped fully into the garage and raised the shovel to deliver another blow. Declan rolled onto his left side as the tool banged against the concrete where his head had been seconds before. Rolling back to his right he raised his gun as the attacker brought the shovel over his head for another blow. Gunshots echoed through the building as three holes appeared in the man's chest and he flew backwards from the close range impact.

Taking a shallow breath, relief was brief as Declan heard the sound of suppressed gunshots. Pushing his feet furiously against the smooth concrete floor and scrambling towards the outer wall of the garage, he raised himself into a sitting position and returned fire towards the red SUV, his first shot impacting the vehicle's windshield. Following the gunman as he skipped sideways towards the front of the vehicle, Declan squeezed the trigger methodically, intent on hitting his target. The man shouted in pain as a bullet tore into his shoulder, followed by another that caught him in the side of the head. The man fell down and Declan stopped firing, breathing heavily as the sound of shell casings hitting the floor abated and the tang of cordite filled the air. The peaceful sound of crickets chirping in the trees lining the driveway returned outside the garage before being interrupted again by a gunshot, this one a distant echo somewhere to the north of the garage.

Standing upright, Declan steadied himself against the side of the black SUV, becoming aware of the injury to his head for the first time as the room spun around him. He lifted a hand and touched a spot above his right eye that was throbbing with pain. Pulling his hand back he noticed blood dotting his fingertips. Turning his hand over, he saw a laceration caused by the shovel striking him. Wiping the warm fluid on his shirt, he pushed himself off the vehicle and moved towards the garage door, stepping over the body of the dead thug.

Outside, he aimed his pistol to the left in the direction the two men had come from. In the distance he could see another building, this one longer than the garage and with a tin roof. The driveway leading to the garage extended past it and turned to gravel about fifteen yards from where Declan stood. Stepping in front of the dark red SUV he peered over the edge of the vehicle to see the gunman he'd shot moments before lying on the pavement. He moved towards him and kicked away the suppressed pistol before nudging the man hard with his foot. The man slumped onto his back and stared eerily upwards, the side of his face covered in blood that had pooled underneath him from the wound above his left ear. Along with an unkempt beard, a black crochet *taqiyah* on the man's head identified him as a follower of Islam, though he didn't appear to be Middle Eastern. He had a slightly pallid complexion and black hair, his skin rough like he'd spent a lot of time in harsh outdoor conditions. Declan turned away towards the north knowing the man was deceased.

Another distant gunshot echoed from the tin-roofed building in the distance and Declan rushed forward, suddenly remembering why he was there. His steps were unsteady and his vision blurred as he made his way forward. Stopping at the base of a tree, he leaned against it for support, realizing the seriousness of the injury to his head. Doing his best to shake it off, he continued forward towards the building fifty yards ahead of him.

Unlike the house and the garage, the building was made of wood that had been blackened by age. Several sets of barn doors lined the outside of it and steel icebreakers jutted out of the tin roof to break up any falling snow as it descended during the winter months. Declan ducked back behind the tree trunk and lowered himself to the ground in a prone position as two black clad men carrying submachine guns appeared around the side of the building and ran up the driveway towards the garage. He watched from the wet ground as the men passed within twenty yards of him. When they arrived at the garage, they slowed to a stop, speaking to each other in a foreign language.

Staying low to the ground and keeping an eye on the two men at his six o'clock, Declan continued forward. Arriving at the building he rested against the aged wood before continuing around the perimeter in search of an open entrance. How many men were there? The vehicle they had arrived in could easily seat six, but could hold as many as eight or nine if they'd used the rear cargo area in addition to the regular seating. Slowly rounding the northwest corner of the building and being sure to stay out of the line of sight of the two men near the garage, he saw another dark red SUV parked next to the building, its passenger doors open. On discovery of the second vehicle he knew he was facing impossible odds. In his injured condition and having expended nine of the sixteen bullets in his magazine, there was no way he could hope to take on what could be as many as twenty men.

The sound of a vehicle starting up and a pair of headlights illuminating the driveway next to the building preceded the appearance of the SUV that had been parked in front of the garage. Arriving around the opposite corner of the building from where Declan was standing, the vehicle came to a stop in front of its twin. The passenger door opened and one of the men who'd run up the driveway got out and entered an open door across from the parked SUV.

"Someone's here," he said in accented English to whoever was inside. "Tariq and Nadir are dead!"

"Get out there and keep a lookout!" a harsh voice bellowed. This time Declan was sure the accent was Slavic and belonged to someone from the old Soviet bloc of countries. "It looks like our fun here has come to an end, little brother, but before you die, I want you to know that I'm going to cut off your head and mail it to your family!" the voice continued. Declan was sure he heard the voice of Abaddon Kafni next, but couldn't make out what was being said. He closed his eyes as two gunshots rang out from within the building. Moments later, as the ringing of the gunshots faded, several celebratory whoops filled the air.

"Allahu akbar! Allahu akbar!" several men repeated over and over again.

Declan moved away from the building towards a clump of trees twenty yards away. He watched from cover as ten heavily armed men exited, aiming their submachine guns and pistols in all directions as an eleventh man moved abruptly out of the building and straight to the parked SUV. In his left hand, Declan could see a white sack with a dark red stain forming at its base. He felt the breath leave his body as a surge of anger erupted within him. Falling back against the trunk of a tree, he slid to a sitting position as the scarlet glare of the SUV's brake lights sliced the darkness. Doors slammed as the men entered the vehicles and a cloud of dust was pushed into the air as they moved out in succession, the tires sliding on the loose gravel as they accelerated around the side of the building and up the driveway towards the house. As the SUVs rounded the knoll next to the teardrop shaped yard and disappeared over the hill, Declan closed his eyes, breathing heavily as darkness took him.

CHAPTER TEN

Senator David Kemiss swallowed the last few sips of the cocktail he'd been drinking and looked at the LED on his cell phone as he pulled it out of his pocket, vibrating. His eyes moved from the LED to the disapproving glare of his wife. Mary Ellen Kemiss was seated on the opposite end of their sofa, the one cushion between them like a thousand snow-covered miles. *Bitch,* he thought as he stood.

"I'll just be a moment," he said.

She rolled her eyes in disgust. Their two children, sitting on the floor of the darkened den, stared on at the glowing television screen and didn't look up or even acknowledge that a real person had spoken. Their faces stayed blank, emotionlessly enthralled in the latest adventure film to grace the store shelves and vending devices.

Tonight was supposed to be their family time, an event the Kemiss family carved out of the busy week to spend together and keep up appearances to their children and any other interested parties. For the last few years family night had meant movie night. If there wasn't a fundraiser, parade or dinner they needed to be seen at, a movie was the only activity where the kids wouldn't notice that mom and dad didn't speak to each other. Two biological children were the only things they had in common and each of them had been seeing other people romantically for years, their marriage a theater production for the eyes of the electorate and the upper crust community they socialized with.

Having exited the dim living room, David Kemiss climbed the open central staircase of the Georgian mansion. When he arrived at his third floor study, he closed the door behind him and flipped open the phone.

"What is it?" he asked, as he sat back in the dark red chair behind his walnut desk. The aged leather protested loudly as he settled his tall frame and made himself comfortable.

"It's me. I'm afraid there's some bad news."

Kemiss took a deep breath. The voice belonged to a longtime friend, Seth Castellano, the man he'd been seeing romantically for nearly five years. They'd been working together for nearly a decade, beginning with Castellano's stint in the Russell Senate Office Building as an intern just out of college, and now Castellano was the ambitious Assistant Special Agent in Charge of the Richmond Virginia Field Office's Counterterrorism Division of the FBI.

"Go on," Kemiss said, feeling the muscles in his face tense.

"Well, as you're probably beginning to see on television if you're watching, everything went off as planned, but we didn't make the goal."

Kemiss closed his eyes and exhaled a long breath. He knew that Castellano was being intentionally vague and careful to avoid using any words that might trigger the vast security measures in place to monitor phone conversations by potential terrorists. On the prepaid wireless devices they were using, words like bomb; target or operation could trigger an electronic monitoring system and create a file that could eventually be traced. Even though the phones were paid for in cash and the farthest any trace could go was the cell tower the call had originated from, it was still closer than he wanted anyone to get. The *everything* Castellano was referring to was the car bomb that had gone off an hour earlier outside of a building at Liberty University, an hour south of Kemiss' residence. The goal had been to kill Dr. Abaddon Kafni. Apparently it had failed.

"And what about our friend," Kemiss asked. "What's the

status of his plan?"

"Done," Castellano said. "Two are gone, including the goal but—"

"You've got the scene closed down? No one's getting in and out of there, right?"

"Relax, David. Both scenes are closed up tight. My department is in complete control of the scene and they report only to me. The investigation is in the right hands."

"So what's the *but* about then?"

"There was an emergency call to the residence and someone has been rushed to the hospital with serious injuries."

Kemiss clenched his teeth. "Someone saw it?" he asked as he exhaled, his lungs tightening along with his grip on the cell phone.

"We don't know that yet," Castellano cautioned. "Whoever he is, he's been rushed to the hospital unconscious. We don't know if he's seen anything or not."

"We can't afford to wait and find out."

"I know. I'll handle it. I'll call you back in a while."

Kemiss closed the cell phone and tossed it across the desk, knocking over a pencil jar. Leaning back in the chair again he wiped the sweat from his face with the back of his sleeve. Guilt settled in the pit of his stomach and acid leapt at the back of his tongue as he sat there thinking. He knew that the people he should be thinking about were the victims who had most likely lost their lives at Liberty University. How many would there be, a dozen, several dozen? He didn't care. He didn't want to think about them. It was all the means to an end. The people he was thinking about were himself and Seth Castellano. The lives they had each built were in jeopardy. If things went wrong, they were both finished.

Standing, he walked over to the long table in front of the bay window that looked out over the Blue Ridge Mountains west of his home. The table was made of the same walnut as the desk. The same walnut as the end tables that sat on either side of the dark red leather sofa, against the wall opposite his desk, and the same walnut as the two floor to ceiling bookshelves that held dozens of thick law books; state, federal and international. They all matched, meticulously handcrafted by American carpenters from North Carolina and, like most of the items in his home, expensive.

On the table was a crystalline tray holding several glass bottles. He opened one with a clink and poured a double shot of bourbon. How had his life and career come to this? David Kemiss, graduate of Harvard, renowned international attorney and the thrice re-elected senior Senator of Virginia was hanging on to the life he'd built by a thread; by something thinner than a thread, by a hair.

He knew how he'd arrived at this dismal place, he wasn't oblivious. The questions in his head were rhetorical. His political career had been in a tailspin since his party had lost the presidential election in 2004, with his name on the bottom of the ticket. Although his party had made a comeback in 2006 and had taken a majority in both the House and the Senate, and had taken the Presidency in 2008, he hadn't been up for re-election until 2010, by which time the so-called Tea Party had risen and the policies he and his colleagues had helped to enact had become extremely toxic.

In the 2010 mid-term election he had narrowly held onto his seat only because of the sharp divide on the conservative side of the ticket which had seen two candidates, one an establishment-backed Republican whose lack of conservative credentials had been sharply criticized and had led to a Tea Party backed candidate who had served to split the Republican vote and hand the election to the Democrats, to him. The circumstances by which he had won had signaled to the national leadership of his party that he was becoming a liability instead of an asset and in Washington D.C. liabilities didn't last very long.

He looked out of the bay window, his eyes stopping on his reflection in the tempered glass. His hair was as gray as his soul felt and his morals had receded along with his hairline: politics was a rough business. He adjusted the wire-rimmed glasses on his nose and looked away towards the skylight in the den below. He couldn't see his children through the frosted glass, but the flicker of the television told him they were still there and likely unaware that he'd even left. He thought briefly about the other families that had been affected by the actions he'd helped set in motion. He didn't know Abaddon Kafni very well, but he was sure the fifty-something Jew had children and that they'd be finding out soon, if they hadn't already, that their father wouldn't be coming home. His thoughts turned to the families that were yet to be affected, but surely would be by the time this was over. There was a term for them: collateral damage. He raised the glass to his lips and drank down the bourbon, willing the sordid thoughts away as the drink burned all the way down into his stomach.

The study door opening gently behind him caused him to stiffen and look suddenly to the room's entrance. A tiny voice surprised him.

"Daddy, why did you leave?" It was his six-year-old son, the youngest of the two.

Luke Kemiss stood in the doorway, his fragile figure illuminated by the dim light in the hallway. The senator turned with a warm smile and sank to one knee, holding his arms open towards his son. The boy accepted the invitation and the two embraced.

"Daddy had to take an important phone call, but it's done now." He brushed the boy's dark hair back off his forehead and marveled for a moment. It was as though he was looking at a photograph of himself, forty years in the past. He smiled again and stood. "Go on back downstairs, you're gonna miss the end. I'll be right behind you."

The boy turned and walked out of the study looking over his shoulder as he neared the door.

"I'll be right there," Kemiss mouthed silently, waving him out. He listened as the boy's bare feet thumped down the stairs before he turned back to the window. The light from the hallway had caused his reflection to disappear, but it didn't matter. These days he barely recognized himself anyway. He poured more bourbon and drank it down, returned the glass to the tray and walked out of the room.

CHAPTER ELEVEN

8:06p.m. Eastern Time – Friday
Virginia Baptist Hospital
Lynchburg, Virginia

Seth Castellano pulled his dark blue Crown Vic under the covered entrance of the smaller of the Lynchburg area's two major medical facilities. Stepping out of the vehicle onto the concrete walkway that led to the main entrance of the multi-storied brick facility, he flashed his badge to the valet who was about to tell him not to park there. The man backed off and Castellano continued walking without a word, shrugging his tan trench coat higher on his shoulders and adjusting the collar as he walked towards a grouping of ambulances closer to the windowed entrance.

"Any of you boys bring in a man from the Cottonwood Road area about twenty minutes ago?" he asked a group of EMTs standing near their buses. His voice rang with a southern tenor and carried briefly on the mist that hung in the humid air, his accent a mixture of Louisiana creole, where he was born, and metro Washingtonian, where he'd lived and worked for over a decade.

The group of EMTs stopped talking amongst each other and regarded him for a moment, looking over his slicked brown hair and slightly rounded features before answering. "We did," a blue uniformed man with blonde hair said, motioning with his cigarette towards another uniformed man next to him.

"And what were his injuries exactly?" Castellano asked.

The EMT started to speak but thought better of it, looking at Castellano instead with a question on his face as if he wanted to say *what's it to you?*

Castellano withdrew the black badge wallet from inside his coat again and flipped it open. "FBI," he said. "What exactly were his injuries?"

"Lacerations to the back of the left hand and to his head above the right eye, he wasn't conscious until about the last two minutes of the ride and then he said something about his wife. We wheeled him to the Outpatient Center. They've turned it into an emergency room to handle the overflow from general."

"And what did he look like?"

"Blondish hair, a beard, kind of slim, he was wearing a blue-button down shirt and tan Dockers. He only spoke briefly but he had some kind of an accent, English maybe."

Castellano closed his badge and returned it to the inner breast pocket of his coat as he walked through the automated glass doors into the spacious, gray carpeted lobby.

"Can I help you find something?" asked a lady behind a courtesy desk just inside the door.

"Outpatient center," Castellano answered.

"Down this hallway to your left and then take a right. Go all the way to the end."

Castellano was on the move before she finished talking. As he made his way down the light blue painted hallway he considered his options. In a modern hospital where patient and medical provider privacy were as critical as the care being given, he knew there would be video cameras and other security measures. While he intended to make sure the man who had apparently been present at the scene of Abaddon Kafni's death never left the hospital alive, this wasn't a movie. He couldn't just walk into a darkened room and snuff the guy with a silenced pistol; he would have to be far more careful.

As he arrived at another automatic door with white vinyl letters identifying the ward beyond as the outpatient center, his thoughts of a stealthy entrance and exit faded. The door hissed open and he was greeted by the sight of a long white hallway filled with ambulance gurneys. Doctors and nurses rushed about wearing uneasy expressions, and patients writhed painfully in their beds, some comforted by family members and others alone, their faces terrified. He'd known the small facility had been turned into a makeshift emergency room to handle the overflow from the larger and more prepared Lynchburg General Hospital, but he hadn't expected to see so closely the destruction caused by the bomb he'd known was going to go off.

He swallowed hard and entered the ward. To his right and left lay people dressed in suits and ties, looking up and down the hallway for the people who were responsible for treating them. "Doctor, doctor!" a man called, reaching out and grabbing the edge of Castellano's coat as he walked by. "I'm in pain. You gotta give me something for this pain!"

Castellano looked the man quickly up and down. From the hastily applied bandages it was obvious that his leg had been injured, and his clothes were covered in dust and ashes, a clear sign that he had been inside the building when the blast had occurred. "I'm sorry," Castellano said, jerking his coat away from the man. "I'm not a doctor."

He moved on through the ward towards the end of the hallway, where the rear entrance to the hospital was marked by a set of automatic glass doors. Directly in front of the entrance stood a nurses' station teaming with men and women in scrubs.

"Are you looking for someone, sir?" asked a loud female voice.

Castellano looked at a blonde haired woman with a no bull expression who sat behind the desk in pink scrubs. "I'm looking for a man who was brought in here from the Cottonwood Road area with lacerations to the head and hands."

"You're going to have to be a lot more specific than that. We've admitted over fifty people in the last hour and lacerations are the flavor of the day."

Her lack of bedside manner didn't surprise him. He'd been in and out of hospitals for the last twenty years during the course of his work, first as a police investigator in New Orleans and then as a field agent in the FBI before obtaining his current position. Doctors and nurses had some of the highest burn out ratios in the country and what normal people considered an emergency barely caused them to break a sweat.

Removing his badge from inside his coat and flipping it open for what seemed like the hundredth time that night, he said, "This man had a laceration above his right eye and on the back of his right hand. He was slim with blonde hair and a beard. He might've been speaking with an accent. I'll need you to check your intake forms and give me a list of the possibilities. It's very important that I speak with him."

The lady flipped through a stack of papers, but before she could answer a harried male voice from behind Castellano spoke. ""I'm afraid you're going to have to come back later, officer. We have an emergency situation here."

Castellano turned around and looked at a gray haired man in a white lab coat who moved from the edge of a gurney to the countertop at the nurses' station.

"I'm Doctor Garvinton. I'm the lead physician on the floor," the man continued. "Right now, I've got three patients to a room and another twenty in the hallway. Your interviews are going to have to wait until later."

Garvinton grabbed a stack of medical charts and began thumbing through them.

"My interviews can't wait until later, Doctor," Castellano said, his voice dripping with contempt. "In case you haven't noticed, we've all got an emergency situation. The man I'm looking for may very well be a witness to the murder of the man we believe was the target of the university bombing. If he's here, I need to speak with him right away and hopefully we can keep whoever did this from striking again."

"If he's a witness to the murder of the target then the target is already dead. No need to strike again if they were successful the first time."

Garvinton moved around Castellano and began to walk away.

"Look," Castellano said, grabbing the doctor by the shoulder and holding up his badge again. "I'm Assistant Special Agent in Charge Seth Castellano of the FBI's Richmond Counterterrorism Division and this is a matter of national security."

Garvinton looked over the edge of his wire-rimmed glasses

for a moment before speaking. "The description you just gave sounds like a man we took to room six about ten minutes ago. One of my physician's assistants is with him now stitching his injuries closed, but you're going to have a lot of trouble talking to him since he's been coming in and out of consciousness. He suffered a pretty hard hit and has a concussion. I won't know the extent of his injuries until I get an x-ray tech in here to photograph him, but I can tell you he'll be held for observation at least until morning and that depends on what the x-rays show. The best I can do for you tonight is to point you towards our waiting room, where his wife is."

Castellano followed the doctor's finger with his eyes as he pointed to an open doorway to the right of the ward's entrance.

Garvinton continued. "I've just finished speaking with her. Her name is Constance McIver and the man you're asking about is Declan McIver. He's the only person here fitting the description you gave and the few words he's been able to say were accented...Irish, if I had to guess."

"Thank you, Doctor."

Garvinton nodded and quickly walked away.

Castellano took a deep breath realizing that there could be more than one witness. Why hadn't the first responders on the scene mentioned a woman? Had she been on the scene or had she arrived at the hospital upon news of her husband's injury? He walked toward the open doorway and leaned in to take a look. A slender woman with auburn colored hair sat alone on a green vinyl bench in the eight-by-ten room, a tissue in her hand.

"Mrs. McIver?" he asked gently.

She straightened herself up and sniffed away a few tears as he entered. "Yes?" she said looking up with a question on her face.

"I'm ASAC Seth Castellano with the Federal Bureau of Investigation."

He stepped fully into the room and opened his badge. She looked at it briefly and then back at him, meeting his stare with sea green eyes.

"I'm leading the investigation into the death of Abaddon

Kafni—" before he could finish speaking he could tell by the look on her face that she hadn't known Kafni was dead.

"I'm sorry," he said interrupting himself. "You didn't know?"

She shook her head as she dabbed at the edges of her eyes with the shredded tissue. He waited a few moments for her to collect herself and then continued. "It was my understanding that your husband, Declan, is it?"

Constance nodded.

"It was my understanding that he was at the scene. Is that correct?"

She nodded again and said, "Yes."

"And were you with him?"

She shook her head. "Only as far as the front gate. We left the university together and when we got to the residence we found the guard at the gate dead. He sent me to call for help because we couldn't get a signal on our cell phones."

Castellano nodded. Just as they had planned, a signal jammer had been used to black out cell service for several hundred yards around the property to prevent anyone from calling for help. What they hadn't planned for was someone arriving at the property after Kafni and being able to leave to summon help. "So you weren't there when he was injured?"

She shook her head and dabbed her eyes again with the tissue.

"Why did the two of you leave the university and go to the Briton-Adams property?"

"My husband was a friend of Dr. Kafni's. He worked security for him for a while. Declan helped get Dr. Kafni out of the building when—when it happened."

There it was. The connection he'd been afraid of. An injured gardener or some kind of other domestic help that just happened to be on the property wouldn't be so bad. Maybe they'd just been in the wrong place at the wrong time, but a trained bodyguard? It was all but certain in his mind that Declan McIver had been directly involved in the scene at the mansion. But if that was the case then why had Ruslan Baktayev and his men left him alive? What did he know? Could he identify the men who'd killed Kafni? Castellano drew in another breath as the questions and potential answers ran through his mind.

He'd been afraid that just such a mistake would happen and had tried to make sure Kafni was dead long before he ever reached the property. While Baktayev wouldn't have been happy about being unable to kill Kafni personally, as he had planned, he couldn't argue with the fact that he had been killed by a bomb originally intended only to evacuate the premises. Castellano wasn't in the business of making terrorists happy. He was in the business of making sure both he and David Kemiss were successful. Unknown to Baktayev, with the help of four hired guns, they had increased the size of the bomb in hopes of killing Kafni and had even placed the four men at the scene to ensure everything went as planned. Now, thanks to the apparent intervention of a former bodyguard nobody had known about, Baktayev's plan had gone forward and everything he and Kemiss had feared was now a fact of life.

"You said he used to work security for Kafni, but he doesn't currently?"

"No," Constance answered. "He worked for Dr. Kafni in the late nineties and for a short while after September 11th. It was before we met so I really don't know much about it. Tonight was the first time I'd met Dr. Kafni. We were supposed to meet him for dinner after the event had concluded. It's been several years since he and Declan have seen each other."

Castellano nodded. "I see."

"Agent Castellano, what happened?" Constance asked, becoming visibly upset.

He didn't know what was going through her mind exactly, but after two decades of experience interviewing witnesses to various types of crime, he had a pretty good idea. Confusion mixed with moments of clarity was common.

"Well," he said, "I don't know yet. That's what I'm trying to put together. We're only in the very early stages of our investigation."

"Declan said there was a bomb in one of the security vehicles," she said, as she sucked in a loud breath and did her best to wipe away the tears falling from her eyes.

"It was in one of the security vehicles?" Castellano asked, trying to sound surprised.

"Yes. He said he saw the vehicle burning as we ran towards our car. He said it was one of the cars that belonged to the security guards."

Castellano grimaced as each word from Constance McIver confirmed to him that her husband was indeed a threat. But how should he handle it? He crossed his arms and felt the grip of his service weapon underneath his coat. With so many witnesses around, it would be impossible for him to act.

"Mrs. McIver," a female voice said from the doorway.

Castellano turned to see a young woman in a white doctor's coat standing just inside the door.

"Yes?" Constance answered, as she stood from the bench she'd been sitting on.

"I'm Lisa Baker. I'm a physician's assistant. I've just finished with your husband and we're moving him up to an observation room in the hospital. You can see him now."

"Can I talk to him?" Castellano asked abruptly.

"No, sir," the P.A. said. "You'll have to wait."

"It's important that I speak with him if he's conscious—"

"I'm sorry, sir. It's Doctor Garvinton's orders. Mr. McIver isn't to be interviewed until his condition has been properly diagnosed."

Constance started to walk out of the room. Castellano stopped her.

"I really need to speak with your husband as soon as possible. This is my card; my cell phone is on it. I'd like you to call me as soon as he's able to speak with me."

Constance nodded. "I will."

Castellano watched as she slipped the card into the pocket of her coat and walked out of the room. Following her briefly, he stopped at the edge of the doorway and looked after her as she walked to the side of a gurney that was being wheeled into the hallway from one of the rooms. As an orderly pushed the cart towards the nursing station Castellano caught his first glimpse of the man he'd been looking for. Declan McIver was just as the EMT had described him and unlike the doctors had said, he seemed perfectly alert as he gripped his wife's hand and looked about the room.

Stepping through the automatic door that led to a covered

entrance at the rear of the hospital, Castellano removed his cell phone from the pocket of his coat. The light rain that had been falling most of the evening had turned to a heavy downpour, the rain drumming against the roofs of the cars parked in the lot beside the outpatient center. He pressed his ear closer into the phone as he listened to it ringing.

"It's me," he said as David Kemiss answered. "We've definitely got a problem."

CHAPTER TWELVE

"Mr. McIver," a doctor said, looking over charts on a clipboard as he walked into the hospital room, "I would say that you're one of the luckiest people I've seen come through here in a long time, but last night would prove me wrong. Thankfully, there were a lot of lucky people in here."

Declan sat up slowly in the hospital bed. After narrowly escaping death at the hands of a group of Islamic assassins, he'd been resting in an observation room since being moved from the makeshift Emergency Room downstairs.

Inside, the Virginia Baptist Hospital looked like any other hospital; white walls, white floors, white drop ceiling, machines buzzing and popping, and overworked nurses and doctors rushing about. Inside his room was dark, lit only in brief flickers and flashes from the television screen that hung angled from the ceiling opposite his bed. A few pieces of particle board furniture occupied the private room and a bathroom barely big enough to turn around in sat off to the side. Not being accustomed to just sitting around, the feeling of going stir crazy was worse than either the pain in his hand or the pain in his head. He closed his eyes and reopened them, gradually allowing his eyesight to adjust as the doctor turned on the lights.

"I guess it's true what they say about the luck of the Irish," the doctor continued, with an arid smile. "You are Irish, right?"

"Aye," Declan said. In fact, he actually thought of himself as an American, having been in the United States for fifteen years, but he was constantly reminded of his heritage whenever he opened his mouth.

"I'd really rather that you not be watching television," the doctor continued. "It's important that you rest for the next several days. It's not uncommon for people who suffer head trauma to have spurts of vomiting and in some rare cases loss of consciousness. You really are quite lucky. If you'd suffered even a shade more trauma than you did, we'd be talking about an entirely different injury. But as it is, the stitches in your hand should be out in a week and you should be back to normal within a week or two at the most. None of the x-rays we've taken in the last twelve hours indicate any continued swelling. Save for that bit of broken skin above your eye, there's no sign you were even hit. I'm going to recommend the doctor on shift this afternoon release you. We should have you out of here in time for dinner, but I still want you to take it easy. Beware of operating any vehicles or equipment."

Declan nodded his agreement, trying to keep his elation at finally being released to a minimum.

"You have a visitor," the doctor said tucking the clipboard under his arm. "I'll show him in."

"Be brief," Declan overheard the doctor saying to someone in the hallway. "He's already spoken to two of your men this morning against my recommendations. As quickly as his injuries seem to have healed, he needs rest, not to be constantly reminded of everything he's witnessed."

Closing the door behind him, a tall, brown haired man in a perfectly pressed three piece suit entered; he was carrying a thick manila folder. His hair was heavy with product and brushed to one side; a soapy fragrance followed him as he strode to the single chair in the room and took a seat, pulling one leg up to rest across his knee.

"Mr. McIver, I'm ASAC Seth Castellano," he said opening the folder. "I'm glad we're finally getting a chance to talk."

An air of youthful superiority emanated from the agent and bells rang out in Declan's subconscious. Unsure of whether it was his bureaucrat BS detector or something else, Declan nodded but remained silent.

"I understand from the staff here that you spoke with the local police earlier, is that correct?"

Declan nodded. "Aye, that's right."

"Let's get one thing straight right off the bat, Mr. McIver; the local police have no jurisdiction over this investigation, none, zero. This is a federal matter and as such it falls to me. It's my case, and you don't talk to anyone about it but me. Clear?"

"Hardly a time for politics and inter-department quarrels, is it?"

"The local police aren't inter-department. They're not inter-anything. Sheriff Andy and Deputy Fife will screw this case up six ways to Sunday and have their men out looking for turban-wearing camel jockeys at the local mosque."

"They were Chechens and Turks. Maybe an Armenian or two, but they weren't Middle Eastern."

"Chechens, Turks and Armenians, that's your story?"

Declan nodded slowly, taken back by the agent's wording. What exactly did Castellano mean by the term "story"? Was he implying that he didn't believe what Declan had told the police?

"I talked to the locals myself," the agent began, with an air of incredulity. "You're saying you witnessed a terrorist cut off Mr. Kafni's head and then hold it up in triumph, is that correct?" Castellano closed his fist and waved it through the air as if he was holding a severed head by its hair.

"That's not what I told them. I heard the leader of the group say he was going to do that." Declan stopped for a moment and took a deep breath. "I heard him say he was going to decapitate Kafni and mail his head to his family. Then I saw the group leave and one of them, the leader, was carrying a white sack with blood pooling in the bottom. Are you watching his family? You can't let anyone deliver anything to them!"

"Well, then, you see my point about the locals," Castellano said, ignoring the plea. "They'd have everyone believing in and searching for the Legend of Sleepy Hollow complete with a flaming pumpkin and a broadsword."

Declan gripped the railing of his bed tightly, his knuckles

whitening. Castellano was baiting him for some reason and he didn't appreciate it.

"So who were these men? You told the locals they were Muslims. Then you told me they were Chechens, Turks and Armenians. How do you know the one carrying the sack was the leader? How many were there? What did they look like? What were their names? How did they get there? What were they driving?"

Declan knew that Castellano was trying to confuse him into making a mistake with the rapid fire questioning, but it wasn't going to work. Despite being injured, he was sure of what he'd seen and of the descriptions of the men involved. "I don't know who they were and I don't know their names. It's your job to find that out and catch them. They were driving two dark red GM Suburban model SUVs and there were thirteen of them. I shot two of them and eleven escaped. In the dark it looked like most of them had dark hair and light complexions, but I only got close to the two that tried to kill me. I know the man carrying the sack was the leader because the others were protecting him as they escaped. He had little or no hair and looked like he could have been sick because his skin was pallid and he was thin for his height. Chechens, Turks and a small percentage of Armenians are Muslims, look it up."

Castellano took a breath and seemed to be fighting back a smile. Was he enjoying this? Declan looked down at the white bedding that was covering his legs and fought back a surge of anger.

"I did look it up," Castellano said, "along with some other things. There are no bodies to back up your assertion that you killed two of these men."

Declan looked up remembering the two men who had run towards the garage to investigate the gunshots and had returned in one of the SUVs. Had they taken the bodies with them? That was the only explanation.

"They must've taken them."

"I see," said Castellano as he looked down at the paperwork in the folder on his lap. "And this leader, the bald sickly man, you told the locals he spoke with a Slavic accent and that you believe he could be a man named Ruslan Baktayev. Is that correct?"

"Aye, that's right."

"But you don't know for sure?"

"I've never seen him, but Kafni told me he'd escaped from a Russian prison and that he had a personal vendetta. It seems like a reasonable conclusion based on the accent, but no, I'm not sure it was him."

Castellano nodded. "Well, let me tell you the problem I have with that and see if maybe you can help me. Abaddon Kafni passed off his suspicions about this Ruslan Baktayev to people in our State Department and they've been in contact with the Russian government in Moscow recently, and they told us this Baktayev is dead. He has been for weeks now."

Declan shrugged. He knew that Kafni had told him the Russians were lying and that there had been someone inside the prison sympathetic to Mossad, but Kafni's first career as a spy was not public knowledge. "Then it wasn't him," Declan said, unwilling to discuss Kafni's connections with Mossad.

Castellano looked up from the folder and stared in Declan's direction. Meeting his gaze, bells again sounded in Declan's subconscious. What exactly was this agent's angle? Why had he been combative from the beginning? Was he not interested in finding the men responsible for the bombing of an American university and the assassination of a man who had tirelessly defended both his adopted home in America and his native land?

"And what about you, Mr. McIver, how exactly do you know Abaddon Kafni and his entourage?" Castellano asked, suddenly changing the subject.

"I worked for him for six years."

"Right," Castellano said closing the folder. "Let's cut the crap. I don't believe this story you've given me that an escaped Chechen terrorist with ties to the *Mujahideen* somehow made it into the United States and took out a man as well protected as Abaddon Kafni. Islamic radicals have been trying for nearly two decades to kill Kafni and so far every one of their mediocre attempts has been foiled by his security."

"I know. I was his security and was personally involved in stopping three of those attacks."

"Which leads me to more questions," Castellano said smugly. "Your immigration file indicates that you arrived in the U.S. from Galway, Ireland, in 1995 and that your occupation there was fisherman, a role you briefly continued in once you arrived here in the U.S. Would you mind telling me how an Irish rodman came to be employed as muscle by a Jewish firebrand?"

Declan had expected this line of questioning to come up at some point, but the confrontational position adopted by Castellano surprised him. He'd been interviewed by federal agents before when he'd been involved in stopping the assassination attempts Castellano had referenced and each time the agents had readily accepted his statements. The fishing industry was rough. Men were employed for long periods of time aboard vessels with less than desirable facilities and forced to endure some of the most vicious weather cycles on the planet. To most it hadn't taken a big stretch of the imagination to believe that someone with that background could end up as a bodyguard, but Castellano didn't seem to be buying it. And, of course, Declan knew he was right not to, the background story was a fabrication. While he'd certainly spent some time fishing as a boy and time aboard fishing trawlers in the waters around Ireland, the trawlers hadn't been bringing in hauls of tuna or lobster, but munitions and armaments intended for use in the IRA's war for independence.

"I met Kafni in Boston in ninety-seven," Declan said. "Some of the Islamic radicals you mentioned made one of their attempts at a restaurant in Beacon Hill. The leader of that group was a man named Deni Baktayev, Ruslan Baktayev's older brother."

Castellano looked up from the file and raised an eyebrow.

"And you rushed in like the boy wonder and saved the day," the agent said in a monotone and looked back at the file.

Declan nodded in confirmation though he knew the question had been rhetorical. It was the truth, or at least partly so. He'd left out the bit where he'd met Kafni a few years earlier in Belfast when he'd still been working for Mossad and that the assassination had been orchestrated in part by Declan's Boston-based employer, a surly maggot named Lorcan O'Rourke who ran a smuggling operation in the American northeast and who'd been paid handsomely by a Palestinian named Hashemi to arrange Kafni's demise.

"So one thing leads to another and you ended up as part of his detail?" Castellano said, looking up again.

"Aye, that's it."

"Let me speak plainly for you, Mr. McIver," Castellano said, standing up, "I—don't—believe—it."

Declan flashed him an amused look as if to say *No kidding.*

"The events at La Jetée in April 1997 are well documented and say that you took out eight Palestinian gunmen who were holding Kafni and his family in the restaurant. It goes on to say that none of Kafni's security was able to return fire because they'd been incapacitated and that you were armed only with a pistol," the agent said, placing his hands on the railing at the foot of Declan's bed. "Now, I'm no military man, but a little bit of experience makes me think that the odds of a fisherman taking out eight heavily armed terrorists are pretty damn lousy."

"I don't gamble," Declan mused, but again he knew the agent had him dead to rights. He'd taken out the gunmen as he moved systematically through the restaurant like the trained soldier he was. One had died in the alley watching the back door, two more in the kitchen, another on the second floor, three on the third floor, and the last one, Baktayev, on the roof.

Drawing himself up to his full height with a deep breath, Castellano said, "You're hiding something, Mr. McIver, and I'm going to find out what it is."

Before Declan could respond the door to the room opened. Constance entered, followed by Okan Osman and Altair Nazari, Abaddon Kafni's remaining bodyguards. Castellano buttoned his suit coat and straightened his tie as the twisted expression he'd been wearing melted away, leaving only a youthful charm.

"Thank you for your cooperation, Mr. McIver," he said in an entirely different voice. "I'll be in touch if I have any more questions."

"I'm sure you will be," Declan said, watching him as he strode from the room with his folder under his arm.

Sensing the tension in the room, Constance looked anxiously at her husband. "Is everything okay?"

Declan smiled and said, "Of course, love. It's grand."

As Castellano clicked the door closed, Declan knew it

wouldn't be the last time he saw the agent and that he would probably like their next meeting even less then he'd liked the first. Whether it was bureaucratic ambition or something more sinister he couldn't be sure, but for some reason the FBI's lead investigator on the case of Abaddon Kafni's assassination and the bombing at Liberty University had pegged him as public enemy number one.

CHAPTER THIRTEEN

"Did you make a new friend?" Okan Osman said, as he and Altair Nazari walked the rest of the way into the room after following Castellano out with a cold stare.

"Yeah, I think so," Declan answered.

"He's a real charmer, isn't he?" Nazari said, as he took the seat where Castellano had been sitting. "We had the pleasure of his company earlier this morning."

"Seems to think the world of me," Declan quipped dryly.

"What's going on?" Constance asked, her face still masked in concern. "What are you talking about? They don't think that you had something do with this whole thing, do they?"

She looked from her husband to Osman and Nazari and then back to Declan.

"It would seem that Agent Castellano certainly wants to believe that," Declan finally answered. While he and the two bodyguards were used to handling bureaucrats like Castellano and tended to do so with a bit of adolescent satisfaction he knew that his wife was a different matter. Raised in a conservative home by an authoritative father, she took people at their word and became visibly upset whenever someone became confrontational with her. She stood solemnly next to the hospital bed with her hands on the railing.

"Hey, it's grand," Declan said, smiling up at her from his reclined position in the bed and placing a hand over hers. "I'm being released this afternoon and we'll straighten this entire thing out. Would you do me a favor?"

"What?" she asked, without the concern leaving her face.

"I could really use a cup of coffee."

Osman and Nazari both agreed audibly and Constance said, "Fine."

It was obvious that she knew the three of them wanted to talk about what was going on and didn't want her to hear. Withdrawing her hands from under Declan's, she walked towards the door. He grimaced as he watched her leave.

As soon as she'd closed the door Declan said, "You have to stop anyone from delivering anything to—"

Osman raised his hands to signal Declan to stop. "We've already intercepted it, Declan. The FBI is supposedly questioning the guy who tried to deliver it but it doesn't look like he knows anything, just a paid delivery boy with no clue what he was carrying."

For the first time since they'd arrived Declan took a moment to take stock of the two men. Neither looked like they'd slept and Declan knew that looks, in this case, probably weren't deceiving. If it hadn't been for the heavy medication he'd received, he likely wouldn't have slept either. He'd witnessed violence before; at times in the past it seemed as though it would be a staple in his life. Having buried many friends over the years, he was no stranger to death. Growing up in Northern Ireland during the thirty year conflict known as the Troubles he'd seen many people die, some at the hands of the British Army, others killed by loyalist paramilitaries and still more in operations run by the Irish Republicans he'd once called friends. Each time the effect was the same, a realization in the pit of his stomach that a person he'd walked and talked with was gone and he would never see them again.

He could remember vividly the last times he'd spent with all of them, and the last minutes he'd spent with Abaddon Kafni haunted him. Had the leader of the group he'd seen at the Briton-Adams mansion really been Ruslan Baktayev? If so, then Kafni had been correct in assuming there was someone else besides Baktayev involved. While it was certainly possible for terrorists to enter the United States, the idea that someone with Baktayev's history could enter a mere two weeks after escaping from a Russian prison and still have time to plan an assault as audacious as the one that had just occurred, certainly supported the theory that a larger network of some sort was involved. And as Kafni had pointed out, whoever they were, they had to be well connected and very powerful, both politically and financially. That fact, coupled with Castellano's confrontational interview, weighed heavily.

"Where were you guys?" he asked. "What happened to you in the Barton Center?"

"Locked in a basement storage room," Osman said. "Led there by one of the security guards who said he'd found something suspicious. Once we were inside, he slammed the door and locked us in. It took the emergency crews hours to find us."

"It was one of the security cars parked outside that exploded," Declan said.

Osman and Nazari both nodded. "It was an inside job," Osman said.

"Aye, who was the security company?"

"We don't know. Their uniforms and vehicles didn't have a name or logo and the investigators are keeping everything very close to their chests. The local police have been completely shut out. The FBI is handling everything and our friend Castellano is in charge."

"It was the same company that was guarding the mansion. You guys didn't vet them?"

"Levi handled all of that. They must've checked out or else they wouldn't have been there."

Declan shook his head. "The FBI has to know it was the security company. They have to be following up on that."

"We assume they are, in addition to giving us a hard time," said Nazari.

"We brought you something," Osman said, handing Declan a manila folder before leaning against the room's waist high armoire.

Osman was tall for an Israeli, mostly owing to the fact that his family was of Arabian descent. With a shaved head, a tightly cropped goatee, a broad chest and an intensity in his eyes that radiated a preparedness found only in a professional soldier, he was an intimidating sight.

Declan took hold of the file and laid it in his lap.

Inside the file a photograph was paper-clipped to a dossier that was written in Hebrew. Although he couldn't read what was written, the picture said enough. A thin man with pale, coarse skin stretched over a bald head stared back with a look only a Russian could muster, coal black eyes staring directly into the camera as if intensely willing the lens to break. Beneath his nose, an untrimmed black beard masked the rest of his face, reaching down out of the photograph.

"That's him," Declan said, closing the file. "That's the guy at the mansion."

"You're sure?" Nazari asked.

Nazari was Osman's polar opposite. Always well-dressed and without so much as a strand of his curly black hair out of place, he looked more like he belonged in front of a television camera reading the nightly news than standing guard. The only evidence of the ordeal he'd been through were the dark circles underneath his eyes, betraying a lack of sleep. Declan knew his employment as Kafni's security wasn't because of his operational prowess, but his intuition and mechanical genius. If it floated, flew or could be driven, Nazari could operate it, fix it or destroy it in a matter of minutes.

"Yes. I'm sure. He didn't have the beard, but it's him."

"How could Baktayev have possibly gotten into the U.S. without Mossad picking up on it?" Osman said. "They've had agents investigating every known connection he has for two weeks and they've turned up nothing. We were beginning to think maybe the Russians weren't lying, maybe he really was dead and we needed to reevaluate our agreement with our man inside the prison."

"They can't be everywhere at once," Declan said. "If the CIA and NSA believed what Moscow said and they weren't keeping an eye out for him, then he could have easily slipped past Mossad."

"He's right," Nazari offered. "Even with the intelligence sharing between our two countries it would have taken a combined effort. Mossad could never track him over U.S. soil without help from the American intelligence community."

"Abe said he had to have had a pretty serious player in the terror world helping him in order to get out of that prison,"

Declan said. "If that's the case then it's possible that that same person helped him get into the U.S. But why? Has Mossad found any connections powerful enough to accomplish this?"

Osman shrugged. "The only person of any real wealth that we're aware of was Sa'adi Nouri, but he's dead and so is his network. But who knows? Al Qaeda or someone else could easily be involved."

Declan shook his head. "None of this makes any sense."

"There's more," Osman said. "We've been ordered to leave the country. Our visas were pulled before Abe's blood was even cold. As soon as the coroner's office releases his body, we're to be on the plane back to Tel Aviv."

"Why? By who?" Declan asked.

Osman shrugged.

"So what do we do?" Declan asked, somewhat rhetorically.

Osman leaned forward, clearly agitated by what he was about to say. "We keep our heads down. We've told them what we know and now it's up to them."

"What other choice do we have?" Nazari said. "In America we are not operators. We're security guards. Kafni gave everything he had on Baktayev to the Americans two weeks ago. It's up to them to act on it."

Declan grimaced and ceded the point. Nazari was right. There was nothing they could do.

"Look," Nazari said, standing. "The coroner is releasing Abe's body to us this afternoon. There's an Israeli C-130 already waiting at Lynchburg Airport to take him home and Mrs. Kafni and the children are being transported here. We're taking both him and Levi back to Jerusalem for burial. You should come with us. We will bury them properly in the land they fought so hard for and loved so much."

Declan paused at the thought of burying his friend. Kafni's death was still sinking in.

"No," he said shaking his head. "I've got to stay here. I'm going to try to get the police on the right track. I saw what I saw, whether Agent Castellano wants to believe it or not."

Both men nodded.

"We'll see what we can do on our end once we're home," Osman said, as he followed Nazari towards the door. "Watch your back, Declan. We're already burying two friends."

Declan watched as they left and as the door clicked closed, their words echoed through his head. He didn't like the picture that was forming in his mind. The law enforcement agencies investigating the matter were looking in entirely the wrong direction and they didn't seem to be interested in being pointed in the right one.

CHAPTER FOURTEEN

Senator David Kemiss buttoned his suit coat as he stepped out of the rear door of the black Lincoln Town Car driven by his government appointed chauffeur. Pushing his thick-rimmed glasses up on his nose like an aging Clark Kent, he prepared for a media onslaught as he walked towards the front door of the non-descript four story building that housed most of the federal offices in Lynchburg. In the twenty hours since the bombing outside of a Liberty University building and the subsequent murder of Abaddon Kafni, the mostly vacant building on the corner of 12th and Court Streets had become a hub of activity. Federal law enforcement officers from every agency under the banner of the Department of Justice and a legion of national news media had descended upon the quiet downtown block like a squadron of flying monkeys.

Kemiss sucked in a deep breath as several reporters took notice of him and ushered their camera men in his direction.

"Senator Kemiss! Senator Kemiss!" a top-heavy blonde said, as she ambled towards him in high heeled shoes and a red pants suit, dragging an obese camera man behind her. "Stacey Courtney, ABC News. Sir, as one of the ranking members of the Senate Intelligence Committee, what can you tell us about the attack last night? Are the bombing and the murder of Dr. Kafni connected in any way?"

"Dr. Kafni was the keynote speaker at the grand opening of the building that was bombed. Of course there's a connection," he answered as he brushed past her. "Excuse me. I really can't discuss this now."

"Senator, why are you here? Has the FBI called you?"

"No," he answered severely. "Why would the FBI call me? I'm a policymaker, not an investigator. I'm here for the same reason as everyone else. I've lived in this region for more than thirty years and I'm a concerned citizen here to make sure our federal government is doing everything within its power to apprehend the men responsible for these events. Now, excuse me."

He pushed past the throng of reporters crowding behind the journalist and entered the building through a glass door that was held open for him by two black-suited federal agents. The two men quickly closed the door behind Kemiss and began blocking off the reporters.

Inside the well-traveled entrance, the building smelled of wet carpet. Aging wallpaper lined the narrow hallway leading to the building's rear entrance; the walls studded with glass doors bearing the logos of several federal agencies.

"FBI?" he asked a man in a white button-down shirt who was walking towards the front entrance.

"They've taken over the fourth floor," the man said, grudgingly. "The elevator's on the left at the end of the hall."

The elevator pinged as it arrived on the fourth floor, and the doors hissed open. Kemiss stepped out and looked around; behind a set of glass doors directly in front of him men in suits buzzed around a hastily prepared office suite. What had probably been a sleepy field office housing only half a dozen agents yesterday had been transformed overnight into a veritable command center. Pulling one of the doors open, he walked inside. Several of the agents looked up from their desks and two men standing in front of an oversized map stretched over a large white board near the back of the room turned around. Kemiss flashed Seth Castellano a knowing look and the agent immediately excused himself from the man he'd been talking to and began making his way towards a corner office.

The entire scene made Kemiss nervous. Under normal

circumstances he would have been proud and possibly even a bit excited at the sight of the law enforcement apparatus of the United States working so diligently to solve a terrible crime, but the circumstances he was here under were anything but normal. Thankfully, Castellano was in charge and would hopefully see to it that no link between him and the events being investigated was uncovered. It was in Castellano's best interest to do so, for both personal and professional reasons.

Castellano held the door open as Kemiss entered, then quietly closed it behind him. Inside the square room was a desk piled high with papers. The pictures in the office weren't of anyone Kemiss recognized; he figured it had belonged to the agent who had been in charge of the field office until the previous night and who was now probably sharing a cubicle outside.

"What's the latest?" Kemiss asked, touching Castellano's shoulder briefly after the agent shut the door.

"State Police found the SUVs near a farm in Spotsylvania County. Both of them were burned down to the axles, just as he was instructed."

Kemiss nodded. "Good. And there's no way to trace them through the rental company?"

"It won't take long for the men outside to trace the vehicles back to the rental company, but all they'll find when they get there is that they were rented by a man working for the Turkish embassy using a diplomatic fleet account and were reported stolen from a parking garage at 5 p.m. yesterday."

"What about the witness? What did you say his name was?"

"Declan McIver. I interviewed him this morning."

"And?"

"Well, it appears that Kafni was much better informed then we realized. Apparently he knew Baktayev was free. He told McIver that Baktayev had escaped from prison and that he might be coming after them both. It seems McIver killed Baktayev's older brother in ninety-seven while he was working for Kafni as a security guard."

Kemiss brought a hand to his head and stroked his clean-shaven face in frustration. "This is what I was afraid of," he said.

He turned away from Castellano and looked out of the window to the city block below. "How the hell could Kafni have known about Baktayev being free?"

"Abaddon Kafni has a long history and most of it, prior to his immigration to the States, is a closely kept secret, but we need to relax, David," said Castellano. "Baktayev's involvement in this whole situation will be exposed eventually anyways. The fact that someone knows of him isn't that big of a deal. What we have to be concerned with is the timing. We have to keep his presence here quiet until after everything is over and done with."

"And how exactly are we supposed to keep this man McIver quiet?" Kemiss hissed over his shoulder. "He's not exactly a known entity that we can keep a close watch on day in and day out. He's a wild card!"

Castellano nodded, as if he'd seen Kemiss' reaction coming. "Yes. Yes he is."

"And we can't afford to have wild cards running around right now! What do we know about him? Everyone has skeletons in their closet. I want you to find them."

Placing his hands in his pockets and rattling the change he found there, Castellano walked around the side of the desk and sat down. Leaning into the black leather chair he said, "I already have."

He pulled a folder off the top of the desk and opened it. "Declan Scot McIver, born 1969 in Galway, Ireland. No parents listed. The file says he was raised in an orphanage in Ballinasloe and then nothing until he showed up here in the U.S. in ninety-seven. He applied for citizenship in o-two and on the INS forms he listed his former occupation in Ireland as 'fisherman.'"

"So he dropped off the face of the earth until he turned twenty-eight? Why don't I believe that?"

"Probably because this immigration file is about as thin as they come. Somehow Mr. McIver went from being a fisherman in Ireland to being a bodyguard in the United States. He did a two month stint in a Massachusetts prison for his involvement with a violent series of events leading up to an assassination attempt on Dr. Kafni and his family, in which McIver intervened and saved their lives. According to the records I dug up on that event he was released from prison after Kafni brought the entire matter to the attention of Adam Ryan, who was the governor of Massachusetts at the time. Kafni claimed McIver was there under his employ and that the proper paperwork from Israel was misplaced by state officials."

"So he went from Ireland to Israel to America?"

"It would appear that way, but there's no documentation to back that up. It seems Governor Ryan was a staunch ally of the Israeli government and had an established diplomatic relationship with then Prime Minister Asher Harel."

"Great. So Ryan back-doored the entire thing and now we're going to pay for it."

"Well, if you ask me, the only place you find these kinds of gaps in a person's history is when you're dealing with some kind of military, but there's no record of any military service anywhere. In fact, there's nothing from the Republic of Ireland at all. Not even a birth certificate."

"What are you suggesting?"

"I'm suggesting that this immigration file is a complete fraud and that Declan McIver is hiding something pretty serious. All we need to do is find it and exploit it."

Kemiss placed his hands in his pockets and stared out the window.

"I don't like that. It could take months to uncover that kind of information and it could very well turn out to be nothing. Even if it is some kind of a whitewash there are plenty of people with secret clearances that do nothing but shine a seat with their asses, and let's say he is some kind of Military Intelligence or Special Forces, how exactly does that help us? If anything it makes him more of a threat."

"Then we'll just have to go with plan B."

Kemiss looked over his shoulder at Castellano with a raised eyebrow.

"Our friends from the security company last night wouldn't argue with additional employment, I'm sure," Castellano said.

"Make it happen."

CHAPTER FIFTEEN

The automatic doors opened with an electric hum and the sun temporarily blinded Declan as he walked out of the hospital with Constance at his side. She hadn't been happy about his private conversation with Osman and Nazari, but he had assured her everything would be okay. Wishing he could convince himself so easily, he shielded his eyes from the glare; it was four in the afternoon and the sun was low in the sky. It felt good to be outside after being held in the hospital all night and most of the day. A light breeze blew across the parking lot and the springtime humidity, aided by the seasonal rainfall from the night before, clung to everything.

As they arrived at Constance's car Declan stopped and said, "I had Regan bring me a company truck."

Constance turned suddenly and looked at him. "So I'm driving back to Roanoke with Regan?"

Declan chuckled. "No, I had Dex give him a ride. I wouldn't torture you like that, would I?"

"Oh, of course not," she said, rolling her eyes. "Where are you going?"

"Abe and Levi are being sent back to Israel in about an hour. I want to be there, for Abe's family."

Constance nodded with a grimace. "The doctor said you

shouldn't be driving for a few days."

"I'm fine," he said, placing his hands on her shoulders. "Really, I am. I have a hard head."

He smiled briefly for her benefit and pulled her toward the driver's door of her car. Opening the door for her, he waited as she got in and placed her purse in the passenger seat.

"I'll be home later," he said. "Probably not until after dark, though. Call me when you get home to let me know you made it safely. I've got one of the company phones with me. Here's the number."

She looked up at him from the car seat as she took the slip of paper he held out. "Why wouldn't I make it home safely?"

She was clearly taken off guard by his statement. Although he doted on her like any loving husband would, he had never been the overprotective type.

Declan shrugged. "I didn't mean to—I don't know, just with everything that's happened and all."

She smiled again. "Keep your phone on."

He closed the door and watched as she started the engine and backed out of the parking space. As she shifted the car into gear, she gave him a small wave and drove off. He stood watching until the pearl white convertible made a right out of the lot and disappeared behind a building. Pulling his keys from his pocket, he walked towards the white utility truck Brendan Regan had parked in the lot beside the hospital. Unlocking the door and sliding up onto the vinyl bench seat, he tapped his hands on the steering wheel as he stared out the windshield. He hadn't seen or talked to Kafni's family in nearly ten years. Seeing them now, under these circumstances, wasn't going to be easy.

CHAPTER SIXTEEN

Declan pulled the white utility truck to a stop in the short-term parking lot in front of the main terminal, a long rectangular building with a glass exterior supported by regular brick columns. In the center, above several sets of revolving doors, was a glass dome. It reminded Declan of a mosque. Engaging the emergency brake out of habit, he left his vehicle and walked toward the front entrance, which in the waning daylight was lit from within by an incandescent yellow glow.

At the front curb, next to a row of taxis, three men in blue uniforms stood checking the bags of passengers arriving for departing flights. Standing near them was Altair Nazari, his ever present dark suit and tie coupled with his naturally dark features making him blend into the shadows created by the well-lit terminal and the column in front of which he stood.

"Declan," he said with a solemn look, as he extended his hand. "I'm glad you could make it."

Declan returned a solemn nod and shook his hand. He knew this was the grimmest business either of them had handled in a long time. Losing a friend was never easy, but saying goodbye to a man who had been instrumental in securing the future he had dreamed of was infinitely harder. Although they hadn't been in regular contact for nearly a decade, he couldn't deny his feelings towards Abaddon Kafni.

They had met on the streets of Belfast in 1993 when Declan, in one of many betrayals organized by the leader of the Black Shuck unit of the IRA, had provided information to a group of British agents about an arms deal between the IRA's Belfast leadership and the Palestinian Liberation Organization. The agents, unknown to anyone at the time, had actually been Mossad led by Kafni and operating illegally in Northern Ireland to stop the PLO from obtaining both arms and essential training from the most successful terrorist organization in modern history: the IRA. Months later, after learning of a plot to wipe out Declan's IRA unit, Kafni had returned the favor.

Not only had Kafni been responsible for saving him from execution at the hands of the IRA's notorious internal security unit, known as the Nutting Squad, but he had also been responsible for his legal status in the United States, without which he would have never been able to build the life he was currently leading.

Following Nazari as he turned and walked through a revolving door, Declan entered the airport terminal. Across a brown tiled floor to his right was a row of neon-signed ticketing counters and in the distance to his left, a baggage claim filled with anxious passengers whose faces communicated the feelings of frustrated travelers. Between the two, a wide hallway stretched past a coffee shop and a newspaper stand to a row of metal detectors operated by TSA agents in bright blue shirts and black trousers. Approaching the security line, Nazari stopped and spoke briefly with a stocky lady with dark curly hair. After nodding several times she walked past Nazari with a handheld metal detector and approached Declan.

"Sir, I just need to pass this over you real quick before I can let you onto the field," she said with a smile.

Declan stood still and raised his arms as she waved the wand around his extremities.

"Thank you, sir," she said, and returned the wand to an agent standing at the row of walkthrough scanners. "I'll take you guys down now."

Nazari and Declan followed the woman to the right of the security checkpoint to a windowless metal door marked with an emergency exit sign. Using a set of keys from a carabiner hooked to her belt loop, the woman disarmed the alarm and pushed open the door. Holding it open, she waited as they entered a concrete stairwell. At the bottom of the stairs she unlocked another emergency door and stood aside as they exited the building onto a concrete staging area occupied by several baggage carrier trains.

"I'll take you over in this," she said motioning towards a white Ford Explorer with an orange light bar attached to the roof, red lettering identifying it as a law enforcement vehicle belonging to the airport.

As they got in and closed the doors the woman's eyes flitted between her passengers as she eyed them nervously. Obviously uncomfortable with the silence, she spoke as they pulled out of the staging area and onto one of the runways. "It's just terrible what happened. No one here could have imagined anything like this. I mean, we all go through training for various types of workplace violence, but you never think it's really going to happen, then it does," she said, her voice trailing off as she finished.

Declan grimaced. What kind of bureaucratic double speak was workplace violence? What had happened at the university was terrorism, plain and simple. He dismissed the thought as a camouflage Hercules C-130 transport aircraft came into view. Parked near the end of the runway, the plane was surrounded on three sides by vehicles. As the Explorer neared the cluster, the woman turned the wheel sharply to the left and stopped.

"Thank you for the ride," Nazari said, as he got out of the passenger side front seat and closed the door. Declan followed suit but chose not to speak to the woman as he exited. The lady pulled away as they walked towards a group of people at the rear of the plane. A sharp breeze blew across the concrete runway. Declan's heart sank as he saw the faces of the bereaved; Kafni's wife and eldest son, David.

Zeva Kafni, a woman in her mid-fifties with long dark hair covered by a multi-colored scarf, looked up at the two approaching men, a look of recognition immediately crossing her face as she saw Declan. Breaking from the small gathering she walked towards them, opening her arms to embrace him as she drew near.

Declan hugged her tightly. Letting go, he tried to communicate his sorrow with his eyes as the words he wanted to say caught in his throat. "I'm sorry," he said, shaking his head. "I—I'm sorry."

He'd attended many funerals in years past and had never known exactly what to say to a bereaved widow or family. Not being the type of man to show emotion easily, most of the time a feeble apology had been all he could choke out. Thankfully, funerals in Northern Ireland had either been large affairs full of pipes and waving flags, where he could easily fade into the crowd, or small, masked gatherings of three or four where a sympathetic priest would open a church and allow a fallen warrior a flag-draped ceremony in the late hours of the night away from the prying eyes of the British army and loyalist mobs. Here on the tarmac of a regional airport with the sun quickly fading over his shoulder, his weakness was on full display.

"Thank you," Zeva said softly. "We're taking him back to Israel to be buried in Jerusalem. While he spent much of his time overseas, Jerusalem was his home. That's where he would want to be."

"And what about you? What will you and the children do now?"

She looked down to the ground briefly before replying. "We will stay in America. David and Hanah have begun building their lives here and although they are adults now and can live on their own, it would make me sad to be so far away from them. Abaddon would not want that."

Declan nodded as David Kafni arrived at his mother's side. A foot taller than either parent, David was an otherwise spitting image of his father, with the same thin-rimmed glasses and dark hair that receded to the very top of his head on which he wore a black *yarmulke*. David embraced Declan tightly as Zeva dabbed tears from her eyes with her scarf. Declan wiped away his own tears as he and David drew apart from their embrace and looked each other in the eye. Somewhere deep inside, each of them had known this day was coming. Declan supposed they had both hoped against hope that it would be many years hence and that Abaddon Kafni would have slipped away during an illness brought on by advanced age.

"Tell me you know who did this and that they will be caught," David said.

Declan looked quickly at Altair Nazari who was standing a few feet away. Had he and Osman neglected to tell Kafni's family that it was Baktayev who had taken Abe's life? The look on Nazari's face confirmed this and Declan looked back to David.

"We don't know anything for sure. The FBI is investigating. They'll find out who it is and they'll catch them. It may take a while, but it will happen," he said, trying to sound as reassuring as possible.

David looked at his shoes momentarily and when he finally raised his head and spoke his voice was angry. "Why are you keeping the truth from us?" he charged.

"David!" Zeva Kafni said as her eyes bored into her son. "These men are your father's friends!"

"I'm sorry, Mother. You may not choose to see it, but they know who killed Dad and they aren't telling us."

Declan watched over David's shoulder as Okan Osman left the three suited men he had been standing with and joined them. Standing next to Declan, Osman looked at David with as soft an expression as his hardened soldier's soul could muster. "Would knowing make it any better? Your father's gone, David. There's nothing we can do about that."

"I want to know," David answered through clenched teeth. "I have a right to know."

Osman looked at Declan and nodded his permission.

Declan placed a hand on David's shoulder and looked him in the eye. "I was there when your father was killed. I didn't see it happen, but I saw his killer afterwards. His name is Ruslan Baktayev."

He continued to look the younger man in the eye as the name bounced around his head and finally sank in. "Baktayev," David said, "just like the man in Boston. The man you killed."

Declan nodded. "Yes."

"Then they finally got him, didn't they? The ones we ran from all those years ago. None of it did any good. They still got him."

"None of it did any good?" Zeva repeated as her eyes narrowed at her son. "It did all the good in the world and I won't have you dishonoring your father's memory by saying otherwise! The hate-filled memories of Islam are long, you should know that better than anyone."

Declan placed his other hand on David Kafni's shoulder. "We're limited as to what we can do here, but you have my word that I'm going to do everything I can to make sure this guy is caught and that he pays for his crimes."

David nodded and wiped tears from his eyes. "They never pay for their crimes. They sit in prison living in luxury while the governments of the world debate endlessly about what to do with them. How do you punish a man who considers himself a martyr? You can't. All you can do is rid the world of him."

Declan nodded. He agreed wholeheartedly. Still, he'd fulfill the promise he'd just made by not letting the police forget about Ruslan Baktayev.

"It's time for us to get going," Osman said, looking at his watch and ushering the small group towards the three suited men standing near the plane's open cargo ramp.

As they arrived Declan looked up and saw two large mahogany coffins strapped down in the center of the plane's cargo hold. Leaving the group, he slowly climbed the metal ramp and looked over the smoothly finished caskets. On top of the first one was a gold plated Star of David with an Israeli and American flag either side. This was the coffin that held the body of Abaddon Kafni, the other bearing the remains of Levi Levitt.

"Goodbye, my friend," Declan said. He kissed his hand and pressed it against the coffin in the center of the Star of David. "I'll miss you."

"He will be missed by many," a deep, accented voice said from behind him.

Declan stood quickly, unaware that anyone had been standing behind him. He turned to see a tall man with a head full of thinning gray hair, a chubby, rounded face and soft gray eyes that looked down on the coffin with the sadness of a father who had just lost a son. Declan recognized him as one of the three suited men who had been standing near the plane. On the left lapel of his suit coat, an Israeli flag pin glinted under the overhead lights in the cargo area.

Declan regarded the man kindly for a moment and then moved to step away. He had no interest in getting into another discussion. As he started to walk away, the man caught him by the arm.

"I'm sorry we are meeting for the first time under these circumstances," the man said.

Declan stopped and turned towards the man. "I'm sorry, but I don't know who you are."

The man smiled briefly. "No, you don't. My name is Asher Harel."

Declan recognized the name immediately. Asher Harel had once been the Prime Minister of Israel and the man whom Kafni had worked under during his days with Mossad. It was Harel and his political connections that had seen to it that Declan was released from a Massachusetts prison after he'd saved Kafni's life in Boston. "I'm sorry. I had no idea. Forgive me for being so rude."

The former prime minister waved off the apology. "It is not rude to be overcome by sadness at the loss of a friend. Abaddon Kafni will be missed by many, but that much more by those who knew him as we did. Such friends do not come along very often in life. You should know that Abaddon thought very highly of you. He was overjoyed at the life you've built for yourself and was very excited to be meeting your wife."

Declan nodded vacantly as he felt an all too familiar feeling in the pit of his stomach. Up until now the events of the last two days had somehow seemed surreal, but now the reality was starting to creep up on him, the realization that he would never be able to speak to Kafni again and that this time he had been too late to save his friend's life.

"He and I have had many conversations over the last month since I arrived in the United States on a diplomatic visit," Harel said, as he put a hand on Declan's shoulder and began walking towards the cargo ramp. "When he learned of the circumstances behind Ruslan Baktayev's escape from prison he was very concerned."

"Last night when we talked he seemed to shrug off the idea

of Baktayev coming after him. I should have seen this coming. In ninety-seven the Baktayevs showed remarkable tenacity to follow him all the way to the U.S. and then to try and kill him the way they did. It wasn't a hit and run on a street corner somewhere. It was well planned."

"I know, but it was not the Baktayevs who were entirely responsible for that. That was the workings and connections of an Iranian named Sa'adi Nouri. Abaddon's concern wasn't for himself; it was for the others that Baktayev could harm."

"Abe told me this guy was involved in some pretty heinous attacks. The Nord-Ost theatre, the Beslan school...I'm sure there were many others."

"Yes, there were. Most of his attention was focused inward towards the conflict between Russia and Chechnya, but there are several video-taped messages from him where he openly threatens targets in Western Europe and the United States. It was one of these tapes that first tipped us off that he was interested in revenge on Abaddon."

Declan nodded. He'd seen such tapes before, both in person and on the nightly news programs.

"The reason why I wanted to talk with you is because, as with the attempt in Boston," Harel said as they reached the edge of the ramp, "we cannot ignore the circumstances of this attack. It, too, was well planned and far beyond anything we have seen from this man outside of the Russian Caucasus."

"What are you saying?"

"I'm saying that Abaddon believed that whoever got Baktayev out of that prison had to be extremely wealthy and very influential. He believed that person had a reason for wanting Baktayev out besides just freeing a fellow warrior of Islam. Now, Abaddon had a long career in Mossad and crossed paths with many people of Islamic persuasion. I don't know if his death was that purpose or if it was something else, but Abaddon's greatest fear was a Beslan-like attack in the United States. Do you know much about what happened there?"

"Aye," Declan said, thinking back to news reports he'd seen and books he'd read on the atrocity. He remembered thinking that in all likelihood, he had probably known some of the soldiers involved. The Black Shuck unit of the IRA had been trained by a Russian Special Forces team known as *Vympel*, or Vega in English. He'd spent two full years with them, and though they'd never totally warmed up to each other, the two teams had developed a teacher-student relationship and garnered each other's respect. "In Beslan there were nearly five dozen, well-armed terrorists holding over one thousand hostages, most of them children," he said. "Russian Special Forces stormed the building three days into the standoff when an explosion went off inside. A massive gunfight ensued with the hostages caught in the crossfire. It redefines the word 'tragedy', if you ask me."

"Correct," Harel said, giving a somber nod. "But what you probably do not know is that in the latter part of September 2004, only a few weeks after the crisis in Beslan ended, a group of twelve Islamists linked to the Chechens crossed the Mexican border into this country. A week later they were followed by another group of twelve. It was feared at the time that these men had come here to do the same thing that had been done in Beslan. Mossad worked tirelessly with the CIA for months, but none of them were ever found. They just vanished. All of them were linked to Baktayev and to a Chechen extremist group called the Crescent Vanguard."

They stood in silence for several moments as Declan allowed the information to sink in. The thought of a hostage crisis inside of a school was something that had kept American counterterrorism officials awake at night for nearly a decade.

Finally Harel spoke again. "If these men were who Mossad believed them to be, then they were waiting for Baktayev to join them here in the U.S. before they attacked. Once they found out he'd been captured and was in jail, they went into sleeper mode and have been waiting ever since."

"And you think whoever was responsible for getting Baktayev out of prison did so because they want him to finish what he started?"

"That was Abaddon's fear, yes. I'm not telling you any of this to scare you or because I expect you to do anything about it. I am telling you because I feel that if Abaddon were here now and he knew what we now know after last night's attack, he would tell you himself. He would tell you that he didn't like the way the investigation was unfolding or that his friends, yourself included, were being handled in such a disdainful way by law enforcement officials. He might even go so far as to say that it seemed like these officials didn't care about finding the truth."

"You're referring to the FBI agent in charge, Castellano," Declan said.

Harel nodded. "Osman and Nazari shared their experience with me and I share their concerns. If Abaddon was correct and there is someone else more powerful than Baktayev at work, well, the possibilities are frightening."

"Yesterday afternoon I'd have said that it was a stretch to even believe Baktayev could make it into the States, but now, now anything seems possible."

"If the events of last night are any indication, I'm afraid we'll be seeing Ruslan Baktayev again, and soon."

Declan nodded his agreement and extended his hand. The notion that Baktayev might not be done yet was one that he had thought of himself and had shared with Osman and Nazari. All around, everyone seemed to think that it was at least possible that there could be another attack, everyone except the lead investigator at the FBI who had seemed very ready to accept the idea that Baktayev was dead.

Harel took Declan's hand and gripped it firmly before walking away towards the other two suited men, who Declan now understood were bodyguards. As he stepped off the aircraft's ramp and onto the paved runway he looked around at the vehicles surrounding the plane. Inside each of them he could make out the faces of stern men. It was obvious that they were there to protect the former prime minister as he visited Kafni's family.

Shivering slightly as a cold wind blew over the runway from the south, Declan rejoined Osman and Nazari, who were standing with David and Zeva Kafni.

"I want you to come and visit us, Declan," Zeva said. "I want to meet your wife."

Declan nodded. "You will. Let us know when you're home again and we'll come."

She placed a hand on his arm and smiled. "Thank you for everything you've done over the years."

"Take care of yourself," Okan Osman said, as he slapped

Declan on the shoulder and gave him a serious look. Altair Nazari gave a nod before he and Osman guided Kafni's family onto the plane for what would be a long journey back to Israel. Declan leaned against a fence bordering the airport property and watched.

The Lockheed C-130 Hercules bore Hebrew markings next to the blue Star of David. Moments later the engines came to life with a deafening whine and the plane rolled to the end of the furthest runway. Declan gripped the fence tightly and breathed heavily as a wave of anger rushed through him. Images of Ruslan Baktayev's knife cleaving the air towards Kafni's head raced through his mind, his own hollow attempt at a rescue cutting his consciousness like shards of glass. The plane's engines roared and drowned out the sounds around him as it sped down the runway. In seconds, the craft had faded to a small spot on the darkening horizon and with it, Declan knew that Abaddon Kafni was gone from his life forever; fading into the shadows of the night much like he had the first time they'd met.

CHAPTER SEVENTEEN

6:56 p.m. Eastern Time – Saturday
Westbound on Route 460
Lynchburg, Virginia

Having been given a ride back to his truck by Asher Harel's security detail, Declan stepped into the vehicle and started the ignition. Backing out of the parking space and driving through the sparsely populated lot, he stopped at the front gate and paid the attendant. Driving around the perimeter of the property to get back to the interstate that would take him home, he watched as several planes took off and disappeared into the dark sky, engines roaring.

A few minutes later he passed the expansive campus of Liberty University. To his left he could see the remains of the C.H. Barton Center for International Relations and Politics, the entrance to its rectangular parking lot blocked by a row of Jersey barriers. In the low light provided by the street lamps he could see that the front of the building had been nearly torn off by the bomb blast. All that remained of the once magnificent architecture were two of the four front columns, which still stood erect but now held nothing, and the statue of Thomas Jefferson, which had somehow escaped any serious damage, the shrubbery around it burned away by a fire that was still smoldering despite the seasonal rainfall. In the grassy area on the left side of the building's entrance was an immense crater, roped off by orange cones and police warning tape. Two white sedans marked with police emblems were parked side by side in the lot, the drivers obviously having a conversation as they watched the area for anyone attempting to get close, whether for pictures or any other reason.

Looking at the two vehicles Declan thought about what he'd seen as he and Constance had left the building the previous night. He was certain it had been one of the security vehicles that had exploded and that the size of the blast meant a bomb too big to have been placed outside of the vehicle. Being familiar with similar devices he knew that for the explosion to have done the damage it did, the bomb had to have been located in the trunk and had probably been manufactured using several hundred pounds of ammonium nitrate fertilizer. He mulled over several questions as he drove west on the four lane highway, but decided it was best to focus on something else. The only thing he could do, though he wished he could do more, was tell the truth about what he'd seen and let the men and women who dealt with these kinds of things for a living handle the rest. Hopefully they would handle it in time to stop any more attacks.

A shrill ring jarred his thoughts back to the present as the LED on his company cell phone, which he'd placed on the dashboard, lit up. Reaching for the phone and touching the screen, he brought the device to his ear and said, "Hello?"

"Hey," a sweet southern accent on the other end said.

Declan smiled at the sound of his wife. "Hi," he answered.

"I'm just calling to tell you that I made it home safely," she said, sounding tired. "It took a while. There was a wreck on interstate eighty-one."

"Eighty-one," he said. "Why did you take eighty-one? You should have used route eleven."

"I did," she said intently. "The wreck on the interstate caused eleven to back up, too. I had to sit through every stoplight like, three times. It took forever."

"Okay, okay," he said in submission, although he was confident that, had he been there, he could've found a side street that would have gotten them through and had them home in half the time. "You sound tired. You should get some sleep."

"What time are you going to be home?"

"I'm on my way now. I should be there in forty-five minutes, an hour at the most. Get some rest."

"Declan, it's just—I don't know, never mind."

He knew what she was getting at. She had never seen or experienced anything like this before. Raised in the mountains of western North Carolina, she had never seen the aftermath of car bombs and sectarian murders. He felt bad, as though it was his fault she had to witness it at all. It was his past that had brought her into contact with such things. Where he'd grown up, bombings had been an almost daily occurrence and a lot of times there just weren't words to express the associated feelings.

"I know," he said softly. "You've never seen anything like this before. I'm sorry you had to see it at all, but the best thing we can do is get on with our lives and put some distance between us and what happened last night. I know it sounds cold, but that's all we can do."

He listened as she sniffed away tears. "But what about his family, how do they move on? What do they do now?"

"The Kafnis have lived with events like this for a long time. Zeva is a strong woman, and she will lead her family on," he said tentatively, as he searched for the right words to comfort her. "Get some rest. I'll be home soon. I'm passing Bedford so I'm about halfway."

He glanced into the rearview mirror as he passed an exit that led to the one horse town of Bedford, Virginia. The two lanes of road behind him were empty of cars, the afternoon commute to Lynchburg's outer areas having ended nearly two hours earlier. As he rounded a sharp left turn he saw a vehicle in the parking lot of a long-closed restaurant on the right hand side of the road near a rundown garage. Instinctively, he moved his foot to the brake and held his breath. The triangular-shaped area full of tall shrubbery where the road went from a widely-divided four lane highway to four lanes separated only by a narrow median strip was a well-known speed trap often used by state and local police. He clicked his tongue as the white SUV's headlights came on as he passed, briefly bathing the interior of his truck in an incandescent light. Passing a large speed limit sign reading *forty-five*, he looked down at the speedometer. He was traveling at just over sixty miles an hour and knew that he was as good as caught if the vehicle in the lot had been a police officer.

"Are you alright?" Constance asked.

"Yeah," he said, distracted as he watched the rearview mirror for any signs of lights or of the vehicle leaving the lot. He breathed a little easier as he saw nothing behind him. Maybe it had just been a stopped motorist. "Yeah, I'm here. I thought maybe I'd passed a cop, sorry."

"Be careful," she said. "You've already had to pay two tickets for Regan in the last three months since he's been traveling to Lynchburg."

"I know. Maybe they have a three for two deal going on," he said flatly.

"Funny."

Declan glanced upwards again into the rearview mirror and caught sight of a vehicle behind him. Looking again, he realized it was the white SUV and that it was approaching fast without its headlights on. "Let me call you back," he said. "I'm about to lose service as the towers switch over."

He ended the call and tossed the phone onto the dashboard as he looked down at the speedometer again. He was traveling at fifty miles an hour and the vehicle behind him was gaining fast. Was it a police officer? If so why weren't there any lights on? A bad feeling crept up his spine as he watched the black grille guard on the front of the vehicle growing closer in the darkness behind him.

Placing both his hands on the steering wheel, he pressed the accelerator and the work truck's diesel engine rumbled as it dispelled a thick plume of black smoke from the tailpipe. "Fifty-five," he said to himself as he glanced between the speedometer and the rearview mirror, "sixty, sixty-five." Still the white SUV was gaining on him at an incredible pace. Suddenly the vehicle's driver turned the headlights on high and flooded Declan's mirrors with a blinding light. Squinting, he braced himself for what he knew was about to happen.

The impact with the rear bumper of his truck jerked him forwards and then quickly backwards again. He pressed the accelerator to the floor and watched as the needle climbed on the speedometer. From behind him he could hear a high growl from the white SUV as its driver revved the engine and again shot forward.

He braced himself against the back of the seat for the impact this time and kept a tight hold on the wheel as the truck was pushed forward. The engine of the SUV behind him whined as its driver kept the accelerator pressed to the floor, pushing the black grille guard against the back of Declan's truck. Sparks from the metal on metal impact shot into the dark night above the vehicles and a metallic screech filled the air. Suddenly the other driver backed off and Declan felt the truck lurch again as the pressure from behind ceased. What was going on here? Who was in the SUV and why were they attacking him? The image of Baktayev or one of his men behind the wheel flashed through his mind. Was this Ruslan Baktayev's revenge for the death of his brother in ninety-seven? With Abaddon Kafni dead, was Declan next on the Chechen's hit list?

The white SUV revved its engine again and shot forward, this time pulling to the left into the fast lane. Quickly changing lanes, Declan blocked the vehicle's attempt to side swipe him and took the impact in the rear. More sparks flew as the vehicles ground against each other.

Antiquated two story homes flew by along either side of the two lane highway as he reached the ninety-four mile per hour limit on the diesel engine. The needle on the speedometer bumped against the small dash mark just before the bold number *ninety-five* on the speedometer and refused to go higher. The SUV backed off again and changed lanes as the engine revved up, propelling the vehicle forward and onto the right side of Declan's truck. The driver swerved towards the utility bed.

Declan steered into the impact in an attempt to keep control of the vehicle. Locked together in a metal on metal duel, sparks flew from the wheel well of his truck as the SUV's grille guard pushed against it. Knowing he couldn't outrun them, his mind raced for another way out. Remembering a section of road ahead where the four lane highway was divided by a steep, rocky hill, he began to form a plan. If he could keep control of his truck long enough to make it to that area, which couldn't be more than a mile ahead of him, then he could hit the brakes and make a quick left onto a dirt road that he'd seen many times as he'd driven home. He didn't know what was down the road or how far it went, but if he could trick the driver of the white SUV into passing him as he took the turn, he might be able to get away.

He pulled the steering wheel hard to the right, pushing back against the attacking vehicle. The SUV backed off again and Declan pulled the wheel left to avoid overturning. The driver's side wheels of the truck left the pavement as he overcorrected, dust and gravel flying as the tires skidded over the unpaved shoulder of the road. Steering right again, the truck weaved back on to the pavement with a thud and he corrected again, this time bringing the vehicle back into the fast lane and continuing forward.

The SUV hit him again from behind before skidding back into the right lane and coming around for another sideswipe. Declan hit the brakes suddenly and the SUV flew past him as his wheels locked up and skidded loudly against the pavement, the smell of burning rubber filling the air. Taking his foot off the brake and pressing the accelerator, the truck continued forward with a begrudging rumble.

He looked ahead towards the SUV. Suddenly a head popped out of the passenger's side of the vehicle, followed by a torso and an arm holding a semi-automatic pistol. Several loud pops sounded as the man sat on the edge of the door and aimed his weapon backwards over the top of the SUV. The windshield of Declan's truck splintered and the back window exploded, covering Declan in chunks of green tinted glass. Keeping his hands on the steering wheel, he ducked low and kept his foot on the accelerator, speeding towards the SUV.

He rammed the vehicle from behind and pushed it forward, the impact causing the gunman hanging out of the window to lurch and nearly fall out. Gripping onto the side view mirror, the man lowered himself back into the SUV as the driver pressed the accelerator and pulled away.

Declan saw the median beginning to broaden to his left. Looking ahead through the cracked windshield he could see the hill separating the eastbound and westbound lanes of the road about a hundred yards away. The SUV shot forward ahead of him as the driver attempted to put distance between them.

Were they running away now? Had the attack become a chase? He had no desire to catch them; he just wanted to get off the road and out of the truck where he could get a better idea of the forces arrayed against him and see exactly who they were. If they moved on and didn't come back in search of him, that would be fine too.

Still traveling at high speed, he watched as the SUV disappeared around a sharp right hand curve that led around the hill. He pressed the brake and slowed down as the dirt road on the left side approached. Pulling off the pavement, the truck bounced hard as it hit a long pothole and started down a steep hill. Instantly he knew he'd been moving too fast to attempt the turn. He steered furiously trying to keep control. As he pulled the wheel hard to the left, the truck's back end skidded around and he felt the vehicle's tremendous weight shift, but he was too late to correct it. Momentum carried the truck over and he braced himself as it rolled.

He crashed hard against the roof and then again against the driver's side door as the truck continued to roll. He felt his head strike the side window repeatedly as he bounced up and down in the seat involuntarily, his body at the mercy of the rapidly changing gravity in the cab of the truck.

The truck stopped rolling with a sudden impact and he felt his torso push hard against the safety belt as gravity continued trying to move him at the former speed of the now still vehicle. Pain shot through his body as it relaxed in the seat. The sound of crushing metal and breaking glass gave way to the stillness of a country night, crickets chirping in the trees surrounding the dirt road. Opening his eyes and breathing heavily, he coughed as dust invaded his lungs. He realized he was upside down and being held to the driver's seat by the safety belt around his waist. His legs hung loosely against the underside of the dashboard and his head throbbed above his left temple where it had impacted with the now broken driver's side window. With painful trepidation he moved his head and looked around the cab as he mentally took stock of his body. He could move his legs and arms and didn't feel any broken bones. Raising his right arm above his head, he reached towards his waist with the left and pressed the orange button on the safety belt, releasing it. With a thud, he fell onto the roof of the overturned truck and lay still, trying to absorb the impact, his legs now sprawled across the passenger side of the vehicle and his left arm caught in the safety belt. Pulling his arm loose, he turned over onto his stomach and crawled towards the broken window.

Wrenching himself free of the truck, he rolled onto his back and grimaced as he brushed pieces of glass off his forearms, leaving bloody dots in their wake. Slowly he raised himself to a sitting position and looked around. He was in an oval-shaped lot just a few yards off the dirt road and was surrounded by construction machinery. Placing a hand flat onto the ground, he pushed himself up onto his feet looking around for any signs of the white SUV or the men who had been in it. He was alone.

Standing still for a second he tested both legs to see if they would hold his weight and was glad to find that he was uninjured, with the exception of the throbbing above his left temple. He placed the fingers of his left hand on the sore spot expecting to find blood and was relieved when there was none. Walking slowly around the front of the truck he noticed that it had come to a stop against a yellow bulldozer bearing the logo of the Virginia Department of Transportation. *So that's what this place is*, he thought, *a storage area for VDOT equipment.*

At least one good thing had come of the situation. He could now cross this road off his mental list of places he'd always been curious about. Bending over and placing his hands on his knees, he took a deep breath and squatted several times to work out the kinks he felt in his muscles. He needed to find a way home and that would mean walking to one of the houses that peppered both sides of the highway.

Dropping to one knee, he leaned over to look inside the truck for his cell phone; in addition to finding a way home, he needed to call the police. The sound of an approaching vehicle reached his ears and he stood upright again, looking in the direction of the noise. A set of headlights pierced the darkness to the west of his position and he stood still, hoping it was just a random motorist, but as the vehicle slowed and made a left hand turn, he knew it wasn't.

Forgetting about his phone, he moved quickly away from the

edge of the storage lot and into the center of the construction machinery where he ducked and weaved his way through the mud-covered equipment looking for a place to hide. As he reached the end of the lot he spotted a large rock formation sticking out of the ground and ran towards it. Behind the rock, the terrain dropped suddenly and he could see the eastbound lane of the highway below him. He carefully climbed onto the rock and lowered himself into a prone position as the sounds of gravel crunching under tires grew closer.

The approaching vehicle bumped over the one lane dirt road adjacent to the lot and there was an audible squeak as its weight shifted on its axles. When it came to a stop ten feet from his truck, Declan could see that it was the white SUV that had attacked him. The sound of the passenger's window coming down preceded the bright beam of a flashlight that was shone on the overturned wreck. The door opened and a man got out, his large frame silhouetted behind the flashlight beam as he moved cautiously towards the truck.

"There's no one here," the man said in a gruff, unaccented voice as he bent down and looked into the cab of the truck.

"We've got to find him!" a voice called from inside the vehicle. "They want this guy dead or we don't get paid!"

CHAPTER EIGHTEEN

From the lack of any noticeable accents Declan could tell the men in the white SUV were not the same men he'd seen at the Briton-Adams mansion the night before. Although he couldn't make out what they looked like in the darkness, their choice of words and style of speech told him they were locals, or at least a lot more local than the men who had killed Levitt and Kafni. Who were they? And more importantly, who was paying these men to kill him, and why? A shiver shot down his spine and through his legs from the cold, damp rocks he was lying on as he watched the bright beams of flashlights pierce the darkness, washing over the dormant equipment like the full moon over an assembly of sleeping grizzly bears.

Two men had left the SUV and were moving about the storage lot searching the cluster of equipment. Declan wondered if there were more men in the vehicle or if the two who had gotten out were alone as he hunkered low against the rock and considered his options. Behind him was a long drop onto the two lane eastbound highway leading to Lynchburg. To his right and left were thick patches of trees that would provide him cover, but would also make noise as he moved among them; alerting the men to his presence and to his location; and in front of him were at least two armed men that were aiming to kill him on sight. If he stayed where he was they would eventually make their way to the end of the lot and if they decided to check out what was behind the rock, he'd be a sitting duck. Considering the fact that they were armed and he wasn't, he decided avoiding a physical confrontation would be best and that meant making a run for it in one direction or another.

"I got nothin," one of the men called loudly to the other. "Maybe he was thrown from the truck during the crash. I've seen bodies tossed fifty or more feet from crash sites and that truck rolled a good distance. He could be anywhere."

Declan stayed still. Would they give up their search and leave?

"Could be, but if we don't bring back pictures of a dead body we've wasted our time," the man who had been driving the SUV answered.

It looked like he was back to making a run for it. Slowly, he moved his head and looked behind him as he heard the sound of a vehicle passing along the highway below. The road rose in elevation as it came around the rocky hill, but in the darkness he couldn't tell exactly how far it was to the bottom and whether the drop was straight down or sloping. If it sloped he could make a run for it, sliding down the hill and crossing the highway into the forest beyond where the men would have little chance of finding him in the dark, but if it was a straight drop, he could end up with a broken leg or worse, complete the men's job for them and be killed. He moved his head again, slowly, looking forward. The men's positions hadn't changed much, they were moving methodically through the muddy lot, checking in and around each machine. He turned his head again and peered into the gloom. The hill sloped down in a rolling fashion as it led to the bottom where the terrain leveled out, bringing the four lane highway back together for the remainder of the journey into Roanoke. Moving downwards would give him some momentum and allow him to move more quickly away from the men despite the fact that they would inevitably hear him and give chase. If he could make it to the bottom of the hill and into the forest across the highway without them catching him, he'd be free to move towards a nearby house where he could call the police. Gripping the craggy rock, he positioned his feet for the maximum amount of push off he could get and prepared to make his move.

"Get over to the truck and call Turner and Allred," one of the men yelled. "I don't want them waiting around for us. Tell them to get in there and take out the wife. I don't want to drag this out any longer than we have to."

Declan's mind raced as his heart rate sped up. *Constance.* How could he have been so stupid? How could he have assumed these men were only after him and not even thought of the possibility that she might be in danger as well? His mind changed in an instant. Now his plan was all about a physical confrontation. Armed or not, these men were not going to reach their vehicle and make that call while he was still alive. Lifting his head, he watched as the man searching the part of the lot closest to him turned and began walking towards the white SUV.

Putting all his weight onto his right foot, Declan launched himself forward and off the rock. Hitting the muddy ground with a squishy thud, he instantly powered forward. His shoulders lowered like a running back heading for the end zone, he darted between the machines towards the man, whose back was still turned.

"There he is! Watch out!"

The man ahead of him started to turn, but his partner's warning was seconds too late. As Declan closed to within a few feet of his target, he launched his arm in a wide circle and formed a knife edge with his hand, striking the man in the carotid artery on the right side of his neck just before colliding with him and driving him face first into the muddy ground. As the momentum caused the man to slide forward in the mud, Declan grabbed his head and twisted until he heard a muted snap.

He braced his feet against the dead man, using the body to hurriedly push himself back up onto his feet and towards a hulking bulldozer for cover. Two gunshots sounded as he ducked behind the machine, one clanging dangerously close as it made contact with the dozer. As the report of the shots faded into the night, Declan stayed low behind the machine, listening to the gunman shifting his stance frequently in an effort to get a shot. He was located at the opposite edge of the lot to Declan's truck, where he had been searching.

"Myers? Myers?" the gunman called in a harsh whisper.

Declan listened for any indication that more men were getting out of the SUV and heard none. The gunman was apparently talking to his fallen friend, confirming that they had been alone in the SUV.

"Ah, you're a dead man when I find you!" the gunman said, raising his voice to address Declan as he realized his friend was deceased.

Moving to the other side of the bulldozer, Declan crouched down and leaned around the edge of the machine. He could see the body of the man called Myers a few yards in front of him lying near the cab of his overturned truck. The guy was white and had a head full of unkempt blonde hair. Just as his voice had indicated, his appearance made it obvious that he wasn't one of the men Declan had seen with Ruslan Baktayev the previous night. These guys were something else entirely, thugs who had been hired by someone to kill him and his wife.

He looked the body up and down for any signs that the man had been carrying a gun. There was nothing in his hands or on the ground near him except the flashlight he'd been using, its beam shining away into the night just like the vacant eyes of its former owner. Did the men really have only one gun between the two of them? Maybe the dead guy had dropped his back on the highway after they'd tried to shoot from a moving vehicle. Whatever the reason, the body had nothing that would be of use in the current situation.

Declan moved his eyes up from the body as he continued to listen to the slow movements of the gunman. The man had crept forward and was apparently working his way towards the bulldozer. The beam of his flashlight, undoubtedly aimed in the same direction as his gun, was shining over the opposite end of the dozer from where Declan was positioned. If the man continued on his current path Declan knew he could double back as he came past the dozer, but he needed a weapon to make sure his attack was effective. This time he wouldn't have the element of surprise.

Retreating behind the tread of the dozer in case the gunman moved suddenly in an unexpected direction, Declan looked around for anything he could use as a weapon. A gun or knife would be preferable, but even a blunt object would work. He just needed to do as much damage as possible on the first strike or else the man could come back at him. Based on the guy's movements, he thought it likely that he was a trained soldier or officer of some kind and had no desire to stand toe to toe with him in a fist fight and find out how well trained he was. Looking over his shoulder to the operator's cab of the dozer, he saw that the windows had been removed. Underneath the operator's seat were a dirty cloth and several hand tools. Slowly he stood upright and reached into the cab. Through the open cab he could see the beam of the gunman's flashlight darting around in front of the dozer, the man himself hidden from view by the dozer's front blade. Inside the cab he felt the handle of a tool and picked it up. Bringing his arm down to his side, he looked to find that the tool was a small garden spade. *Perfect.* Memories of his training in Russia surfaced and he thought about the entrenching spades that each member of the Black Shuck Unit had been given on their first day. These, they were taught, were your life line; one part tool, one part weapon.

Holding the spade, he slowly rolled out around the edge of the dozer and began making his way towards the front blade. The gunman was still at the front of the dozer, his location given away by his flashlight beam which glanced off the trees next to the machine. Apparently the man was wondering whether Declan had taken off into the woods beyond or had gone around the other side of the machine. He was about to find out.

Suddenly the flashlight beam stopped moving and Declan held his breath as he stood still. Had the man heard him approaching? He waited, watching as the beam slowly began moving again. The gunman was about to roll out around the bulldozer's blade and aim his gun at the spot where Declan had been hiding moments before.

As the movement of the beam sped up suddenly, Declan stepped forward around the blade and saw the gunman's back as he aimed his weapon at the rear of the dozer. The man's eyes flitted quickly to his peripheral right and Declan knew that he'd been seen. The gunman made a quick quarter turn, bringing the gun around to fire. Throwing the spade at the man's head as a distraction, Declan dove headfirst into him and drove him to the ground with his right shoulder. Rolling over top of him and into a standing position, he turned and came back at the stunned gunman as he scrambled to his feet. Kicking the gun to the left as the man tried to aim, he threw a punch and his fist connected with the man's jaw, pushing him against the blade of the bulldozer. Declan pinned him there with his body while he grabbed for the pistol.

Gripping the barrel of the gun for control and pushing the gunman against the dozer, he wrestled for the weapon. The gunman held on tight with both hands and tried to push him away. Shooting his head forward, he caught Declan's nose with a strong head-butt, driving him back. Declan held onto the gun as his eyes filled with tears and his legs buckled. He felt blood run over his upper lip and into his mouth. Breathing heavily, he spat it from his mouth, covering the man's tan coat in dark red dots. The gunman put the entire weight of his body against the gun and tried to force it down to get off a shot, but Declan planted his feet and pushed back. With the man now standing over him and his feet slipping against the muddy ground, he knew he couldn't match the man's leverage for long. Throwing his foot up and falling onto his back, he caught the man in the groin and pulled him forward, throwing him over onto his back. Standing up quickly, but staggering for a moment, he looked at the gunman who was sprawled out on his back and fighting hard to recover from the shock of the two hits, the pistol still in his hand.

Declan moved quickly and dropped his knee on the man's wrist, pinning the pistol to the ground. Adrenaline pumping, he drove his fist into the man's face, dropping his weight into each punch. Blood exploded from gunman's nose and he choked as it flowed into his mouth. *How dare they try to kill me?* Declan thought as he pounded away.

"How dare they try to ruin my life!" he growled, unaware that he was speaking aloud.

The sound of his own voice surprised him and jarred him back to reality. One last punch fell limp onto the man's face as Declan struggled to catch his breath. He fell onto his backside and sat there staring at the scene. He knew by the gunman's vacant eyes that he was dead, his head crushed between a rock on the ground and the fist that had been pounding on him moments before. Blood leaked from the wound on the back of his head and mixed with the mud underneath.

Declan brought his legs up slowly and pushed himself into a standing position. Breathing heavily from the fight, he looked around for anyone else nearby. He was alone. Stooping down, he pulled the pistol from the gunman's hand and checked it over. It was a Smith & Wesson Sigma style handgun with a standard sixteen capacity magazine. The man had fired two shots at him which meant there should be fourteen left including the one in the chamber. He released the magazine and looked at the tiny holes in the side of it. Counting eleven rounds, he reinserted it into the grip and moved away from the bulldozer. He had to get to his house fast; to his wife who wouldn't be able to defend herself the way he just had against the two men that were apparently waiting for confirmation from their now dead compatriots. How long would they wait? If they didn't receive the call would they move in anyway or abandon their mission and return to their employer?

With his own truck overturned, Declan approached the battered white SUV that sat idling in the middle of the dirt road, its fenders dented and scratched from the impacts with his vehicle as the men had attempted to push him off the road. With the pistol aimed in front of him, he moved around the vehicle checking to be sure no one was waiting inside. He opened the driver's door and got behind the wheel, looking over his shoulder at the empty passenger compartment behind him. He tossed the pistol onto the passenger seat and pulled the SUV into gear. The engine rattled as it chugged grudgingly forward. Moments later, after craning his neck to look for oncoming traffic, he pulled into the westbound lane of route 460. The road was empty. He pressed his foot down on the accelerator and drove for home, images of Constance's vacant eyes staring at him from just beyond the windshield.

CHAPTER NINETEEN

7:59 p.m. Eastern Time – Saturday
Verndale Drive
Roanoke, Virginia

Turning right, Declan drove south towards his home. Just beyond the windshield two more sets of dead eyes haunted him. Until last night it had been a decade since he'd had to pull the trigger and end a person's life. Now he would have four new faces to reconcile with when he closed his eyes at night, even though he knew his actions had been in self-defense. Some of the dead glared at him with hatred, rightly blaming him for their deaths. Others, most of them friends, stared at him in mute warning, cautioning him that he would end up the same way; staring eternally into the eyes of his own killer.

His headlights flashed over the parked cars and manicured yards that lined Verndale Drive. His neighbors sat comfortably in their homes for the night. Paying mortgages, keeping their families happy, and trying to find some time leftover for themselves were their biggest challenges. Most Americans had no idea what it was like to wake up each morning wondering if today would be *your* last, or someone else's. He had tried to forget, to be one of them. He'd succeeded for a while, but it seemed that no matter what, death was a part of his life. It might lose track of him for a time, but eventually it would catch up with a vengeance, just like it had in the last twenty-four hours.

He forced himself to focus on the situation at hand as he

guided the white SUV around the last bend in the road before his house. Constance was in danger. As fast as he'd tried to drive, the SUV only had so much power in its damaged state. Several times along the way he'd wondered if the vehicle would even make it. White smoke poured from its tail pipe and the accelerator vibrated heavily each time he pressed it.

Who could these men be working for? The two men who had attacked him along the road hadn't been Chechens or even Muslims as far as he could tell. By every indication, they were Americans and not all that different from the kind of men he dealt with on a daily basis, although it was clear they had some kind of military or law enforcement training. He didn't know much about Ruslan Baktayev, but he doubted that a man who had been imprisoned in Russia for over eight years could know too many Americans. Like Kafni and Harel had suggested, there had to be someone else involved.

Suddenly his thoughts were interrupted by a flash of light in the darkness of the park across from his driveway. He slowed the SUV and made a quick left. Circling into the driveway of a darkened house like a homeowner returning from an evening out, he doused his headlights and watched as the cherry on the end of a cigarette floated alone in the air, providing the only visible evidence of the person sitting there. As the person inhaled the outline of a human jaw appeared followed by the outline of a car door frame. The person was seated in a car watching the driveway of his house.

He knew the streets of the neighborhood well and knew that he could easily make his way around a few houses and get the drop on the man, but his instincts told him he wasn't alone. He looked up and down the parts of Verndale Drive that he could see for any vehicles that seemed out of place, but saw nothing. The minivans, utility trucks and economy sized sedans all fitted the area and there was no sign of anyone inside any of them. A thought crept up on him, slowly at first and then accelerating like a splinter into the end of a finger. A sick feeling settled in his stomach as the realization hit him: what if the man in the park was only the lookout for more who were already in his house?

He had to know if Constance was safe. Rooting around

in the vehicle he found a cell phone and retrieved it from the dashboard. He dialed her number, keeping the phone in his lap so the light from the LED wouldn't alert anyone to his presence. He clicked on the speaker phone as the call connected. Five rings later her voicemail answered.

"Hi you've reached Constance McIv—" he hung up, pounding his fist lightly against the steering wheel, biting his bottom lip. He pressed the resend button.

"Hi you've reached Con—" he hung up again and again pressed the resend button. Images of his wife lying on the floor of their house in a pool of blood flashed through his mind, her eyes wide open and staring into the void, like so many others he'd seen.

"Hi you've reach—" Declan threw the phone forcefully against the windshield, a spider web of cracks bursting across the laminated glass. He placed his face against the steering wheel and tried to force the images from his head. The sound of his heart beating and the blood racing through his veins pounded in his ears and his fingers began to numb as he gripped the steering wheel. He could live with all of the other faces, but he couldn't live with hers, her eyes forever asking him why, the question eerily permanent on her delicate features.

As he began to contemplate rushing past the watcher and charging up the driveway in a hail of gunfire, luminescence flared in the foot well, followed by the sound of the phone vibrating against the rubber floor mat. The sound jarred him back to reality and he opened his eyes to see that the phone had come to rest beneath his feet, its display undamaged by the impact and clearly showing a familiar phone number. *Constance.*

Picking the phone up, he imagined the voice on the other end, rough and gravelly, a smile playing on the lips of his wife's killer. He'd called three times with no answer. Maybe it had taken the men that long to find the phone in her purse. He barely recognized the sound of his own voice as he answered.

"Are you okay?" he said, nearly out of breath.

"Declan? Where are you? When are you coming home?"

All at once the moaning ghosts of his past vanished. Her voice was heavy with sleep but angelic to his ears. Her tone told him she was safe, she had no idea of the danger that lurked just a short distance from their house.

"Declan?"

"I'm here," he breathed.

"Where are you calling from?"

He remembered that he wasn't calling from his own phone and that perhaps the reason she hadn't answered was because she didn't recognize the number. "It's a company phone," he lied. "Are you okay? I'm sorry to wake you."

"I'm fine. Where are you? Why aren't you home yet?"

The sound of her sweet voice broke his heart. She had no idea what was going on and soon he would have to tell her. She'd handled the news of his injury and of Kafni's death well enough, but the events of this evening would mean big changes in their life, changes that had to happen fast and without any time for explanations. They had to get away now. Whoever had sent these men after them wouldn't be likely to give up easily and he still had at least one more to deal with.

"The truck broke down," he said, thinking quickly. "I need you to come and get me."

"What do you mean, the truck broke down? It's a brand new truck!"

"I don't know. Just won't start. Come get me. I'm downtown by the old railroad yard. You know where your Uncle's produce warehouse used to be?"

"Yeah, okay. Why are you down there?"

"I was taking the back way home. I'm in his old parking lot. Hurry up. I don't want to be down here for long. It's a rough area."

"Okay. I'm coming."

"Call me when you leave the house."

"Okay."

He heard the rustle of the bedsheets as she pushed them back before she ended the call. He looked up the hill through the trees and could make out a faint light in their bedroom window. He turned to watch the smoking bandit in the car. If the nicotine addiction hadn't gotten the better of him, he might have been successful in staying undetected in the darkness. Suddenly the flame moved through the air to the right and gave birth to a twin. *So there are two men in the car.* That was a good sign that they were still waiting for orders from their now deceased cohorts.

Ten minutes later the headlights of Constance's pearl white convertible moved out of the garage and onto the driveway. The men in the car chucked their cigarettes onto the gravel path of the park and faded into the darkness as they saw her approaching. She made a left turn out of the driveway and drove thirty yards up a small hill where she made a right, heading towards downtown Roanoke.

Declan watched, waiting for the men to make their move, and seconds later they did. The taillights of the car blazed to life in the darkness, casting a red hue on the trees behind it, followed by the sound of an engine turning over, then a white Crown Victoria with two passengers pulled out of the lot and passed within thirty feet of where Declan was parked. Watching closely for them to signal anyone else nearby, Declan saw nothing. It appeared that they were alone after all. He watched for any signs of another vehicle behind him as he followed them at a safe distance. He looked down as the phone in his lap vibrated.

"You on your way?" he said to his wife. "Good. Listen to me carefully. I'm not at the produce warehouse. I'm two hundred yards behind you."

"Decl—"

"Don't talk! Just listen," he ordered. "Look in your rearview mirror. You see the headlights?"

"Yes. But why are you—"

"Just listen," he ordered again. "That's not me in the car. I'm behind it in a white SUV. You're being followed."

He watched ahead and saw the Nissan's brake lights come on. "Don't react. Just keep going," he said.

"Declan what's going on?"

"Just keep going. I don't have time to explain. Just stay on the line with me and head towards the produce warehouse."

"Okay."

He could hear the fear in her voice and hoped what he was planning would work. Constance had no training for this kind of thing.

Up ahead the Crown Vic followed the Nissan closely, a sign that its driver didn't have a lot of experience. Apparently whoever had hired this crew had run out of experienced men to do their dirty work and had been forced to rely on rookies.

"I want you to get on the highway as quick as possible," Declan said.

The Crown Vic backed off and was now following at a more experienced distance. Declan realized immediately that the driver had been using the headlights to try and determine how many people were in the vehicle he was following; maybe he was experienced after all.

Ahead, Constance was approaching a stop light. Only a few vehicles were on the road at this time of night and the normally busy four lane intersection was empty. The green glow of the traffic signal changed suddenly to amber and then to red as she approached.

Damn, Declan thought as he saw her slowing down to a stop. The Crown Vic came to a rest two car lengths behind her. Watching carefully as he approached, Declan looked for any sign that he'd been noticed. He leaned over and pulled the Smith & Wesson pistol he had taken from the men who'd attacked him off the passenger seat of the vehicle. Preparation was the key to survival and although he had hoped he would never have to use them, he'd stashed weapons, mostly semi-automatic pistols, throughout his house and vehicles; unfortunately he wasn't in his vehicle.

"Declan, I wish you would tell me what's going on. Why are there people following me? Is this about Abe's death?"

"Yes," he said, and let his words hang in the air for a moment before continuing. "I'll tell you more once we're both safe, but for now, just keep going."

The traffic signal turned green and Constance made a left hand turn heading west towards the highway. Slowly, apparently being careful not to be too aggressive and tip her off, the Crown Vic rolled after her.

"Remember, just keep going and lead them to the warehouse. I'll tell you what to do when we get there. Everything will be okay," Declan said hoping he was right.

*

Sixteen minutes after leaving the house, Constance turned right off the interstate at the downtown Roanoke exit and drove east. She continued through two stop lights then made a left, heading into the city's southeast neighborhoods.

Between the downtown market area and the expansive ward known commonly as "old southeast" were rows of dilapidated warehouses that had once been used by the Norfolk & Southern railroad and other businesses that had supported it. The railroad still maintained a working yard that occupied a large quadrant of Roanoke's south side, but it was a shadow of its former self. Staying about a hundred yards behind the Crown Vic, Declan could see to his left the dormant shapes of the hulking locomotives across the Roanoke River, their engines kept running throughout the night to avoid freezing.

"Alright, we're almost there," he said to Constance. "Do you remember your uncle's favorite parking spot? The one around the back between the building and the fence, just big enough to fit a car into?"

"Yeah, yeah I think so."

"Grand. I want you to pull straight ahead into that spot and stay in the car until I come and get you. Whatever you hear, do not get out of the car. Do you understand?"

"Yes."

Declan knew he was scaring her. He could hear a quiver in her voice. He was doing it on purpose. He had a pretty good feeling that he had avoided being made, but that was about to change. The last thing he wanted was Constance out in the open when the shooting started. He hoped that the men in the car were only carrying smaller firearms, certainly nothing bigger than the one he carried. While he trusted his aim, he was using a firearm that wasn't his own and he had no desire to take on a sub-machine gun or some other automatic weapon.

"Turn off the engine and the lights as soon as you're parked."

"Okay," Constance said, her voice a high squeak.

He hung up the phone and watched as she turned right into the fenced lot that belonged to a two story white concrete building with a loading dock wrapped around it. The gate that once prevented people from accessing the property after business hours had now rusted off its hinges and was lying in the muddy dirt lot. Weathered signs along the road and on the building identified it as *Star City Fruit & Produce*. The business had once shipped locally grown goods all over the southeast United States and had belonged to Constance's uncle, Nathan Cobrian. Upon his death six years earlier his two sons had taken over and run the company into the ground. All that was left of it now was the abandoned building, which Declan had bought out of foreclosure, and a few rusting box trucks that sat along the rear fence.

Declan pulled his truck to the side of the road and watched as the Crown Vic cautiously entered the lot, trying to remain undetected. Constance had done exactly as he had told her and was now around the far end of the building out of sight. The driver of the Crown Vic turned off the headlights and proceeded forward. Declan turned off his truck and got out. He would have to be quick to avoid any chance of his wife getting hit during the fight that was about to erupt. With any luck he would get the drop on the goons before they could get a shot off.

Getting out of the SUV, he tucked the pistol into his coat pocket and started off in a jog. Entering the dirt lot, he stayed in the shadows close to the fence as the Crown Vic came to a stop. The cloudy night and the tall, leafless birch trees that lined the rear of the property shrouded most of the one acre lot in darkness.

The men got out of the car and Declan watched as they each drew a handgun from under their coats and chambered a round. He pulled his own pistol from his pocket.

The men moved cautiously towards the far corner of the warehouse, their pistols raised and following their line of sight, as if they realized that there was a good possibility that they'd been led into a trap.

Silently, Declan pulled himself up onto the loading dock and crept along the smooth concrete floor, his dark clothing and the lack of natural light concealing him perfectly. Flattening himself against the wall, he made sure the men were looking away when he moved.

The men arrived at the corner of the warehouse, first pointing their weapons down the side of the building and then in the opposite direction, into the yard, towards the decaying box trucks. Moving down the side of the building they momentarily passed out of Declan's view, their pistols still aimed towards the back of the property.

Declan moved quickly across the loading dock to the far corner and turned quickly, taking aim. The men swept from right to left with their backs to him as they looked for any signs of Constance's vehicle. They were twenty yards from where she was parked in the narrow but deep parking spot her uncle had used for thirty years, the ribbed sheet metal siding of the building easily hiding the slender sports car from view.

"Looking for someone?" Declan announced.

The men turned counterclockwise in a fraction of a second, aiming their weapons.

Declan didn't wait. He fired three times, the report of the shots echoing against the metal building. His first shot hit the driver in the face, where he'd been aiming, and the other two struck the passenger center mass. Both men collapsed into the dirt lot and lay still. He jumped off the loading dock and breathed slowly but deeply as he approached, his gun ready. Standing at the feet of the passenger, he looked down at both men. Like the ones who had attacked him earlier, these two also appeared to be Americans. Their short haircuts and the movements they had been making also indicated that they were trained police or military. He watched for any signs that they were still breathing and saw none. To be sure, he aimed and fired twice more, sending blood and brain tissue splattering into the tire tracks made by Constance's Nissan in the muddy parking lot.

He did a full three hundred and sixty degree turn to be sure there was no one nearby and then moved quickly to the back of the building. His wife's convertible sat exactly where he had told her, a consistent tapping sound from the engine as it cooled in the night the only clue as to its presence. Through the rear window he could see his wife sitting in the driver's seat. As he approached the side of the car she stared straight ahead. He tapped on the glass but she did not move. Tears ran down her face and her chest heaved. Slowly she looked out at him.

Declan felt his insides tighten as regret washed over him. As long as he lived, he would never be able to apologize enough for what she was going through.

"Move over," he said, as he opened the driver's door. She slid silently across the console into the passenger's seat. He could hear her sniffing away tears as he got in and removed the pistol from his pocket, laying it on the black vinyl dashboard. He turned the key and revved the engine. All six cylinders whined as he shifted into reverse and stomped on the accelerator, guiding the vehicle straight back. He turned the wheel suddenly and ground the gears as the convertible slid to a stop in the wet mud. He heard Constance sob as she saw the two men a short distance away. He knew as they tore past the wrecked bodies that she would never look at him the same way again.

CHAPTER TWENTY

As his children slept in the luxurious bedroom suites below, David Kemiss sat at the desk in his third floor study. The television in the walnut armoire along the opposite wall flickered with images of the plane carrying Abaddon Kafni's body leaving the Lynchburg Regional Airport. The talking heads of the major media networks were aglow with speculation as to what could have happened to the outspoken professor and author who had frequently appeared on their shows defending Israel and America's war on terrorism, as well as analyzing dozens of other events, from the Arab Spring to the mass casualties in Syria at the hands of that nation's own government.

Their experts, many of them Kafni's colleagues, seemed sure of only one thing: the Islamic extremists who had been trying for years to kill Kafni without success had finally achieved their goal. But who were the extremists? Had it been the act of a lone wolf? Was it a sign of a larger attack to come? The news media seemed barely able to contain itself at the thought of the possibilities. Peppered with bits and pieces of Kafni's life story, this event would give them something to report on for at least a week, maybe longer. But there was only one thing about the entire situation that Kemiss wanted to know as he leaned back in his red leather chair: had the witness to Kafni's death been neutralized? Nervously, he flipped his cell phone around in his hand. Suddenly the phone vibrated and he switched off the television, tossing the remote back onto the desk as he flipped open the phone. Looking at the display, he recognized Castellano's number.

"Have you heard anything?" he asked as he heard a car door slam on the other end of the line.

"Not a thing."

Kemiss sighed loudly. "It's been over an hour since they were supposed to report. Something's gone wrong."

"We don't know that yet. Maybe they had to take him somewhere else. These guys know what they're doing. They handled the situation last night, didn't they?"

"Yes, but I'm not waiting to find out. Every minute that goes by, this guy could be contacting the press or someone else. I don't want anything left to chance."

"He doesn't have anything to go to the press with, David. He can't even make a one hundred percent positive identification."

"That won't stop them from spreading his story all over the airwaves and turning this thing into more of a three ring circus than it already is. All we need is one tabloid journalist to wave some money under this guy's nose and he'll be on the front page in every grocery aisle in America."

"Okay...okay. I'll call them and find out what's going on, but it needs to be kept short and to the point. We have got to maintain as much silence on this as possible. These throw-away phones are only so secure."

"I don't like forcing your hand," Kemiss said, "but you're not the only one with contacts that might be able to help if need be. Use the three-way calling feature. I'll wait."

He listened as Castellano tabbed through the calls received to the only other number that had ever called the phone, the number belonging to the throw-away phone of the man who should at that very moment be trying to wash Declan McIver's blood off his hands. He tensed as the phone rang, followed by the sound of someone picking up the call, a rustling sound perhaps caused by the mouthpiece brushing against facial hair as the phone was raised into the proper position.

"Hello? Who's there?" an accented voice asked.

"Who is this?" Castellano asked severely. But as the words left the agent's mouth Kemiss knew who it was. Declan McIver was alive and had just answered the phone of the man who was supposed to have killed him. He terminated the call by closing the phone and slowly placed the device on his desk, his mind racing as he sat forward in his chair. The owner of the phone not answering could only mean one thing: he was dead. What did they do now?

The phone vibrated again on the desk.

"Yeah," Kemiss said as he picked it up.

"They're dead," Castellano said. "We have to get rid of these phones. Take out the battery and the SIM card and keep them separate from the phone. I'll take care of destroying them, but don't turn it back on or try to use it for any reason."

"Then what?"

"I'll call the state police and monitor any traffic reports. We need to find out what happened and where. You said you had contacts that can help? Now would be the time to call them. This guy knows there's someone after him now and if he's smart he's going to run. We need someone that can catch him."

"I know just the person to handle that."

Kemiss closed the phone and pressed down on the back of it, removing the battery covering. Taking the battery and the tiny black SIM card out, he placed all three items in a neat line on the side of his desk. Castellano could take care of the rest.

Picking up the land line phone on his desk, he dialed a number and waited for an answer.

"Yeah, Allan? It's David Kemiss."

CHAPTER TWENTY-ONE

"Were you present during the Bush administration, David, or were you just voting that way?" Allan Ayers asked pointedly as he brushed a hand over his goatee. "I know you were there because you were leading the charge against warrantless wiretaps in the Senate."

He listened to the uncomfortable silence on the other end of the line as he rested his elbows on the black Government Issue desk in his office, on the seventh floor of the National Security Agency's headquarters fifteen miles southwest of Baltimore. In his position, the last thing he wanted when he came to work was a phone call from a sitting senator, even if that senator happened to be a friend of the family.

Under normal circumstances, the politicians that called expected a favor to be done for one of the many new recruits that passed through the Live Environment Analyst Development, or LEAD, facility that sat just outside of Ayers' office. The recruit would likely be the offspring of an influential but not necessarily wealthy constituent. He or she would have recently graduated from college and have somehow figured out his or her way through the absolute maze that was the federal hiring process, and now their parent's political connections would be brought into to play to ensure that they received as high a pay grade as possible at the agency of their choice, which for computer science majors, was always the NSA. Ayers had seen many of these individuals rise through the ranks rapidly after his aid in securing them the highest possible scores on the agency's systems and some had even surpassed him in the chain of command, which made filling more such requests far more difficult. But tonight, just as he was about to begin loading in a fresh batch of targets for a class, Senator David Kemiss had called for an entirely different type of favor, one that Ayers didn't want anything to do with.

"Don't insult me, Allan," Kemiss said, after allowing the uncomfortable silence to grow to a cacophony. "I was there and so were you, thanks in no small part to my intervention on your behalf. It's time to pay the piper. I need wiretaps and a team of analysts searching for two individuals and I needed it done five minutes ago."

There it was. The advancing locomotive that Ayers had seen coming a mile away, his dirty little secret plastered to the front of it like a windswept Christmas wreath. He too, as an unemployed IT worker from Silicon Valley, had once reached out for help the same way many of his students did. He'd always reasoned to himself that his situation had been different, that he'd had a family to feed and that waiting for the dot-com industry to repair itself after the bust in the late nineties would have meant stocking shelves at Wal-Mart for a decade while his children were raised on food stamps. But in reality, the scenario was the same as for a recent college grad needing to pay back the student loans taken out to finance their education, and as Kemiss had so pointedly put it seconds before, the piper always came calling.

"So you're telling me that this is a matter of national security and that these people are suspected of involvement in the attack in Virginia?"

"He is; she just has the misfortune of being married to him."

"Then why isn't this going through the Surveillance Court and up to one of the analyst centers with a warrant attached?"

"Because we don't have that kind of time. Within the last hour this guy killed at least two men sent to apprehend him and he's going to be on his way out of the country in a matter of a few hours more. Now, if we find him this way the Richmond Field Office can put a collar on him before he even leaves the region and no one, including him, will ever know the NSA was involved."

Ayers looked over the two dozen computer terminals lined up in rows of four in front of a 216" x 96" blank LED monitor that, during a training operation, would be filled with the images of whoever it was he had loaded into the system for his students to hunt down. These days most of the individuals, known as mice, that he would load into the system were terror suspects that had already been caught or killed, but whose movements had been sporadic and had led authorities on a global chase as they left clues in, out, and around businesses, airports and other facilities, clues that the budding analysts could track until they found where he had placed the mouse.

Could a real individual be traced with the training system? Of course, it was the same system used in the upper floor analyst centers and, just like those centers, all the data collected by the analysts went directly to their team leader before being sent up the line. Being the team leader in this case, he made sure the collected data was stored in a training file where it would be scored by senior analysts and then deleted from the live system. So what Kemiss was proposing was not only possible, but also easy to do. Was the risk of turning him down really worth it? He thought it very likely that every senior analyst and team leader at the agency had probably had a little fun with the system at least once in their career. Whether it was something as innocuous as checking out an old high school flame or something more nefarious like listening in on your neighbor's phone conversations, it happened. Was losing his job for something that could be so easily covered up worth it? The immediate answer was no. He wasn't willing to risk the federal pension he would be enjoying in less than a decade for someone who had just killed two federal agents.

"Alright, send me everything you have."

"It's all located in an attachment in the draft folder of an email address set up at mailer.com; I'll give you the login information."

CHAPTER TWENTY-TWO

10:10 p.m. Eastern Time – Saturday
Porter's Exxon Station – Route 60
White Sulphur Springs, West Virginia

"Who do you think it was?" Constance asked. "Do you think there are more of them?"

She had asked the same questions at least twice in the last several minutes and the same quiver was still present in her voice when she talked. The look on her face spoke volumes about her frame of mind. She was afraid and she had every reason to be.

"Oh, there's definitely more of them," Declan said, as he looked at the cell phone he'd taken from the heavily-damaged SUV that had attacked him on his way home. He and his wife had been parked at a gas station on the corner of West Virginia State Routes 60 and 92 for half an hour, ever since the phone had rang, a male caller on the other end. "Those guys weren't acting alone. The ones who came after me talked about someone paying them to be there."

"Paying them to be there? You mean they were hired to kill us? By who?"

He could tell by her voice that his wife was nearly at the point of hysterics.

"I don't know, but I suspect that was one of them that just called."

He picked up the phone and flipped it open. Hitting the

green "send" button again, he lifted the phone to his ear. An electronic voice immediately picked up the line and repeated the same message he had heard when he'd tried to call the number back three previous times. *The TelPay Wireless user you have dialed is not available and has not setup a voicemail account. Please try your call again later.*

He closed the phone and tossed it onto the dashboard. The first time he had called it the number had rung busy, but each time after the electronic message had picked up. He wasn't familiar with the company, TelPay, but he suspected it was one of the many prepaid wireless services that could be found in just about every convenience store or grocery chain in the United States. The only clue he had was the number's area code, 434, and that meant the phone had likely been purchased somewhere in Central Virginia and that the person using it was located there as well.

"Do you have any service on your phone?" he asked, as Constance sniffed away new tears.

She reached down to the tan leather handbag that sat on the floorboard between her feet and pulled out a dark red Samsung smartphone. "Two bars," she said.

He reached out and took hold of the phone, allowing his hand to touch hers softly for a moment.

"Hey," he said with a quick smile and a comforting look. "I'm not going to let anything happen to us, okay?"

She wiped her face and nodded as he took the phone from her hand and thumbed the display. Opening the android phone's web browser to the Google home page, he flipped it sideways and typed "TelPay" into the search engine. Moments later the search engine returned the page of a prepaid wireless provider based in Chula Vista, California, confirming his suspicions.

"Damn."

"What? What is it?" Constance asked, her head snapping up to look at him.

"Nothing," he said, raising his hands slowly, hoping to calm her startled movements. "The phone is from a prepaid wireless service, that's all."

"What does that mean?"

He shrugged. "It just means that the caller didn't sign a

contract when they bought the phone. The service was paid for in advance which usually means the buyer either has bad credit or wants to remain anonymous for some reason."

"So there's no way the police can find out who it is that's after us?" she asked rhetorically.

Declan nodded. "Aye, that's what it means."

"There's got to be someone we can call, someone that can help."

Declan nodded. "Yeah, maybe. But if we call them we have to explain all of this, and we don't have time for that right now."

"Why don't you want to explain it, Declan? Tell me! Someone tried to kill you! People go to the police when that happens, they don't run away and hide!"

"So you've said."

"Stop saying that!" She stomped her foot hard against the floorboard.

"Look, we've covered this. I'm not going to anyone until I know you're safe. We don't know who these people are and we don't know who's involved."

Running directly to the police was a typical civilian response and in most cases it made sense. Most of the murders in the United States were committed by jealous lovers or enraged spouses and going straight to the authorities was the right thing to do, but not in this situation. It wasn't a coincidence that Abaddon Kafni had been killed the night before and that now someone was trying to kill the only people who had been within a few hundred yards of where he'd died. Declan was certain there was more to what was happening than could be plainly seen. What he needed to do was to get his wife to a safe place where he wouldn't have to worry about protecting her if someone came at him again. She may not agree with what he was doing, but she didn't have to – as long as she was alive.

"Look, I already know these phones can't be tracked down very easily. That's why people use them. I'm not trying to hide from the police; I just want to make sure you're safe. You have to believe me when I say this....I've never experienced a worse feeling than I did tonight, driving home knowing there were people that could be hurting you at that very moment. I won't risk that again."

Constance's expression softened.

"I just want you to be safe," he said, continuing to drive the point home that what he was doing was for her own good, "and then I'll go to the police and start trying to figure this whole thing out. You didn't see anything so there's no reason for them to talk to you anyways. There's no reason that you can't be holed up somewhere for a few days." In actuality, he had no intention of going to the police. While he hadn't told his wife, he'd recognized the voice on the phone. Picking up on the croaky sounding Creole accent, he knew the caller had been ASAC Seth Castellano; the police, for all intents and purposes.

"If these people can find our house and can find you when you're driving along a road then why can't they find a cabin in the woods?"

"Because it doesn't belong to us and no one knows we're going there," Declan said, although he knew the statement wasn't entirely accurate. In fact the cabin they were going to, which was still another thirty miles away, did belong to him. He'd bought it several years ago shortly after they'd been married, and had been preparing it over the last few years as an emergency shelter. He had, however, been very careful as to how the cabin was owned and his name didn't appear on any of the paperwork. Instead, it was owned by what was commonly called a dummy corporation, this one based in the Grand Cayman Islands. Without some serious international investigation backed up by legal proceedings, its ownership would be impossible to determine.

"Without powerful connections," he continued, as he shifted the sports car into gear and left the gas station's parking lot, "it would take a very long time for someone to trace us to this location."

CHAPTER TWENTY-THREE

Declan had insisted Constance stay in the warm car while he got the fire going. Now that the place was beginning to warm up, he escorted her inside and she stood still in the center of the room, taking in the rustic decor. After helping her out of her coat, Declan pushed a wooden Adirondack chair to the edge of the stone hearth so she could sit by the fireplace.She took her seat gingerly, as if she was being asked to sit on a rusty nail. He watched for a moment, and then moved to the galley kitchen at the right side of the cabin to begin a pot of coffee.

Standing on the edge of a lake at the end of a half mile dirt road that was barely passable without four wheel drive, the cabin's sturdy log construction was testament to a bygone era of rugged craftsmanship. Inside, it consisted of one large room, a small bathroom the only area with privacy. Directly across from the front door a stone fireplace jutted out from the back wall and tonight, for the first time in years, smoke spewed from the chimney.

The lake was situated ten miles west of the Virginia / West Virginia state line, in the Monongahela National Forest northeast of the tiny, unincorporated town of Lowry's Mill. With nearly twenty miles of one and a half lane road between it and anything closely resembling civilization, the cabin was as safe a place as someone wanting to hide out would find. Whether you were a dedicated homesteader, a paranoid survivalist, or someone delusional enough to want a hideout from the zombie apocalypse, you'd be hard pressed to find a more remote location and still be within driving distance of a few modern amenities. For Declan, the place was all about preparation.

Declan had bought most of the property he owned at auction, after a bank or some lien holding agency had foreclosed on it. In the case of the cabin, its original owner had been a retired widower who'd moved there to take up gold prospecting in the nearby creek beds after a life of working on aircraft for the United States government. The man had drowned while trying to retrieve some mining equipment during a storm and since he had no relatives the Greenbrier County government had ended up owning the property. By law, they'd put it up for auction to the highest bidder. Declan had shown up at the county courthouse despite a snowstorm and in a small bidding war between himself and two area residents, he'd paid twice what the property was worth.

Leaning against the green laminated counter top in the galley kitchen, he watched his wife as she stared into the fire. Here he was sure they would be safe for however long they needed to be, but living in a place this small and this secluded was out of the question long term. The presence of two obvious outsiders in the small town of Lowry's Mill would surely bring attention and eventually someone would put two and two together. He needed to come up with a plan, but it could wait until morning. Right now, he had something else on his mind.

Constance sat still, her hands in her lap, staring into the flames as they licked the top of the stone fireplace. Declan had no idea what she was thinking. Despite the brief argument in the parking lot of the gas station, few words had passed between them on the journey from Roanoke. He supposed she was just trying to take it all in. Having been raised in a devoutly Christian home, he knew that her experience with violence likely amounted to what she had seen on television. Seeing the bodies of the two men who had been following her had been a shock, for sure. He hated the idea of burdening her with even more information tonight, especially the revelation that he'd lied to her for nearly a decade about who he was and where he came from, but on the drive he'd worked things over in his mind. He'd tried to convince himself that there was no need to tell her, no need to cause her further pain and risk driving a huge wedge between them in their relationship, but ultimately he'd decided it was time that he came clean about his full history with Abaddon Kafni. If she was going to trust him throughout this situation, she needed to know everything.

"You know...I...uhh...I want to tell you more about how I know Abe and how all of this came about," he said, as he walked over and handed her a cup of hot coffee.

She looked briefly up at him and then back to the fire, taking the cup without a word.

In the last twenty four hours he had reacquainted himself with a way of life he thought he'd left behind nearly two decades ago and had hoped he'd never have to revisit. He'd faced down six trained killers like an old pro, but telling his wife how he'd done it scared the hell out of him.

"I wish I could tell you that none of this was my fault. That somehow I just happened to get caught up in this. But the truth is that Abe and I go much further back than just working security for him when I first arrived in the States."

Constance looked up at him, her interest renewed. The expression on her face scared him; it was vacant with the slightest hint of' *what now?* in her eyes. Disappointment settled in his stomach and he couldn't avoid the feeling that he would never look the same in her eyes again, no matter what he did.

"I'm not from Galway in the Republic," he began. "I was born in a town called Ballygowan about twenty miles south of Belfast and I lived there until I was eleven."

"Northern Ireland?" she asked rhetorically.

"Aye, Northern Ireland, and my family weren't fisherman who had a bad bout of pneumonia and left me orphaned."

The look on her face told him that she knew what was coming. While most Americans had only a slight notion of the thirty year war in Northern Ireland known as the Troubles, mostly from romanticized books and movies about the IRA, he knew that she was better educated on the subject. Not only was she married to someone from Ireland, but she also held a master's degree in history and had more than a passing interest in the British Isles. In fact, their first conversation had been about the subject when they had met at a book store just over nine years ago.

"My da' was Paul McIver, elected MP of the North Down constituency located just south of Belfast. He and my mum were killed in 1980 by men linked to a loyalist paramilitary group called the Ulster Volunteer Force."

Tears formed in Constance's eyes, sliding slowly down her cheeks. She knew exactly where he was going with this. For a moment it looked as if she might try to comfort him, but instead she buried her face in her hands without a word.

"They were killed because the UVF said my da' was a traitor. My mum was Lorna Flynn, a Catholic from Derry. Da' hid me in the backseat of our car under a blanket just before the masked men approached the car. I heard the whole thing. I heard my da' beg them not to hurt my mum, I heard my mum screaming, and then I heard them both being shot. I was eleven years old."

He recounted the story without emotion. For him it was just something he lived with every day and he hadn't felt one way or another about it for years. It was just a fact, a sad part of the story of his life, a life he'd hoped had moved away from death and violence and war towards a successful marriage and a family of his own. He sat down on the edge of the queen bed and waited for her to gather her thoughts.

"So there's more?" she said, finally looking up at him and wiping away tears. "You didn't just lie about where you were born and who your parents were, did you?"

He winced. Her words felt like a razor blade being dragged repeatedly across his conscience.

"Yeah, there's more," he said, after a moment. "After my parents died I was sent to live in a Catholic orphanage in County Armagh. I lived there until I was fourteen. I ran away with an older boy after we intervened in a rape being committed by one of the clergy."

He stopped talking momentarily as Constance's face softened, but she continued to dab away tears.

"On the streets I met up with and joined the IRA as an angry young man who thought revenge for the wrong done to him was all that mattered. I spent nearly ten years in their ranks before I realized I wasn't solving problems, I was perpetuating them."

"So you were a member of a terrorist organization?" she asked. Her voice was full of indignation, but the look in her eyes communicated sorrow, although whether it was sorrow because he'd lied and wasn't who she thought he was or because of the story he'd just told her, he wasn't sure. "Why did you feel like you had to lie to me about it?" she asked, and he took his time forming his reply. He knew exactly how important this was.

"Because I wasn't exactly proud of who I was, who I had been and the things I'd done," he said, eventually. "I just wanted to move on. I wanted someone to look at me as more than just a sad son of a bitch who'd picked up a gun to solve his problems. I wanted to be someone different, and I was, in your eyes, it seemed. America was my chance to start over. To have the life my da' always wanted his family to have, but never got the chance to give them. Now all of this has happened and I feel like I'm right back on the streets of Belfast."

For some reason that he couldn't put his finger on, Declan was angry. He felt like he couldn't breathe. Pulling his coat on, he opened the door and walked out into the cold mountain night.

Minutes later he stood at the end of the rickety pier thirty yards from the front door of the cabin. He lit a match and placed it into the end of his churchwarden pipe, inhaling the first burst of smoke from the cherry tobacco. He only smoked when something was bothering him. Flicking the lit match into the air towards the black water in front of him, he watched as the orange light moved through the air and vanished with an audible hiss. In its absence he realized exactly how dark it was at night without any street lights nearby.

A brief light broke the darkness again as the front door to the cabin opened. He took another drag from the pipe and exhaled slowly as he felt a pair of slender arms slide around his waist in a light embrace, followed by a head resting against his back. He held the pipe between his teeth and placed his hands over his wife's arms.

"None of this is your fault," she said after several moments of holding him silently. "I didn't marry you because you were a fisherman from Galway. I married you because I loved you, and I love you now. I don't understand everything that's happened, but my feeling is that the outcome would have been much different if you weren't who you are."

One of the things he loved most about her was that she never held a grudge. No matter how angry she got, she worked through it quickly and always had a clear way of thinking about things afterwards. This time, as usual, she was right, whether he liked it or not. If not for his past experiences, the outcome of several situations would have been much different. For starters, he'd be dead, the two goons on the highway would have seen to that, and the other two waiting in the park would have killed Constance. Despite the sins of his past, they were both alive now because he was a trained killer. He silenced the thought that if he hadn't been, he never would have met Kafni and none of this would have even happened. Following such thoughts led a man in circles.

"It's not that I didn't want you to know that I'd done some bad things," he said. "I wasn't running from you, I was running from myself. I'd been running for years. When we met, for the first time I actually dared to believe that I could have a normal life."

"And we do have a normal life," she said, moving around to face him. "Or at least we did."

He snorted a short laugh and said, "Yeah, past tense. Abe's timing has always been an issue."

She hugged him tightly and rested her head against his chest. "How'd you meet him?"

"He was a Mossad agent working illegally in Belfast. He was acting on intelligence Israel had received that Arafat's PLO was being aided by the IRA. The 'ra was helping to train some of Arafat's men in the use of IEDs in exchange for shipments of weapons and semtex. I was on the outs by then, most of the right-wingers I'd run with were dead. I supplied him with some dates and times. Earned myself a right good beating for it, too," he said, tracing his index finger down a small scar beside his right eye. "They'd have killed me that night for being a tout if Abe and two of his men hadn't shown up."

"He saved your life?"

"Aye. Moved me to the Republic that same night, to a Mossad safe house in Galway. The Brits didn't have anything on me so I was able to leave the country on a freighter heading to Boston."

"And once he quit Mossad and came to the U.S. you two met up again," she said.

He nodded. "I worked in Boston doing the only thing I knew how to do, smuggling and gun running. I got wind of an assassination plot that my employer was involved in and found out that Kafni was the target."

"And you saved his life to return the favor he did you?"

"Aye."

Several minutes passed as they stood holding each other in silence.

"What do we do now?" she asked, finally breaking the silence.

Declan shook his head. "I don't know. My mind keeps going back to that FBI agent, the one who interviewed me in the hospital. He was combative from the very beginning and stopped just short of accusing me of being involved. It was his voice on that phone a while ago, I'm sure of it."

She drew back and looked up at him as if she was studying his face to see if he was serious.

"I met him too," she said finally, "in the waiting room last night. I didn't really think much of it at the time, but I got a weird feeling from him. He kept insisting that he needed to talk to you right away, but the doctors and nurses wouldn't let him."

Her voice trailed off and he knew she was thinking the same thing he was. If an FBI agent was involved then they were in a lot of trouble. Not only did it mean that the people against them weren't just some two bit thugs, it meant there was a much wider conspiracy that could involve countless numbers of people. What did they do now? Run?

Declan felt a surge of anger rise inside him as he considered the options. He and Constance had built a life together and if they ran then that life would crumble away into nothing. Sure, they could rebuild somewhere else and probably even live safely, but they'd never be able to stop looking over their shoulders and he didn't want that kind of life. He'd been down that road before and had determined to leave it behind.

"That's why I didn't want to go to the police. If there's some kind of conspiracy going on, then we'd just end up back in the same situation. By coming here, by disappearing, we've got the advantage. We get to decide when and where we surface, or even if we surface."

CHAPTER TWENTY-FOUR

Seth Castellano sat alone in the fourth floor field office his counterterrorism unit had taken over thirty-six hours earlier. The other agents assigned to the case were either out, following the hundreds of leads that had poured in through the FBI's eyewitness hotlines, or had taken a few hours off to freshen up and get some rest. He'd spent most of the night going over ways to spin the fact that Declan McIver had killed the four assassins that had been sent to make sure that what he knew never reached the ears of the public at large.

Castellano had had a pretty good idea that McIver was hiding something when he'd first begun to pull information on the man after learning his identity at the hospital, and the deaths of the four men all but proved it. Now the question wasn't *if* McIver was hiding something, but *what*.

Shortly before 11 p.m. the previous night, Castellano had received word from the Virginia State Police that a vehicle belonging to DCM Properties had been found overturned along a deserted section of a four lane highway between Lynchburg and Roanoke and that two bodies had been nearby. He'd immediately ordered his agents in the field to secure the scene and to prevent any of the local or state police from contaminating it. By the time he'd arrived to have a closer look, he'd also learned that the Roanoke City Police had found two more bodies near a warehouse owned by the same company.

Now, with four suspicious bodies attached to property ostensibly belonging to Declan McIver, he was beginning to feel much better about their chances of success. Even with McIver still on the loose, the bodies meant a huge hit to his credibility and he would have a lot of questions to answer when he was located. In the meantime, Castellano was sure that he could make the four dead men work in his and David Kemiss's favor if he could figure out the right angle.

Castellano's thoughts were interrupted by the bell on the elevator. He turned in his chair to see an agent entering the office. "Good morning, Agent Kelly," he said.

Kelly placed a black computer bag on one of the many desks and took a seat. "Good morning, sir. Have you been here all night?" She was one of the newest agents in his unit, but one of the most experienced investigators on the team, having had many years of prior service in the FBI. She was middle-aged with scraggly, dark hair and a lined face. Not the most attractive person, but certainly one of the most motivated agents he had under his command.

Castellano nodded. "No rest for the wicked, I suppose."

"No rest here either, sir, I spent most of the night trying to locate a lead that I thought you might be interested in, in light of last night's discoveries."

"Oh?"

Kelly zipped open the computer bag and withdrew a tip sheet. "I remembered seeing this yesterday morning and didn't think much of it. At the time it seemed like just another nutjob calling in conspiracy theories, but since those bodies were found near Kafni's former bodyguard's property...I thought maybe there was more to it."

Castellano reached out and took the tip sheet. Looking it over he said, "What kind of name is Lorcan O'Rourke?"

"Irish, I believe, sir."

"Well, let's see if we can get him on the phone, shall we?"

Kelly took the tip sheet back and dialed the phone number listed. Pressing the speaker button, the agents listened as the phone rang on the other end.

"Yeah?" a gruff voice answered.

"Is this Lorcan O'Rourke?" Castellano said, over-enunciating the name.

"Depends on who's asking, boyo." The voice was accented and when the man spoke it sounded as though he was gargling broken glass. Whoever he was, he needed to lay off the cigarettes or else he was going to have a serious disagreement with cancer before long.

"You're speaking with Assistant Special Agent in Charge Seth Castellano, at the FBI. I understand that you phoned one of our tip lines and said you had information on the Kafni investigation, is that correct?"

"Well, boyo, I have some information that might be related to your investigation and it might not be. It's more of an additional direction you could take a look in, besides Islamic terrorism."

"You indicated that your information had something to do with a former bodyguard. Why don't you tell me more about that?"

"Aye. Have you run across a man named Declan McIver in your investigation yet?"

Castellano couldn't believe his ears. Had the man just said Declan McIver? He sure as hell had, and now Castellano was listening intently. "I can't comment on an ongoing investigation, sir. You'll have to tell me what it is that you have and I'll decide from there whether it's something we need to pursue."

"McIver used to be a member of Kafni's security detail back in the late nineties, but before that he worked for me, as a smuggler. Turned out to be quite a lot of trouble, too, and cost me a damn fortune. After thirty years at sea, I can tell you that he's the worst thing I've ever plucked out of the Atlantic Ocean."

"I'm sorry, plucked out of the Atlantic Ocean?"

"That's right, boyo. McIver's an immigrant, and not the legal kind, at least not originally. He came to the States aboard a freighter that originated in Ireland. That freighter was carrying, well, we'll call it undeclared cargo, and when we offloaded it onto our own boat, McIver came with it. We used to get a lot of guys like him in the late eighties and nineties, all running from the British Army or the Royal Ulster Constabulary or some damn agency or another over there."

"Running? Why?"

"Three words, boyo: Irish—Republican—Army."

"The IRA?" Castellano said rhetorically.

"Yeah, the IRA, revolutionaries, terrorists, whatever you want to call them. My point is, Declan McIver was one of them, and if I was looking for a man close to Abaddon Kafni who was capable of the kind of violence that happened Friday night, I'd be looking right at this man. Do some digging and you'll see what I mean. And when you do...I want you to jam him up really hard and tell him Lorcan O'Rourke sends a hearty up yours."

The caller hung up with a laugh that quickly turned into a wheezing cough. Agent Kelly picked up the receiver and hung it up again to turn off the speaker system. "Sorry, sir, I guess he was a nut after all."

"Maybe," Castellano said with a shrug, "maybe not."

"I don't see how that could help our current investigation, sir."

"Well, it's a bit of possible background on McIver, which has been hard to come by, but no, you're right. It doesn't help us much at the moment. Good effort though, Agent Kelly. Keep it up. I'll be in my office for a while before heading out if you find anything else."

"Yes, sir."

Castellano stood from the chair he'd been sitting in near a wall mounted map of the Western Virginia area. He walked into the office he had commandeered and closed the door behind him. The caller hadn't given them anything that was really pertinent to the official investigation, but that didn't matter. Whatever the guy's angle was, three words that he'd uttered were more than helpful to the goals that Castellano wanted to accomplish.

CHAPTER TWENTY-FIVE

David Kemiss turned up the collar on his black wool overcoat as he stepped onto the concrete porch of his house; he expelled several short breaths, which quickly evaporated into the cold air. Placing his hands in the oversized pockets of the coat, he suppressed a shiver as he strolled quickly down a brick walkway that led to a circular motor court, about twenty yards in front of the three story Georgian mansion.

He turned and looked back at the house as he arrived in the motor court. Four gray pilasters held up a triangular gable, under which stood his front door. That there were many rooms in the brick-built industrial era house was evident from the eight windows that studded the front elevation on each of the two lower levels, with four more sitting just below the roof line. He looked over each of the windows for any sign that he'd woken his family and saw none. He himself hadn't slept more than a few hours, and even that had been sporadic. He had tossed and turned and slept for only brief periods, his troubled mind unwilling to let go of his problems.

He tried to distract himself with thoughts of the beautiful landscape surrounding his home as he plodded along the narrow gravel driveway: rolling hills that looked out over the tall peaks of the Shenandoah Mountains to the west and a sloping valley to the south overlooking the Revolutionary era city of Charlottesville, glimpses of the Rivanna River trickling down the wooded expanse toward the city's many brick-fronted institutions. The nearly one hundred acres around him had been in his family since the 1950s when his father had moved to the area and opened the law firm of Kemiss, Cronk and Caulfield. Since then the Kemiss name had been synonymous with the area and both he and his father had served as the elected representative for what was known politically as the 5th District of Virginia. In 1992, he'd given up that seat to run for the more influential position of senator and had held it in each of the three elections since.

Kemiss' heart leapt as a familiar buzzing sounded from inside the left breast pocket of his coat, and he reached inside to retrieve his cell phone, hoping this was the call he'd been waiting most of the night for.

He looked at the 410 area code and took a deep breath. The caller was from the Fort Meade area of Maryland, which meant that it was indeed the man he'd been waiting for.

"What do you have, Allan?"

"Not much, I'm afraid. I've had my entire class at it since ten o'clock last night and the only thing I've got for you is a few GPS pings off the woman's cell phone. They came in shortly after we started our search, but we've had nothing since."

"But we know where they're at, right?" Kemiss felt his stomach tighten. The NSA had to have a location. That's what they did.

"No. We have no idea where they're at."

"What do you mean *no*?" Kemiss snapped. "Isn't locating people what you do?"

"Yes," Ayers said dryly, "but sometimes our work can take days or even weeks to find an actionable location. The pings came from a cell tower in the Lewisburg, West Virginia area. Now the satellite can trace the location, but unfortunately they were stationary at the time and then the signal disappeared, which means they either turned the phone off or lost service."

"Well, where were they?"

"In the parking lot of a gas station in White Sulphur Springs, but that isn't going to help you much. There's a major east-west interstate going right past there so they literally could have been going anywhere."

"Why didn't you call me sooner? We could have had someone in the area on the lookout!"

"We've been on the lookout and found nothing. No more pings in any direction for two hundred miles and we've been checking every airport, bus station and train terminal within the region continually. More than likely they turned the phone off and continued on. This class is over at ten and I'm pulling the plug. I'll keep the search parameters open for another twenty four hours and see if the system returns anything. I'll let you know if anything comes back, but I'm not risking my head any further for this."

"Fine, maybe I'll pull the plug on you, too." Kemiss slapped the phone closed. He'd let Ayers twist in the wind for a while and see what the gnawing idea of being fired motivated the man to do, but for now it was time to move onto another plan. If they couldn't find Declan McIver then they couldn't kill him. But maybe they didn't need to kill him. The idea of discrediting him somehow had been tossed around, but had been ditched in favor of dealing with the problem more permanently. Since that idea had obviously failed, it was time to revisit the other options.

He flipped open his phone again and dialed Castellano's number. "It's time to move on to Plan B. What do you have?" he said as Castellano picked up the call.

He could practically hear the smile in the agent's voice as he answered. "I've got four bodies, each near a piece of property belonging to our man. That's enough probable cause for me to get search warrants and to open up an official investigation, which will put a lot more resources at our command. As far as I'm concerned, Declan McIver just did us a big favor and eliminated four witnesses to Friday night's events. And I'm going to paint it to look like he eliminated four witnesses to *his* involvement."

"That's good—"

"That's not all I've got, either."

"Well? Don't keep me in suspense."

"What was going on in Ireland sixteen years ago when this

guy first showed up in the U.S.?" Castellano didn't wait for an answer. "Terrorism," he continued, "the Irish Republican Army. We tie this guy to the car bombing, which the IRA had a proclivity for, and we brand him a terrorist."

"How the hell are you going to tie him to the IRA?"

"We got a tip from a man who knew McIver in the mid-nineties before he hooked up with Kafni. He gave me a name and I did a little checking. He was a smuggler out of Boston who operated a ship called the Saint Malachy's Revenge. He was involved in the first assassination attempt on Abaddon Kafni in ninety-seven, the one I told you about yesterday? The one that our man McIver did a prison stint for, before Kafni sprung him? This guy who called, this Captain O'Rourke, was arrested for a whole host of charges after that and spent a decade in prison himself. He's probably just trying to get a bit of revenge by muddying the waters for McIver, but I don't care about that. What I do care about is how he said McIver got to the States and why."

"Go on."

"He was running from the British because of his involvement with the IRA."

Kemiss stood in silence as he let the information sink in.

"This will take some connections to pull off," Castellano continued, "but you need to see these bodies to understand exactly what I mean. The shorthand version is that there's no way this guy is just a fisherman from Galway. Two of these guys have been shot and the other two look like they were mauled by a bear. It's just like I thought. There's a lot more to Declan McIver than what's on the surface and it lines up very well with what O'Rourke said about the IRA."

"I'll start making some calls right away," Kemiss said. "With this becoming an official inquiry it's like you said, we have more resources. I'm sure somewhere in my Rolodex I can come up with someone that can help us sort out this guy's past. If he's a goddamn terrorist we need to know. In this situation that kind of information could prove very useful."

"In the meantime, we should leak it to the press and get them stirred up about the possible connection."

"No, no. Not yet. Let me see what I can come up with first.

We don't want a flock of reporters combing over every inch of this guy's life just yet. If at all possible we want to keep him out of the public eye, so when he's eliminated there's not as many questions. We'll keep this IRA thing to ourselves for now, an ace up our sleeve, if you will."

"Fine, good idea. I'm heading to the McIver house now," Castellano said. "I'll make sure everything needed to connect him to the bomb is found on the property when my men search it later on. I've already put in a call for the warrants."

"Keep me posted."

Kemiss closed the phone and returned it to his pocket. Sometimes when a door closed, a window was opened. All you had to do was find it. Mentally he began cycling through the names of people he'd had contact with over the years that might be able to help. Having been a sitting Senator for twenty years his list of contacts was long and included a number of influential people, but the person he needed was someone who would have access to classified information in the Republic of Ireland and the United Kingdom. Soon a name came to mind and as he arrived at the end of his driveway and turned to walk back to his house, he dispelled a frozen breath and hit the call button next to a contact listed in his phone.

CHAPTER TWENTY-SIX

"It's an '81 model," Declan said, pulling a gray canvas cover off a Mercedes Benz 280SE. The slate blue four door sedan sat parked on a concrete pad in a narrow space between the rear wall of the cabin and two tall piles of firewood, effectively hiding the vehicle from the view of anyone who might be passing by in the winter months while the leaves were off the trees.

"And you've had it stored here for how long?" Constance asked, as she folded her arms across her chest in an attempt to stay warm. "How do you know it's going to start?"

"Oh, it'll start. My da' had one just like it. With the exception of my mum and me, I think that car was his favorite thing in the world."

Constance flashed a brief smile and Declan suddenly realized that he'd never spoken openly about his family in front of her. It was a new experience and it felt absolutely liberating. He leaned against the hood of the Mercedes and looked at her as she stood there in the same green knit sweater and blue jeans that she'd been wearing the night before. Her auburn hair was tied behind her head and instead of meeting his gaze, she looked down at her feet and flexed her toes up and down inside the brown sandals she was wearing.

"Hey," he said with a smile, as he moved over towards her

and touched her lightly on the arm. "It's too cold for sandals."

She grimaced slightly and his smile faded as he looked at her for a moment. He'd thought she had her arms crossed due to the chilly weather but on a second look, she seemed to be holding her stomach. "Are you alright?"

"Yeah," she said shaking her head. "Sorry."

"Whoa—hey—hey—it's alright," he said as she bent over and threw up. He moved beside her and held her hair back as she retched several times. Rubbing her back as she tried to stand upright, he said, "Let's get you inside."

Inside the cabin the fire was still smoldering from the night before and the small space was warm, the pleasant smell of burning hardwood thick in the air. He closed the door behind them and guided her over to the bed where she stepped out of her shoes and lay down. He pulled the covers over her and sat on the edge of the bed.

"What's going on?" he asked, as he stroked the side of her face. "Are you alright?"

"I'm okay," she said, tentatively. "I just felt sick all of a sudden. I don't know why."

They sat in silence for several minutes until he stood and retrieved a wet washcloth from the bathroom. He hoped that whatever had come over her had just been a short-term result of stress and not something more serious. With Constance not being accustomed to seeing any kind of violence, he worried about the long-term effects the events of the last two days might have on her.

"You're leaving, aren't you?" she said, as he laid the damp cloth over her forehead. "That's why you're getting the car ready." She wiped away tears as he looked down at her and nodded.

"Not until tomorrow, though. I wanted to get you someplace safe and you are, but this place isn't set up for long-term living."

"You say that like we're never going to be able to go home, like we're just going to have to vanish forever. Declan, we can't just go away forever. What about my family? What will my parents do if I just go missing?"

"Hey, it'll be grand. It'll be grand," he said reassuringly. "No one's going missing. We just had to get out of there and get to a safe location where I could think this thing through, come up with some kind of a plan."

2:47 p.m. Eastern Time
Intersection of Rts. 92 & 60
White Sulphur Springs, West Virginia

"I don't like it," Constance said, as she reached over from the passenger side of the Mercedes and touched his cheek lightly.

"Aye, I know," Declan said, as he felt her hand on his freshly shaven face. "I'll grow it back soon."

They had waited awhile for whatever had been ailing her to pass and had then prepared for a quick trip into the town that lay about forty minutes south. He had stored a lot of survival supplies in the cabin, but he didn't think the situation they found themselves in was quite that extreme. They could risk coming out for some creature comforts and real food.

She forced a smile. "Just one of the many changes I'm going to have to get used to, I guess."

She reached for the door handle and pulled it, then opened the car door.

"Take this," he said, withdrawing a small wad of bills from his coat pocket and handing it to her. "No cards, only cash for now. I'll be next door." He pointed in the direction of a small public library on the opposite end of the parking lot.

Constance made a face as she took the money before closing the door and disappearing into the entrance of the small grocery store. Declan watched through the large glass windows as she took a shopping cart and moved past the cash registers into the aisles. Wearing a burgundy knit beanie and heavy winter coat she stood out a bit, but the air outside was still cold enough that no one would think too much of it. While Constance felt the cold, the garb was intended more as a disguise. He wasn't sure yet, but he had a feeling that pictures of both of them were probably being displayed in the media. Unless the whole thing had somehow been covered up by the people who had tried to kill them—and he couldn't imagine anyone involved with

Ruslan Baktayev being that powerful—you didn't witness a bombing and an assassination and then kill four people without attracting some attention.

He put the Mercedes into gear and coasted through the lot to the other end, where he backed the car into an empty space and got out. With his beard shaved off, a heavy coat and a West Virginia Mountaineers baseball cap on his head, he was sure that no one besides the most astute of observers would be able to recognize him from any photos that were being circulated. He climbed the four concrete steps and pulled the door to the library open.

Inside, the building smelled like aged paper. Two librarians looked up from a circulation desk as he entered, one saying, "Hello," with a halfhearted smile before returning to the stack of books in front of her. He quickly surveyed the room and made a note of the handful of people inside, most of them located near a bank of computers along the rear wall and none of them paying attention to the fact that someone had entered. He took a slip of paper from a basket marked *Computer Passes* and walked to an empty terminal at the end of the row. Logging in with the number and password on the slip of paper, he watched as the library's chosen search engine appeared on the screen. He scanned the page for a moment before his eyes fixed on a link near the top of the site's news feed.

Former bodyguard sought in connection with bombing; deaths of FBI agents and popular news personality.

He read the headline again as a feeling of panic washed over him. Unconsciously, he shrugged his coat higher on his shoulders and pulled the baseball cap lower on his forehead as his mind began to race. He clicked on the link deftly and tapped his fingers on the mouse as he waited for the article to load. His body went rigid as he scanned the article, which contained two paragraphs that not only claimed the four men who had tried to kill him and his wife were undercover FBI agents, but also that he was being treated by the investigators as a person of interest in both the bombing and the assassination. He closed his eyes and willed himself to think clearly. Opening them again, he scrolled through the pictures in the article. They showed Abaddon Kafni and the remains of the C.H. Barton Center, plus there was a photo of him that had been taken in ninety-seven while he was a guest at a Massachusetts Correctional Institute. For once, he wished that he'd aged a little rougher than he had, as the fifteen-year-old photo still looked very recent. There was also an image of Constance from the Roanoke County Public School system's website where she'd worked for several years as a history teacher. In the article she was listed as being missing and wanted for questioning.

Clicking the red *X* at the top of the screen, he knew that he'd dramatically underestimated the men that were involved in covering up Abaddon Kafni's assassination at the hands of Ruslan Baktayev. While he'd known that he was facing a conspiracy, the extent of it was only now becoming clear. Whoever these people were, they had power and access beyond anything he'd imagined and they were trying to frame him for a crime he hadn't committed.

9:09 p.m. Eastern Time – Sunday
County Route 141
Lake Sherwood, West Virginia

"Declan, you can't just go to the university and start asking questions," Constance said. "These people know who you are. They've blamed you for killing four cops."

"I don't have a choice, Connie. You said it yourself—we've built a life together and until two days ago we were very happy. Now, do you want to abandon that life, your family, our friends, our business, everything? Because that's the other option; we run and we don't stop running, ever."

"There's got to be someone out there somewhere that can help us."

Declan knew there were two people that he could reach out to that were guaranteed to help without asking too many questions or getting other people involved. Fintan McGuire and Shane O'Reilly were both men he'd served alongside in the IRA. Being the only three surviving members of the Black Shuck Unit, they'd made a promise to look after one another and to keep their true histories a closely guarded secret. As far as Declan was concerned, that was a connection he would make only as a last resort. All either man could possibly do was help them run and hide, and right now Declan didn't want to run and hide. He had another idea.

"Aye, there is someone who I think would help us," he said. "Asher Harel."

"Who?"

"He's a friend of Abe's and the former Prime Minister of Israel. That's the problem, though, I can't just pick up the phone and call him."

"What about Osman or Nazari? Could they reach him?"

"I've already tried. They're traveling to Jerusalem for Abe's funeral. I left a message. We'll just have to wait and see."

"Then we just wait. You can't go back to the university. There's going to be federal agents crawling all over that campus, Declan. These people have told everyone that those men last night were cops and that you killed them. There's no way you're even going to get close."

"The campus is closed down. Classes have been stopped for the rest of the week, at least. All I have to do is get in, put a few pieces together and then get out. Someone there has to know who that security company was."

"Even if you get the name of the company, what's that going to prove? I guarantee you the FBI or whoever is already all over them."

"Maybe they are and maybe they aren't. You forget we're not dealing with a normal investigation here. They've covered up what happened to us. They've kicked Kafni's people out of the country. Who knows what else they might have done. Now, I know that Seth Castellano was the voice on that phone the last night, but I can't prove it. I have to be able to prove it if we're going to have any chance of telling the world and returning to our normal lives. Even Asher Harel can't help us if we don't have any proof of what's going on. We'd still be running away."

Constance sat down on the edge of the bed. "I'd rather run away than be a widow."

"You're not going to be a widow," he said, taking a seat beside her on the bed. "And running isn't a realistic option. These people aren't going to stop. At best, even with Harel's help, we'd be in hiding for the rest of our lives."

"Why are they doing this to us? What did we do to them?"

"The other night when I talked to Abe before his speech, when you asked me what it was all about? He told me that Ruslan Baktayev had escaped. He told me as a warning so that I could take steps to make sure both you and I were safe. One of the men I killed when I was working for Abe, one of the men who tried to kill him, was Baktayev's brother. Abe played down the idea of Baktayev being able to come after either of us, but he wanted me know just in case. Then last night, before the plane carrying Abe's body left, Asher Harel approached me. He told me Abe was concerned about Baktayev committing the kind of attack in America that he carried out in a town called Beslan in southern Russia, because of the circumstances surrounding his escape from prison."

"What kind of attack?"

"Taking a school full of children hostage and holding them until his demands are met, only his demands can't be met. On American soil it would be a suicide mission and Baktayev knows that."

"So he'd kill the hostages before the police killed him?"

Declan nodded. "Aye, and whoever these people are, Abe was right, they've got to be the same people that got Baktayev out of jail. They want him to commit this attack and they want to keep his presence in this country quiet until he does. That's the only reason I can think of that anyone would have to try to harm us. Because we know Baktayev is the one who killed Abe, not just some random extremist like they're pushing in the media."

"Declan, I work in a school," she said. "Why would anyone in this country want to help terrorists kill children?"

"In Russia the Beslan attack was used by the government as a major power-grab and a lot of people have suggested that the government either organized it themselves or at least knew about it in advance, but allowed it to happen regardless."

"So whoever these people are they want to use this attack to gain power and Castellano is working for them?"

"Apparently so. Castellano's the link to finding them, but I can't just walk up to him and stick a gun in his face. I'd never even get close. But if I can find out who those men last night were I'd have something to work with, a lead to follow. The vehicles they were driving were just like the ones the security company at the Barton Center had, both the SUV and the sedan. They have to have been working for that company and that's where I need to start looking."

"But if that company is involved and you go there, they'll try to kill you again. What if you're not so lucky this time?"

He shook his head and smiled. "I may be Irish, but it's like you said last night, it wasn't luck that saved us the first time around."

CHAPTER TWENTY-SEVEN

1:46 p.m. Local Time – Monday
Sandford Road
Dublin, Ireland

Fintan McGuire swung his newly completed Newtonian Reflector telescope gently around on its axis. He was very proud of it, having ground the mirrors personally. Looking over the distant buildings of Dublin's skyline from his roof in the affluent Donnybrook neighborhood, south of the downtown area, he had to admit that he was impressed with his own handiwork. He swung the telescope to the east and smiled as he caught sight of the ferries that moved in and out of the Irish capital to the United Kingdom throughout the day. Even the venerable gates leading into his home looked tremendous through the telescope.

Diligently, he moved the scope again and refocused the lens on the crumbling, time-worn rock walls that surrounded his one acre property on Dublin's R117 Sandford Road. He'd purchased it a few years ago and was restoring it, and they were to be his next project, to be started just as soon as the weather warmed and the seasonal rains lessened. The only challenge that stood between him and its completion was figuring out exactly how, with his considerable disability, he would manage to spread mortar through the cracked stones. He shrugged off the doubt; it was a minor complication at best. There were few feelings in the world that matched that of a successfully completed project and there was nothing he loved more than taking on a challenge from an amateur's point of view.

That attitude, and his love of the country that surrounded him, were what had led him to run for office as *Teachta Dála* in his home county of Monaghan. County Monaghan was a five seat constituency in the north of the Irish Republic, near the border with the six counties of Ulster that were part of the United Kingdom. As a newly elected member of the *Dáil Éireann*, the Irish Parliament, the free time he was currently enjoying would soon be at an end. The economic bubble that had burst in 2008 and left Ireland's economy in shambles needed to be undone and as one of Ireland's most successful entrepreneurs and a longtime member of the country's center-right *Fine Gael* party, he'd agreed to take on the job.

The mechanical sound of the stately home's elevator rising to the roof drew his attention away from the telescope and he turned in his chair to face the old freight door as it was pulled open.

"Pardon the interruption, Governor," his assistant, Dean Lynch, said as he stepped off the car, "but I've just come across something in this morning's edition of the *Independent* that I think you need to see."

Fintan pushed himself away from the telescope and towards his assistant as the dark haired, muscular man held out a copy of Ireland's largest selling newspaper. Taking hold of it, he spread it open and looked at the page Lynch had marked.

Former bodyguard sought in bombing of American university; deaths of Israeli celebrity Kafni and undercover FBI agents.

He scanned the article quickly and looked over the accompanying picture, a photo of a face he hadn't seen in over a decade, but one that was still very familiar to him. "Take me to my office, now," he said.

"Aye, Governor."

Lynch stepped behind him and gripped the handles on the back of the wheelchair. While McGuire much preferred to move about on his own the process could be laborious at times, especially when navigating the upper floors of the eight thousand square foot house below him, and at the moment, he didn't have any time to spare.

Lynch pushed him into the freight elevator and pulled the door closed behind them. When the car had reached the second floor, he tugged it open again and pushed the chair down a narrow hallway past the grand central staircase to a large office on the northern side. "I'll take it from here," Fintan said, as he gripped the wheels of the chair and propelled himself into the room towards a long, oak desk.

The room's decor was elagantly rustic and the walls featured the mounted heads of a number of large animals in addition to several antique hunting rifles. The floors were deeply stained wooden parquet and large windows looked to the north at the Irish capital's skyline. Not caring much about hunting or wild game, Fintan had made the room into his personal library and office. Where there had once been large lounge chairs and probably an antique floor globe, there was now a row of bookshelves, wooden file cabinets and an aquarium that boasted a variety of exotic fish, mainly from the Indian and South Pacific Oceans.

He pulled himself up to the oak desk and gripped the mouse that sat alongside a computer terminal boasting several monitors. As the various screens came to life, he pulled a keyboard from underneath the desk and typed in a web address. Lynch stood beside the door as if he already knew what his boss would soon find and was anticipating the order that would surely come if his intuition was correct. Once the site of an international, subscription based mail server in Switzerland had loaded, Fintan punched in a username and password. The login information accepted, he clicked quickly to the inbox and opened the draft folder.

"No messages. Why are there no messages?" he said aloud, the question rhetorical.

Lynch stepped into the room. "If everything this article says is true, Governor, he's got to be on the run. Maybe he just hasn't been able to contact you yet."

Fintan knew that Lynch was right. Whatever had happened in Declan McIver's life to bring him under the media's microscope in such a way had to have happened very fast and unexpectedly. Of his fellow surviving members of the Black Shuck Unit, which Fintan's father had founded and operated until being murdered in 1993, Declan McIver was the most careful and capable of all and the man Fintan least expected to need his help. But it was obvious from the article that he now needed all the help he could get.

"We have to find him, Lynch. Before anyone else can. Have Cummings meet us in Waterford within the hour. We have a sudden need to visit the United States."

CHAPTER TWENTY-EIGHT

10:26 a.m. Eastern Time – Monday
Intersection of Lee Jackson Hwy & Boonsboro Road
Lynchburg, Virginia

Declan pulled off of the Lee Jackson Highway and made a right onto Boonsboro Road. He'd decided that it would be safer to enter Lynchburg by coming over the Blue Ridge Mountains and across the James River instead of having to pass by the place where he'd been run off the road and nearly killed. He'd been listening to AM radio stations since he'd left the cabin looking for any word on what to expect when he arrived. The news anchor had just finished reading a statement from the university's chancellor, Jerry Fallwell Jr., in which he talked about the university's response to the attack, his narrow escape due to the health concerns of his mother and offered prayers and support for those effected, but Declan had yet to hear any indication that the police or FBI had roadblocks or checkpoints setup around the university.

He removed a navy blue baseball cap from the passenger seat and placed it on his head, pulling it down over his forehead to rest just above his eyebrows in an effort to disguise himself as much as possible. He was hoping that showing up at the university was the last thing anyone would expect him to do and that no one would be looking for him there for that reason, but he couldn't be too careful.

Driving the blue Mercedes sedan south onto the Lynchburg

Expressway, the campus of Liberty University came into view. Leaving the four lane interstate, he drove a short distance onto the commercial street known locally as "Hamburger Row" and crossed a set of railroad tracks onto the campus. This was the rear entrance to the university and was marked by far less traffic than the more widely used entrance east of the main campus. He passed by several faculty parking lots and finally found a visitor parking area along the sidewalk adjacent to Arthur DeMoss Hall, the university's most recognizable building. The Hall had two levels of concrete steps and eighteen stone columns supporting a towering Jeffersonian portico, which made the building look a lot like the Supreme Court in Washington D.C. In front was a statue of an eagle with its wings spread wide as it perched atop a marble column.

Declan reached over the front seat and grabbed a dark red backpack before stepping out of the car and locking it. Placing the bag on the ground at his feet, he pulled on a black Gore-Tex raincoat, zipping the collar up as far as it would go to further hide his facial features. With a cold wind blowing off the mountains and the ever present threat of seasonal rain from the heavy clouds above, the weather was providing the perfect environment for such a disguise. He slung the backpack over his shoulder and walked onto the sidewalk. Unlike most of the people he would be passing as he searched for the university's faculty offices the contents of his bag weren't textbooks and notepads, but instead a collection of first-aid and survival gear, including two to three days' worth of ration bars, butane lighters, duct tape and light sticks. In addition were some items he'd placed in the pre-made kit himself, including a lock picking kit, two pre-paid cell phones and a Glock .26 pistol with two extra magazines. He didn't plan on starting a firefight in the middle of campus and he didn't expect anyone else to, either, but if any more of the men trying to take him out showed, he was prepared.

Allowing the bag to slide off his shoulder and around to his chest as he walked, he unzipped it and reached inside to retrieve the campus map he'd purchased from a convenience store several miles outside of town.

He had come to visit Michael Coulson, wanting to ask the

man several questions that would hopefully shed some light onto what exactly had happened at the Barton Center two nights prior. He didn't suspect Coulson or anyone else at the university of being involved, although he couldn't rule out the possibility, but they certainly would know who the security company was and how to contact them. Returning the backpack to his shoulder, he spread open the glossy campus map and looked over it.

"Are you new here?" a female voice asked from behind him.

Declan turned to see a young woman with dark brown hair partially stuffed into a multi-colored stocking cap, her hands held close to her body inside the large pockets of a tan parka.

"Aye," he said, "just arrived today."

"You're kind of late," she responded with a quick smile. "Classes started two months ago."

"Okay," he said with a nervous laugh as he returned her smile. "You got me. I'm not a student, at least not yet. I'm here for a meeting with Dr. Michael Coulson. I'm hoping to start my master's degree here in the fall."

"I'm surprised Dr. Coulson is seeing anyone with everything that's happened over the last few days, but you'll find him in the Helms School of Government. I'm heading that way if you'd like a guide."

"Aye, that would be grand. I didn't call ahead to confirm the appointment, but I suppose I should have. I heard about what happened."

"It's been a rough couple of days for everyone around here," she said, as she started walking towards the front of DeMoss Hall. "Even with the shootings on the Virginia Tech campus a few years back you still don't think that it can happen to you, until it does. People here are in shock, classes have been canceled for the rest of the week. Grief counselors are all over the place for people who need to talk. I've just been trying to keep myself busy and not pay attention to the news and everything."

"Aye, I thought it looked a little desolate. Things like this used to happen all the time where I come from."

She looked over at him with a question on her face as they ascended the steps of DeMoss Hall and entered the relative shelter of the portico. "Ireland?" she said.

"Aye, Belfast area. It's not so bad anymore, but when I was a kid it was a violent place."

"I don't know much about it, I guess," she said with a shrug, as he held the front door of the building open for her. "I'm a math major."

"Oh," he said with a sarcastic laugh, "my favorite subject."

As they entered the building the girl removed her hand from the pocket of her coat and pulled off her stocking cap. Declan watched as her dark brown hair spilled down around her shoulders. He couldn't escape the thought that people just like her had been working in and around the Barton Center two nights ago. He'd noticed several of them as he and Constance had entered. How many of them had been killed or seriously injured? Did this girl know any of them? He grimaced as she led the way through the bottom floor of the building. Innocents like her were always the ones who got hurt and the people who planted the bombs or fired the guns dismissed their lives with petty political reasoning that, when you really stopped to think about it, held about as much water as a wet Kleenex. He felt anger rise from the pit of his stomach. He used to be one of those men. How many innocent girls and boys had been killed in IRA operations he'd played a part in? He'd realized early on in his days with the IRA that the type of attacks they were committing were doing little for their cause and only harming innocent neighbors. He'd tried to limit his involvement to attacks on the kind of men who had murdered his parents, but he was certain there had been unintended consequences, there always were.

"You okay?" the girl said, as he nearly ran into her. He hadn't noticed that she'd stopped walking and turned to face him.

"Aye, sorry, I was just thinking about the people in that building the other night."

Her brown eyes suddenly looked sad. "I didn't know anyone that was there, but some of my friends did. My roommate is over at the counseling center. Her ex-boyfriend was killed in the explosion. I thought I would just keep my mind off of it by studying. I'm heading to the learning center on the third floor, but I'll show you where Dr. Coulson's office is first."

"Oh, you don't have to go out of your way like that for me. If you'll just point me in the right direction I'll wander around until I find it."

"Nope, can't do that," she said as her smile returned. "I'm duty-bound to see you there. It's the Liberty way."

"Well, I appreciate it," he said, as they continued walking and neared a set of doors leading out of DeMoss Hall. They exited the building into a rectangular courtyard filled with evergreen shrubbery and descended a flight of concrete steps.

"I think I took my hat off a little too soon," the girl said as a gust of wind blew her hair over the top of her head and she hurriedly placed the stocking cap back on. They walked past several rows of hedges towards a one story concrete block building with a sign identifying it as the *food court annex* and turned left before they reached it. At the end of a long row of shrubs next to the building they turned left again and the girl pulled open a door leading into a long hallway.

"Well, this is it," she said. "This is Dr. Coulson's office." She motioned towards a closed door on the right side of the hallway just past the entrance. The shingle on the door read; *Michael Coulson, Ph.D.*

"Aye, that's grand. Thank you," Declan said, looking at the door.

"It doesn't look like anyone's here, so I hope you didn't come all the way from Ireland just for this."

"Oh no, I'll be in town for a while," he said, with a smile.

"Well, my name is Brooke," she said, as she removed a hand from her coat pocket and held it out.

"Paul," Declan lied, as he took her hand and shook it politely.

"Well, maybe I'll see you around then, Paul," she said with a smile.

He smiled back at the expectant look in her eyes. He couldn't be sure, but he was getting the impression that she wouldn't mind seeing him again. He continued smiling knowing that he was likely old enough to be her father. "Aye, I'll be around."

"Okay," she said nodding slightly as she turned to the exit. Declan slid his backpack off his shoulders and allowed it to fall to his feet. As soon as Brooke had exited the building and was out of sight, he turned and looked down the hallway. All of the twenty or so doors in the hall were closed and he couldn't hear any noises indicating that there were people present. He tried the door to Coulson's office: locked. Taking a last look through the glass door leading into the courtyard, he bent down and opened the backpack.

The fact that Coulson wasn't in his office wasn't going to deter him from trying to find the information he wanted. Maybe there was something inside, some paperwork, perhaps, that could tell him what he wanted to know. In many ways that would be ideal. If he could find what he needed without having to speak directly with anyone, then maybe nobody would ever know he'd been there. He looked up and down the hall again, this time with his eyes on the ceiling, looking for any sign of security cameras. Seeing none, he removed a fist-sized leather case and opened it, revealing a set of metal lock picks and a black pick gun. He withdrew the pick gun and closed the kit, setting it on the ground beside him as he leaned in towards the door and inserted the end of the pick gun into the keyhole. Pulling the trigger on the gun, he counted in his head until he heard an audible click. Removing the gun quickly, he turned the doorknob and pushed the door open before the tumbler returned to its locked position.

Declan picked up the lock kit and his bag and retreated inside the dark office, searching for a light switch as he closed the door. Finding the switch on the wall, he turned on the light and looked around. The office was windowless and it was obvious from the number of opened boxes sitting on the floor and in the chairs that Coulson had been preparing to move to his new home on the third floor of the C.H. Barton Center. In the right hand corner of the square room was a corner desk with a computer and printer on it. On the monitor, several images of the campus flashed around the screen and Declan realized that Coulson probably hadn't been gone very long. Most screensavers were only set to a maximum of thirty minutes before the computer would enter power save mode and turn itself off.

Before touching anything, he reached into a side pocket of his backpack and pulled out a pair of black leather police gloves. Setting the backpack on the floor, he pulled on the gloves and opened a box sitting on a red upholstered chair near the door. Inside he found several plaques with various academic awards listed, and quickly closed it and moved on. In another box was a stack of binders containing test materials for the many courses that were taught in the university's government programs, and again he closed the box and moved on. Taking a seat in the leather office chair behind the desk, he swiveled back and forth, opening drawers. Inside, everything was neat and labeled, but he found nothing that told him what he wanted to know. He bumped the mouse and the computer screen came to life, revealing a desktop background picture of Michael Coulson, his wife, and what were apparently the couple's children, sitting atop a high rock overlooking a valley. He recognized the location as being the top of McAfee's Knob in Roanoke, a popular local hike that connected in several locations with the Appalachian Trail. He and Constance had hiked it many times and had similar photos at home.

The sound of someone opening the entrance door to the hallway caught his attention and he quickly stood from the seat and hit the power button on the monitor, making the screen dark. He moved over to the door and listened as someone entered, whistling. The person stopped just outside the office and Declan turned the lock to the open position and removed the gloves. Stuffing the gloves in his coat pocket, he picked up one of the boxes and moved it to the floor so he could take a seat. He watched the door intensely as the sound of a key being inserted into the hole came from outside. The sound stopped and the person trying to enter turned the knob and pushed the door open.

Declan sat with his foot casually propped up on his other leg and leaned back in the chair. "Good morning, Dr. Coulson," he said, as surprise registered in the eyes of the professor. "The door was open so I thought I'd wait inside."

Declan could tell by the look on Coulson's face that, unlike the student he had run into on his way in, Coulson had been paying attention to the news.

"The door was open?" Coulson asked suspiciously. "I could've sworn I locked it."

Declan shrugged. "Must not have, because it opened when

I turned the knob."

"Hmm." Coulson stepped fully into the room, running a hand through his neatly combed brown hair as he looked around. His thick mustache twitched as he spoke. "I wasn't expecting anyone, much less you."

Declan could sense that the man was nervous. "I came to ask you a couple of quick questions and then I'll be on my way."

"Questions? About what? I've been over everything with the FBI a dozen times."

Now the professor sounded frustrated instead of nervous.

"I'm sure you have been," Declan said, trying to sound reassuring. "I just wanted to know if you knew who–"

"They're looking for you, you know?" Coulson interrupted.

Declan stopped talking as the professor withdrew a business card from inside his coat.

"One of the agents gave me this card and told me to call them if I saw you."

Declan stood and looked at the man. "Did they tell you why?"

"No. Only that they were looking to question you in connection with the—with everything. They asked if I knew you and said you hadn't been available since you left the hospital."

Declan reached for the business card. Flipping it over in his hand he read the name of Seth Castellano. "Funny thing about that, someone tried to run me off the road and kill me when I was heading home after I left the hospital."

Coulson looked up in surprise. Although he didn't speak, the words *you're serious?* were pasted on his face.

Declan nodded. "They were driving a vehicle that closely matched the type of SUV that some of the security officers had the night of the gala. That's why I came. I was hoping you knew who the security company was and could direct me to them."

Coulson stroked his mustache and chin with his hand as he took a deep breath. He seemed to be contemplating his next words carefully. He shook his head as he spoke. "We have our own police department here and they usually take care of any and all of the university's security needs. If we're expecting a big crowd for an event, for example, then our department hires off-duty police officers from the city for extra manpower."

"The guys the other night looked more like a private firm, not off-duty officers."

Coulson shook his head again. "I don't know who they were. I didn't plan the event. That was handled by our scheduling department. They coordinate all campus events."

"Can you call them and find out?"

Coulson brushed a hand through his hair again. "I don't think I should. I think you need to call the agent on that card and talk to him. He's in charge of investigating this, not you."

Declan stepped closer to the professor, who continued his nervous and frustrated movements. "Look," he said, stepping to within a few inches of Coulson and allowing the obvious threat to hang in the air for a moment. "I've already spoken to Agent Castellano and he all but told me he didn't believe what I was saying. I was part of Abaddon Kafni's security detail for five years. You were with me in the Barton Center when that bomb exploded. Why would I put myself and my wife in that kind of danger if I knew what was going to happen? I followed Kafni to the home he was staying in after we evacuated him from the building and I saw his attackers carry his head out in a bag."

Coulson swallowed hard at the mental images as Declan continued.

"Since then someone has tried to run me off the road. When they succeeded, they came back to make sure I was dead and I overheard them talking about killing my wife next. Luckily, I'm not an amateur when it comes to such situations and those men and the men I found watching my house are no longer with us. The men I saw kill Kafni were Islamists, the same type of men that have been trying to take him out for over a decade, but the men who came after me were different. They were Americans, and until I find out who they are and who was running them I'm not going anywhere near Agent Castellano or anyone else involved in this investigation."

Reading into the professor's wide-eyed look, he knew he had the man on the ropes and decided to go in for the final blow.

"Now all of that, to me, adds up to a conspiracy and that means the bombing wasn't a terrorist attack and that there are other people involved. Since you opened that door and saw me you've been sweating bullets and fidgeting like a hyperactive child. Do you have something you want to get off your chest, Dr. Coulson?"

The professor broke eye contact and looked at the floor. "I'm an academic. I don't know anything about bombs or murders or any of this stuff. All I know is that two nights ago I watched a lot of my colleagues get killed or injured in that explosion and the investigation has yet to come up with any kind of an explanation as to exactly what happened and why. You want the name of the security company? Fine, I'll get it for you and then I want you out of my office."

Coulson's eyes were filled with emotion. He removed his glasses and wiped his face with a handkerchief before reaching for the telephone on his desk. He punched a button and a dial tone sounded over the speaker. After he dialed a few numbers, Declan heard a female voice pick up the line.

"Scheduling, this is Nikki."

"Nikki, this is Michael Coulson over at the Helms School of Government. I'm standing here with an investigator who has asked me the name of the security company that was used the other night and I'm afraid I can't help him. Would you know who they were?"

"Yes, sir, but I've already given that information to the investigators that came here."

"Well, I'm sure they're just trying to build as complete a picture of things as possible. We're on speaker phone, would you mind telling him again?"

"It was a company out of Moneta called Sweat Security. They were providing the security for the home Dr. Kafni was staying in as well."

"Thank you, Nikki," Coulson said, as he terminated the call. "There, Sweat Security in Moneta."

Declan softened his demeanor and looked at Coulson. "Thank you, Dr. Coulson. I'm truly sorry for your losses. Abaddon Kafni was good friend of mine. We all lost people close to us. I'm just trying not to lose anymore."

CHAPTER TWENTY-NINE

10:48 a.m. Eastern Time – Monday
Verndale Drive
Roanoke, Virginia

Seth Castellano looked over the living room of the house located at the end of a long driveway on Verndale Drive in the northern part of Roanoke County. If not for the fact that the home was set apart by an acre of forest, it would stand in direct contrast to the working middle-class neighborhood that bordered it. Behind the stone-columned gate, the long paved driveway and the forest, the house wasn't the anomaly it would otherwise have been, but instead a neat gem hidden perfectly in a little valley. He'd been here once before, but hadn't gone inside. Everything he'd needed to do he'd accomplished inside one of the two garages on the property.

"Found another one, sir," a young man in a suit and tie said as he entered from the basement steps and walked down the short hallway to the living room, carrying an AR style rifle.

"That makes nine," Castellano said. "Put it on the kitchen table with the others."

"What the hell do you think this guy's doing with all these weapons anyway, sir?"

"No idea, Agent Carter, but my guess is he wasn't planning a safari."

The agent laid the rifle down on the oval kitchen table next to the others they'd found stashed in various locations throughout the house. In total there were nine guns; six semi-automatic pistols, two AR style rifles and a Mossberg pump action shot gun. "You want me to start on the master bedroom?" Carter asked.

"No," Castellano answered. "I'll handle that. Head out back and help the others search the garage. I'm betting there's more hidden there than there is in the house."

"Yes, sir."

The young agent disappeared out of the back door that led onto the wrap around porch. As the door banged closed Castellano withdrew a pair of nitrile gloves from his pocket and put them on. He walked slowly around the living room, looking at the two curio cabinets filled with pictures. Declan and Constance McIver certainly looked like the typical, upper middle-class American couple and in addition to the photos of the smiling couple, their house testified to it.

Despite its private setting, the house was small by most upper crust standards with only three bedrooms and two bathrooms. One of the bedrooms upstairs was used as an office and two technicians from the FBI's Computer Crimes Division were there searching the filing cabinets and two computers located in the room. He doubted they'd find anything. Although Declan McIver clearly had a penchant for concealing weapons, they'd found nothing else to indicate that he was involved in any criminal activities. As far as Castellano could tell there was nothing that would help him tie either of the McIvers to the murder of Abaddon Kafni, but that was okay. He had placed all the evidence they would need.

Craning his neck to look out of the home's windows for any of his men that might still be nearby, he slowly pulled out a gallon-sized ziplock bag from the oversized pocket on the side of his overcoat. Inside was a suppressed pistol that he'd obtained from Ruslan Baktayev through an undisclosed shipment with DHL. While it was technically against the company's policy to ship firearms, what they didn't know wouldn't hurt them. Opening the bag, he walked down the hallway off the living room towards the master bedroom which, except for being cleared of any occupants upon their initial arrival, had yet to be searched.

Inside the bedroom it looked as though someone had left quickly and he had no doubt that someone had. The comforter and sheets on the bed were tossed back as though someone had gotten out of bed and a pair of pink fleece pajamas lay crumpled on the floor near a pair of slippers. The local police had found the bodies of two men that he knew had been watching the McIver house and from the scene at both locations it was obvious what had happened. Declan McIver had killed the two men who ambushed him on the highway and had driven their vehicle to his house where he'd found the other two men waiting. He'd then called his wife and used her leaving the house as a decoy to draw the remaining assailants into a less populated area so that he could take them out as well, which he'd done with the kind of precision only an experienced killer could muster.

The bedroom, like the rest of the house, showed no signs of anyone having returned since then for clothes or anything else, so wherever the McIvers had gone it was obviously a place that had been prepared in advance. That fact, coupled with everything else, played right into the idea that Declan McIver was some sort of terrorist in hiding.

Checking his surroundings again, Castellano lifted the edge of the mattress on the side that hadn't been slept in and placed the suppressed gun underneath. Its presence in the home and the ballistics tests that would be done on it once it was found would be more than enough to prove Declan McIver had killed the guard in front of the Briton-Adams mansion and would cast serious doubt on his story of having seen terrorists kill Kafni. Castellano stuffed the ziplock bag back in his pocket and left the room.

"Agent Schultz?" he called, as he reentered the living room.

A man dressed in a dark blue Windbreaker with yellow letters on the back reading *FBI* appeared from one of the upstairs bedrooms and looked over the landing bannister. "Yes, sir?"

"Kindly start searching the master bedroom, will you? I've got to make some calls."

"Yes, sir."

Castellano heard the agent's footsteps on the stairs as he walked into the kitchen and left the house through the back door. He fished his cell phone from the inside breast pocket of his coat as he strode across the porch to where his car was parked on the wrap around driveway. Opening the door and getting inside, he pushed and held a key on the phone until the sound of a number being dialed could be heard.

"What do you have?" David Kemiss answered.

"I've got enough illegally converted automatic weapons to put Declan McIver in jail for the next twenty years if we take the charges before the right judge."

"Good, but we still need a motive."

"I've got men upstairs pulling their personal financial records now and I have a warrant to search the company's offices as well. With the real estate market being what it has been over the last few years I'm sure we won't have a problem finding a financial motive."

"That'll work. I don't care if this guy brings in two hundred thousand a year. All we have to prove is that he's brought in more in previous years and that he's not happy about the cut in pay."

"Like I said, shouldn't be hard." Castellano looked up into the rearview mirror as he heard a vehicle pull in behind him. "Let me call you back, David. Someone's just arrived."

He closed the phone and opened the car door, stepping out at the same time as a stocky woman from the white mini-van behind him. "Can I help you, miss?"

The woman looked stunned at the number of unmarked police cars in the driveway.

"I guess I uhh came at the wrong time," the woman stammered.

"Why are you here?"

"I'm Carol Minnix from up the road. I'm here for the dog, Shelby."

Castellano looked towards the house. "There's no dog here that I'm aware of. Did the McIvers call you and ask you to come?"

The woman shook her head. "No. I always take care of Shelby when Declan and Constance are away."

"And how do you know they're away?"

"I just figured they were because of what the news was

saying."

"I see. Well, as I said, there's no dog here."

"She's under the couch. That's where she hides when someone she doesn't know is around."

"We've searched the entire house, miss. There's no dog. Agent Carter, did you find a dog?" Castellano asked, as the young agent strode up the driveway from around the other side of the house where the garage was located.

"No sir, but I found traces of ammonium nitrate fertilizer in an old Jeep inside the garage."

"I'm sure you did."

"May I go in and get her, sir? I know where she is," the woman pleaded.

Castellano pointed at the door. "Don't touch anything. Get the dog and get out."

He followed the woman onto the porch and watched as she stepped inside. "Oh," she said solemnly as she saw the assortment of firearms laid out on the kitchen table.

"'Oh' is right," Castellano said. "Do you have any idea why the McIvers have so many weapons?"

"No, sir. I didn't know they did. I didn't even know Constance knew how to fire a gun."

"Of course not, it's just like an episode of the Greatest American Hero around here, or so everyone tells me."

The woman looked ashen as she stood there apparently wondering what to do next.

"The dog," Castellano said, pointing into the house.

"Oh, right. Okay," the woman stammered as she moved quickly into the living room and sank to her knees in front of the couch. She whistled and said, "Shelby, it's Carol. Come here."

Castellano watched as the woman reached under the couch and pulled a beefy beagle out by its collar. "I'll be damned," he said. "Some guard dog, huh?"

The woman picked up the dog and moved quickly out of the house.

"Do you have any idea if the McIvers have any properties that they stay at for vacations or anything?" Castellano asked, as he followed her out.

The woman shook her head as she loaded the beagle onto the passenger seat of her van and closed the door. "No," she said as she moved around to the driver's side. "They travel a fair amount, but not to the same places, so far as I'm aware. I'm usually jealous when they go out of town, to be honest. They've been all over the world. Paris, Madrid, all over."

"I see; and what about Mr. McIver? Does he have any place that maybe he'd go without his wife?"

"Declan's got property all over the place, sir. He's in the real estate business. Always buying and selling something. Constance mentioned a fishing cabin that he liked to go to sometimes, but I don't have any idea where it is."

"A fishing cabin," Castellano said, raising his eyebrows. "Interesting, and you have no idea where it is?"

"No. She never told me. To be honest I'm not even sure if she knew where it was."

Castellano nodded. "Thank you. You take care of that dog now," he continued with a smirk. "It looks a little underfed."

As he turned away from the woman he heard his phone ringing in his car. Walking over and opening the door, he reached in and picked up the device. *Call From (434)565-2674* flashed on the screen. "Castellano," he said as he thumbed the display and brought the phone to his ear.

"Agent Castellano, this is Michael Coulson from Liberty University."

"What can I do for you, Dr. Coulson?"

"You asked me to call you if I saw or heard from Declan McIver, sir. He's just left here a few minutes ago."

CHAPTER THIRTY

11:03 a.m. Eastern Time – Monday
7th Street & Pennsylvania Ave.
Washington D.C.

David Kemiss watched as the wait staff moved promptly around tables set in well-defined rows. He was in the large rectangular restaurant that made up the ninth floor of the Frederick J. Cooper building. No clanking dishes or noisy push carts. No breaking china or dropped silverware. No banter with the clientele, as there was in most restaurants. Like phantoms that appeared and disappeared at the most opportune moment they went about their jobs silently, every move planned well in advance like a Black Ops team whose goal it was to liberate dirty dishes and half-eaten entrées, safely extracting them beyond enemy borders before allowing them to make a sound. Such was the atmosphere of the exclusive 701 Restaurant, adjacent to the United States navy memorial and six blocks from the US Capitol building.

Between the hours of twelve and two the ornate restaurant and jazz lounge would be packed with congressmen, senators, aides, lobbyists, attorneys, wealthy businessmen and anyone else who had the connections to garner a reservation. But it was eleven, and the crowd had yet to arrive from the nearby government institutions.

Kemiss sat alone in the corner of the room, the morning edition of the Washington Post open on the table in front of him. Without a word, a waiter deftly set before him the club's signature Scottish salmon then retreated as the senator's guest approached. Kemiss closed the newspaper and looked over the table with a question on his face as the maître d' pulled out two chairs instead of one. Looking up, he saw the man he was meeting had a guest of his own. He looked over the two men as the maître d' set down two menus, and silverware wrapped in dark red cloth napkins, before leaving at a brisk pace.

The first man, the man Kemiss had been expecting, was wearing a blue pinstriped suit with a red tie and wore a pair of gold bifocals that sat high on his nose. His demeanor was confident but not cocky, and his receding, brownish-gray hair formed two horns on his forehead.

"Good morning, David," Lane Simard said, as he took his seat. There was a slight British hue to his voice. As the CIA's Station Chief in London, Simard spent most of his time in the British capital and had apparently picked up a hint of the accent. Simard looked up at the man who accompanied him. He was a broad man with a rosy complexion, dark hair and a neatly trimmed mustache, flecks of gray throughout both. He unbuttoned his charcoal suit as he sat and loosened his burgundy tie.

"Nothing to eat, thank you, just a pot of hot tea," he said in a pronounced British accent to the waiter who had appeared beside the table.

"The same," Simard said, as he sat back in his chair and brought a leg up to rest over his knee.

"Good morning, Lane," Kemiss said, as he set the newspaper aside. "Thank you for meeting me on such short notice."

"David, this is Jones Forester. When you called yesterday and told me what you needed I couldn't think of anyone more apt to help than Jones, so I brought him along."

"How do you do?" Forester said with a nod.

Kemiss returned the nod and extended his hand. The Brit grabbed it and gave it a firm squeeze. Kemiss could tell right away that the man was former military. The look in his eyes as he shook hands told him so.

"Jones here has a unique perspective on all things British," Simard said. "After our days at Oxford together he spent several years in the army and then joined the Metropolitan Police Service in London where he retired as the Deputy Commissioner. He works for the British Embassy here in Washington now as the Police Attaché. His military career includes a tour in Ireland, but he only likes to talk about that when he gets a few drinks in him."

The men chuckled.

"I'm sure they have a twelve year old scotch or something here that's sure to loosen his tongue," Kemiss said with a smile, before his face turned grave again.

Sensing that the conversation was about to turn serious, Lane Simard straightened up in his chair and said, "Why don't you start by telling us a little more about what you need and how you think we can help."

Kemiss sat forward in his chair and rested his elbows on the table. "We're dealing with a matter of national security here so I'm sure I don't have to tell either of you that anything I say isn't to leave this table."

Simard and Forester both grimaced and nodded. Kemiss could tell they knew how the game was played. It was always about deniability. That's why he'd chosen a meeting place away from his offices. In the 701 Restaurant there were no guest logs and no witnesses that were likely to know who Simard or Forester were. Neither man was high enough in the pecking order to frequent the establishment.

"As you both probably know from news reports, the United States was again hit by terrorists the other night. This time the target was a university and we believe that the attackers were aided by someone on the inside. I've been asked by the Richmond Field Office of the FBI to pull a few strings and see if I can't help them out with a particular matter."

"The attack was an attempted assassination, was it not?" Forester said. "News reports have said that the Israeli that was killed was the target and not the university itself."

Kemiss nodded. "That's partially true. Whoever committed the attack was indeed trying to kill Abaddon Kafni, but our sources indicate that whoever financed the deal also wanted to make a statement."

"And you think it was this Irishman you mentioned," Simard

said. "What was his name again?"

"Declan McIver. He was close to Kafni and was familiar with his security personnel, which in the FBI's working theory allowed him to move about without suspicion."

Forester tilted his head at the mention of an Irishman, his expression revealing that the reason for his being invited had suddenly become clear to him.

"And why is the FBI so stumped with him that they need my help?" Simard asked, the old agency rivalry audible in his voice.

"The problem is with his background."

Simard raised an eyebrow.

"He hasn't got one," Kemiss continued. "He immigrated from Ireland in the mid-nineties and turned up in Boston working as part of Kafni's security detail, but nothing in his personal history indicates any military or police experience that would lead him to such a position."

"So the feebs think it's a whitewash and they want to get their hands on the real thing?"

Kemiss nodded. "I've seen the file myself and it's about as vague as they come."

"So what *do* you know about this guy?" Simard asked.

"He left Kafni's employ shortly after September the 11th. He and his wife now own a small business in Roanoke, Virginia, and according the neighbors and employees they're only two-point-five kids short of being the perfect family."

"Doesn't sound like much of a threat," Forester said.

"Well you wouldn't think so, but he's certainly proven otherwise. Saturday night, four undercover men were sent to question him. Those four men are now dead and Mr. McIver hasn't been seen since."

"He killed four men?" Forester said with an air of incredulity. "Who were they? Were they trained to handle a fight or were they just your average gumshoes?"

Kemiss shrugged and grimaced. "All of them were experienced, but to what degree I don't know. Two of them were taken down hand to hand, the other two shot from a distance."

As an experienced politician, Kemiss knew how to stick to a well-prepared message, whether it was true or not, and this time he was lying through his teeth. He was making it all up as he went along and hoping his position would be enough to convince the two men in front of him that any holes in the narrative were due to a lack of actual field experience. As an ex officio member of the Senate Intelligence Committee he dealt with these types of issues frequently, but always from behind a desk and no matter how detailed the reports in front of him were, they still lacked a certain immediacy. It was like watching a football game from the booth as opposed to watching it from the sidelines, an entirely different point of view.

"Sorry about your men," Forester said. "Nasty business, terrorism always has been."

Kemiss waved off the condolences. He couldn't care less about the men Castellano had hired, they were pawns, useful when they were needed but certainly not missed now that they were gone. "I don't want your sympathy; I want you to help me catch this guy. I was supposed to be a guest at Kafni's speech the other night and although we didn't agree on much, I considered him a friend. I could have been killed and he was, so I'm taking this personally. I want to see this McIver's head on the end of a stick. Now, if you did duty in Ireland, what can you tell me? This guy isn't just some lowly potato farmer who came here for a better job. There's more to him and I want you to help me find it. It's imperative that we know who this guy is."

"So what are the ideas that are being thrown around?" Simard asked.

"There have been a few tips called in that they're looking seriously at, one in particular that I think you might be able to help with, Mr. Forester. How much do you know about the IRA?"

"Heavens, everything," Forester said. "I spent thirty-six months with 14 Intelligence in the eighties. But if you're thinking this man is IRA, then the question isn't how much I know about them, but how much you know."

Kemiss shrugged. "What the hell is that supposed to mean?"

"Well, the group you're most likely referring to is the Provisional IRA and they had upwards of ten thousand men at one point. A lot of whom are still out there somewhere, although probably living on the dole since the peace accords. Their particular expertise isn't very useful in the job market. These men are far from being professional operators. They were third and fourth tier revolutionaries with too much time on their hands because of the high level of unemployment in Northern Ireland. The entire organization was riddled with spies, known locally as 'touts'. By the mid-seventies they couldn't sneeze without us knowing where every bit landed."

"But it's a documented fact that they had ties with the PLO and other jihadi organizations that might want to take out someone like Abaddon Kafni."

"Oh, yes." Forester nodded. "Indeed. That lot never had any love affair with the Israelis and there were definitely ties to other terrorist organizations. Qaddafi was a major weapons supplier, the Syrians and Palestinians too, sometimes we'd even let a shipment get through to protect informers or track the weapons, but that's about it."

"I'm telling you the men that were sent to question him were experienced men and this guy took all four of them out without suffering a scratch, as far as we can tell."

"So he got lucky," Simard said. "When you have the element of surprise, that happens, David. Those men weren't expecting an attack."

"No offense intended, senator, but to hell with your experienced backgrounds," Forester said sitting back in his chair and crossing his ankles. "Our men make your boys look like they could use a lollie."

Kemiss let the insult slide. "That was my next thought...that this guy was British Special Forces or something."

Forester shook his head as if he didn't believe what he was hearing. "Unlikely," he said.

"Well, tell me it's not possible."

"It's not *impossible*, but it's damned unlikely. Her majesty's government was very careful about allowing Ulstermen to join the ranks of the military in those days. Most that were allowed to serve did so in more support-orientated positions, and they did it in places far away from Ireland. Occasionally we'd pick out some men we thought were particularly suited to becoming spies for us and we'd send them home to join up with the subversives, but we didn't want to be training our enemies like you lot did in Afghanistan with the *Mujahideen,* just so you could stick it to the Ruskies."

"You all were involved in Afghanistan, too," Kemiss said, again ignoring the insult. "I refuse to believe this guy just got lucky. Somewhere and at some point this guy was trained by someone."

"The IRA could have trainded him themselves. They always operated in what was known as Active Service Units or ASUs," Forestor said, "usually four men to a team, and they were almost always trained at terror camps in the Republic of Ireland or Libya, if the leadership in Belfast could manage to get their men out of the country without us tracking them. That didn't happen very often, especially in the latter days. We had some information that the Soviets were involved at one point, but it was pretty thin."

"Sounds like there's certainly more to him then what you see on the surface, but who could he possibly be working for?" Simard said. "From what you say he doesn't need money and that's the only reason I can come up with that would lead him to ally himself with anyone who'd be interested in taking out an Israeli or committing a terrorist attack against the United States. The IRA were nationalists, they had no interest in any country beyond the borders of Ireland. The few attacks they committed outside of Ireland were all British targets and were designed for the same purpose as their attacks in Northern Ireland, to force the British out of 'their' country."

"The IRA certainly did a lot to influence the *jihadis,*" Forester put in, "but there's no connection there anymore. The *jihadis* would detonate a bomb in Belfast or Dublin just as quick as they would in London or New York and the Micks know it."

"So you guys can't help me?" Kemiss said, his face becoming a cold stone.

"Oh, we're not saying that," Simard said hurriedly. "We're just not sure about the IRA idea."

"Like I said, senator, it's not impossible to think that this guy somehow slipped through the net and was either enlisted or part of a paramilitary group. I have some contacts on the inside still. If it will help, I'll have them run his name against everything they have access to and see what comes up. We certainly used our share of spies in Northern Ireland, maybe he was one of them. I should be able to let you know in a day or two."

"Fine, thank you."

"Don't mention it. You can owe me one," Forester said with a toothy smile. "Honestly, I doubt anything will come of it. That kind of information used to be stored at Briagde Headquarters in Lisburn or even the RUC headquarters on Knock Road, but not anymore. Not since the peace accords and the supposed end of the Troubles. Now it's all stored in Thames House, I suspect. If you really want to find out what's in this guy's past, Lane here would be able to help you more than I. He's the man with the connections to the JIC."

Kemiss knew JIC was an acronym for the Joint Intelligence Committee, a part of the British Cabinet Office that was responsible for directing the national intelligence-collecting services of the United Kingdom.

"That's why I called you," Kemiss said, looking at Simard.

Simard shifted in his seat and sat forward to rest his elbows on the table. "I can certainly take a look and see what there is to find. It will take a few days, though. I'll have to tread carefully. I'm only there as an observer unless something being discussed affects U.S. security."

Kemiss glared. "This affects U.S. security, for sure. Let me know what you find as soon as you get it. You get this done for me and you'll have all the favors you could ever need from my office."

Simard smiled. "I'll be in touch."

CHAPTER THIRTY-ONE

Driving on a two lane highway, Declan kept a close watch on the rearview mirror. Like many other companies in recent years, Sweat Security had chosen a rural location, east of Roanoke and west of Lynchburg, known as Franklin County. Home to the largest lake in Virginia, the area was a popular destination of residents in both cities. In addition to the county's booming construction industry, low corporate taxes and less burdensome regulations by the local government had made it a haven for companies that didn't rely on a commercial storefront. In the case of Sweat Security, the company was located a few miles north of the small farming town of Moneta and about five miles northeast of the waterfront.

Declan slowed the car as he approached the company's property, keeping a sharp lookout for any signs that the FBI or other law enforcement agencies had the building under surveillance. Seeing none, he turned into the gravel parking lot in front of a split-faced block building with a blue metal roof. Immediately, he was struck by the lack of cars in the parking lot and hoped he hadn't made a terrible mistake in coming. Stopping directly in front of the business's main entrance, he shifted the vehicle into park. Drumming his fingers on the steering wheel, he craned his neck to scan the horizon behind him. Satisfied that no one was around, he looked through the Mercedes' windshield at the hastily drawn sign hanging on the front door: *closed until further notice.*

The front of the building was lined with rectangular windows, but no lights appeared to be on inside. He stepped out of the car, closing the door quietly behind him. Approaching the front door, he cupped his hands around his eyes and peered through the tinted windows. Inside the front office was deserted, filing cabinets were wide open and papers littered the gray carpeted floor. Standing back from the door, he again scanned the horizon behind him for any signs of surveillance before he began to make his way along the side of the building.

The adjacent lots were wooded and provided him the perfect cover as he arrived at a chain link fence that surrounded a rear lot where some of the company's service vehicles were parked. Seeing several of the vehicles, he knew he'd found the right place. In the lot there were a dozen police style Crown Victoria sedans and several white Dodge Durango SUVs, just like the one that had tried to run him off the road. Some of the vehicles were marked with red letters reading *security* and some weren't. Grabbing ahold of the fence, he pulled himself up, using the diamond-shaped holes in the fencing as footholds as he climbed up the eight foot barrier and swung his legs over the top, jumping onto the gravel lot beyond.

Standing from his landing crouch, he made his way cautiously to the back of the building where a metal door with a thin window above the latch stood. He tried the latch but just as he'd expected, the door was locked. Knowing the building likely had an alarm that would sound if he broke a window or picked a lock, he considered his options as he looked around. On the opposite side of the building from the fence he'd climbed was a row of four garage doors with small half-moon ports in the bottom for attaching vehicle exhaust hoses. Apparently the building had been used as a repair facility in the past or else the company performed the maintenance on their own fleet. Noting that the exhaust ports were an older style that sat at the very bottom of the door near the cement instead of further up, he got an idea.

Turning and looking around the lot, he spotted an old

stake back truck that was missing most of its windows in the far corner. Walking over to it, he reached through the window opening and raised the lock. The hinges protested loudly as he opened the door and got into the driver's seat. Looking at the floor between the driver and passenger seats, he spotted what he was searching for in a metal box attached to the truck's back panel. Lifting two latches, he opened the vehicle's tire changing compartment and withdrew the separated sections of the angled tire iron and the manual vehicle jack. He slid out of the truck and returned to the garage door furthest from the front of the building. Using the hubcap removal side of the tire iron, he pried open the door on the exhaust port and slid the manual jack underneath. Fitting the pieces of the tire iron together to create the long pole used to operate the jack, he inserted it into the end and began pushing it up and down causing the jack to lift. When the door had raised about four inches it stopped, obviously held in place by an internal locking rod. Taking a deep breath, he pushed down on the pole with all of his weight, lifting himself off the ground. Slowly the door raised as the metal locking rod inside was bent downwards by the pressure. With the garage door now about a foot from the concrete floor, Declan removed his Glock pistol from his coat, lay down and slid underneath into the building.

Raising himself slowly into a standing position, he looked around the spacious garage, pistol aimed in the direction of sight until he was sure he was alone. Inside, eight vehicles in various stages of repair sat dormant, the smell of antifreeze hanging in the humid air. Only the natural light allowed in by the building's windows lit the room, the tinted glass giving the interior a greyish hue. The ceiling was at least fifteen feet high with an arched center, and a sliding glass window sat high in the wall closest to the front of the building. As he walked down the center between the two rows of vehicles, a hissing sound caught his attention. The sound was coming from a maroon colored BMW SUV that was parked in the very first bay and indicated the vehicle's water pump was leaking. Declan moved towards it and reached for its hood, knowing that the only way the water leak could make the hissing sound was if the vehicle's exhaust manifold was still hot. Sure enough, as he placed his hand flat on the hood, he could feel warmth through the metal. The SUV hadn't been parked there very long. Had its occupants left in another vehicle or were they still in the building?

He moved to a doorway at the front of the garage and entered a hallway beyond. From the hall he could see the door that he'd peered through earlier and the papers littering the front office floor. Clearing the few rooms off the hallway, he made his way to the front office. The first floor of the building was empty, but he needed to make sure the second floor was, too, before he could begin searching for anything that might identify the four men he'd killed. Inside the office, he searched for a staircase that would lead him to the second floor he knew was there. Spotting a closed door in the far corner of the room, he strode towards it, raising his pistol in one hand and gripping the doorknob with the other. He pulled open the door and aimed the pistol up a set of stairs that hair pinned around a corner and out of view. Keeping his weapon aimed, he climbed the steps slowly, one at a time. On the landing halfway up, he rolled out around a wall, securing the second flight of stairs. There was no door at the top and whatever room was beyond sat off to the right. Nearing the last step before reaching the second floor, he moved as far to the left on the stairs as he could to get a view of the room. Suddenly he heard a loud blast and a piece of drywall disintegrated a foot from him.

"Stay away from here," a gruff voice shouted. "Get out!"

"I'm not here to hurt anyone!" Declan shouted in response. "I just need to ask some questions!"

"The hell you do! Get out!"

Another gunshot sounded, the bullet tearing loose more of the white drywall and causing it to fall to the floor in a dusty heap. Declan stayed put on the steps; unable to see who it was that was firing at him.

"I'm warning you, I'm not going down without a fight! I'll shoot you!"

"I believe you," Declan said, putting his pistol in his coat where it was hidden from view but still accessible. "I'm not here to hurt you. I'm one of the good guys. I'm unarmed. Now, who am I talking to?"

"You know who I am! I'm Tim Sweat, the guy whose family

you've been threatening for the last month!"

"I think you've got me confused with someone else. My name's Declan McIver. I'm the owner of DCM Properties in Roanoke."

There was silence in the room for several seconds.

"Do you always go around breaking into people's buildings?"

"No. No, I don't. Now I'm going to step onto the landing slowly with my hands up. Don't shoot."

Declan raised his hands to shoulder level and stepped up onto the last step, gradually exposing one hand and stepping sideways onto the second floor, facing the direction the gunshots had come from. The floor creaked under his weight.

In the rectangular room beyond a heavyset man with white hair, a rose-colored complexion and a thin mustache crouched behind a long desk, aiming a .38 revolver. Perspiration beaded and rolled down his face.

"Easy," Declan said, keeping his hands up and stepping forward into the room. "Now, surely you can see I'm not the man whose been threatening you."

The man sniffed loudly and wiped his sweaty face with his hand. "There are four of 'em. How do I know you're not just a fifth sent here to keep me from talking?"

"I'm here because a vehicle belonging to this company ran me off the road last night. Then its occupants tried to kill me."

"Kill you? Oh, God." The man's grip on the revolver loosened a bit and he raised himself up a few inches to support his body against the edge of the desk. Breathing heavily he said, "I don't know anything about it. Oh, God." Tears streamed from his eyes and he wiped frantically at them.

Declan relaxed and lowered his hands, keeping them just far enough away from his body that the man could see he wasn't going for a weapon. "You said your name is Tim Sweat? Are you the owner of this company?"

"Yeah, at least I was until yesterday afternoon when the FBI walked in and shut us down."

"Why did the FBI shut you down? Because the car that blew up at the university belonged to your company?"

"Yes," Sweat said, nodding. "But I didn't have anything to do with it. I swear. They were threatening my family."

"I believe you," Declan said, being sure to maintain eye contact. "Let's put the gun down and talk about this. I'm here because someone's threatening my family, too."

Sweat stood and slowly lowered the revolver, his face contorting as he fought back tears.

"Now tell me who *they* are," Declan said, though he thought he probably already knew.

"Four men, they came in just a little over a month ago when we first booked the job at Liberty. I don't even know how they knew about it. They said they wanted in on the job but I've got a good crew here. Most of them have been with me for over a decade and I wasn't about to bump them so I could hire these guys. Something about 'em, I don't know, something just wasn't right."

"But they didn't go away when you said no?"

Sweat shook his head. "No. They came back here that same night. I'm always the last one to leave and they approached me as I was getting in my truck. Told me that if I didn't agree to hire them on as part of the security team for the university, they'd hurt my family. They had pictures of my granddaughters getting on the school bus, pictures of my wife in the garden at home. I didn't have a choice."

Declan nodded. Sweat was obviously scared and was showing no signs of deception. The revolver quaked in his hand and clamshell-shaped stains formed in the underarms of his white button-down shirt.

"I knew they were up to something bad," Sweat continued, "but I couldn't have imagined anything like this. I wanted to call the police, but then everywhere we went one of them was there. My wife and I would go out to eat and one of them would walk in and sit a few tables away from us, making sure that I saw him. At night they'd drive one of my own company vehicles by my house and park in the cul-de-sac, watching. I thought you were one of them. I thought you'd come to make sure I didn't talk."

Declan shook his head. "Until two days ago I was just a real estate investor attending the grand opening of the Barton Center where a good friend was the keynote speaker. Now he's dead and there's men trying to kill my wife and me."

Sweat's face contorted again as he said, "Until these four men walked into my life, I was just the owner of a small, family-run security company in Moneta, Virginia. Now the business I started with my two sons in 1986 is gone and I'm going to end up in jail."

Declan could understand both the fear and the frustration Sweat was feeling. Like Sweat, he'd worked hard to build his company and his life. What effect the current situation would have on his business, he didn't know. First, he had to survive, and that meant taking the fight to those responsible. "When was the last time you saw these men?"

"Yesterday morning," Sweat said. "They left just before the FBI arrived. It's like they knew they were coming."

"They might have," Declan said, thinking about Castellano. He'd yet to find any evidence to prove it, but his gut instinct still told him the agent was involved. "Do you know anything about these men, their names? Can you tell me what they look like? I need to find them."

"The FBI raided the office downstairs completely and searched the entire building. They took all of my employee files and years of financial documents, but I made copies of the paperwork these guys filled out for their DOJ clearance and kept them up here, tucked away in a filing cabinet full of instruction booklets and warranty information. That's why I came here, to get the files."

"DOJ clearance?"

"Yeah, we do a lot of guard work for government buildings so our guys have to have a security clearance from the Department of Justice. I don't know if the names and information they put down are real, but it passed DOJ, so if not they're damn good fakes."

Sweat spread out a stack of four folders side by side on his desk and opened them. Declan stepped around the desk and looked down at the passport-sized picture on each one. "I don't think you've got anything to fear from these men anymore," he said as he looked at the photos of the men who'd tried to kill both him and Constance. "They're all dead."

Sweat looked up abruptly, fear evident in his eyes as if he

was thinking that he'd let his guard down to soon. His grip tightened on the revolver held at his side.

"Relax," Declan said. "These are the four men who tried to kill my wife and me Saturday night."

"But you got them first," Sweat said, as his grip on the gun loosened again.

Declan nodded.

"How? I mean, I'm a twenty-year police veteran, I know a dangerous man when I see one and those four guys were dangerous. Ex-military for sure, maybe even Special Forces. They were killers. I could sense it."

"I guess I didn't have time to be scared."

"Yeah, right, what were you, British military or something?"

Declan shrugged. "Something like that."

Sweat nodded. "Yeah, I thought so, the way you carry yourself and all. That's why I thought you were one of them."

"We need to get these files to someone who can tell us if the information is real or not. Maybe that will help us find out who they were working for, because they definitely weren't alone."

"Noone's getting these files. "

Declan looked up as Sweat backed away from him and raised the revolver. "I'm not risking anyone coming after my family," the white haired security man said.

"So that's your answer to this? You're going to blow your brains out and just hope that whoever these men were working for will leave your family alone when you're gone?"

Sweat grimaced, tears streaming down his face. "What other choice do I have? If I'm dead I can't talk and they've got no reason to hurt anyone."

"These guys have the word 'henchmen' written all over them. They were doing someone's dirty work. I've seen people like this operate before. If you think they're going to leave your family alone because you're dead you'd better reconsider. Men like that don't leave loose ends hanging."

Declan heard the sound of gravel crunching underneath the wheels of a vehicle outside; he reached towards the picture window and flipped up a single section of the blinds. Outside a police cruiser had pulled onto the company's parking lot.

He could see the officer inside was on his radio, his attention focused on Declan's blue Mercedes alone in front of the building. Moments later a second cruiser came up the road and made a left into the lot, stopping beside the car already there. Declan had no doubt that they were there looking for him. Just as he'd thought would happen, Michael Coulson had called Castellano and now the police were closing in. He'd found what he was looking for, information that identified the four attackers, but now he needed to get it and himself out of here fast.

"Who is it?" Sweat asked.

"The police."

"The police?" Sweat said, as he strode towards the window with a hand out.

"No, wait," Declan said, moving to stop the man, but he was too late. Sweat reached the other window, pulled down a large section of the blinds and looked out. Over his shoulder, Declan watched as the sudden motion in the upstairs window attracted the attention of the officers sitting in their cruisers. The officer in the first car brought his radio to his mouth and began talking, without taking his eyes off the window.

Sweat backed away quickly as he sensed Declan behind him. "Stay back," he yelled, raising the gun to his temple. "I'm not going to jail!"

"You don't have to do this," Declan said urgently. "I can help you. We just have to get out of here!"

The sound of crunching gravel as more vehicles pulled onto the lot reached the second floor office and Declan held his hands out in a stop motion. "Let's go! We can make it out the back door before they get the—No!"

Sweat's hand tightened as he pressed the stout barrel hard against his temple, closed his eyes and pulled the trigger. The report echoed through the small room as blood and brain tissue spattered the white drywall. Sweat's body fell to the floor with a heavy thud.

"No! Dammit!" Declan yelled, throwing his hands in the air and turning away from the grisly sight of the man's eviscerated head. He could feel liquid warmth on his face, droplets of blood that had been cast from the self-inflicted wound. He wiped his face with the sleeve of his coat. His mind raced as car doors slammed shut outside and officers left their vehicles, having heard the gunshot. He scooped up the four files and placed them under his arm. Sitting underneath them was a note written in chicken-scratched handwriting, a capitalized T and an S obvious in the signature at the bottom. Declan shook his head and moved quickly towards the stairs. Taking them two at a time, he looked through the tinted front windows as he reached the first floor. The police presence had multiplied to at least a half dozen and a group of officers was at the front door trying to get it open.

"Hey! There's someone inside!" one of the officers yelled, his voice muffled by the glass but still audible. Without making eye contact, Declan ran through the office to the hallway leading into the fleet garage. "He's going out the back!" he heard an officer yell.

Declan ran between the eight cars parked in the garage and reached the back door as the shouts of officers swarming over the front fence reached his ears. Tearing the door open, he exited the humid garage into the crisp spring afternoon and ran straight for the fence at the rear of the property. Jumping onto the hood of one of the parked Dodge Durangos, he ran over the roof and jumped the fence behind it, landing with a painful gasp from the eight foot drop.

"Where's he at? Where'd he go?" voices shouted from the fenced-in lot as the police reached the rear of the building. Declan darted into the thick brush that surrounded the building, branches tearing at his face as he pushed past the trees trying to get out of sight. He crested a small hill and stopped, breathing heavily. With his back against a tree, he craned his neck towards the building. Through the thick brush he could see parts of the fenced-in lot, now thirty yards behind him. Officers searched between vehicles, others gathering at the back door and preparing to enter. They hadn't seen him jump the fence, but he knew it wouldn't take them long to figure it out.

CHAPTER THIRTY-TWO

11:50 a.m. Eastern Time – Monday
Offices of Sweat Security
Moneta, Virginia

Seth Castellano slowed the dark blue Crown Victoria as the female voice on his GPS unit told him he needed to turn right and that he had nearly reached his destination. "Damn," he said aloud, as he saw the mass of police cruisers in the parking lot. He'd told the local dispatcher to make sure the deputies didn't approach the property until he got there and he had reiterated that statement to the Franklin County Sheriff minutes later when the man had returned his call. How could they screw up an order so simple? Clearly Seth's decision to call them in to make sure Declan McIver didn't leave the area before he could arrive had been the wrong one.

Pulling the car to a stop, he shifted it into park and stepped out. He folded his badge over the breast pocket of his suit coat as he walked around the vehicle towards the front of the building. Men in brown police uniforms looked up at him as he approached, but clearly saw the badge and chose not to address him. Maybe he was lucky and they'd managed to apprehend McIver. While that would be problematic in another way, at least he wouldn't be running around loose where he could cause other problems.

As he neared the front door of the building he saw a hastily written sign saying *closed until further notice* and wasn't surprised. He'd sent a team of agents to this building the previous morning to obtain as much of the company's paperwork as possible and to interview the employees about the company's involvement in the car bombing outside of the Barton Center. The interviews had turned up exactly what he wanted them to: nothing. None of the employees had known about the four men placed inside Sweat Security, which meant that the company's owner had done as he was told. Likewise, the paperwork would show no record of them either. The glass door swung open and a broad man with salt and pepper colored hair stepped out.

"Are you Castellano?" he asked. Castellano nodded. It was clear from the white shirt of the man's uniform that he was the Sheriff and his introduction a moment later confirmed it. "I'm Steve Scruggs, Franklin County Sheriff."

"ASAC Seth Castellano, Sheriff. What the hell is going on here? I thought I told you not to approach the property."

The man seemed to bristle for a moment at the obvious rebuke. Taking a deep breath, he answered. "Two of my deputies heard gunshots from within the building and decided to enter the premises."

Castellano grimaced. As much as he'd like to, he couldn't really argue with that kind of judgment call and it was clear from the Sheriff's expression that he knew it. "And what did they find?"

"They witnessed a man coming down the stairs from the second floor as they attempted to get the door open. The guy ran through a hallway towards the garage, but he was gone by the time my deputies got over the fence and around the building."

Castellano closed his eyes and sighed. Fighting hard to control his anger he asked, "Does this man have a description?"

"Blonde hair, about six foot, and thin. He was wearing a black raincoat and blue jeans."

"Sounds like my guy. Any idea what the gunshot was about?"

The Sheriff pointed over his shoulder with his thumb. "Upstairs," he said, as he turned around and held the door open. As they entered Castellano saw the typical handiwork of a crew with a search warrant. Desk drawers and filing cabinets were wide open and papers that had apparently been outside of the scope of the warrant littered the floor. The sheriff led the way through the rectangular office to the left side of the room, where a door led to a set of steps. Following the sheriff up, Castellano turned the corner to a second set of stairs and saw two large holes and a pile of crumbled drywall on the landing above them.

"What happened here?" he asked, as they topped the steps and he looked closely at the holes and the drywall. "Looks like gunshots."

"That's what I thought and this seems to confirm that," the sheriff said, as he stepped further into the room.

Castellano followed the man and saw blood spatter on the wall near one of the two windows that overlooked the parking lot. As he stepped around one of the desks he knew what he was about to see wasn't going to be pleasant. He grimaced as the body of a large man came into view. Around the man's head a massive pool of blood mixed with the gray commercial carpeting and created a dark halo. In the man's meaty hand was a .38 caliber revolver.

"Who is he?"

"Tim Sweat. He owns the company. We haven't touched anything so what you see is exactly how things were when my men arrived. It looks self-inflicted to me and there's a suicide note on the desk."

"Or it was made to look that way," Castellano posited.

"Exactly," the sheriff confirmed. "I spent a decade investigating homicides in Richmond before moving here so I've seen my share of bodies. I'm sure your people can tell for sure by the presence of gunshot residue on the hands."

Castellano nodded and looked from the position of the body to the holes in the wall near the stairs. "Those holes look consistent with gunshots so I'm going to go out on a limb and say he was shooting at someone who came up the stairs."

"My thoughts exactly, and we found evidence of a break in by the garage. Someone used a manual tire jack from one of the vehicles to pry open a garage door."

Castellano fought a smirk as he looked from the body to the gunshot holes. If he didn't know better he would swear that Declan McIver was trying to help them frame him, because he sure wasn't helping himself. Not only was he on the run, as far as the public knew, but now they had another body tied to him and no witnesses to offer an alternative version of events.

"What's the suicide note say?"

"It's right here on the desk. It's an apology to his wife and children and talks about some men threatening them, fits the murder idea more than the suicide one if you ask me. I've known Tim Sweat for nearly twenty years and he's not a man to be threatened by anyone."

Castellano nodded and turned around to look at the legal-sized piece of paper sitting on the desk, blood droplets soaking through it onto the wood beneath.

"It says something about some files with the identities of the men doing the threatening," Sheriff Scruggs continued, "but I don't see any folders nearby. My deputies said the guy running away was carrying something, but they couldn't tell for sure what it was. Sounds like a motive to me."

Castellano felt a sinking feeling in his stomach. Just when everything seemed to be going his way there had to be some bad news. Had Sweat somehow managed to get information on the four men, or did the files just contain pictures? He dismissed the bad feeling. Surely the four had been smart enough not to give their real names and it wasn't like he had to worry about them talking to anyone. Declan McIver had again solved that problem for him when he killed them.

"Then we need to find him before he has a chance to destroy those files. Any idea where he could have gone?"

"Well, we're guessing the blue Mercedes out front belongs to him because Tim Sweat's BMW is in the garage. So that means he had to have left here on foot. He must've jumped the fence before my men got around the building. I made a call to a guy with some dogs. He's on his way. We'll get a scent off of something in the car and start tracking him."

"What's around here that he could get to?"

"The only real development is several miles to the east and my men had the building blocked off from the front so he had to have gone out the back. There's nothing back there but several dozen acres of forest and beyond that some country roads. I sent my deputies to the nearest houses and put out an

APB to all of my patrols. They'll be searching along the roads and visiting the homes of the few residents that live out that way."

"Good. When will the dogs be here?"

"Should be here any minute, the guy just lives over the way," the sheriff said, making a motion towards the south with his hand. "The way I figure it, this guy has been on foot for less than thirty minutes. If you take into account the fact that the average human male runs five to eight miles per hour, and with the kind of terrain around here there's no way he could keep up a full run that entire time, I'm thinking he can't be more than a mile away, if that."

"This guy is full of surprises so far, so I want you to expand that APB to the neighboring counties, triple the patrols along the roads and set up checkpoints at every major road into and out of the area. Do you have enough manpower for that?"

The sheriff nodded.

"Good. Get it done. I'm calling in the area field agents to assist us and I'll see what kind of help the other agencies in the area can offer."

"It's going to be kind of difficult to hold every thin, blonde-haired male we come across until you get there for a positive ID. Do you have a picture of this guy?"

Castellano reached into his suit coat and removed a picture he'd taken from one of the curio cabinets in the McIver's home. "His name is Declan McIver and he speaks with an Irish accent. That ought to narrow it quite a bit."

"I'll get this photo out to everyone," the sheriff said. "He won't get far."

CHAPTER THIRTY-THREE

12:04 p.m. Eastern Time – Monday
Wooded Area between Rts. 806 & 122
Moneta, Virginia

Leaning against the trunk of a pine tree for support as he caught his breath, Declan looked back in the direction he had come as the sound of baying hounds filled the air. He placed his hands on his knees, taking deep breaths. He knew what the sound meant. The police had brought in dogs and were on his trail. He stood upright and tucked the file folders containing the identities of the four men who had been threatening the Sweat family under his arm like a football and set off at a light jog down a steep incline. Ahead he could see large breaks of sunlight through the thick trees and realized the forested area was coming to an end; soon he would be in open ground. Even in such good shape, there was no way he could cover the kind of distance he needed to on foot. He needed to find a vehicle if he was going to avoid being chased down and caught.

Undoubtedly the police were looking at him as a suspect in Tim Sweat's death and why shouldn't they? He'd run from the scene as soon as they'd shown up. It would take time for a coroner to determine that the gunshot had been self-inflicted and in the meantime they'd arrest and hold him. Declan didn't have that kind of time. On his own, he held the cards and could communicate when and how he wanted. In a jail cell he wouldn't have that choice; plus he didn't want to risk losing the four folders of information he'd got from Sweat. They could help him identify who it was that was trying to kill him and whether or not they had any connection to Seth Castellano, as he suspected they did.

At the bottom of the incline he stopped briefly as the tree cover gave way to a broad, rolling field that was just beginning to show signs of life in the early spring. It was a hayfield, if he had to guess, and in the distance he could see sunlight glinting off a tin roof. He didn't know if it was a barn or a house, but either way it was the only building he could see and might be his only chance for several miles of finding a car. The baying of the hound dogs sounded again in the distance and he looked over his shoulder. It sounded like they were searching the forest southeast of his current location, where he'd stopped at a set of three metal outbuildings that had been used as a storage area for a nearby farm. He hadn't been able to see the farm from the storage area and there hadn't been anything useful inside so he'd kept moving. Although it had cost him some precious time, in hindsight he was thankful he'd stopped. Hopefully the buildings would slow the pursuing officers as they would surely approach the area cautiously in case he was hiding inside and armed.

He moved in the direction of the tin-roofed building at a steady pace and as he got closer he recognized the pungent odor of a chicken coop. The smell assaulted his nostrils and brought water to his eyes as he crested the last hill before the end of the field. In front of him a small valley between more hills opened up and he could see that the tin roof did indeed belong to a long rectangular chicken coop. He surveyed the area around the coop for vehicles, but saw none. As his eyes moved across the adjacent fields, he spotted the rear of a brick ranch house surrounded by several tall trees on the opposite side of the property. A one lane gravel road forked about a hundred yards from the house and led past it and over more hilly terrain. He would have preferred to find a vehicle near the farm buildings where there was less chance he would encounter the landowner, but it looked like the house was his only choice; parked next to it he could see a blue pickup truck.

Declan kept his eyes on the house and the road leading to

it as he made his way out of the field on a rough pathway that he thought had likely been made by the frequent passing of a tractor. He didn't like the idea of stealing a car from someone, but how else was he going to get out of the area and to a more secure location where he could take a long look at the information he was carrying? He didn't know exactly what he was expecting to find in the files that would be so valuable, but there had to be something that could help him find a lead.

Keeping his eyes focused on the house and his ears tuned to the road in case any vehicles approached, Declan carefully stepped over a waist-high barbed wire fence that separated the hayfield from the home's spacious yard. He darted between several tall pine trees as he moved across the yard towards the short driveway that ran off the gravel road in front of the house and ended where the truck was parked.

The house was a one story brick ranch with its exterior mostly surrounded by tall evergreen shrubs that hadn't been trimmed back in many years. From the looks of the lawn and the lack of any kind of homely decorations, he suspected the owner of the property was elderly and that could work out in his favor. With any luck, if there was anyone inside, he would have the truck started and be rolling out of the driveway before they even heard a sound. Keeping his eyes on what little bit of window he could see through the thick shrubs, he approached the truck low and slow and reached out to touch the hood. The metal was cold, signaling that it hadn't been driven recently. The truck was a navy blue Chevrolet and from the body style he was guessing it was an early nineties model; hopefully it still ran. He moved around to the passenger's side where the body of the vehicle hid him from view, and pulled up on the door handle. He paused briefly to see if anyone had seen or heard him, then rested easy as no sounds came from the house. Looking over his shoulder, he cleared his six o'clock position. The door came open with a low clunk as the latch released and he leaned inside as he pulled it the rest of the way open. The cab smelled heavily of cigarette smoke and the passenger's floor area was littered with old receipts and sales paper inserts that had been trampled by wet shoes and were now a permanent part of the worn carpeting. On the seat sat a bucket of white spackling and a rusted paint scraper. He grabbed ahold of the paint scraper and reached across to the steering wheel to begin prying the casing off so he could get to the wiring underneath.

As he placed the blade of the scraper into the joint between the upper and lower casings, the sound of crunching gravel drew his attention. He ducked quickly down onto the seat and turned around as he slid out of the truck. Looking towards the gravel road, panic rose as he saw a brown and white Crown Victoria turn right at the fork and head towards the house. He pushed the truck door closed and moved around the front of the vehicle, his eyes darting between the house and the approaching police car as he crouched to hide from the deputy's view. He needed a place to hide before he was seen, assuming he hadn't been already. Spotting a low porch on the front of the house, white plastic lattice work across the bottom to hide the edge of the wooden boards, he moved towards it, looking for an opening. At the meeting of the lattice work and the edge of the house, time had loosened whatever nails or staples had been holding the white vinyl to the wood. He leaned down and tore a piece loose before lying on the ground in a prone position and pulling himself under the porch on his elbows. Sliding around in a circle, he reached out and picked up the piece of lattice work, leaning it against the edge of the deck to hide his entry point. He squinted and held his breath as the dust from the dirty ground underneath the porch settled.

Looking through the triangular holes in the lattice work, he watched as the Crown Vic, clearly bearing the logo of the Franklin County Sheriff's Office, turned right into the short driveway and pulled to a stop behind the parked truck.

He could hear the muffled sound of the deputy's radio unit through the closed doors of the vehicle and wondered if the man had seen him as he'd approached the house. The sound of the door latch being released preceded the sound of two feet hitting the gravel driveway as the deputy left the cruiser. Declan scooted back from the edge of the porch, hoping the shadows would hide him from view if the man happened to look down. The short distance still gave him enough visibility to watch the deputy's actions.

"Dispatch this is 2-Adam-23. I'm 10-62 for a 10-66 at 608

Rucker Road, copy?"

"10-4, 23, advise 10-8. Over?"

"Copy dispatch, will advise."

The deputy walked over the ten foot distance between his cruiser and the edge of the porch. Declan could hear the boards of the weathered porch creek under the man's weight as he passed over him. The sound of a screen door being pulled open preceded a forceful knock on the front door. Slow footsteps sounded heavy on the aged floorboards of the house as the occupant made his or her way to the front door and opened it, metal hinges squealing in protest.

"I'm Deputy Rogers with the Franklin County Sheriff's Office." the deputy said. "How do you do, Ma'am?"

"I'm fine, Deputy," an elderly woman answered, a question audible in her raspy voice.

"Ma'am, I'm here because we're searching for a suspect in a crime that happened a few miles southeast of here. Now, I don't want to scare you, but have you seen anyone you didn't recognize around here this afternoon?"

Declan grimaced as he waited for the woman's answer. Had she seen him through a window as he'd approached?

"No. No, I haven't."

He breathed easy.

"Okay, Ma'am. The man we're looking for is approximately six feet in height, he has blonde hair and he's kind of thin. At this point he's considered armed and dangerous, so please do not open your door for anyone and call us immediately if you see someone matching that description. We'll be patrolling the nearby areas frequently until we find him."

"Oh, dear. Alright, then."

Declan could hear the fear in the woman's voice and he shook his head. He didn't mean anyone any harm; he just wanted to get back to his wife. There were people out there that did mean harm, though, and they had already killed a lot of good people. If they weren't stopped, chances were that they'd kill a lot more.

"One last thing before I leave, ma'am," the deputy said. "Would you mind if I had a look around the barn and the chicken coop just in case someone may have tried to hide there?"

"No, go right ahead. I'm going to call my son and ask him to come over. Will you notify us when you've found the man you're looking for?"

"Do you have a television or a radio, ma'am?"

"Yes."

"We'll be keeping people updated through the local stations."

"Thank you, Deputy."

Declan listened as the woman closed the door with a thud and the deputy released his hold on the screen door allowing it to bang closed. The deputy's heavy footsteps sounded over the porch and Declan watched as he made his way back to his vehicle and entered, closing the door behind him. Muffled voices sounded as the man radioed his dispatcher and informed her of his return to his vehicle. The cruiser's engine started up and the deputy backed out of the driveway and drove towards the barn that was a short distance past the tractor path Declan had traveled a few minutes before.

Waiting until he was sure the deputy was out of sight, he pushed the loosened lattice work aside and slid out from under the porch, his black coat and blue jeans tan with dust. He had no idea how close the lady's son lived, but he knew he needed to get out of the area quick before anyone saw him. He looked at the truck and grimaced. He wasn't as concerned about the woman inside seeing him, but was there really any chance that he could get the thing started and get away without alerting the deputy? He doubted it, but it was the only option he had. He crossed the untrimmed grass to the driver's side of the pickup and opened the door. Closing it as quietly as possible, he tossed the file folders onto the passenger seat and grabbed the handle of the paint scraper that was sticking out of the steering wheel casing where he'd left it. Good thing the deputy hadn't checked the truck or else he would have known someone was around by the obvious attempt to hot wire the vehicle. Prying the casing down far enough to get his fingers inside, he pulled off the bottom casing and revealed the wires underneath. After a quick inspection he identified the two wires that would complete the circuit. With the bladed end of the scraper he tore them loose and twisted them together before allowing them to touch the starter wire. The truck sputtered as he held the wires together and the starter began to squeal. After what seemed like a solid minute but was probably only a few seconds, the engine turned over and the truck came loudly to life. He sat up in the seat and pulled the gearshift into the drive position. The truck lurched into gear and he backed out of the gravel driveway, skidding to a stop as he shifted quickly through the gears and pressed the accelerator to the floor. The truck's rear wheels spun against the loose gravel and churned a cloud of dust as the vehicle shot forward towards the fork in the road. He didn't know exactly where he was, but he took a gamble that the deputy had been coming from the main road when he'd arrived at the house. He made a left at the fork and sixty yards later the road turned from gravel to pavement and he knew he'd made the right decision. As he passed a row of more modern homes he could see the intersection of the main road ahead. He slowed as he approached the intersection. The brakes ground loudly against the bare rotors and he fought to keep the steering wheel from pulling to the left. With his attention on keeping control of the truck, he glanced through the pitted windshield just as another Crown Vic pulled onto the road and blocked his way. He stomped hard on the brakes and brought the truck to a skidding stop, his eyes locking with those of the deputy behind the wheel of the cruiser, who now had his radio to his mouth and was shouting into the mic.

Declan slammed the truck into reverse as he pressed the pedal to the floor. The nearly bald tires slid against the smooth pavement before finally gaining traction and pushing the vehicle backwards. Placing his arm over the back seat he looked over his shoulder as he backed the vehicle up the road as fast as it would go. The back end fishtailed and he fought to keep the badly aligned truck from swerving off the road and into one of the manicured yards on either side. As he cleared the last of the homes, he stomped hard on the emergency brake and slapped the gearshift into neutral as he turned the steering wheel sharply, causing the truck to skid sideways and around in a half circle.

Declan braced for impact as the deputy pursuing him

collided with the rear bumper of the truck and pushed it forward. Declan shifted back into drive, popped the emergency brake and again pressed the pedal to the floor. White smoke plumed from the rear wheels as the truck struggled to gain traction. With only inches between his rear bumper and the front bumper of the police cruiser, he swerved the truck, deliberately trying to get the deputy to back off, but without success. The truck bounced violently as the paved surface ended and a cloud of dust cascaded into the air. With the fork in the road just ahead of him, he looked through the truck's windows trying to determine which way was more likely to lead him back around to the main road, but his choice was made for him when he saw a cloud of dust trailing behind a vehicle coming down the road to the right. The deputy from the old lady's house was trying to cut him off at the fork.

He pressed harder on the accelerator and tightened his grip on the wheel until his knuckles turned white. As he approached the fork he allowed the vehicle to glide to the left and braced himself for the impact he knew was coming. Giving the accelerator a last push, he managed to clear the fork with the cab of the truck before the oncoming police cruiser hit him.

The car collided with the rear quarter of the truck and Declan steered hard to the left as the truck was knocked into a sideways skid. Correcting the steering, he brought the truck back into a forward trajectory and looked into the rearview mirror. Through the dust he could see that the two deputies had narrowly avoided a collision and were now trying to back out of each other's way so they could continue the pursuit. The temporary delay allowed him to distance himself from his pursuers, but he knew the advantage wouldn't last. There was no way the old truck could outrun the amped up engines of the police cars and any hope of making a sudden turn to throw them off his trail was foiled by the dust cloud being churned up behind him. It was clear as he wound his way furiously over a curvy section of the dirt road that he needed to find a place to ditch the truck and get back into the forest on foot. Without being able to outrun the police cars, it was his only way of escaping. Glancing into the rearview mirror again, he could see the blue lights of the police cars through the dust, closing the distance. Ahead another fork in the road became visible and he looked to the right and left. On the right the dirt road continued winding its way around the grassy fields and to the left a thick patch of forest was cleared at the crest of a hill where a water tower broke the tree line. Taking the road to the left he gambled that there was some kind of building at the base of the water tower that might slow the approach of the pursuing deputies. Any law enforcement officer with more than five minutes of training wouldn't approach with any speed a building that potentially held an armed suspect, and that could give him all the time he needed to make a run for it through the woods and put some distance between himself and the police.

The road narrowed as it became tree lined and he slowed slightly as overgrown branches slapped the sides of the truck. The water tower was less than fifty yards ahead of him and he could already see that his gamble wasn't going to pay off. There was nothing at the base of the water tower but a ladder leading to the top and a dead end. *Damn* he thought as he moved his foot from the accelerator to the brake and slowed the truck to a skidding stop. Quickly he gathered the folders into a stack and left the truck. Behind him he could hear the crunch of gravel as the police cruisers approached, their progress slowing as they entered the tree covered area. Maybe his idea had panned out after all. Maybe the deputies were worried he would take up a position on the water tower and try shooting at them as they approached. With the truck hopefully blocking their view of him, he ran into the woods as fast as he could.

Fifty yards behind the water tower, in the cover of the trees, he stopped and listened. He couldn't hear any sounds from the vehicles and assumed the two deputies had stopped their pursuit. He took a minute to look around and to try and decide what direction he was headed. In the ferocity of the chase he hadn't been paying attention to where he was going and quickly began retracing his movements in his head as he moved forward in a jog. The sudden bark of a large dog at his back jarred him and he jerked his head over his shoulder towards the water tower. Had one of the deputies been a K-9 unit? He couldn't afford to wait and find out. He broke into a run, grabbing onto trees and pulling himself forward through the forest as he heard the barking continue behind him.

Jumping over a downed tree, he landed in a clearing created by a set of high-tension wires that cut through the forest. Wading quickly through the waist high scrub brush he crossed into the forest on the other side before continuing to run. Ahead he could tell that the patch of forest he was in was coming to an end and he knew he had no chance of outrunning a dog on open ground. As he broke the tree line he saw several weathered buildings in the clearing. Sliding down a hill on his heels and grabbing at tiny scrub pines to keep himself upright, he landed at the bottom and ran for the biggest building.

Dodging around several piles of cut trees, the property he was now on appeared to be a saw mill. The buildings were made from split boards that were weathered black with age and he could see a conveyor belt coming through the side of the biggest building's A-frame. As he ran he looked for any signs that the place was occupied and saw nothing. No vehicles appeared to be present and a dirt driveway cut through the forest to his right. Several barks bellowed from behind him and he picked up his pace, his breath coming in rapid gasps. Arriving at the side of the biggest building, he ran around it until he found a door. Pulling it open by the twisted metal handle, he entered and pulled it shut behind him, holding it closed by the interior handle as he felt something leap against the door with a frustrated bark. Breathing heavily, he looked around the area near the door and found a rusted screwdriver on a workbench that was thin enough to fit into the door handle. He jammed it through the hole to hold the door closed and turned into the building.

Inside, the place was like a large barn with a conveyor belt in the center that was used to bring in the logs from outside so they could be sawed and split into boards. The room smelled heavily of sawdust, and thin beams of sunlight exposed the dust floating in the air as they pierced through the spaces in between the boarded walls. He looked for any other entrances, but didn't see any. The only hole in the building besides the door he had come through was for the conveyor belt and it was too high for either a dog or a human to reach. He breathed easily and considered his next move as the barking continued from outside the door. He knew the two deputies wouldn't be far behind the dog and that they would be radioing for more units to back them up. He walked a little further into the building and noticed a set of steps that led to a room off a second floor catwalk. Maybe there was a door there that he could sneak out of. He climbed the steps two at a time, the weathered boards creaking under his weight and the catwalk shaking slightly as he stepped onto it. He crossed it carefully to a closed door and slowly opened it.

Inside was an employee break room with a refrigerator, microwave and a square table in one corner. It was clear from the settled dust that it hadn't been used in quite a while. On the opposite side of the rectangular room was a door that obviously led to what was intended to be the front of the building. Faded vinyl lettering on the window in the door read *Walterman's Lumber*. He crossed the tiled floor to the door, and looked outside. The doorway led to a second story porch that had a set of stairs leading down to the small parking lot in front of the building. The driveway he'd seen on his way in ran off the lot and up into the woods where he assumed it connected with the dirt road he had been on a short time ago. A cloud of dust coming through the trees attracted his attention and he watched as it moved closer. Knowing exactly what it was he wasn't surprised when a police cruiser appeared at the top of the driveway and stopped. The officer inside surveyed the lot and the buildings below and brought his radio to his mouth. Ducking out of the window, Declan reached down to make sure the door was locked.

Standing against a counter he could see out of the window to the right side of the lumber yard where he'd first approached the property. Two men in brown and tan uniforms appeared at the crest of the hill and one yelled a command in a language that Declan didn't understand. From the other side of the building a tan and black German shepherd bounded between the piles of uncut lumber and up the hill to his master's feet. The men stood beside a row of trees looking over the property for any sign of him and prepared to take cover if he began shooting.

They had him cornered now and they knew it. The driveway was blocked by the police cruiser and if he tried to make a run for it out of the back door that he'd come in through, the dog would be on him in a matter of seconds. He knew that the one deputy in his cruiser at the top of the driveway would soon be joined by more vehicles and that within a few minutes the entire place would be surrounded. He wiped his face with his hand and took a deep breath as he considered his next move. For the moment he had time on his side and while he wasn't willing to harm innocent men, they didn't know that and would be extremely cautious and well prepared before attempting to enter the building after him. He turned around and placed the files on the counter top in front of him. Spreading them out, he opened one and looked at the face of one of the men he'd killed.

The face the paperwork identified as Jack Turlington stared back at him and he recognized the man as the apparent leader of the four, the man he'd beaten to death beside a bulldozer two nights earlier. He set the folder aside and opened each of the other three.

Scanning briefly over the information on each man's DOJ application he settled on the fact that the information was likely for real. Nothing in the documents looked out of place. By all appearances they were just four men who had applied and were working at a small security company in central Virginia. Somehow Declan needed to find a way to get the information out of the physical folders because there was no way he was going to be leaving with them still in his possession.

"Attention," a voice from outside bellowed over a bullhorn. "This is Franklin County Sheriff Steve Scruggs. We have the building surrounded. This place hasn't been used in several years now so we know you're alone. Give yourself up or we're prepared to come in after you."

Declan turned towards the window and leaned his head so he could see outside. Three more police cars had arrived at the top of the driveway and behind them a white SUV bearing similar law enforcement markings was parked. A total of nine men were now gathered near the cars, all taking cover behind the open doors of the vehicles. He scanned the tree line quickly and didn't see anyone else in position, but it didn't matter. There was still no way he was going to make it on foot with as many men as were out there and there was still the presence of the dog to consider.

He turned back towards the countertop and looked at the folders. He pulled one of his prepaid cell phones from the pocket of his coat and flipped it open. The camera on the phone took a low megapixel image but it would have to do. He snapped several photos of the DOJ applications and bundled them into an email. Pressing the "send" button, he waited as the service connected and uploaded the pictures. When it was done, he laid the phone on the countertop as he looked around the room for something he could break it with. He didn't want anyone being able to turn it on and find out what he'd sent and where it had gone. Seeing nothing that he could use he picked the device up in both hands and snapped it in half at the joint between the receiver and the LED display. Crossing the room to the door that led back into the saw mill, he opened it and peered out. No one had tried to enter the building after him yet. He stepped onto the catwalk and threw the LED part of the phone as hard as he could across the building. Taking the back off the remaining piece he removed the battery and the SIM card and repeated the process of throwing them as far as he could before finally dropping the receiver through the holes in the floor of the catwalk and listening as it clattered onto the cement floor below and shattered. Hopefully the pieces wouldn't be found and if they were, he was hopeful that they were beyond any kind of use.

"Attention," the amplified voice of the Sheriff said again. "This is your second and final warning. Come out now or we are prepared to come in after you."

The voice echoed over the small valley that the saw mill sat in and Declan turned back towards the interior of the break room. He knew there were only two ways he was going to get out of the building, in a body bag or by giving up and allowing himself to be arrested. He unzipped his coat and slid it off, laying it on the floor at his feet. He released the magazine in his Glock pistol as he removed it from the holster on his belt and laid them both on the counter side by side. The last thing he wanted to happen was for an antsy deputy to pull the trigger nervously upon seeing that he was carrying a gun. He stepped towards the door and unlocked it before pulling it open and allowing it to bang against the wall. "I'm comin' out," he yelled as he raised his hands and stepped onto the porch.

The sunlight temporarily blinded him as the cool spring air touched his sweaty face. With his hands raised up past his shoulders he walked fully out to the edge of the porch and looked towards the grouping of police cruisers at the top of the hill. He felt his chest tighten as he noticed that a new face had joined the group. Seth Castellano now stood beside the sheriff, his Glock .22 service pistol raised over the top of the cruiser's door.

"Turn around slowly and stand with your back to us!" the sheriff announced over the bullhorn. Declan took a deep breath and slowly obeyed. He didn't like the idea of turning his back on Castellano when he had a gun aimed, but he didn't have any other choice. He listened closely as the sound of men in uniforms moved into position at the bottom of the steps. Moments later two deputies with their weapons drawn moved cautiously up the steps and confronted him.

"Turn around and stand still," one of them barked in a southern dialect. Declan turned around again and waited until the man reached for his hands and pulled them down one at a time behind his back where a pair of handcuffs were snapped over his wrists.

"C'mon," the deputy said, as he tugged backwards on the cuffs. Declan allowed himself to be guided to the stairs and walked to the gravel lot below. As he and the two deputies reached the bottom, the sheriff and Castellano walked towards them as one of the police cruisers was moved down the hill and pulled sideways to a stop where they could load him inside.

With his dark red tie blowing in the slight breeze, Castellano leaned in close as the deputy pushed Declan towards the rear door of the cruiser, now being held open. "Thanks for the help," he whispered in a snide tone as Declan felt a hand placed on top of his head to push him into the car. He closed his eyes as he entered the vehicle, his hands uncomfortable between his back and the edge of the seat. Slowly the car pulled forward and he opened his eyes again to look forward as the car moved up the hill. How was he going to get out of this?

CHAPTER THIRTY-FOUR

"I don't want to be here, Vakha."

And Sharpuddin Daudov didn't. He had crossed into America over the Mexican border in 2004 along with his brother and ten other men. What he had found when they'd entered the country was very different to what he had expected. The leader of the group he had belonged to in his native Chechnya, a man who called himself Abu Tabak in place of his more Slavic sounding birth name, had preached for years about the imperialistic attitudes of the people who lived in places like America and Great Britain. He had told the group time and again about the endless atrocities committed by these people. Sharpuddin had witnessed such events at the hands of the Russians, whom Tabak assured the group were just like the Americans. "They may not be killing your brothers, your sisters and your neighbors, but they are killing your fellow Moslems across the world and taking their land." Those words had echoed through Sharpuddin's mind for months when he'd first arrived, but after a few years of living in American neighborhoods, shopping alongside Americans in supermarkets and working with them at the various jobs he did to support himself and his brother, he'd settled on the fact that Tabak's words had been one of two things; a lie, or the voice of a man who really didn't have the experience to back up what he was talking about and was only repeating a message that had been passed to him from someone else. Americans, as far as Sharpuddin could tell, were generally accommodating, kind and curious people who were far more interested in what was going on in the lives of their families and friends than in hurting or taking anything from anyone else. But here he was with his older brother, who still believed in and hung on every word and teaching of Tabak and other radical Imams. Here he was parked in front of a dilapidated building in an out of the way suburb of Baltimore, about to meet Abu Tabak for the first time in eight years.

"I'm not going in. I don't want any part of this anymore."

Vakha Daudov turned in the driver's seat of the tan, two-door Chevy Cavalier and stared at his younger brother. "Do not embarrass me, Sharpuddin!"

"Embarrass you? You're an embarrassment to yourself! You don't work, you live in squalor and you drive this rundown car just so you can say you still adhere to a way of life that we left behind a dec—"

Vakha lashed out and struck Sharpuddin on the face with a closed fist. The young man's head thumped against the passenger side window.

"Ah, c'mon man! What the hell?" Sharpuddin looked back at his older brother. He could feel tears in his eyes and the side of his face stung from the ferocious strike.

Vakha's nostrils flared with anger. "You're not going to embarrass me! The only reason you're in this country is because of Abu! You will do what he wants or so help me I will beat you senseless!"

"The hell with you, Vakha!" Sharpuddin pushed open the car door and stepped from the vehicle.

"Where are you going to go?" Vakha said getting out and rounding the car after him. "Where are you going to go?" he repeated as Sharpuddin felt himself being grabbed by the shoulders and pulled back until he hit the side of the car. "You're two hundred miles from home! Where are you going to go?"

"Anywhere but here, I don't want any part of what you're about to do!"

Vakha held him against the car as he struggled. "Stop, just

stop!"

Sharpuddin gave up.

"Now," Vakha continued, "we're going to go inside and you're not going to say a damn word."

"You're going to get yourself killed."

"Not a damn word! Do you understand me?"

Slowly Vakha let go and turned towards the vacant-looking garage they were parked a few hundred feet from. "Not a damn word," he repeated.

Ruslan Baktayev got up from the stool he was sitting on, a cigarette hanging from his mouth, and looked to the workshop entrance as the metal door to the office of the former welding service banged open loudly. The laughter in the grimy workshop came to a quick halt as the door to the workshop was slowly pushed open. A tall man with dark closely cut hair and a vertical scar down the left side of his face leaned his head around the door and looked inside.

Baktayev grinned. "Vakha!"

The tall man stepped fully into the room and smiled. "Abu."

The two embraced tightly, their hands slapping over each other's backs loudly.

"I'm sorry I missed it," Vakha said as he drew back. "I missed your victory over the Jew."

Baktayev grinned and raised his arm, the sleeve of his coat covered in dried streaks of dark red that appeared to have run down his hand past his wrist. "I held his head up high! You were with me in spirit, little brother."

Vakha grinned broadly. "Glory be to Allah, you haven't changed a bit."

"The Russians could not break him," Anzor Kasparov said, as he stood from a lawn chair in the center of the room, where several men sat smoking and drinking. "Not in years of war or imprisonment could they break him! Abu Tabak!" The obviously intoxicated Kasparov raised a can of beer and several men followed suit with elated cheers of, "Abu Tabak!" A toast to their leader, Ruslan Baktayev.

The hinges of the door whined as it was opened again and a

thin young man with shaggy brown hair and an almost sickly complexion stepped in, his face full of disgust.

"Sharpuddin," Baktayev said, as he looked past Vakha at the boy. "You've grown."

The boy leaned up against a workbench and folded his arms across his chest, turning his head to hide the reddish welt on his cheek.

Vakha turned slightly. "My little brother has gotten too used to American life. He has forgotten what it is to be one of the Nokhchi! But we'll remind him, won't we?" Vakha raised his fist in triumph as more cheers came from the small gathering of men.

The cheers stopped as the ringing of a phone echoed loudly through the high-ceilinged room.

Baktayev walked over to the workbench where the phone was located and picked it up. "Nokhchi Welding Service, how may we kill you?"

A barely contained snicker passed through the group of drunken men but Baktayev's face quickly turned serious. "Quiet," he barked. A hush fell over the room and the twenty men present looked at their leader, a question on each face as Baktayev listened to the caller.

"I'm not an errand boy," he said. "Find someone else!"

"You'll want to do this yourself, I promise," a tinny voice said over the phone. "The man we are talking about was once the bodyguard of the Jew. He is the man who killed your brother."

Baktayev's grip tightened on the phone as he thought about what Levent Kahraman was saying. "You told me that you didn't know where he was, that you couldn't find him."

"I couldn't. But glory be to Allah, he came to us."

"Where is he?"

"He is in the custody of the American FBI in a place called Rocky Mount in Virginia."

"And how the hell am I supposed to get to him if he's with the police?"

"I promised you I would help you get revenge on Kafni and, if possible, the men who worked with him to kill your brothers. This is me keeping that promise. They'll be transporting him from the jail tomorrow morning, with only one agent; I want you to follow them until you find a safe place and then kill them both."

Baktayev nodded as a smile formed on his face. "We will do it."

"Good. Make sure they are both dead. The agent cannot become a witness." Kahraman hung up and Baktayev lowered the receiver back to its cradle. Looking at the faces staring up at him from the center of the room he said, "I need three of you to gather some weapons and leave tonight. The Sheikh has found another of Kafni's men who needs to meet his maker."

"Me, Abu. I will go." Vakha said. "I will not miss another chance at victory."

"Vakha, you can't do this!" Sharpuddin said from across the room. "You're going to get yourself killed!"

Every eye in the shop moved to the boy standing near the door and a laugh passed through the room.

Vakha blushed. "I told you not to talk, Sharpuddin! If I die, it will be for Ichkeria in the service of Allah!"

"We left Ichkeria nine years ago! This isn't a game!" Sharpuddin shouted. "Do you think this man cares anything about you? Look at him! All he wants are mindless soldiers to do his dirty work for him!"

Baktayev strolled back to the center of the room, his eyes on Sharpuddin as he gripped Vakha by the shoulder and said, "Tomorrow you will kill a man for me, the man who killed my brother."

CHAPTER THIRTY-FIVE

David Kemiss hung up the phone and dialed another number.

"I made the necessary calls. There'll be a federal warrant releasing McIver into your custody by morning," he said, as he poured two fingers of Glenmorangie into a glass and turned towards the window behind his walnut desk. With his office located on the fifth floor at the corner of Delaware Avenue and C Street, he could see the entirety of the Upper and Lower Senate Parks from his window. With the sun setting behind it, the waterworks of the Senate Garage Fountain glowed orange and the cherry blossom trees swayed in the light breeze; within the next month their pink and white flowers would be at full bloom.

"And what am I supposed to do with him once he's in my custody?" Castellano asked, over the secure connection.

Kemiss was certain Castellano already knew the answer. "This has gone on long enough, Seth. No more hired guns." He took a sip of the amber-colored spirit in his glass and listened as Castellano took a deep breath.

"Unless you want this entire thing to unravel at our feet," he continued, "you need to take care of this guy personally this time. You're a creative guy, I trust you'll find just the right place and time to make sure Declan McIver is no longer a problem for us. Any idea what he was looking for?"

"It appears that the owner of the security company somehow got our men to fill out DOJ paperwork."

"That could have been disastrous. I thought you said this guy, this Jack Turlington, was a professional soldier?"

"It doesn't matter what he was. He's dead. McIver saw to that and now I've got the paperwork, or rather I *had* the paperwork."

"Still, McIver's seen it. Any chance that he was able to transfer it to anyone?"

"I don't think so. He didn't have it that long and he was running the entire time. Besides, it really doesn't matter. Turlington was paid in cash and now that he's dead, he can't talk about who hired him. Either way you look at it, it's a dead end. What about the wife? What do you want me to do about her?"

"According to your interview with her at the hospital she didn't actually see anything, correct?"

"Yes."

"Then we'll deal with her later when she surfaces from whatever hole her husband has hidden her in."

"I found out earlier today that she mentioned a fishing cabin to a neighbor. The lady didn't know where it was, but it can't be too far away. There are probably two dozen rivers and at least a handful of lakes within a short drive of Roanoke, but we'll find it. I've got people on it now."

"Good. Call me in the morning once you're done and we'll get this thing back on schedule."

He set the receiver loudly down on its cradle before turning back to the window. He watched as the flashing lights of a Capitol police car patrolled the closed off section of Delaware Avenue, its driver shining a spotlight into the grove of cherry blossom trees at the edge of Upper Senate Park. Kemiss didn't like the idea of killing innocent people, but if he played this right than there wasn't an office in the land that was out of his reach. After all, it had been the war hawks in the previous administrations that had brought them to this point. Their constant imperialistic attitude towards other sovereign nations was what had set men like Ruslan Baktayev and those allied with him against the United States and set the stage for the continued acts of terrorism being suffered around the world. In the last year alone there had been three successful attacks on US embassies abroad and one had resulted in the death of a prominent ambassador. Bringing the kind of attack that was planned to the home front after nearly twelve years of avoiding any serious disasters on U.S. soil was a natural progression and with the electorate's distaste of lengthy wars and the expenditures that came with them, the success of such an attack would be a devastating blow to right-wing candidates and could all but ensure the victory of the opposite party in coming elections. And with the renewed vigor of leadership during a crisis under his belt, he'd be poised to regain much of his former prestige. What else could happen, a full scale invasion of Chechnya? He nearly laughed at the idea.

His thoughts were interrupted by the shrill ringing of the phone. Could a man not get some peace and quiet? Who would it be this time? Certainly it wasn't some petulant voter wanting to take issue with him over a piece of legislation; constituents were only given the switchboard number and more often than not asked to leave messages. The few constituent phone calls he took were scheduled for only a few times a month and normally only lasted for a maximum of half an hour. It was probably some overly dedicated reporter looking for quotes about the latest sleazy story to ooze out of the beltway. Who did he have to pretend to be outraged by now? He had staff that was supposed to handle such things. He glanced at his watch as the line stopped ringing.

From outside the office he could hear a male voice; he quietly stood and walked around his desk. Apparently someone was still around. He'd thought that he was alone and that his conversation with Castellano couldn't be overheard, but perhaps that was too much privacy to ask for in Washington. He should have been more careful. He didn't recognize the voice but it had to be one of the interns who were constantly buzzing around during the day. Their faces were a blur to him and he had to be reminded of their names constantly, but they had their uses. He stepped through a set of double wooden doors and into the outer room where his secretary normally sat. Sitting at her desk was a thin young man with gelled hair and glasses.

"Thank you for calling," he said, as he hung up the phone and looked up at Kemiss. "I didn't realize you were still here, Senator. Sorry."

"Working late, are you?" Kemiss asked, making a motion with his hand for the boy to say his name.

"Colin Bellanger, sir."

"Right, Colin. A bit late to be answering the phones isn't it?"

"Sorry, sir."

Kemiss knew the boy could have easily overheard the conversation just by sitting where he was, but what could he do about it? This was how secrets became headline news. Castellano had started out sitting in the same chair fifteen years earlier and had probably overheard his share of private exchanges as well. That relationship had certainly blossomed so Kemiss quickly decided the best way to handle Bellanger was the same approach; give him exactly what people who applied to be interns wanted; a foot in the proverbial door.

"Why don't you put the phone through to the switchboard and come talk to me for a bit. I like getting to know the new faces around here, especially the ambitious ones that like to work late."

CHAPTER THIRTY-SIX

7:02 a.m. Eastern Time – Tuesday
Franklin County Jail
Rocky Mount, Virginia

Vertical beams of sunlight cut through the barred window a few feet above Declan McIver's head as he lay staring at the underside of the empty metal bunk bed above him. Hearing the birds chirping in the early morning light, he swung his feet off the bed and stood. Resting his elbows on the concrete window sill he looked through the six inch spaces between the heavy iron bars onto the quaint town of Rocky Mount. From his vantage point in the third floor window of the 1920s era jail house that stood adjacent to the Franklin County courthouse in the heart of the small town, a person could see the two story brick storefronts of a bygone era and in the distance behind them the tall smokestacks of the furniture factories that provided the area's primary employment. But he wasn't seeing any of it. His mind was focused on his wife.

He had promised her that he would return to the remote cabin they were hiding in by nightfall of the previous evening and he had no idea what she was doing now that he hadn't shown up. While the jailers who were holding him had offered him the standard phone call with which to contact an attorney or loved one, he'd declined. Such a call could be traced and he didn't want her location to be known. As far as he knew there were still people out there looking to kill them and by all accounts it appeared as if the FBI's lead investigator was one of them. All he could do at this point was hope that word had gone out through the local media that he had been arrested and that Constance would hear it and at least know that he was alive.

He turned away from the window as he heard the sound of a key being inserted into the lock of the cast iron door at the end of the hallway, which contained nine cells including the one he'd spent the night in. At nearly eighty years old and probably not having been updated since, the jailhouse had none of the mechanisms of more modern facilities. Each cast iron door was still opened by a key on the set carried by a deputy stationed at the end of each of the six hallways, known as blocks, and a team of two to three deputies responsible for transporting or releasing prisoners carried another set of keys containing a key for each of the forty eight cells. Declan had seen them come and go throughout the night to release prisoners being held on much lesser charges than the ones that would soon be filed against him. He imagined that the average inmate in the facility was probably guilty of little more than a DUI or petty theft. Having someone in their facility that was suspected of murder was probably a new experience. If only he could convince them of the truth, that he wasn't guilty of murder and hadn't in fact done anything other than being in the wrong place at the wrong time; but in jail everyone was innocent and his words would be wasted.

He listened as the door at the end of the hall slammed and two pairs of boots began walking dutifully down the hallway. Who were they coming for this time? The drunk across the way, who had finally woken up and seemed to be getting more lucid by the minute? He leaned against the edge of the metal bunk bed as the two deputies stopped in front of his cell and looked in.

"Turn around and place your hands against the wall," one of them ordered, his slow drawl clearly identifying him as a native of Franklin County. Declan looked them up and down for a moment, wondering why they were removing him from the cell. He knew he had to stand before a magistrate at some point to have the charges against him certified, but he was pretty sure that wasn't going to happen for a few hours since it was barely seven o'clock in the morning. Slowly he turned around and placed his hands against the window sill in a push up position, his legs spread wide. He listened as the deputy inserted the key and pulled open the cell door. The two men stepped inside and stood on either side of him, one holding a pair of handcuffs attached to leg irons.

This wasn't the first time in his life that Declan had been held in a jail. Internment, as it had been known in Ireland, had been commonplace and he'd been taken in at least a half a dozen times during his years with the IRA. The police in Northern Ireland, the Royal Ulster Constabulary, would hold people for as long as two weeks while they pumped them for information on the movements and plans of suspected IRA volunteers. The treatment was harsh and the governing authority routinely turned a blind eye to the abuses dealt out by the prison guards, known throughout the land as *screws*. While American jails were a dramatic improvement, he didn't like being held in one any more than he had in the Irish one.

The last time he had been a guest at such a facility had been after he'd saved Abaddon Kafni's life for the first time. As an illegal immigrant at the time, he'd been held on a variety of charges stemming from the violent incidents surrounding the attempted assassination. He'd spent two months in the Massachusetts prison known as MCI-Norfolk until Kafni had recovered from his injuries and pulled the necessary political strings to have him released. This time he doubted he would be so lucky.

After snapping the cuffs around his wrists and ankles and securing the excess chain with a heavy leather belt around his waist, the two deputies pulled him out of the cell and slammed the door behind him.

"Where am I going?" Declan asked.

"Transport van's here to take you to Regional," the shorter of the two deputies responded.

While Declan hadn't spent any time at all in any of the local correctional facilities, he knew that the term "regional" referred to the large prison that had been constructed on the southwestern side of Roanoke County and was used to hold the longer-term inmates of at least four different jurisdictions.

Shuffling down the hallway six inches at a time due to the leg restraints, he waited as they opened the door and pushed him onto an elevator that descended three stories to the bottom floor of the adjoining courthouse, where the sole interrogation room and the small cubicles of outdated computer terminals belonging to the Sheriff's Office were located. The two deputies led him past the office marked *Sheriff* with gold vinyl lettering and out onto the small parking lot behind the jail.

There, surrounded on three sides by tall pine trees and a chain-link fence, the cars of the county's civil servants sat, along with many of the police cruisers that he'd seen the previous afternoon. Parked just inside the manually operated gate was a long cargo van with green and gold markings identifying it as a vehicle belonging to the Western Virginia Regional Jail. Upon seeing the deputies approaching, two green-uniformed correctional officers got out of the van with their own set of restraints and prepared to take custody of him and load him into the secured cargo area in the rear.

"Hold on, boys," a familiar voice said from behind the two deputies holding Declan, "looks like he's not being transported to regional after all."

"Why the hell not?" the taller deputy asked, as he turned to face Sheriff Steve Scruggs as the superior officer walked around and stood between them and the two COs from the regional jail.

"Mind your tone, Deputy," Scruggs said with a grimace.

"Sorry, Sheriff," the deputy said, looking towards the ground. "I know the Sweat family well."

"I know you do," Scruggs said with a nod, "but this one's outta my hands. There's been a federal warrant issued for him and we've been ordered to hand him over to the FBI. They're here to collect him. It seems Tim Sweat isn't the only person Mr. McIver is wanted for murdering."

Declan craned his neck over his shoulder and saw a man in a suit and tie walk out of the glass door behind them. Even though he could only see him in his peripheral vision, he recognized the smug face of Seth Castellano.

CHAPTER THIRTY-SEVEN

Declan felt Castellano grasp his shoulder at the same time the agent grabbed the security belt around his waist and began pushing him towards the light blue Crown Victoria that was parked in one of the four spots marked *visitor* near the front of the lot.

"You're transporting him alone?" Sheriff Scruggs asked, as Castellano released his grip on Declan's shoulder so he could reach for the handle of the rear passenger-side door.

"You can thank our current leaders in congress for that," Castellano quipped, "they've cut our budget to the bone."

"I can send a man with you, and a car to follow and bring him back if you like."

Declan knew Castellano would turn down the offer before the words were even out of the agent's mouth. Wherever they were going, he had a feeling it wasn't to another jail.

"I'll be fine. I'm only taking him as far as Roanoke and then he'll be turned over to the Marshals."

"As you wish," Scruggs said with a wave of his hand, as he turned to look Declan in the eye. "I'll be seeing you again, son. We don't take kindly to murder around here so you can bet this jurisdiction will be pressing maximum charges after the feds are done with you. We'll get our pound of flesh."

When the deputies had finished releasing the restraints, Castellano cuffed Declan's hands in front of him and pushed him down into the back seat. Declan didn't respond to the Sheriff. He could understand Scruggs' anger, even if it was misdirected. It was the same anger he felt over the deaths of

Abaddon Kafni and Levi Levitt.

After pausing briefly beside the car to sign the necessary paperwork, Castellano moved around the vehicle with a bounce in his step and got in, slamming the door behind him and starting up the car's engine. A deputy unlocked and pulled open the gate leading out of the parking lot and Castellano gave a slight wave as he turned onto East Court Street and the jail began to fade from view.

After passing the mid-nineteenth century shops and industrial era homes that made up the town of Rocky Mount and crossing into the more commercial section of Franklin County that housed the area's gas stations and fast food joints, Castellano turned north onto the four lane road that would take them all the way into Roanoke, thirty miles to the north, and pressed the accelerator to the floor. As the sedan reached the edge of the acceleration ramp, he spoke.

"You sure turned out to be a lot more trouble than I'd have thought. I knew I was onto something when I saw your immigration paperwork and it looks like I was right."

Declan didn't respond. He kept his eyes on the passenger side mirror, watching the vehicles traveling along the road behind them.

"There's no reason we can't be friends for the short time we have left together," Castellano said, as he glanced into the rearview mirror and flashed a toothy smile. "You know I actually owe you some gratitude. You did me a big favor when you killed Turlington and his men the other night."

Again, Declan refused to give the agent the satisfaction of an answer.

"Don't take this so personally," Castellano continued. "We've all got our secrets we want to protect."

"My secrets don't bomb universities and assassinate decent men," said Declan, finally giving in to the temptation to speak.

"Like hell they don't." The agent laughed. "Maybe not anymore, but I'm willing to bet you've got a cemetery full of headstones you're responsible for, directly or indirectly."

Declan fixed his eyes on the road ahead. "So what's the plan? Get me a good ways out of town and then execute me, beat the hell out of yourself and tell everyone I tried to escape?"

Castellano looked into the rear view mirror. "I'll think of something."

They rode in silence for several miles. Declan glanced several time at the vehicle's mirrors.

"What are you so interested in back there?" Castellano finally asked.

"White cargo van with two visible occupants," Declan said. "They've been on us since we left the jail."

Castellano moved his eyes from the side mirror to the rearview mirror and his expression confirmed what Declan had already suspected. He hadn't known the vehicle was there and that meant the men following them weren't part of his team. He dialed a number on his cell phone and raised it to his ear. "Dammit," he said under his breath as he ended the call after several seconds and the car crossed a concrete bridge over the Pigg River, a broad tributary of the Roanoke River that created the border between Franklin County and Roanoke.

"Not your guys, old son? Well, we've got one thing in common then," Declan said, his eyes fixed straight ahead so the men following them wouldn't know they'd been made. "We're both expendable."

A brief flash drew his attention as Castellano piloted the vehicle up a sharp incline a hundred yards from the bridge they'd just crossed. "Watch out!" Declan shouted, as the smoke trail from an RPG shot across the road towards them. Castellano saw the attack a second later, slammed on the brakes and turned the vehicle sharply to the right. The sedan bounced over a concrete curb and into the gravel lot of a public dumping area as the pavement behind them exploded, an orange fireball throwing chunks of black pavement into the air and shattering the rear window. Fighting to keep control of the vehicle, Castellano turned the steering wheel hard and collided with a metal dumpster.

With no seatbelt or airbag in front of him to deploy, Declan felt his head connect with the back of the passenger side seat as the impact threw him forward, then slammed him back again. Pain shot down his spine and through his legs as he landed sideways on the back seat. He closed his eyes and made a guttural noise as he heard the hiss of steam escaping from the front end of the vehicle. Slowly he raised himself into a sitting position and looked into the driver's seat. The airbag in the steering wheel had deployed and Castellano's head was buried in it, his arms sprawled across the dashboard. Declan couldn't tell whether he was conscious and reached towards his shoulder with his cuffed hands.

The agent sat up suddenly, drawing his gun from his shoulder holster. His hands outstretched, Declan grabbed the gun barrel with one hand and Castellano's wrist with the other as the agent swung the gun around towards the back seat. Placing his thumb behind the trigger, he prevented the agent from firing. Castellano turned in the seat and grabbed the gun with his other hand, trying to regain control. Declan felt intense pain shoot through his hand as Castellano tried to squeeze the trigger of the Glock service pistol, and he felt the handcuffs tighten against his wrists as he tensed his arms and tried to keep the gun away from his head.

"We have to get out of here before they come back to make sure they've succeeded," Declan said through clenched teeth.

"*I* have to get out of here," Castellano growled. "I just need you to die!"

Squealing brakes preceded the sound of tires quickly leaving the pavement and bumping onto the gravel lot, and Declan knew the men who had been following them had arrived. Castellano suddenly let go of the gun and pushed open the driver's side door, exiting the car and running towards one of the dumpsters for cover. The reverberation of automatic gunfire erupted from behind the Crown Vic and Declan allowed himself to fall flat onto the back seat as he tried to adjust the pistol in his cuffed hands. He could hear the ping of bullets hitting the row of metal dumpsters in front of the crashed sedan as someone sprayed the area with gunfire. Getting his grip straight on the service pistol, he raised his hands toward the sound of the gunfire and squeezed the trigger rapidly. He heard the sound of his shots hitting metal and glass as the automatic gunfire stopped.

Launching himself to the other side of the seat, his back braced against the passenger side door to steady his aim, he looked out of the shattered back window as he fired more rounds towards the cargo van that had pulled onto the lot.

The rounds shattered the vehicle's windshield and the two occupants ducked into the cargo area for cover. Declan kicked at the opposite passenger side door, trying to get it to open, but quickly realized the futility; this was a police-style vehicle, it could only be opened from the outside. Firing two more shots, he threw himself over the back of the front seat before firing two more as he scrambled out of the driver's side door, left open by Castellano.

Knowing the magazine in the gun was close to empty, he aimed it towards the van as he escaped from the car and ran towards the row of dumpsters, following Castellano's lead. Two shots exploded from the barrel, followed by a faint clicking sound as the trigger went limp.

As he ducked behind one of the dumpsters he saw Castellano leaning against another alongside, a red stain formed on the side of his light blue button-down shirt signaling that he had been hit. "Get down!" Declan yelled, as he ran between the dumpsters towards him and pulled him onto the ground by the shoulder. Castellano groaned loudly in response to the impact as the sound of one of the van's doors opening preceded more automatic gunfire. Holding the agent close, Declan hunkered them both as close to the ground as he could as the bullets cut through the thin metal containers like they were made of warm butter and into the sparsely covered hill beyond, creating clouds of dust on impact. He couldn't tell what kind of weapon was being fired at them, but he thought by the sound of the firing mechanism that it was likely something smaller, an Uzi or an MP5 perhaps.

"Get over there and find them," someone shouted as the gunfire stopped "Make sure they're dead! We have to get away before the police get here!"

Declan sat up quickly and looked at Castellano, who was obviously incapacitated by his injury. Reaching for the agent's shoulder holster, he unsnapped the compartment that held the extra magazines and pulled them loose. With the press of a button he dumped the empty magazine and slid in a new one. Snapping the slide back and chambering a round, he braced his back against the dumpster as he stood and rolled out into the space between the two containers. He squeezed the trigger rapidly as a heavily jacketed man holding an MP5 machine pistol came into his line of sight. The man was tall, with a narrow scar down the side of his face, and his skin had the same sickly Caucasian tone as the men Declan had seen the night Kafni had been killed. Undoubtedly this man was a Chechen and part of Ruslan Baktayev's crew. But why would they attack Castellano if he was allied with them? The three shots hit the man center mass as he was surprised by the sudden attack, the impact pushing him back into the cargo area of the van.

"Damn!" the driver yelled. The van's tires spun, shooting gravel into the air as it left the lot and pulled back onto the paved highway, its cargo door wide open and the body of the fallen gunman hanging out. Declan quickly cleared the dumpsters and looked in the direction the van had fled. Several motorists had pulled to the side of the road nearby and were looking on in confusion and fright. With the van now out of sight, he turned back towards the dumpsters and ran between them to where Castellano lay. He bent down and gripped the agent by the shoulder as he laid the pistol on the ground.

"C'mon, you're not dying on me!" he said, tearing at the man's bloody shirt to inspect the injury. "I need you!"

Castellano groaned as an agonized look spread across his face. With the bloody shirt torn open and moved aside, Declan felt for the gunshot hole. He applied pressure as best he could with his hands still cuffed together when he found the hole in the agent's side.

"C'mon," he yelled, "stay with me!"

He moved his head towards Castellano's mouth and listened for breathing. Hearing none, he looked at the man's face. The serious loss of blood was evident from the ashen color of the agent's skin and Declan knew he'd be dead within minutes without medical treatment.

"Talk to me! Tell me who's doing this! They tried to kill you, too!"

He pressed hard against the wound to try and stop the bleeding, but the jagged hole was too hard to cover with his hands cuffed together. He released the pressure and reached for Castellano's pockets to find the keys.

"C'mon, c'mon!" he said, searching desperately and finding

nothing. He stood and ran quickly towards the crashed Crown Victoria, quickly checking up and down the road before exposing himself. He backed into the driver's seat and reached around the steering wheel for the keys that were hanging in the ignition. Pulling the set of keys loose, he thumbed through them frantically until he found a tiny metal key with a loop on the end. He pushed the metal cuffs hard against his wrists as he tried to position his hands correctly to insert the key. Feeling the cuffs dig into his skin, he inserted the key and twisted it with his fingers, causing the cuffs to fall loose with a snap. He quickly repeated the process on his other hand and tossed the cuffs onto the floor as he left the vehicle and ran back towards the dumpsters.

Reaching Castellano, he dropped to one knee and leaned over to place pressure on the wound again. The earth beneath the agent had turned black as blood mixed with dirt. Declan was too late. ASAC Seth Castellano was dead.

CHAPTER THIRTY-EIGHT

7:36 p.m. Eastern Time – Tuesday
Northbound on Interstate I-581
Roanoke, Virginia

"Awful news, David," a male voice said, as Kemiss picked up the phone in the back of his limousine. "I'm very sorry this happened."

Kemiss grimaced. The voice belonged to Lukas Kreft, an influential campaign donor and his partner in the terror attack that was set to happen in less than a week. Together they had created the character of Levent Kahraman, a mysterious Turkish sheikh whose identity Kreft now used to communicate with and give orders to Ruslan Baktayev.

"It's over, Lukas. It has to be. Seth's dead and McIver's back in the wind where we may never find him. We can't afford to keep going with this or we'll both lose everything."

"That's your grief talking, David. What would Seth want? He'd want you to keep going, to see you on top of the world again like you were in 2004. It's at your fingertips. After twelve years in Afghanistan and countless attacks and casualties around the world, the American public is ready for the kind of change you were offering. The election in 2016 is going to be all about new realities, both economic and defensive. The United States cannot keep playing guardian around the world and it's your job—our job—to push them just a little further and get them to that realization."

Kemiss looked out of the rear windows of the car as it traveled over an arched concrete bridge in the small railroad city of Roanoke. Below the bridge to the left he could see the empty field that once held a World War II era stadium in which he'd delivered many campaign speeches over the last two decades. Now, with only a few mobile goalposts and metal bleachers, the site looked the way he felt; empty, a hollow reminder of his former self. As visions of his past speeches in front of heavy crowds during the 2004 presidential campaign flashed through his mind, he willed himself to look ahead. In the distance beyond the end of the bridge he could see the interstate exit ramp that would lead him to the facility where Seth Castellano's mother and sister were about to officially identify his remains.

"Baktayev killed Seth, Lukas. How can we continue to have any confidence in him? We should bury this animal before he causes us any more problems. We'll move on. Find another way."

"We've got millions invested in this, more than either of us can afford to lose with the situation being what it is. We can't turn back, David."

Kemiss knew that Kreft's situation wasn't all that different to his own. Like wounded animals, they were both striking out in desperation. After a decade of warfare in the Middle East, Kreft had been backed into a corner and his empire was on the verge of collapse.

Oil was the life's blood of Kreft's business and the despotic regimes in the Middle East were its cornerstone. Despite Kreft's careful warnings, the regimes had attacked, riding militant Islam like a galloping steed and finding themselves impaled on a spear of red, white and blue after awakening a sleeping giant. Now their scattered hordes clung to life by a thread and the caliphate they so desperately desired was a fleeting dream without the strong central support of their governments.

With the oil fields of Iraq opened to capitalist competition at the end of Saddam Hussein's rule and the recent instability of the Libyan fields after Qadaffi's death, Kreft's organization was badly in need of a transfusion. His only hope of keeping his expensive organization from snapping like a toothpick was to convince the West that the war on Islamic terror could not be won and to deliver the newly freed, but abandoned, Middle Eastern countries back into the hands of dictators who would return control of the resources to him, a goal he intended to accomplish with Kemiss' help and in return, Kemiss would receive unending financial support for his future political endeavors from American corporations that Kreft owned a significant interest in.

"Baktayev needs to be made to understand who's in charge. Seth would have handled McIver if he hadn't gotten in the way!"

"Baktayev had a personal vendetta against McIver for killing his brother. Seth told you that when he found out who McIver was. I can't say I'm exactly surprised that Baktayev did what he did now that McIver's involvement in this has gone public. Seth getting caught in the crossfire was unfortunate."

"Unfortunate? This whole thing is a first rate screw up with Ruslan Baktayev's name all over it! Whose side are you on?"

"Easy, David, I'm on your side. I want what you want. I'm just telling you that we can't afford to quit and start over. It's this, or we both go into the history books as bankrupt and defeated."

The limousine Kemiss was riding in made a sharp left into the parking lot of a two story brick building with narrow windows and no identifying signage. Kemiss thought for a moment as the car circled around the lot to a rear entrance. Kreft was right. If the status quo wasn't changed in a major way then the next election cycle would see him packing his belongings and leaving Washington with his tail tucked between his legs.

"Fine," he said. "We'll go forward, but this is personal now, Lukas. It might have been Baktayev's bullet that killed Seth, but McIver was the reason either of them were there at all. I want the world to know that one of the finest law enforcement officers this country has ever known was killed by a second-rate backwater terrorist, and I'm not talking about Ruslan Baktayev. He'll get his when the whole of American law enforcement descends on him next week."

"Alright, David, if there's any kind of victory to be had in this it's the fact that there's now a nationwide manhunt for an inmate who killed an FBI agent. McIver can't avoid the country's entire law enforcement apparatus for very long and that's what's going to be after him now. As far as they know, Seth's murder was part of his escape. Do you know who's going to take over the investigation?"

"Yes," Kemiss said, as he looked out of the window and saw a broad man with a balding head standing near the entrance of the building, an FBI badge folded over the breast pocket of his dark suit. "I know exactly who will and I'll make sure he keeps us informed the entire time."

"Great. I'll make sure everything stays sewn up on our Chechen end."

Kemiss ended the call. Wiping his face with a handkerchief, he opened the car door and stepped out into the cool night. Straightening his suit as he strode towards the entrance, he made eye contact with the suited man who stood grimly by the door.

"Robert," he said with a curt nod, as he extended his hand.

"It's good of you to make the trip, Senator," Robert Evers said, as he gripped Kemiss' hand firmly. Evers was the Special Agent in Charge of the FBI's Richmond Field Office, Seth Castellano's direct supervisor and the man who oversaw both the Counterterrorism and Criminal Investigation Divisions of the FBI for the entire central and southwest Virginia region.

"I've been friends with the Castellano family for two decades. How could I not have?" Kemiss asked rhetorically as their hands separated and Evers turned to walk with him into the building.

"We're all shocked and heartbroken," Evers said with a shake of his head, as they walked down a long corridor towards a set of elevators. "Seth was as careful an agent and investigator as there was. The idea of him transporting such a violent individual alone simply goes against everything we knew about him. I just can't imagine what he was thinking."

Here Kemiss had to be careful as he realized that he knew far more about the circumstances surrounding Castellano's death than he should or that anyone else he was about to meet with did.

"Well, he certainly was thorough. He worked in my office for three years while he finished graduate school and I helped him get into the FBI, despite his mother's objections. I can't help but feel partially responsible."

"There's no one responsible but the animal that killed him, Senator. When we find him, I'm going to snap the cuffs on personally and make sure he trips a few times on the way to the squad car."

"Well, put your foot out in front of him once or twice for me, will ya?"

"Yes, sir," Evers said, as they entered the elevator and he pressed the button to take them to the basement.

"How much did Seth tell you about the man he was transporting?"

"Not much, really. He kept me abreast of the investigation's progress, but he and I had an understanding, as I do with all my agents. I trusted him to do his job and didn't get in the way."

Kemiss nodded.

"Apparently," Evers continued, "he was an Irish immigrant with ties to Kafni, which allowed him to get close enough to set up the assassination without looking suspicious. Seth was hot on his case from the moment he set eyes on him. He had a sixth sense about people, he knew he'd found his man, and it was just a matter of time before he ran him down."

"Hmm," Kemiss said, as he nodded again. Evers was telling him exactly what he wanted to hear. For a senior G-man, Evers had been eating right out of Castellano's hand and accepting without question every word the agent had fed him about the assassination of Abaddon Kafni.

The bell on the elevator chimed and the doors separated with a low hum. Kemiss followed Evers as he stepped out into a dimly lit hallway and walked towards a wooden door at the end. As they drew closer, Kemiss grimaced as he read the word *morgue* on the sign above the door.

"This way, Senator," Evers said, as he stopped at one of several doors that led off the hallway and held his hand out for Kemiss to enter as he pulled it open.

Kemiss stepped slowly into the bleak room beyond and his eyes fell immediately on two women standing side by side, their backs turned to the men, the younger of the two with her head on her elder's shoulder, holding her hand lightly. The two were looking towards a four foot by eight foot window with a curtain tightly drawn over it and either didn't hear or didn't care that people had entered. From behind he knew they were Seth Castellano's mother and sister, not only because they were the only two in the room, but because they each had the same build and hair color as their son and brother. Both Seth and his sister, whose name he was trying hard to remember, had taken after their mother's side of the family in looks and temperament.

"Mrs. Castellano," Evers said in a hushed tone, as he stepped up beside Kemiss. He stood with his hands in his pockets as if he didn't know what else to do with them. Kemiss couldn't imagine having to be the one to deliver the kind of news he was sure Evers had delivered only a few hours earlier.

The older of the two women slowly turned and looked towards them, her eyes swollen and red from crying. At once Kemiss could see the family resemblance and had to fight back a surge of anger. Castellano's mother had the same chestnut brown hair, youthful features and rounded face as her son. He fought hard to keep his face from twisting up in anger as he remembered the way Seth's face had felt as he'd brushed a hand across his cheek after a recent shave.

"Elizabeth," he said solemnly, as the woman's eyes fell on him. The younger woman beside her turned and again he could see the resemblance as he waited for the elder to speak.

"David," she said finally, her voice hoarse, and she stepped away from her daughter to embrace him.

"I'm very sorry for your loss," he said meekly as he opened his arms, his suit making a swishing sound.

"It's good of you to come," she said, as she pulled away and turned sideways towards her daughter. "You probably don't remember, but this is my daughter, Emily."

"I remember," Kemiss lied. "You were what, twelve, thirteen when your brother came to work for me at my office?"

The young woman nodded.

"I remember the two of you and his father accompanying him up the stairs with his things. He was so embarrassed."

The young woman flashed a brief smile that disappeared as the sound of a metal door swinging open came from the side of the room. The party of four turned as a gray haired man in a white lab coat entered, carrying a metal clipboard.

"I'm Dr. Chambers, the Medical Examiner for Virginia's western district," he said, as he stopped and stood near the corner of the window, "you all are the Castellano family?"

"Yes," said Evers, "his mother and sister, and a family friend."

Chambers gave a slight nod and tried to muster a sorrowful look, although it was obvious that this was business as usual for him. "Well, first off, I'm very sorry for your loss. I know this is a very difficult time for all of you."

He waited briefly for a response, but quickly continued when it was obvious that one wasn't forthcoming. "This won't take very long. We need you, as the next of kin, to positively identify your deceased relative for us and to sign off saying that the person in our possession is Seth James Castellano. I'll also need you to sign off on the autopsy that we are required by law to perform when criminal activity was involved in order to determine the cause of death. Do you all understand what I've just said?"

Elizabeth Castellano gave a nod and sniffed away tears as Chambers turned slightly and knocked on the glass window with a knuckle. From behind the glass, an arm appeared around the curtain and quickly pulled it aside, revealing a small rectangular room with white walls and a concrete floor that was just big enough for the hospital gurney that was positioned in its center, a thick white sheet covering the outline of the human being lying on it.

Castellano's sister began to cry audibly as a man in a white lab coat wearing a blue face mask and hairnet positioned himself beside the gurney in preparation for removing the sheet. The man looked out of the window towards Chambers who gave a quick nod.

Kemiss and Evers both stepped forward to stand beside the two women as the man in the room slowly pulled back the sheet and revealed the head and shoulders of Seth Castellano, his eyes closed as though he were sleeping soundly, his hair wet and slicked back with a fine toothed comb, and his skin a chalky white that was in equal parts due to the lighting in the room and the lack of blood circulating in his body.

Both women's distress became audible and Kemiss slipped an arm around Elizabeth Castellano's shoulders, trying to be as comforting as he could be in spite of the emotions that he was feeling, but couldn't show.

Taking the anguished cries as an affirmative identification, the medical examiner made a few marks on his paperwork and motioned for the medical technician in the room to close the curtain. The man obeyed and the room quickly disappeared behind the heavy polyester.

"I just need Mrs. Castellano to sign these two forms for me and you all can go. I know you have a long night ahead of you," Chambers said, as he stepped away from the window towards the group, his clipboard held out.

"Did he suffer?" Elizabeth Castellano asked, as she took hold of the clipboard.

Chambers grimaced as all four faces looked to him for an answer. He shook his head. "I've only completed a preliminary examination. At this time, I really don't know. I'm sorry."

Kemiss gave the doctor a nod of gratitude before glancing towards the clipboard as Castellano's mother scribbled her signature on the two forms and handed it back.

"Let's go," Evers said, pulling lightly on Emily Castellano's shoulder. "I'll see to it that you both get home safely."

"SAC Evers," Kemiss said loudly; everyone stopped and turned to him.

"Senator?" Evers answered.

"I want you to find the man that did this," Kemiss said, wiping a tear from his left eye with his fingers. "My office will make sure that you and your men have every possible tool at your disposal and I want you to keep me informed of any developments every step of the way, and of anything you need, *anything*."

Kemiss' eyes bored into the Special Agent for several seconds.

"Yes, sir. It's a nationwide priority, he won't get away."

"See to it that he doesn't," he said, as he adjusted his suit and looked at the two women, doing his best to soften his expression. "I'm very sorry for the loss of your son and brother. He and I remained in contact after he left my employment and

I promise you that we will capture the man responsible. The United States Government will not rest until Declan McIver is either behind bars or dead."

Minutes later he re-entered his limousine and picked up the phone as his driver closed the door behind him. He dialed a number and waited for an answer. Someone picked up on the other end and he listened as they fumbled their phone. He looked at his watch; it was one o'clock in the morning in Great Britain.

"Simard?" a sleepy voice finally said.

"You'd better have something for me."

"The committee meets first thing in the morning, Senator. I'll have answers for you by the time you're eating breakfast."

CHAPTER THIRTY-NINE

8:19 p.m. Eastern Time – Tuesday
County Route 141
Lake Sherwood, West Virginia

The headlights of the stolen Chevrolet Trailblazer flashed over the roughly hewn driveway that led to his cabin as Declan McIver turned into the property. All he could see as he drove were the crooked branches of the area's many maple trees, the cabin itself being located a safe distance away from the road and only visible in the winter months when the leaves were off the trees. As the vehicle bounced over one of the many potholes in the road he glanced up to look in the rearview mirror out of force of habit, momentarily forgetting that he had removed the mirror from the vehicle in order to disengage the OnStar system, which could be used to track the vehicle's location via GPS. The last thing he needed at the moment was a team of FBI agents descending on the rustic hideaway.

Pulling the vehicle to a stop where he had once parked his 1981 Mercedes, now in the possession of the FBI, he shifted it into park and looked around as he exited onto the concrete pad that stood between the small house and a tall stack of firewood. The smell of burning wood filled his nostrils and he inhaled deeply. Stepping around the side of the house towards the front door that faced the shores of Lake Sherwood, he stopped as a bright light stabbed the darkness from the front of the house and a figure slowly stepped around the side of the log structure.

"It's me," he said, as his wife stepped off the front porch. She walked over the small patch of wet grass that stood beside the house and embraced him. There were no tears and no surprise at seeing him. Along the winding country roads he'd taken to get there, being sure he wasn't followed, he'd stopped and risked a call from a pay phone to the pre-paid cell he'd left with her the day before.

"What took you so long?" she asked.

"Just being careful," he said. It had taken him nearly twelve hours to make a drive that under normal circumstances could've been made in less than three. Along the way he'd travelled in several different directions and had used multiple vehicles. Knowing that the vehicles would eventually be reported stolen and that he had likely been seen at least once, all of his movements had been designed to make his actual destination a mystery.

"The radio said you'd been arrested," she said, holding him tightly. "I thought they'd kill you."

"They tried," he said, as he drew back from her and looked down into her eyes. He gave her a quick smile. "But that's not as easy as it looks."

"What happened?"

"It was Castellano, just like I thought."

"Was?"

"He's dead."

"Then this is over?"

He took a deep breath and shook his head, mouthing the word *no*. She buried her face in the flannel shirt he wore, found in the back of the stolen SUV, and sniffed away tears.

"Let's get inside," he said, placing his hands on her shoulders and guiding her towards the front door.

On the porch, he turned and scanned the area around the house as she stepped inside. The inky darkness of the mountain night made it quickly apparent that there was nothing to see and even if there was, seeing it would be nearly impossible. He stepped inside and closed the door behind him, silencing the sound of the grasshoppers in the trees.

Inside the cabin a glowing red log crackled in the fireplace and emitted warmth that felt good after standing outside. He unbuttoned the flannel shirt and removed it, revealing the prison jumpsuit he'd been given at the Franklin County Jail. Spots of dirt and blood covered the torso and knee areas of the green garment and Constance made a face as she looked at him.

"It's not mine," he said, although he thought she probably knew that. "I tried to save Castellano after he'd been shot, but I couldn't."

"You didn't shoot him?" The crestfallen look on her face said everything about how she was feeling. Slowly, she took a seat in the Adirondack chair next to the stone hearth.

"Whoever these people are," he said, "they decided he was expendable if it meant getting me."

"Did you get what you needed, did you find out who those men from the other night were?"

"Aye, but I don't think it's going to do us any good now that Castellano's dead. Maybe it will help provide some proof of what's going on if there's ever a real investigation launched, but without Castellano, the identities of the people he was working for are going to be impossible to determine. I don't even have an idea about where to begin searching."

She sat forward and reached for his hand. Gripping it softly she asked, "What do we do now?"

"We can't stay here," he said, looking over the rustic interior of the cabin. "We have to get to a place where we'll be safe as long as we need to be. I'm not giving up on this. There's a conspiracy going on and sooner or later someone is going to figure that out. We'll be able to get back to our old lives." He squeezed her hand a couple of times and smiled. Inside he was beginning to feel concerned, they were running out of options, but he couldn't let her know that. He had to maintain the appearance of confidence if he was going to keep her from completely falling apart. In the last seventy-two hours she'd been through more danger than in the previous thirty-five years combined.

"Have you heard anything from Osman or Nazari yet?" she asked.

"Not yet. The problem is that I'm calling their American cell phones, which I'm not even sure will work in Israel where they're currently located."

"Why wouldn't they work?"

"Because there can be a big difference between American cell networks and those of other countries, it all depends on the carrier. I don't know a whole lot about it but I know that they're incompatible with each other in a lot of cases. Just like when we travelled to France and Spain, remember?"

She nodded. "What about the place that Dad and Mom have near Hilton Head? It's on a private island. We'd be okay there and it's a lot more comfortable than this."

He shook his head. "We can't. It's too predictable. We can't go near anyone we have an obvious connection with. It would only get them hurt, or worse."

"So we're going to just keep running from place to place?" she said, starting to sound desperate. "You can't have hidden that many cabins in the woods from me."

"No," he said, trying hard to maintain a calm appearance despite the emotions he was feeling. At this point it looked like the only realistic choice they had was to run, at least for a while. "There are two more people I can reach out to, but it means leaving the country."

"Where would we go?"

"Home," he said looking at her, "to Ireland."

CHAPTER FORTY

Lane Simard sipped a steaming cup of dark blended Creole coffee from his weekly stop at Carluccio's as the late model Range Rover glided smoothly onto Horse Guards Road from Great George Street. His driver sounded the horn several times as a group of gawking tourists scattered away from the front end of the vehicle as the two car caravan pressed towards the gated rear entrance of Downing Street. Like many other people that were milling around Whitehall Road with cameras and sightseeing maps, the tourists were probably wondering if it was a member of the royal family sitting behind the deeply tinted windows of the SUV.

The driver lowered the passenger side window and handed the necessary credentials to one of the Custodian helmeted officers standing at the wrought iron gate holding MP-5 machine pistols across their chests, a staple at the two entrances since the mortar attack in 1991 by the Provisional IRA. The police officer leaned down and glanced into the back seat. Simard lifted his coffee cup in acknowledgment and the officer gave a curt nod before standing up and waving the vehicles on.

As the wrought iron gate opened and the officers stood aside, the Range Rover began to vibrate as the driver pulled onto the cobblestones of Downing Street and passed the black wooden door bearing the famed number ten at the front of the Prime Minister's official residence. Turning into the narrow entrance of a parking lot next to the three story black brick townhouse, Simard readied himself for another meeting of minds as the two Range Rovers pulled to a stop.

A blue uniformed police officer stepped off the stone staircase that led to the first floor of the Whitehall Government Complex and said, "Good morning to you, Mr. Simard," as he opened the rear door of the government-owned SUV.

"Good morning to you, constable," Simard said with a nod and a smile, as he stepped from the vehicle and buttoned his suit. The meeting he was about to attend was the highlight of the London CIA Station Chief's job and the gray cobblestoned area between the Prime Minister's residence and the four story concrete complex known as the Cabinet Office always amazed him.

It wasn't the expensive sedans, or the suited drivers of the various committee members, or the tall oak trees that covered the lot from above that impressed him, but rather the sheer amount of hard work and years of networking that had finally landed him one of the most coveted positions in the Central Intelligence Agency. He was now, and had been for the last four years, able to count himself among a precious few foreigners who had passed through the gates at either end of Downing Street into the heart of the United Kingdom's government. Presidents, vice presidents and heads of state from around the world were the members of this exclusive club and the fact that he, an Iowan farm boy, was among them was a source of great pride.

One of the four agents responsible for transporting him through the capital city stepped around the back of the vehicle and handed him his briefcase as he turned and climbed four marble steps to a green wooden door and pulled it open. While the four agents with him might be able to describe the setting in the courtyard, only he could pass through the doors and into the massive complex of conference rooms and offices that made up number seventy, Whitehall.

"Good morning, sir," a guard sitting in a black leather chair said as he stood up. "I'll show you in."

Simard nodded as the guard led the way down the white hallway to a narrow elevator and inserted a key. The surroundings inside the Cabinet Office were as bland as anyone would expect of a government office, but the fact that no camera had entered the building in recent history gave credence to the constant speculation as to what went on behind the green doors on Whitehall Road, one block from the River Thames in the heart of London.

The bell on the elevator let out a hollow ring as the car arrived on the first floor where Cabinet Office Briefing Room A, more commonly known as COBRA in the media, was located. The guard stood aside as Simard stepped off directly in front of the briefing room's heavily secured door. With a set of metal rods that secured the door closed in the case of a national emergency, the room appeared to be a bunker, and in fact it was. Only one picture had ever been published of the empty room beyond and no one beneath the position of a member of parliament had entered while the weekly Joint Intelligence Committee meeting was taking place. Two more guards stood on either side of the door and one leaned over and inserted a large metal key, like that of an antiquated jail cell, into the center of the lock causing the metal rods to unlatch with a thonk. Without making eye contact or allowing his face to change from the blank stare he was required to hold, the second guard pulled open the door and Simard stepped inside.

Eight people seated around an eloquent marble table looked up as he entered. Some murmured a good morning and others just nodded as he passed and took his seat at the corner of the table near eight LED screens used to monitor emergencies and intelligence throughout the entire country. Just before the doors were closed after his entrance another figure stepped past the guards and into the room. Everyone adjusted themselves in their seats knowing that the arrival of the Joint Intelligence Committee's chairman meant the meeting had begun.

Sir John Morris, a white haired and rounded man with thin-rimmed spectacles seated on his nose, set down a leather briefcase and took his place in the green upholstered swivel chair at the head of the table as the doors latched behind him. "Good morning, everyone," he said in a thick English accent, "we'll begin straight away by hearing your individual reports of the Requirements & Priorities discussed at last week's meeting–"

"Mr. Chairman, if I may?" Simard interrupted raising his hand slightly.

The seven men and two women present looked in his direction, curious as to the reason for his interruption.

"The committee recognizes the CIA's London Station Chief," Morris said slowly, with a wave of his hand in Simard's direction. "You have the floor, Mr. Simard. Proceed."

"Thank you, Mr. Chairman, members of the committee," Simard said with a nod, as he clicked open his briefcase, withdrew a file and stood up. "As you all likely know my country has again been the target of international terrorism in recent days. The detonation of a car bomb outside of a prominent university has been responsible for thirty-seven deaths and one hundred and fifty-three injuries. Many of those inside the building were policymakers of one sort or another, but we believe the target was this man," he said, holding up a picture from the file. "Dr. Abaddon Kafni, an Israeli national with dual citizenship in both the U.S. and Israel. Prior to the detonation several members of Kafni's security detail were drawn away from their posts. The investigators in charge of the case believe that the bombing was a diversion designed to elicit an emergency response from the remaining members of the detail so that the perpetrators could attack Dr. Kafni while he was without his usual protection. Again, as you all likely know, this was successful and Dr. Kafni as well as his chief of security, Levi Levitt, were executed at a house a few miles away."

The heads around the table nodded, indicating that they had all heard the news reports and were aware of the situation. Simard leafed through the papers inside the folder and withdrew several.

"Now I'll get to the part where this concerns the government of the United Kingdom," he continued. "The investigation into the matter has proceeded quickly and has become centered on a particular individual named Declan McIver, who is a former member of Dr. Kafni's security detail. We believe that fact allowed him to move about without suspicion and to set up the attack that has cost so many lives. As you've probably guessed by his name, McIver is a British citizen, or at least he was until about ten years ago. The problem we have run into is that his history prior to his immigration to the U.S. is a black hole, there's nothing there. He was simply born and then fell off of the grid. Now, as everyone in this room knows very well, that's not possible unless you're dealing with a particular type of individual and McIver's actions to date support the idea that he is just such an individual."

Simard stopped talking and allowed the idea that Declan McIver was a military operator of some kind or another to sink in.

"I'm assuming from his name that this McIver is one of our Irish cousins," Chairman Morris said, from the head of the table.

Simard nodded. "The immigration paperwork obtained from our Citizenship and Immigration Service supports that, although we had to go to great lengths to uncover his real place of birth. The paperwork originally filed with our government was full of fraudulent statements indicating he was born in the Republic of Ireland. McIver was actually born in a place called Ballygowan," he said, as he read the name of the town from a piece of paper in his hand.

"Northern Ireland," someone at the table said, though Simard hadn't seen who. He turned and looked at the people seated at the table.

"You say this man's actions support the notion that he is some kind of military agent," the man continued, revealing himself to be the head of the Secret Intelligence Service, a broad man with bushy gray eyebrows and severe facial features. "Can you be more specific?"

"Yes, of course," Simard said, nodding and turning to face the U.K.'s spy chief. "McIver was initially hospitalized for an injury he supposedly received trying to save Dr. Kafni's life, but the truth of that has been in doubt since his first interview with an FBI agent. Since it became obvious to McIver that his ruse had failed, the actions that he has taken to avoid being caught have made it obvious that he is a man of some experience. Those actions include murdering four men that we believe were working with him at the university's event and that we have established a financial connection with, as well as the murder of a business owner whose company provided additional security at the university and whose family was being threatened. It was shortly after that last murder that McIver was cornered and arrested. However, during his transfer yesterday morning to a federal facility where he would have awaited trial, he escaped, taking the life of agent Seth Castellano, the lead investigator on the case, in the process."

"I see," the director of MI6 said, "and do you have any idea as to what kind of experience you think it is that has enabled him to do these things?"

"The reports that have been given to me by my government indicate that two of the murders were carried out hand to hand and the other three by gunshot, all showing signs of precision with the firearms used. In addition to the deaths of these men there were numerous weapons found in his home that were modified in ways that only an individual with military experience could achieve without considerable expense. We're considering all the possibilities. Obviously with him being Irish, connections to groups like the IRA and the INLA are being looked at, but without a paper trail to go on, we're quite frankly flying blind. Every hour that goes by is an hour that a terrorist with obvious international ties is at large and a danger to the populace of the world. For all we know this guy could be well outside of the United States by now."

"So your government wants this committee to unseal any records the intelligence-gathering agencies of the United Kingdom have on him and to provide you with that information?" Chairman Morris asked.

Simard nodded. "Yes, sir. That is what we are requesting."

"Well, I for one don't see any detriment to the United Kingdom or to its overseas interests by agreeing to such a request. Our problems with certain elements within Northern Ireland are ongoing, but from the sound of it any connections this McIver has with that community date back quite a way and are unlikely to affect any current operations. Does anyone else present see this as a problem or have any questions?"

"The fact that he is actively involved in a terrorist act would call that observation into question, Mr. Chairman," one of the ministers said. "We cannot afford to risk our current operations against the extremist elements in Northern Ireland until we know more about this individual."

"I can appreciate your concern, Minister," Simard answered, "but my government would handle this information with the utmost delicacy. It would only be used to effect an arrest within our borders and any international actions required would, of course, be cleared with the governing authorities of that nation or territory."

"Dr. Kafni was an Israeli Jew who had made quite a few enemies in the Islamic parts of the world. Those enemies have threatened him on more than one occasion," a female voice said from the chair diagonally adjacent to Morris. "Why is it that you think an Irishman is responsible for his death instead of one of the more radical Muslim groups? The only benefit I can see coming from Kafni's death would be to one of those groups."

"You're correct, Madame Advisor," Simard said. "That is why we are looking at possible connections with terrorist groups like the IRA. Their previous dealings with Islamic militants are well documented. I don't want to speculate about what McIver's motivation may or may not be, but I think it's clear that he's a danger. Having access to his past, his real past, would provide us with any potential connections that he may use to hide out and will reinvigorate an investigation that has essentially hit a dead end at this point."

The Prime Minister's advisor on foreign affairs nodded her satisfaction with the answer and Morris looked around the table for anyone else to speak. When no one did, he said "Then it's settled. The Joint Intelligence Committee approves the request by the CIA for access to its records relating to Declan McIver. Since Mr. McIver was a British citizen, those records would be held in Thames House by the Security Service. Can you see to it that this request is handled, Dennis?"

Simard looked towards the end of the table to a thin man with graying blonde hair that he knew as Lord Dennis Allardyce, the acting Director-General of the United Kingdom's Security Service. Allardyce nodded. "I'll inform the head of our Irish and Domestic Terrorism Department as soon as this meeting is concluded. He'll see to it that you have what you need by the end of the day."

Simard nodded his thanks. Soon Declan McIver would be on his way to a federal prison.

CHAPTER FORTY-ONE

11:17 a.m. Local Time – Wednesday
Thames House
London, England

"Relax, old son," Shane O'Reilly said into the receiver of his phone. "I'll have the expenditure approved by the morning and we can both go about our merry ways."

"Aye, you'd better have. I'm not doing this for me health, you know."

The voice on the other end of the phone belonged to a man named Patrick "Paddy" Murray, but of course, he, Shane O'Reilly, and his direct supervisor at the Security Service were the only ones who knew that. To everyone else in the Imperial building that sat on the north bank of the River Thames and covered nearly two blocks of the Millbank district of London, Murray was simply agent 4606, a random number with a numerical prefix that indicated his location, if you were high enough in the pecking order to actually have access to the documents that deciphered the locations.

"I'll have it approved and you'll be off to see your mum, I promise."

"Well, grand. I'd hate to have to start forgetting parts and pieces of certain conversations."

"Aye, we'd hate that, too," Shane responded, trying hard not to let the exasperation he was feeling creep into his voice. "We'll have you off soon enough. Call me tomorrow at sixteen hundred hours."

"Four o'clock? You said you'd have it done by morning. She's ill, might not make it through the week, you know? Do you bastards care about anything but yourselves and your bloody politics? I'm starting to rethink this whole thing."

"Aye, now calm down, Paddy, I care about you and your mum and I will get you off to see her. I'll have the expense approved by tomorrow morning and I'll have the travel arrangements made by the time you call. This isn't the easiest thing in the world to pull off, you know? In the eyes of the U.S. government you're a convicted terrorist, and they don't take kindly to that fact. Do you want the FBI swooping down on you as soon as you're off the plane?"

"No—"

"Then let me do my job and call me tomorrow at sixteen hundred."

"Aye, grand. I'll talk to you then."

He listened as Murray set down the receiver of the pay phone he was calling from before he let out a deep breath and allowed himself to sink back in his chair. There were times, a lot of times recently, when all he felt like was a high-price babysitter.

As an intelligence officer assigned to the Irish and Domestic Terrorism Department within the United Kingdom's Security Service, more commonly referred to as MI5, or just 5, his job was to manage the Service's many assets throughout both the mainland and Ireland who regularly provided the British government with information on the plans and whereabouts of known Irish dissidents who continued to plot bombings and shootings. While their activities were on a much smaller scale than the fevered pace that had been the norm when he'd first joined the ranks as a spook seventeen years earlier, they persisted.

O'Reilly returned the receiver of his phone to its cradle before taking hold of his coffee cup and turning around in his chair to look at the empty workspaces surrounding him. Seventeen years ago, every desk on the sixth floor of Thames House had been full and they'd been pilfering unused space in other areas of the expansive government complex. Now those doing the pilfering were located far below him in the Joint Terrorism Analysis

Centre and the International Counter Terrorism Department, in charge of investigating Islamic terrorist activity.

Along with the fevered pace of Irish terrorism had gone many of the colleagues he'd come to genuinely enjoy working with. Now their desks, computers and personal effects were gone, some transferred to other areas of the building where the Service thought their expertise was more needed and others, the old stalwarts like him, moved to the Security Service's Northern Ireland HQ inside the Palace Barracks in County Down. The only reason he hadn't been moved as well was because he had vowed never again to set down roots in Northern Ireland. The memories there for him were too painful and rather than face them each day he'd have quit, and he'd made that known.

"If you're done boring a hole into that mug, O'Reilly, I've got something to talk with you about," a gruff voice called from the other end of the office. He straightened up and placed the coffee cup on his desk, glancing out the antiquated window into the gray waters of the Thames as a black barge made its way down the river.

Standing up, he looked towards the corner office at the end of the room about thirty feet away. Standing in the open doorway was the broad figure of his boss, Harold Thom, a part Irish, part English, but one hundred percent British company man whom he'd worked with for the last twenty years starting with his role as an informer in Northern Ireland. While Thom's hair had gone from flaming orange to mostly gray, the scowl he wore and the beady eyes that seemed as though they could cut through steel hadn't changed since they'd first met in an abandoned textile mill in Belfast.

He nodded in Thom's direction as the man turned and disappeared into his office. Walking around the edge of his desk, he caught the *oh crap* glances of the two dozen or so co-workers left in the IDT's half of the sixth floor, which they shared with the Northern Ireland Office. Stopping halfway along his route, O'Reilly briefly considered his reflection in the glass covering a large picture of London's skyline and straightened his tie. Every time he looked, the lines on his face seemed deeper and the red fuzz he called hair seemed grayer. It was fitting given the mood he found himself in most days. It felt like it had been years since he'd experienced any real excitement, and by excitement he wasn't thinking of the kind he'd endured as a younger man traipsing around the hills and loughs of Ireland, the deserts of Libya or the mountains of Afghanistan. No, he'd be more than happy with a bottle of wine and a good lay every once in a while.

Stepping into the office and closing the door behind him, he watched as the barrel-shaped Thom descended into the leather chair behind his long, L-shaped mahogany desk.

"How's it, Shane?" the big man asked, as he labored to get comfortable in the chair.

"Well enough, sir," he said, with a raise of his eyebrows, "just trying to keep Her Majesty's Government from being completely shaken down by my countrymen."

Thom flashed the briefest smile in history. "I've had a call from the Deputy Director this morning. It seems there's a matter the JIC would like us to look into. I thought you'd be particularly suited to the assignment."

"You mean they've actually remembered we're here?"

Thom again flashed a smile that faded almost as quickly as it had appeared on his thin lips. "Yeah, it seems that some sad bastard from your old stomping grounds has turned up in an American investigation into the car bombing of that university and the death of that teacher, or whatever he was. The Yanks want everything we have on him and the JIC has agreed to give it to them. That means you need to blow the dust off some really old stuff down in the file room and hope it's still readable."

Shane nodded. He'd heard about the bombing in America and about the subsequent death of Abaddon Kafni. To him it was a tragedy that was compounded by the fact that he'd actually met the man on one occasion and believed him to be an all-round good person with a family life that differed greatly from the heated rhetoric that consumed his professional time. Like everyone with a television license and even a passing interest in politics, he had followed Kafni's career to a degree and he couldn't say his death was a surprise. Like the fatwas issued against people like Salman Rushdie, the ranks of Islamic militancy didn't take kindly to being so loudly and publically excoriated. The idea that someone from his old stomping grounds, as Thom had put it, could be involved piqued his interest and immediately a sinking feeling settled on him as one name in particular came to mind.

"Does this sad bastard have a name?"

Thom nodded and slid a file across his desk. "This is what the Yanks have on him. They want us to fill in the blanks."

Shane bent down quickly and picked up the file. Opening it, the sinking feeling turned to the twist of a knife in his stomach as he looked at the photo paper-clipped to the top of dossier.

"Sir, there must be some mistake here," he said.

"Oh?" Thom said, raising his eyebrows.

"Aye, this file belongs to Declan McIver."

"And that's a mistake because?"

"Because he's one of the most decent men I've ever known. He saved my life, sir."

CHAPTER FORTY-TWO

"Well be that as it may, Agent O'Reilly," Thom said, after briefly considering the story that Shane had just recounted for him. "He was enlisted in the ranks of a subversive organization and things change. It's been a number of years since you and this McIver have had any contact."

Shane nodded with a grimace.

"If you're not up for this, I understand. I'll have someone else get on it straight away. This one comes directly from the top, so I can't afford to have it messed up."

"No, sir," Shane said, closing the file and gripping it tightly. "I'm good with it. As you said, it's been a number of years and things change. Who's my contact when I've gathered everything?"

"Me. This one is going straight up the line." Thom motioned towards the door with his index finger indicating that it was time for Shane to leave.

"Alright then, I'll get busy just as soon as I've had a smoke," Shane said, as he tucked the folder under his arm and withdrew a full bent Peterson tobacco pipe from his coat pocket, "the lounge is on the way to the file room."

He heard Thom grunt as he stepped out of the office and pulled the door closed behind him. With rare haste in his step, O'Reilly moved quickly through the maze of desks towards the hallway of elevators that separated the shared sixth floor. This was a moment he'd waited nearly twenty years for, but had hoped would never come.

Outside, he turned up the collar of his tan trench coat as a cold wind blew off the Thames and up Thorney Street, the narrow alleyway that ran along the rear of Thames House. The windowless bronze door at the top of the one story flight of stairs he'd just descended slammed shut behind him and he turned right along the sidewalk, leaving the alcove of entrance number six. Passing the building's official rear entrance, he nodded at an armed guard that stood watch. The guard nodded in return but didn't pay any further attention to him. He was a common sight, walking by every morning and every afternoon on his way to his mundane flat in Newington, just across the Lambeth Bridge.

He held his pipe between his teeth as he withdrew a leather pouch from the inside breast pocket of his coat and grabbed several pinches of his favorite whiskey-flavored tobacco. Filling his pipe, he rounded Thames House and crossed Millbank Road onto the Lambeth Bridge. A cold, seasonal wind blew north off the river as he turned downwind to light up. When the tobacco was lit evenly, he inhaled deeply as he placed a hand in his pocket and strolled slowly onto the concrete walkway beside the road that led into the Lambeth and Newington neighborhoods on the opposite side of the river.

At nearly midday, traffic rushed past him a few feet away and he nodded as he passed the occasional pedestrian without really seeing them. His mind was focused on the file he'd just been given. Exhaling a bluish haze and watching it waft away across the walls of the bridge, he considered the photograph he'd seen paper-clipped inside and remembered a younger but no less friendly face. Even in his early forties and in what was probably a prison mug shot, Declan McIver hadn't lost his boyish looks and the slight sparkle in his eyes that made you believe him when he spoke. It had been that look and the actions that followed that were responsible for the fact that Shane was still breathing and counted among the living.

"Ah, I'm screwed, Declan!" a younger version of his own voice said, as it echoed through his head.

"You're not screwed, neither of us are!" Declan had responded, as he'd grabbed him by the shoulders and looked him in the eye as the barbaric calls of the Russian soldiers pursuing them echoed through the mountains outside of the cave they'd been held up in.

The memory faded and he wondered what the circumstances were that had brought a file containing Declan's image into the offices of the Security Service. When you were a former Irish dissident, the offices of the Security Service was one of the last places you wanted anything to do with you to end up, and the idea that Declan had returned to the kind of life that would send him there just didn't seem possible. Still, he had to consider the words of Harold Thom, things changed and it had been a number of years since he'd had any kind of lengthy contact with his old friend. While it hadn't been as long as Thom probably thought, it was still long enough for the circumstances in anyone's life to change for the worse, but bad enough to murder a friend? He didn't believe it.

He inhaled again from his pipe as he leaned on the columned walls of the bridge and watched the boats sail underneath. In his mind, there was no way Declan could be guilty of what the Americans thought he was. It was a mistake, it had to be. Declan and Abaddon Kafni had been friends for years and he'd seen these kinds of things happen before during the course of an investigation. In their haste to capture terrorists, someone had stumbled upon Declan's past and had simply drawn the wrong conclusions. But the damage done to Declan's life could be irrevocable. As the only remaining members of the IRA unit they had once belonged to, they'd made a promise to each other to take the necessary steps to ensure each other's safety and while he knew he was risking everything his life had been for the last seventeen years, a promise was a promise. He pulled a Blackberry from his pocket and typed in a web address. He knew that the Security Service had eyes and ears on just about every location within a few blocks of Thames House and that they were notorious for watching their own people as much as they watched everyone else. Making the transmission that he was about to make could amount to a charge of high crimes and misdemeanors, but then, technically, he wasn't sending anything. He punched in his login information to a subscription based Swiss mail server and opened the draft folder. Quickly, he typed out a message and hit the save button.

Five has received a request for records regarding DM. Will stall it as long as I can but trouble is coming. Acknowledge. – SO

CHAPTER FORTY-THREE

"It's Allan Ayers, Senator," a voice said, David Kemiss having removed his cell phone from his jacket pocket and answered a call. "I've found it."

Kemiss smiled. You could always rely on a bureaucrat to be spineless. It was in their nature and Allan Ayers was no different. Thirty-six hours after his threat to fire the man, Ayers had been back on board and had been helping Castellano locate McIver's cabin. "Where is he?"

"I centered my search on areas within a hundred miles of Roanoke and I paid special attention to the areas northwest of Roanoke since that's the direction McIver was last heading when his wife was known to be with him—"

"I didn't ask where you centered your search, Allan. I asked where he is."

"Greenbrier County, West Virginia, sir, near a small reservoir known as Lake Sherwood."

"You're sure?"

Ayers was silent for a moment. "As sure as I can be without actually seeing McIver there. The property's registered owner is a corporation out of the Grand Cayman Islands called Kirkgrim Incorporated. I've run the company name through every search engine and program I can think of and the only thing it seems to be associated with is this property. There's no tax returns, no website, nothing. It's just a holding company with one property, which is pretty unusual, especially in as remote a location as this Lake Sherwood."

Kemiss took a seat at his desk and drummed his fingers on the smoothly polished mahogany as he thought things through. McIver had disappeared twice now, so it certainly made sense that he was hiding somewhere nearby his home in Roanoke. Kemiss was familiar with Greenbrier County. It was the home of one of the finest resorts on the east coast of the United States. He had spent many weekends there and the surrounding area was definitely remote enough to make a good hideout. That being the case though, the resort attracted many high profile guests and the cabin could easily be a getaway for someone entirely different, someone who had a legitimate reason for hiding their ownership of the property and who just enjoyed living off the grid for a few days here and there.

"There's one other thing that makes me a little more sure it's his," Ayers continued. "The name Kirkgrim, it's an Irish folk legend about a ghostly dog that protects graveyards, sir."

"Then it's him. It has to be. Make me a file with all the pertinent information on this place and forward it to my email," Kemiss said, deciding that whoever owned the cabin would just have to forgive him if he was wrong. "I'll handle it from here. Call me the minute you find anything else."

He closed the cell phone and returned it to his pocket. Who should he call now? If he called Kreft, then it was a certainty that whoever was at the cabin would be slaughtered, and if it wasn't the McIvers then that could cause even more trouble than they currently had. But if he called Robert Evers and had a team of federal agents raid the place, there was a chance the McIvers could be taken alive, and that was problematic as well. He picked up the receiver of the SCIP-enabled phone on his desk and allowed his finger to hover over the dial pad for a moment as he considered his options. Making a decision, he dialed a number and waited. "It's Kemiss," he said when the line was answered. "I think we've found him."

CHAPTER FORTY-FOUR

5:36 p.m. Eastern Time – Wednesday
County Route 141
Lake Sherwood, West Virginia

Constance gripped Declan's hand lightly as they pulled into the cabin's driveway. The last twenty four hours had been rough on them both, but they'd managed to get some sleep and had even risked a late afternoon trip to the town of Covington, Virginia, to pick up some supplies. While they were there, Declan had again used the wireless internet access at a small public library to find out the latest news on the manhunt for him. The efforts had now gone nationwide and the media coverage had grown more intense. On the various network websites he had seen photos of his house, quotes from his employees, who seemed beside themselves, and even an interview with the neighbor who took care of their dog whenever they were out of town. The entire scene made him dizzy. Even if he succeeded in identifying the people who had actually killed Abaddon Kafni and he and Constance were able to return to their normal lives, he wasn't sure there was going to be anything left to go back to.

"You don't think anyone recognized you, do you?" Constance asked.

He'd chosen to go to Covington instead of a closer town because, in his travels around the area over the years, he'd learned that the small city had a sizeable amount of Western European immigrants that had come to the area in search of employment at the large textile and paper mills that were the primary employers. Their presence meant that his accent wouldn't stand out as much, but he'd still been careful not to speak to anyone he didn't have to and he'd let Constance do the shopping while he waited in their car. Even driving her Nissan sports car at this point was a risk, but the only other option they had was the Trailblazer he'd stolen from a car lot the day before. It was a toss-up as to which vehicle would attract more attention.

"Nah," he said with a smile. "But I'm sure they recognized you. The most beautiful woman in the world doesn't walk into a store in backwater U.S.A. and not get recognized."

"Yeah, yeah," she said as she rolled her eyes and opened the car door.

As he got out of the car and followed her towards the cabin he was glad that the mood between them had begun to lighten. They'd always enjoyed a jovial relationship. He'd certainly done his share over the years to strain the marriage, but nothing made him feel worse than getting the cold shoulder from the person who had become his best friend.

"Let's go for a walk," Constance said, as she set down a bag of groceries on the porch. "It's almost warm out here tonight."

Declan stopped and scanned the shores of the lake that she was looking at. Seeing his reluctance, she said, "Did you try to contact your friends? The ones you said could help us."

"Aye, I left an e-mail for them. If news of what's going on has been picked up internationally, and I'm sure it has, they'll check it and be in contact. I'm sure of it. Now, what direction should we go in?" he said, clapping his hands loudly and rubbing them together. He was trying to be reassuring. He had, in fact, left word for Fintan McGuire and Shane O'Reilly and was sure they'd get back to him. The problem was when and how. In such a remote location they had no Internet access and would have to rely on periodic trips to the few libraries located in the region. The more he showed his face around, the more chances they had of getting caught, and trying to arrange travel out of the country with such limited contact wasn't going to be easy.

Half an hour later he wrenched his hand loose from his wife's and placed his arm over her back as they strolled slowly along a narrow path that wound its way around the remote mountain lake and through the many rhododendron thickets that sat along its shores. The sun had retreated behind the pine tree-covered Allegheny Mountains to the west and the path in front of them was growing steadily darker.

Constance brushed a hand through her auburn hair as the trail came to an end and the cabin came into view. "I'm not exactly suited to mountain life," she said, looking down at her sandals and wiggling her toes as if to say she wasn't smart enough to have worn the right shoes out of the house. The bottoms of her jeans were stained from the wet mud on the ground.

"Oh, I don't know," he said, looking down at her feet with a laugh. "You'd probably fit in better than you think. Ellie May never wore shoes either and she wrestled bears for honey. C'mon. Let's get back inside before you freeze. The temperature's dropping faster than the sun." He suddenly lifted her off the ground.

"Oh—Declan!" she protested, as he swung her over his shoulder and carried her like a wounded soldier.

As they walked across the uneven terrain she grunted loudly with every step he took, making it seem as if she was bouncing hard against his shoulder each time. Ten yards from the door, he stopped suddenly and lowered her to the ground.

"You're gonna pay for that," she said, slapping him playfully.

"Quiet," he said seriously, holding up his hand and looking off into the darkness.

She followed his gaze and a moment later watched as a pair of headlights shone through the thick forest and quickly disappeared again as a vehicle made its way over the highs and lows of the driveway.

"Who is it?" she asked. "Are you expecting someone?"

"No," he responded, as he withdrew a Glock pistol from his belt.

The headlights rose again, slowly washing over them. A twig snapped to their right and Declan knew he was too late.

"Put down the weapon!" a voice shouted from the

darkness.

Professionals. Declan knew by the way they'd positioned themselves, one at his three o'clock and the other at his seven. With his eyes adjusted to the darkness, he could just make out the two men, each with M4 carbine assault rifles aimed for the kill. There was no way he could take them both and they knew it.

He didn't know how they'd found him, but they had. He should have moved on faster and been out of the area, but he'd allowed the remote location and his emergency preparations to lull him into a false sense of security. He hadn't wanted Constance to live a life on the run so he'd delayed their leaving as long as he could; now they were caught and he was cursing himself. Instead of living a life on the run, neither of them would be living at all.

"Put down the weapon!" the man at his three o'clock shouted again. "We're not here to hurt you!"

The headlights of the approaching vehicle rose over the last incline of the driveway and bathed the small clearing where the cabin stood in incandescent light.

"Well, you're sure as hell not here selling hoovers, old son," Declan said, keeping his arms straight by his side but not releasing the Glock from his grip. He stared straight ahead at Constance who stood perfectly still, her arms straight up in the air and her eyes darting from left to right looking at each of the men in turn.

"Like you said, bud, we're not here sellin'...whatever. Someone wants to have a chat with you, but he can't very well do that if he's got a gun stuck in his mug." The seven o'clock's accent was local, for sure, the voice deep and raspy, probably from years of smoking.

The approaching vehicle took the last left hand curve of the drive way and pulled to a stop next to Constance's Nissan Z, revealing itself to be a dark-colored late model mini-van with deeply tinted windows. The rear passenger side window in the cargo door came down with a low hum but revealed only darkness beyond. Declan heard the pneumatic hiss before he saw anything.

"Get down!" he said pushing Constance to the muddy

surface of the driveway, but it was too late. As he dived on top of her a sharp pain stabbed the side of his neck. He pulled the dart out as he rolled onto his back and raised his pistol to fire, but the poison was acting fast. He'd pulled the trigger twice before he realized he was aiming at nothing, the shots echoing into the night. A black boot came from the darkness and pinned his arm at the wrist, holding his hand and the gun in it tight against the ground. Trying to fight through the fog that was steadily overtaking his mind, he brought his leg up to kick the kneecap of the man holding him. But instead of landing a crippling blow, he found his leg held above him at the ankle and twisted into a stress position by a second assaulter. His vision began coming in quick, blurry flashes.

"Damn. He's almost out. That's some good stuff."

The voice was a slow drawl, but Declan couldn't tell if it was a real accent or just the effects of the poison. "You bastards," he breathed as he felt himself losing consciousness.

"You got that right, bud."

CHAPTER FORTY-FIVE

"The cabin was definitely theirs, Senator," the voice of SAC Robert Evers said, as David Kemiss answered the line. "But it looks like they cleared out just before we got there."

"Dammit!" Kemiss slammed his fist on his desk. He still hadn't heard a word from Lane Simard and the FBI had come up empty. With every hour that ticked by, Declan McIver could be getting further and further away. "Have you got anything, anything at all?"

Evers was silent for a moment and Kemiss realized he was overstepping the invisible boundaries between being an interested policymaker wanting to help and a desperate man with an ulterior motive. "Sorry," Kemiss said bringing his voice back to a normal level. "The Castellanos are good friends, and I'm taking this very personal."

"I understand, sir. We think they cleared out minutes before we got there. Somehow they saw us coming and took off. There were still groceries in a bag on the front porch. We have police patrols all over the area, checkpoints set up and their pictures will be in the local media outlets within minutes. If they're still in the area, we'll find them."

"Good. The Castellano and Kafni families deserve justice and don't even get me started on the families of those people at

Liberty University."

"It's the Bureau's top priority across the nation, Senator. Declan McIver's been moved to the top of the most wanted list and we're moving heaven and earth to find him. We just have very little to go on."

"I told you that my office would help, so I have. I'm working on getting you more information on his past."

"I'm sure that would be very helpful, sir. Judging from the cabin, they left in a hurry and on foot. They can't have gotten far."

"Hopefully not. Keep me updated every step of the way, will you?"

"Yes, of course, sir."

Kemiss set down the phone and looked at his watch; so much for Simard having answers for him by breakfast. It was already evening in the U.S. and after midnight in the United Kingdom. If Simard wanted to keep his posh job as the London station chief and not find himself transferred to a remote substation in the Ukraine, he'd be making a phone call soon.

Kemiss stood from his desk and stretched. It was late, but if he hurried he could still catch the last train to his nearby apartment and at least try to get some rest. He began to gather some files containing legislation that he would soon be asked to vote on, but set them back on the desk. What good would reading the bills be if he wasn't in the Senate to vote on them? And that's exactly what would happen if his plans didn't come to fruition soon. He'd be washed out of American politics on a tidal wave of scandal.

His phone sounded suddenly and before it could produce even half a ring, he'd picked it up and brought the receiver to his ear. At this time of night the Capitol's switchboard staff had left for the day and any calls would be from someone who had the private numbers of any legislators that happened to be working.

"Kemiss?"

"It's Simard, sir," the voice on the other end said. "I apologize for the delay, but it seems the files in London were quite old and some of the information had to be reconstructed before it could be passed on."

"Fine, fine, what's it say?"

"I'm sending the files to you now, but as it turns out Declan McIver doesn't have a file at the Security Service. His name only appears in a file dedicated to a unit known as Black Shuck."

"What the hell is Black Shuck?"

"Do you remember what Forestor said the other day about having evidence that the Soviets may have been involved with the IRA?"

"Yes."

"Well, he was right. The files the Security Service sent over indicate that in the mid-eighties there were rumors being spread around the paramilitary groups that some ultra-right wing members of the IRA were busy preparing a secret unit. Supposedly someone fairly wealthy within the ranks of the IRA had connections with some military brass in the Soviet Union and sent some men to be trained by their version of the Special Forces, the *Spetsnaz*. Officially, the group was known as Black Shuck."

"Jesus Christ," Kemiss murmured. "So this guy's a Russian trained terrorist?"

"Maybe. His name appears on a list with about a hundred possible suspects and it appears in a number of individual reports within the file, but there's nothing concrete. The British intelligence agencies never finished the job. The investigation was abandoned in ninety-four after a supposedly rock solid source, codenamed Homeless Viper, said that the unit was wiped out from the inside. Apparently the IRA was infamous for eating its own children because of the infiltration of British spies throughout their ranks."

"Intriguing." Kemiss was interested in the concept whether Declan McIver was involved or not. If he could pin McIver as a member of a specially trained unit of terrorists, then nothing the man said to anyone would ever be believed and he'd be on the run for the rest of his life–which wouldn't be very long if Kemiss had his way.

"When it comes to Northern Ireland, David, I have to caution you, you're dealing with an extremely difficult to understand situation."

"I don't care about understanding the situation," Kemiss

said, being careful not to make the same mistake he had with Robert Evers moments ago. Like Evers, Simard was trying to capture a man whom he believed was guilty of a crime, not eliminate the only witness to it. "I only want this information because it might reveal where this guy's hiding and who he may reach out to for help."

"There's a lot here, David. It's going to take some time to go through and pick out anything useful."

"Have you seen the amount of regulations generated by the federal government lately? Send it all to me. I've got people around here that deserve purple hearts for the amount of paper cuts they've suffered."

"On its way, sir. I'll warn you, though. Some of the names and locations have been redacted to protect the identities of undercover agents. There was nothing I could do about that."

"Thank you, Mr. Simard. I'll be sure and send word of your helpfulness to your superiors."

"Thank you—"

Kemiss pressed the button on the phone's cradle to end the call before the man could finish speaking. Dialing another number, he waited.

"Colin?" he said as a young man's voice answered. "It's David Kemiss. I have a job I need you to get on right away. Are you up for it, son?"

"Yes, sir, of course."

"Good. Get in here and I'll explain everything."

CHAPTER FORTY-SIX

9:10 p.m. Eastern Time – Wednesday
The Greenbrier Resort
White Sulphur Springs, West Virginia

Declan felt a rush of cold air as the cargo door on the van slid open, followed closely by the stench of garbage. He'd been conscious for only a few moments and his head was still buzzing from the effects of whatever poison he'd been hit with. His wrists and ankles were bound tightly together; a blindfold that stunk of grease and felt like it had been fashioned out of an old dishrag had been placed over his eyes. He felt two large hands grip him under the arms and pull upwards.

"Let's go, bud, your date's waiting."

He recognized the voice as the seven o'clock gunman from outside the cabin. He tried to drop his weight and make himself as heavy as possible, but realized quickly that his muscles were useless. He was already being supported one hundred percent by the two men, each with an arm looped under his, holding him up as they dragged him out of the van. His legs stung like they'd been asleep as his feet impacted with the floor and he felt himself being pulled forward. The stinging continued as his feet bounced against the edges of steps as he was dragged upwards.

The smell of grease hung thick in the air and from the sounds around him he guessed he was in some kind of loading area in close proximity to a restaurant. How long had he been out? Where was Constance? He tried again to struggle against the two men carrying him, to no avail. He drew in a breath of putrid air and tried to ask "Where's my wife?" but all that came out was slurred babble.

"Bring him through here," he heard a voice say from up ahead. The two men dragging him stopped for a moment and he heard a door unlatch and open before they pulled him inside.

The unmistakable sound of a metal chair being pulled across a concrete floor filled his ears and when it stopped, the two men dumped him into the seat. He sat completely still concentrating hard on staying upright in the chair as he fought against the lingering effect of the drugs. He heard the shuffling of feet as at least two men moved around him and then a loud slam as the door he'd been brought through closed, leaving the room in silence. Was he alone? No, he felt someone nearby, standing in front of him.

"Welcome to the Greenbrier Resort, old friend. Sorry the accommodations aren't a bit better, but it seems you've gotten yourself into some trouble."

Declan recognized the voice immediately. It sounded older now, more experienced somehow but it was still close enough that he knew who it was even though he couldn't see him.

The blindfold was pulled off and the cold air attacked his sweaty face as he looked around. His vision was still blurry but his eyes finally settled on the person in front of him.

"Fintan?"

"Aye, you look like hell, old son."

"Screw you," Declan said his voice weak and catching in his throat. "How'd you get here so fast?"

"Fast? We've been looking for you for three days."

"Why?"

"Well, if you've been reading the same newspapers I have, you're in a lot of trouble."

"They killed Abe and set me up because I saw it."

"I figured it had to be something like that. Here, drink this. It'll help clear your head."

Declan felt cold condensation drip from a bottle as a hand held it to his mouth.

"Oh, cut him loose already," Fintan ordered. "He's not gonna hurt anyone. He can barely sit upright."

Declan felt the bindings on his wrists tighten momentarily as something pushed against them. With a small pop his hands fell to his sides as the restraints were cut. Sitting forward, he placed his hands on his face, wiping sweat away. The bottle was tapped against his right hand. He took it and gulped cold water, allowing it to spill over his chin and onto his shirt. Placing the bottle on the floor, he took another moment to collect himself. He rubbed his eyes as his vision began to clear and the buzzing in his head slowed.

He looked around to see that he was in an empty walk-in freezer. A tall, dark-haired man with a square chin stood behind him, wearing a black trench coat, his face threateningly blank. Fintan sat a few feet in front of him and as Declan looked toward him he was surprised. He'd nearly forgotten he was wheelchair-bound, a gift from their days in Northern Ireland.

Fintan patted the armrests of the chair and smiled. He still had the same neatly combed blonde hair and angular features as the last time Declan had seen him. His face was a bit more lined, but his eyes still gave off the same *I'm smarter than you* look they always had. "A bit sportier a model than the one you last saw," Fintan said. "I can actually walk with the assistance of crutches, but with all the twists and turns in this place, well, it's just easier this way."

Declan remembered the night Fintan had been injured; a gunshot to his lower back had left him paralyzed from the waist down. In 1993, a group of left wing IRA leaders from Belfast had paid an assassin to attack the McGuire family home in Mullaghmore, just over the border with the Irish Republic. Their goal had been to put an end to an internal power struggle within the IRA that had pitted them against right wing commanders from around the six counties of the north who disagreed with the consolidation of power in Belfast and with the political ambitions of Sinn Fein.

Angered by what they saw as the Belfast leadership being more interested in pandering to the IRA's enemies in Stormont and Westminster, and using the armed struggle only as a negotiating tool to gain political power and garner small fortunes for themselves, the commanders united under the leadership of Eamon Maguire, Fintan's father and commander of the IRA's South Armagh Brigade, to begin a quest to take back the military council and continue the battle for a united, thirty-two county Irish state. Being independently wealthy, the culmination of McGuire's plan was a specially trained group of operatives that he'd codenamed Black Shuck and had sent to train in Afghanistan under the supervision of a rogue Russian commander in charge of a unit of special forces soldiers known as *Vympel*.

Naturally the politicians of Sinn Fein hadn't taken kindly to the challenge and with the help of a traitor named Torrance Sands, they'd attacked and eliminated the team. Declan had served as the leader of one of the four active service units that made up Black Shuck under Eamon McGuire's command and his tenure had ended the same night Fintan had been shot. Although Fintan was never involved directly in any operations, the assassin had spared no one. Eamon McGuire, a half dozen other commanders and a dozen of the IRA's most lethal operators had been killed, and Fintan had been left for dead. Declan and his fellow operative Shane O'Reilly had survived only because they'd arrived after the assault and had found only carnage.

Declan placed his head back in his hands. *Dammit,* he thought. Although the buzzing had stopped, his vision had cleared and he could finally move his arms and legs again, he still had a severe headache.

"What was that your guys got me with? Where's Constance?"

"Ah, your wife, you did well there, Dec," Fintan chuckled. "She's fine, just fine, upstairs in a suite probably enjoying a facial and a massage. I have no idea what they hit you with. Only two of these guys are mine. The rest were friends of friends. A fact I'm not exactly happy about, as I'm trying really hard to keep my presence here under wraps, but I didn't have much choice. I knew it would take some damn good training to handle you."

"So no one knows you're here?"

"No. The staff here is used to quiet visits by political figures so I'm hoping it will stay that way. I'm on a plane back as soon as we're done."

"How'd you find me?"

"Christ, Declan, you're not that hard to predict. I knew you'd have a bolt-hole somewhere remote, probably within a hundred miles of home, someplace nice and quiet. As soon as I saw the news I had one of my guys make some calls. He found this nice old boy, former U.S. marine recon as it was, who works here in the kitchen. He outlined all of the possibilities and between him and some friends they sat on them until you showed up."

"Jesus, Fintan. This whole thing has way too many hands on it. How do you know this guy isn't going to turn me in or hasn't already?"

"Well, my friend here says he's trustworthy," Fintan said, motioning towards the man standing behind Declan. "Met him in Desert Storm, says he's no friend of the government. You know, one of those conspiracy types. Seems trustworthy enough, but that's all the more reason why you need to get your arse on a plane out of here. If he found you, the peelers won't be far behind. I have some contacts in Switzerland that can set you and the missus up with a nice cabin. All the skiin' and screwin' you'd care for until this thing blows over in a few months."

Declan shook his head. "Its not going to blow over. We have to find these bastards and stop them. Abe isn't going to have died for nothing and they aren't going to get away with taking away the best life I've ever had. I've worked too hard to put the past behind me to have it all destroyed."

"Jesus, Declan. You always did buy into all that stuff about the American dream, didn't you? You've got bigger problems than you realize. We all do. Whoever's after you has gone all the way to the Security Service in London. Shane's department received the order earlier today. The service is to release all the information they have on you. Shane'll delay the order as long as he can and even try to figure out who made it, but that won't help much. You've got to go to ground as fast as you can and I don't mean hiding in a cabin by the lake. I mean real hiding, new names, new paperwork, everything."

"I've got all of that; have had for years, French passports and papers, German passports and papers. It's not like they're going to stop looking for me just because I'm running and hiding. As long as I'm alive and I know the truth, they're going to be hunting me. Six days, six months or six years, any way you look at it, they're coming. We'll be running for the rest of our lives and I'm tired of running, Fintan. I've seen too many people die because the people in power were in collusion with the psychopaths out trying to murder everyone."

"How the hell do you plan on finding these guys? You don't even know who they are, do you? They made it all the way to Whitehall without breaking a sweat. What're you gonna do if this whole things goes all the way up to the presidency or something like that? You can't take on an entire government."

"I don't have to. This isn't the 1980s and we're not in Northern Ireland anymore. This is America and whoever these people are, they're on the fringe. They may have power and access, but that won't save them when the truth of what they're doing is revealed."

Fintan shook his head in seeming disbelief. "I should know better than to try to talk you out of anything. You're worse than a dog with a bone, always have been."

Declan thought for a moment. Slowly he sat back, took a deep breath and another long drink of water. He didn't like any of the options, but that was usually the way things worked in these situations. You always had to go with the best of the choices in front of you and Fintan was right. Staying in the U.S. didn't make much sense, Declan had settled on that fact the night before. The more distance he could put between himself and the conspirators trying to kill him the better off he'd be and the better his chances would be of finding out who they were without them finding him in the meantime.

"London," he said aloud, though he wasn't speaking to anyone in particular.

In all likelihood he didn't think there were any significant ties to London. His history in the U.S. was barely over a decade old and the information he'd supplied to the INS when he'd applied for citizenship left out as much as it told. That was where the Security Service came in. Whoever was after him had needed information and had reached out to contacts within the British government to get it. Still, someone there had to know where the request originated and that person might just be the best chance he had at finding out who was responsible for everything that had happened since Friday night.

"Look," Fintan said, as if he could read minds, "your best chance of finding these guys is Shane. Let him stay on the London link while you lay low. When he's got something, we can decide the next move from there. You and the missus can shack up at the estate in Mullaghmore. No one will ever think to look for you there. It hasn't been used in years. You'll be close enough to act when Shane comes up with something and you'll be far enough away from the mess you're in here."

Declan nodded. "Hopefully you've cleaned up since the last time I saw Mullaghmore."

Fintan grimaced and Declan realized the insensitivity of his comment. The last time he'd seen the McGuire estate was the night Black Shuck had been wiped out and Eamon McGuire had died.

"Sorry," he said. "I didn't mean to—"

"Forget it. We need to get moving," Fintan said, as he pushed himself towards the door. "My pilot will get my jet ready and then we'll be off. You can be safe in County Monaghan by this time tomorrow."

CHAPTER FORTY-SEVEN

6:53 a.m. Eastern Time – Thursday
Piney Ridge Trailer Park
White Sulphur Springs, West Virginia

Nate Crickard knew that he was many things to many different people. To his thirteen-year-old son he was a father, or at least he had tried to be. To his ex-wife he was a deadbeat dad with a drinking problem. To his boss, Karl Lindgren, Executive Chef of the Greenbrier Resort, he was one of seven sous chefs, which translated to peon. To the staff at the VA Medical Center in Beckley, he was a veteran; and to untold thousands of Americans he was a patriot for his service to his country. He'd been called all of these names and more, but one thing he'd never been called was a traitor.

Sitting alone in the single-wide trailer that he called home, a bottle of Jack Daniel's beside him, fingers stroking the gray beard he'd grown during his first vacation in five years, he felt like a traitor to his country and he felt betrayed. He set the latest edition of the *Lewisburg Mountain Messenger* down on the cheap particle board coffee table in front of him and read the words again to be sure he hadn't imagined them. *Terrorist sought in connection with bombing and deaths on the loose in Greenbrier County?* was still emblazoned in bold black letters at the bottom corner of the page, over a photo of the suspect.

"Goddammit!" he swore out loud and threw the half-full glass he'd been drinking from onto the newspaper. A rust-colored stain soaked quickly through the paper. This was just his luck. How was it possible that everything he touched literally turned to excrement in front of his eyes? Was it damned bad luck or was he just flat-out damned? He slammed his fist down, cracking the particle board, and swore again as pain shot through his hand and up his arm. For the last ten years of his life, things had gone from bad to worse.

The downward spiral had begun when he had left the Marine Corp where he'd served for over a decade in the 2nd Reconnaissance Battalion, after he'd badly beaten a man he'd found sleeping with his wife. After a court martial, the choices had been made clear; resign his commission with the special operations battalion known as Marine Force Recon and never speak of the matter again, or receive a dishonorable discharge and a two-year prison sentence. He'd chosen the former and then watched as his wife packed up and took their then one-year-old son to live with her bruised and battered boyfriend in Charleston, South Carolina where, as far as he knew, they still lived.

He'd like to have said that things got better after that, but he'd be lying. He'd moved back to White Sulphur Springs where he'd been born and raised and where the employment for unskilled workers was limited to putting nuts on bolts in nearby factories or taking out the trash and maintaining the grounds of the Greenbrier Hotel. Nobody cared that he could break apart an M4A1 rifle in less than fifteen seconds or that he could put a single round between the eyes of a target from hundreds of yards away.

After choosing the Greenbrier, he'd slowly worked his way into the good graces of the hotel's Executive Chef and earned promotions from dishwasher to line cook to sous chef and another forty dollars a week, bringing his take home pay to just over three hundred. Somewhere in between, he'd gained fifty pounds and been diagnosed with type 2 diabetes and neuropathy, which often left his hands and feet feeling numb. The doctors at the VA had told him that his drinking would kill him and he'd told them to shove off. It wasn't like he wanted to live anyway, he just lacked the courage to pull the trigger and end it.

The last good memories he had were of his days in the marine corp running black operations in countries like Iraq, Somalia and Yugoslavia, or whatever they were calling it this week. For years he'd entertained his coworkers at the Greenbrier with tales of bloody daring and steel testicles, and for their part they'd smiled and nodded, allowing him his illusions of grandeur, or so they thought.

For that reason he'd jumped at the opportunity when he'd received a phone call from an old friend, a fellow Special Forces man with the British army, offering him a chance to work side by side again. The last time they'd met was a NATO mission in Kosovo in 1999 and Dean Lynch was one of the few people he'd kept in contact with over the years of his exile.

To the best of his knowledge the Brit had no idea of the circumstances in which he'd left the marines or the shambles in which he found his life. If he did, then he'd never mentioned it, which was fine by Nate. In their occasional e-mails, which Nate read at the Greenbrier County Public Library every Wednesday on his day off, they swapped bloody stories and traded barbs, with Nate always signing off, *God shave the Queen.*

The +44 country code in front of the calling number had caused him to look twice at the caller ID on his night stand and the British accented voice on the line when he'd picked up had come as a complete surprise. Dean Lynch now worked in the private sector and had needed help locating a specific individual who was thought to be hiding somewhere in the vicinity of Roanoke, Virginia. Lynch couldn't tell him who the man was or why he was wanted, and at the time, Nate hadn't cared. It was a chance to forget the pathetic existence he called a life and to be a marine again, even if it was only for a day or two.

Now, looking down at the image of a suspect in an international crime, he cursed himself for not paying more attention to the national media and realized all he'd been was a convenient patsy in the right geographic location. *In the right place at the right time,* he thought.

With the help of some other veterans he knew from the VA, Nate had identified four likely areas for a hideout. With the promise of good money and the excitement of reliving the old days, they'd fanned out and watched the areas until the man they were looking for had shown up. Then, together with Lynch, Nate had cornered the suspect, whom Lynch had assured him was extremely dangerous, and they'd managed to take him down without firing a shot, a fact that Nate wasn't all that happy about. He'd just as soon have had the whole thing hit the fan and just maybe he'd have caught a bullet and gone down shooting.

He would certainly have preferred that to feeling like he'd betrayed his country and realizing that he'd been used by a man he'd thought was his friend. Now a man that the newspaper said was guilty of countless murders on U.S. soil was safe in the air, having been hustled away in the middle of the night by Lynch at the behest of some bigwig whose name Nate had never been given and whom he'd never been allowed to see.

I should've known better. That limey bastard better never show his face near me again. I'll kill him and display his decapitated head. Nate's face flushed two shades of red and he unscrewed the cap on the bottle of Jack, taking a long swig directly from the bottle and exhaling loudly as it burned all the way down into his stomach. *I can still fix this,* he thought, looking at the Washington D.C. phone number listed at the end of the article. The paper identified the number as that of a taskforce that had been setup to find and arrest the suspect, a man named Declan McIver. Surely the FBI could make contact with the authorities in other countries and they could intercept the plane when it landed, wherever it landed.

Why Lynch's employer had cared so much about the fate of an Irish terrorist was beyond him. Who knew why the micks did anything? All Nate Crickard cared about was setting things right and maybe, just maybe, he could salvage some of his former honor in the process. He took another sip from the bottle and screwed on the lid before picking up the phone and dialing the number.

CHAPTER FORTY-EIGHT

"The boy is a danger, Abu," Anzor Kasparov said. "All he has done for the last two days is stare at his brother's body. He is making the others nervous."

"Vakha was a good soldier. But Sharpuddin, he is no longer one of us," Ruslan Baktayev said, as he stood at the back door of the abandoned welding service with Kasparov and looked into the fenced-in lot behind the building. Baktayev assumed that at some point in the past valuable equipment had been stored on the lot because wooden pallets had been hung across the entire fence to keep anyone from seeing what was inside. Rusted strands of barbed wire prevented people from climbing over and signs reading b*eware of dogs* had been placed throughout the property. Whatever had once been there was now long gone. Only three empty sea containers and stacks of rusted junk remained. At the mouth of one of the sea containers, Sharpuddin Daudov knelt, looking mournfully into the trailer where the bodies of his brother and two other men lay.

"I will talk to him," Kasparov said, and started forward.

"No," Baktayev said, holding up his arm to stop Kasparov. "We don't have time for this. I will deal with him myself, but later."

Kasparov nodded. Baktayev turned back inside. "Albek," he

said to a bearded man who sat near a workbench covered with Kalashnikov rifles. The man looked up. "Anzor and I are leaving now. We will be gone for most of the day. Do not let Sharpuddin leave under any circumstances."

"What do I do if he tries?"

"Stop him. Any way you can."

Albek nodded. "I will take care of it, General. Where are you going?"

"To do some reconnaissance."

11:34 a.m. Eastern Time
Southbound on Rt. 40 – Main St.
Victoria, Virginia

Baktayev craned his neck as Kasparov drove through a small, desperate-looking town made up of empty brick storefronts with haphazardly hung *out of business* banners, sidewalks with clumps of weeds growing between joints in the concrete, and medians with tall, uncut grass. Every building in the one mile stretch of real estate that was marked as *Main Street* had an antiquated and uncared for appearance, even the court-like building marked *City Hall*. Overall, Baktayev was surprised. This was the kind of place that he was used to seeing in cities throughout Russia, not the kind of place he had expected to encounter in the United States of America, a country as famous for its wealth as it was infamous for its military excursions around the world. "What happened here?" he asked.

Kasparov shrugged. "A drug called meth, General. The Americans are their own worst enemies. The manufacturing jobs that supported areas like this left for places in other countries with cheaper workers and the idle minds and hands of those who lived here found solace in drugs and alcohol."

"Hmm."

Kasparov turned left and entered a residential area as the town itself came to an end. Here the situation seemed much the same. Small houses with unkempt yards and broken down cars dotted the ill-maintained streets. "This is where I live."

Baktayev sat forward and looked at a one-floor, wood-sided house that appeared to be no bigger than two, maybe three rooms at the most. Tall trees that loomed over the property had covered the exterior of the house in a brownish dust, and a cracked concrete porch with two plastic lawn chairs led to a badly dented screen door.

Kasparov pulled the white cargo van he was driving into the property's pine needle covered driveway and shifted the vehicle into reverse. Backing out, he returned in the direction they had come and said, "I moved here five years ago. I knew that I had chosen the perfect place when I received your first letter from Sheikh Kahraman."

Baktayev nodded. "You've done well, Anzor."

A mile after making a right back onto the main road through the town of Victoria, Kasparov pulled the vehicle to the side of the road a few dozen yards away from a one-story brick building with narrow, metal-rimmed windows. It was clear from the obvious disrepair of the exterior that it suffered from the same blight as the rest of the town. Baktayev smiled as he read the sign that stood in the building's foreground.

"W.N. Page Junior High School," he said aloud. "Praise be to Allah and his servant Sheikh Kahraman. It is perfect."

"Wait until you see the inside."

CHAPTER FORTY-NINE

2:49 p.m. Local Time – Thursday
Over The Atlantic Ocean
500 Miles from Waterford Airport – Ireland

Constance gripped the upholstered armrest tighter, her face as white as her knuckles, as turbulence bumped the Embraer Legacy 500. She had never been comfortable on airplanes but had finally gotten used to the large commercial jetliners they'd frequented in their travels. The smaller business class jet they were currently on seemed to have to reawakened her fear. Declan smiled at her. "It'll be grand," he mouthed.

Compared to the average commercial airliner the plane belonging to Fintan's company, McGuire & Lyons Industries, was testimony to the expense of private aviation. Its interior was a palette of soft shades of gray and featured plush leather seating, multiple LED monitors for both in-flight entertainment and corporate duties, lay-flat accommodations for overnight trips, and a generous number of windows big enough to give the cabin an open and airy feeling. It was easily the most comfortable and well-equipped aircraft Declan had ever seen.

"We should be in Waterford within the hour," he said, looking across at his wife, trying to be reassuring. She managed a smile but said nothing. On top of her fear of flying and everything else that had happened, she hadn't slept since the previous day. He knew that she had to be near rock bottom both emotionally and physically. Even once they landed in Waterford, there was still a three hour drive north to County Monaghan before she'd be able to rest. The jet lurched violently, causing their drinks to turn over, spilling liquor and water across the lavish wooden surface of the collapsible table standing in between their seats. Constance hurriedly unbuckled her seat belt and rushed towards the lavatory at the rear of the cabin.

Fintan opened his eyes and looked over from the seat across the aisle as the door slammed closed. "Will she be alright?"

"Aye," Declan said vacantly. "It's been a rough couple of days, so."

"Aye, sounds like it."

Declan had told Fintan and his assistant Dean Lynch about everything that had happened, on the first leg of their flight. They'd left the U.S. at 3 a.m. Eastern time via a small airport located in Bath County, Virginia, just over the state line from Declan's cabin, and had traveled six hours to the Azores, where they had refueled the plane before leaving again for Ireland.

The lavatory door opened and Constance came out, retaking her seat shyly. "Sorry. I thought I was going to be sick."

Fintan spoke first. "It's alright, love. Soon enough you'll be in the care of the staff at the McGuire family's country home. You'll be back to tip top in a matter of hours. You can put all of this mess behind you for a while."

"Thank you for your hospitality," she said, without making eye contact. "I think I'd just like to get some sleep."

"Understood. You'll have your choice of seven bedrooms all with warm sheets right out of the dryer."

Declan leaned back in his seat and closed his eyes. He still felt bad about her being involved, but he tried to keep self-doubt from overtaking him. Maybe she'd have been happier if she'd married someone else. Maybe he should have known better than to think that his life could ever be normal. Maybe the Beatles wouldn't have broken up if he hadn't joined the IRA when he was fourteen. That line of thinking was absurd given their current situation and he banished the thoughts from his head. They were counterproductive and would do nothing to help. He was determined to identify the leaders of the forces against them, and once he found them, he would find a way to exploit their weaknesses and bring them down.

While he would never say that his years in the IRA were good times–he certainly carried the scars and the guilt of the wrong he'd done–he couldn't say that in some ways he wasn't thankful for them. It was those formative years that had made him the man he was today, the kind of man who could survive the situation he currently found himself in. It was what he had been trained to do. Kidnappings, assassinations, bombings, any means necessary to bring his target crashing down from the bottom up. It was state-sponsored terrorism, Soviet style.

His thoughts were interrupted when the door to the pilot compartment swung open and banged loudly against the wall. He opened his eyes to see Dean Lynch stride towards them, his expression serious.

"We have a problem, governor."

All eyes were on the former British paratrooper and retired Irish Garda as he took a seat in front of Fintan, across the aisle from Declan.

"Captain Cummings just received word from ground support that we're to be boarded as soon as we land. Apparently your situation has gone public and someone in the States has informed the authorities in Ireland. It seems our aircraft being registered in Ireland and having taken off near locations associated with you was enough to attract someone's attention," he finished, looking at Declan.

Fintan tapped the screen of his smartphone. "I dare say it has gone public, old son," he said, handing the phone to Declan. "It looks like your friends have decided to enlist the aid of the public at large in their search for you even more so than they already have."

Declan tapped the screen and the phone's BBC News app came to life, displaying the headline: *Former IRA terrorist officially named a suspect in US bombing; murders of Israeli and lead investigator.*

He moved a hand through his hair as he thumbed through the article containing two paragraphs that identified him as a former member of a Provisional Irish Republican Army unit that once targeted the city of London in a plot to bring down the British Government, a plot that had been abandoned in 1993 when the Black Shuck Unit had been targeted and killed by their own.

"I guess Shane couldn't delay them any longer," Fintan said.

"Apparently not. It says here that I'm wanted for taking part in the Brighton bombing in 1984."

Constance's face was ashen. The bombing had taken place at the Grand Hotel in Brighton, England on October 12th 1984 and was an attempt by the Provisional IRA to assassinate then Prime Minister Margaret Thatcher. The attack had largely gone as planned and five people in Thatcher's party had been killed, with a further thirty-one injured. Thatcher herself had narrowly escaped injury. "Are you?" Constance asked incredulously.

"No. I was only fifteen at the time. I was still taking pot shots at passing motorcades. I guess they decided to fancy things up a bit in hopes of convincing folks I'm a really bad guy."

"A bit of media make believe, more than likely," Fintan said. "Da' was all over the bombing in Brighton, but you had nothing to do with it. I guess it could be safely said that that was before your time. Might as well pin the Mountbatten and Warrenpoint attacks on you as well. What were you then? Ten years old? Old enough, I suppose."

Declan shot him the middle finger and mouthed a good natured *screw you.*

The attacks Fintan was referring to had occurred in August of 1979 and had resulted in the assassination of Lord Louis Mountbatten, a member of the Royal Family, as he made for Donegal Bay in Ireland aboard his yacht, and eighteen soldiers in the British Army's Parachute Regiment as they had approached Narrow Water Castle near the border town of Warrenpoint in Northern Ireland. In total, the two separate attacks were responsible for twenty-two deaths and had been the single greatest loss of life for the British Army during the Troubles.

"This might be a joke to all of you, but I'm not laughing!" Constance said, her voice shrill, tears in her eyes.

"You're right. You're right," Declan said, reaching out to her. "It's not funny and we're not laughing about it. A lot of people died on those days, but I had nothing to do with it. These people that are after us are just trying to make me look as bad as possible."

She pushed his hands away. "We're going to be raided by a SWAT team when we land! Declan, you're going to be arrested and taken to jail, and probably me too, if they don't just shoot us dead!" She stood up and looked around frantically as if there was some way off the plane.

"It's okay," Declan said, standing to meet her and placing his hands on her shoulders. "They're not going to shoot us unless we put up a fight."

"But if they arrest you, they'll take you back," she said, embracing him and crying, "and those people will find a way to kill you."

She was right. He would be taken back to the U.S., but he doubted he'd ever make it to trial.

As if he could read minds, Fintan said, "She's right, mate. You and I both know there'd never be a trial. You'd meet with an unfortunate gang riot in some prison somewhere, or else there'd be a bad traffic accident while they were transporting you. Something like that, anyway. Might even accuse you of trying to escape and just shoot you in the back."

Constance sobbed into Declan's T-shirt.

"How long 'til we land?" Fintan asked Lynch, who stood and walked quickly toward the cockpit.

"Thirty minutes, Governor," he answered as he reemerged a few seconds later, shutting the door behind him.

"Tell Captain Cummings to call ground support and arrange it so that we'll be landing from the east. I have an idea."

"Yes, sir," Lynch said, and disappeared back into the cockpit.

Declan looked at Fintan and Constance lifted her head to do the same.

"This plane was built specially for me," he said. "Cost a bloody fortune and it sits most of the time, but it may just have been worth it after all. Help me up."

Constance moved away from Declan, wiping her eyes on her sleeve, and grabbed hold of the two forearm crutches Fintan supported himself with when he walked. Declan took hold of Fintan's hands and lifted him, supporting him with a hand under each arm as Constance strapped a cane around each of his forearms.

Making his way slowly towards the rear of the jet, Fintan said, "In most jets the staircase is at the front, but I had it installed in the rear on this one because of my condition."

Declan thought back to when they'd entered the plane and Fintan was right. They had entered on a ramp from the rear of the plane. He hadn't thought much about it at the time, but now it was obvious to him that it was because of Fintan's occasional use of a wheelchair.

"My da' was a big fan of Mr. Cooper's apparently successful jump back in the early seventies. You remember that, love?" Fintan said, looking at Constance with a smile.

"Yeah, D.B. Cooper. What American doesn't? 1972 I think— wait a minute," Constance said, stopping suddenly. "You're not suggesting that we jump out of this plane, are you?"

"No, of course not, love," Fintan said, continuing to smile, "not all of us, anyway. Just Declan. He's the one they're after."

"There's no way! Nobody even knows if Cooper survived! His money washed up in a river! Declan, you can't seriously consider this!"

Declan kept moving towards the rear of the plane. "It's a moot point unless you have a parachute," he said, looking over his shoulder at Fintan.

"Well, it just so happens," Fintan said, opening a door next to the lavatory, "that I have several. Like I said, Da' was a fan and more than a bit paranoid. As the wealthiest member of the 'Ra's army council, he had good reason. The company jet back then was an old Boeing, not that different from the one Cooper hijacked."

"But your dad wasn't even involved in the company. Your uncle ran it." said Declan.

Fintan's company, McGuire & Lyons Industries, founded by his great-grandfather and a business partner, had been around since the late 1800s and had made the family a fortune during the heyday of shipbuilding in Belfast's harbors. The company had since branched out and was involved worldwide in a plethora of technical fields and was among the top industrial engineering firms in the world. Declan didn't know how many people the company employed or how much its annual revenue was, but he wouldn't be surprised to learn that it was in the thousands and hundreds of millions respectively.

"True, but that didn't stop Da' from taking advantage of its resources," Fintan said, "much to my uncle's chagrin. Da' was convinced the Brits would try to assassinate him if they found out who he was. He kept emergency preparations everywhere, including parachutes on the plane."

"Christ, Fintan, they've got to be what, at least twenty years old?"

"No, not actually, I suffered a fit of paranoia of my own once, like father, like son, I suppose. I had Lynch replace them with the latest and greatest about six years ago. He's maintained them ever since."

"This is mad," Declan said, smiling, as he took one of the black-bagged chutes out of the storage compartment and checked it over.

"But you've never jumped out of a plane! This isn't something you can just do," Constance said, grabbing him by the shoulder as if she could shake him back into his right mind.

"Actually, I have, over the Wakhan Valley in Afghanistan, multiple times. Russian special forces insist on all their soldiers being able to jump over any kind of terrain."

"Russians, what are you talking about?" Her face twisted into a painful question.

"I'll explain later," he said, looking at Fintan. "What's the plan?"

"Right then," Fintan said. "The runways in Waterford run east and north. We're going to fly south of the island and circle around it bringing us in from the east. Now we'll have to make a wide turn and that should put us over the southern part of Wales. That's where you'll exit."

"That'll put me on the mainland where I can link up with Shane."

"Exactly. It's probably barking mad, but it's the best plan we've got unless you fancy a trip to Mountjoy Prison or some such."

"Aye, it's mad."

"And what about me?" Constance said. "They're looking for me, too, and I'm not jumping out of this plane!"

"I think we can get by with that. While I'm sure they'd love to get their hands on you it appears they're assuming you're going to be with Declan."

"And you didn't actually see anything. All you know is what I've told you. The best they could hope for would be to use you against me and that would be extremely difficult with all of this going public," Declan said, turning his attention from Constance to Fintan. "Can you get her by the police with the French passport I have for her?"

"This whole thing is a crapshoot, to be honest, but I am a member of parliament. That'll give me a lot of leverage. Once they see you're not on board I'll insist they got a bogus tip and proceed to throw a real fit. As long as her French is good and the paperwork is realistic, we should be grand."

"Her French is fluent and the paperwork is the real deal."

"Then we're golden, old son."

"Quit talking about me like I'm not even here. This whole thing is insane," Constance said, moving between Declan and Fintan. "You can't be serious!" She stood perfectly still, staring him directly in the eye. Declan could tell from her expression that she was feeling both desperation and fear, a volatile mixture.

"Look, it's like Fintan says," he said, taking her by the shoulders and trying his best to sound reassuring. "If they catch me, I'll be extradited back to the U.S. and I'll never make it to trial. Abe's dead. Levi's dead. I'm the only one left that knows Baktayev is in the U.S. If I'm out of the way, then there's no one left to stop them. Whoever these people are, they didn't break Baktayev out of prison for his company. They have plans for him and he's only good at one thing: killing innocent people."

Slowly she backed away and took her seat without another word. He'd won this argument because there really wasn't any other way out. Neither option was any good, but he'd much rather take his chances with a risky jump out of a plane than sit around waiting to see who would stick a knife between his ribs in an American jail.

Twenty five minutes later Declan sat on the floor near the rear of the plane with the parachute rig secured around him. He'd changed into a black jumpsuit and held a plastic helmet and goggles. He could see the sun glinting off of the vast ocean below through the oval windows as the plane made its descent. In a short amount of time the deep blue would change to the rocky cliffs of Wales and the jet would make the sharp left-hand turn that would take them around towards Waterford.

Dean Lynch exited the cockpit and walked to the back of the plane. Fintan got slowly to his feet, with the aid of his crutches, and followed.

"Captain says we're about five minutes out, mate. You sure you're ready for this?"

Declan glanced over and saw Constance place her head in her hands. "Aye. No other way that I can figure. If I'm on this plane when it lands, we're all in a lot of trouble."

"You can say that again," Fintan said, arriving behind Lynch. "I'll have a damn hard time explaining that to the *Dáil*. If we ever get back to the U.S. I'll be sure and pay Mr. Crickard a friendly visit. It had to be him that gave us away. He's the only one that ever saw Declan."

"You'll have to get in line, Governor," Lynch said. "I'm sure there's a long list of people that would like ol' Nate's head on a pole. Myself included, after this go round."

"I'll let you have a go at him for the both of us—" he was interrupted by the voice of the captain over the plane's intercom.

"Three minutes, sir. I'm bringing her in low and slow."

"Christ this is dangerous," Lynch breathed as the engines whined. "If the plane slows too much it'll stall and we'll all end up in the Irish Sea or worse, plastered into the side of a Welsh mountain."

"Cummings is the best, old friend." Fintan said. "All that's missing for him is some bullets flying at us."

The lopsided grin that stretched across Lynch's face told Declan that he knew Fintan was right. Declan had never met Cummings until they'd arrived at the airport, but he'd been told the man was good, a former RAF fighter pilot now employed privately by McGuire & Lyons.

"Alright," Lynch said, looking at Declan. "This part of the plane seals off from the rest, so it'll just be you and I back here." He reached up and clasped a carabiner to a metal rod above the exit ramp. Although he wasn't jumping, he had a full harness and chute on just in case. "I'll make sure the door's closed after you're out. There's no internal stairs so you won't have to worry about that. The handicap ramp retracts into the underbelly of the jet, so this is just a wide open hole. Just dive straight down and you'll clear fine. Inside your pack there are several things you're going to need. For starters, there's a shovel to bury your rig with once you're on the ground. You don't want a parachute blowing around the moor, might cause a lot of questions. The second item you need to know about is a satellite phone. It's encrypted, but I'd still limit the usage. Let us know when you're on the ground and safe. The rest of the items are self-explanatory. Got it?"

"Aye, got it."

"Grand. Let's do it." Lynch gripped the lever that would open the door and waited for the captain's signal.

"Hey, Dec," Fintan called. "Look on the bright side, if you don't make it, Constance will be free to date." His grin was ear to ear.

"See you on the ground, old son," Declan said, grasping him hard on the shoulder. "And hands off my wife, or you'll need a lot more than crutches to get around."

He let go and Fintan moved back towards the main cabin, sliding the door closed behind him.

"Now or never," said Cummings over the intercom. Lynch pulled the lever and the door opened inwards, revealing a rectangular shaped hole where the handicapped ramp descended for the plane's passengers to unload. The sound of the engines outside was deafening and cold air rushed into the tiny compartment from the open door. Lynch held tight to the railing along the wall.

Declan pulled the goggles on his head down over his eyes and crossed himself as he unhooked his carabiner. He gripped each side of the doorway and with a *one-two-three* motion, pulled himself out of the plane. In a fraction of a second the noise of the engines disappeared, replaced by the sound of the earth rushing towards him as his body entered terminal velocity.

CHAPTER FIFTY

The Constitutional Condominiums stood six blocks northeast of the U.S. capitol building and overlooked both Stanton Park and the medievally designed Imani Temple. The eighteenth century brick building with its aged stone accents and arcuate windows was four stories tall, six stories wide and housed twenty-four one-floor, two bedroom apartments, all occupied by employees of the United States Senate, or in the case of David Kemiss, the senator himself.

Kemiss massaged his temples with one hand as he sat in the fourth floor, fully furnished corner unit the U.S. taxpayers were providing for his lengthy stays in the nation's capital. The residence was small by his standards, but luxurious, and it was all he needed during the week. Breakfast, lunch and dinner were served at the capitol building and he took advantage of it as he worked long hours.

He stood up from the leather sofa, crossed the room to a doorway leading into a small bathroom and turned on the faucet. He was tired, having barely slept in nearly five days. The dark circles around his eyes looked familiar. He was used to late nights, and little sleep. Politics in the United States had become so divisive over his last term that negotiations and filibusters lasting into the early morning were common. Thankfully the crisis he was currently handling, the reason for his complete lack of sleep, would soon be over. A tip called into the FBI hotline had placed Declan McIver on a plane belonging to an Irish entrepreneur and by now, the Irish Garda would have taken him into custody and would be making the necessary arrangements to have him transferred back to the U.S. Hopefully, there wouldn't be any lengthy delays over whether the death penalty would be sought in any trial. As far as he was concerned, the Federal Government could guarantee that McIver wouldn't get more than a slap on the wrist because, as he saw it, the chances of him making it to trial were slim.

He splashed cold water over his face and toweled off his hands before exiting the bathroom through a different door, into his bedroom. He pulled back the sheets on the king-sized bed and kicked off his shoes. As he sat on the edge of the bed and prepared to lie down, he heard the sound of his cell phone ringing inside the computer bag he'd left in the living room. He crossed the tiled bathroom floor quickly and retrieved the phone from the bag.

"Tell me they've got him," he said, as he answered the call.

He gripped the phone, his body rigid, as he listened to the answer. Placing a hand to his forehead, he sighed in aggravation. "How can one man keep dodging the complete manpower of every government agency sent after him?"

"I don't know, sir," the voice of Robert Evers said. "The tipster must've been mistaken. It looks like the United States Government is going to owe the executives at McGuire & Lyons Industries a big apology."

"So we'll send them a big basket of fruit!"

There was silence on the other end of the phone line. Kemiss held the phone away from his head and took a deep breath. "So we're back to square one?" he asked, when he'd collected himself.

"It looks that way, sir. I'm sorry to have disturbed you with this tip just for it to turn out to have been bogus. We'll go back over everything we have and I'll let you know what we come up with, but until then, I'm afraid he's still out there somewhere."

"Thank you, Mr. Evers," Kemiss said, with a tone of resignation.

"Sir, if I may?" Evers said, before Kemiss could hang up.

"Go on."

"I hope the people of Virginia realize the kind of man they have representing them in the Senate. And I'm not saying that to kiss ass. You've been an integral part of this process and without you we'd be much further behind this scumbag than we currently are. I hope you'll use this in your next campaign. Men of your integrity are hard to come by in Washington these days."

Kemiss bathed in the glow of the compliment for a moment before responding. If only he could use this in a campaign. "Thank you, Mr. Evers. Please call me with any updates as soon as you have them."

"Of course, sir," he heard Evers say, as he moved the phone away from his ear and closed it. He turned around and caught sight of his reflection in the window behind his desk. He looked even more tired than he had moments ago in the bathroom mirror. With Seth Castellano dead, he didn't know how much longer he could keep up the charade he was putting on. He crossed the bathroom floor, quickly undressed, and slid into the bed.

As soon as he'd closed his eyes, his phone rang again.

"David," a familiar voice said as he picked up the line. It was Lukas Kreft.

Kemiss adjusted himself in the bed and took a slow breath. "What is it now?"

"Baktayev's made his choice. We need all the documentation there is on it, now."

"Okay. Okay. I'll take care of it."

CHAPTER FIFTY-ONE

3:56 p.m. Local Time – Thursday
Pembrokeshire Coast National Park
Wales, United Kingdom

Declan dragged himself slowly up onto the beach, grabbing handfuls of wet sand with each reach. Cold, salty waves washed over him, doing their part to push him ashore. He stopped and turned over onto his back, breathing heavily. The late afternoon sun peered down from behind a springtime haze. He'd survived the jump from the plane and the free fall down; it was the landing that had nearly killed him. As soon as he'd opened his parachute he'd known he was in trouble. At four thousand feet, the wind had been blowing in from the southeast, up the rocky Welsh coastline, pushing anything brazen enough to be aloft to the west and into the Irish Sea.

Despite his best efforts to steer the ram-air chute onto one of the several islands that dotted the coastline, nature had won and he'd ended up taking a swim. In the northwest corner of Europe, early spring was no time for swimming. The temperature had to be near forty degrees and, coupled with the surging wind, it felt even colder. The risk of hypothermia notwithstanding, the riptides had been merciless and had grabbed a hold of his chute as soon as he'd hit the water, like the tentacles of some vengeful sea beast. Had Dean Lynch not so diligently prepared the two escape chutes, he'd have been pulled out to sea and drowned. Instead, the six inch bowie knife secured to the harness around his waist had allowed him to cut the tangled lines of the nylon noose. *So much for burying the parachute so it won't be found.*

Dragging himself the rest of the way onto the beach he became aware of a sharp pain in his right wrist. He cleared the salt water from his eyes to see that it was swollen badly. As he stood and took stock of himself a tear in the left leg of his jumpsuit caught his attention. Leaning down and doing his best to spread the polyester with his one good hand, he revealed a twelve inch gash on the outside of his calf. Blood dotted the sand beneath him, but he felt no pain; apparently his legs were numb from the frigid water. He didn't remember hitting anything as he'd struggled to swim ashore, but he must have, more than likely one of the many jagged rocks that populated the coastline like naturally formed Czech hedgehogs awaiting an invading army.

Slowly his legs began to regain feeling and he limped over to a nearby rock. Sitting against it he released the black skydiving rig from his torso. The main compartment that had been strapped to his back was now empty except for the ends of the severed nylon cords that had once held the parachute in place. Strapped to his front had been the tightly packed twelve inch by twelve inch compartment that held what little equipment the rig allowed a skydiver to bring along. Standing up and setting the rig against the rock, he unzipped the compartment and began removing the items Lynch had packed. On top was a Glock 17, two extra magazines and a suppressor, secured together with a Velcro strap. *A man after my own heart,* Declan thought, smiling to himself as he set the weapon aside. Next out was a compact first aid kit, followed by a foldaway shovel the size of a fist, a roll of paper money secured with a rubber band, a Thuraya satphone and a firmly packed piece of thin, square nylon with a another Velcro strap around it. He turned the square over in his hands wondering what it was. As he undid the Velcro strap, the square fell loose and began to unfold. Shaking it the rest of the way open he was surprised to see a miniature duffel bag complete with two handles and a zipper. *I love you, Lynch* he mouthed jokingly as he unzipped it and began placing the gear inside, leaving only the first aid kit out.

Opening the first-aid kit and removing the jumpsuit with

one hand was slow going, but he eventually managed to clean the jagged laceration with antiseptic and wrap sterile gauze around it, using the tiny role of tape included in the kit to secure it in place and keep pressure against it at the same time. It was far from perfect but hopefully it would hold until he could get some proper treatment. Using the bowie knife, which he'd hung onto after cutting the chute loose, he sliced up the black nylon straps that held the rig together and gingerly wrapped them around his right wrist, securing the brace with more of the tape. Having inspected his wrist as well as possible, he was reasonably sure it wasn't broken, just sprained. The pressure from the makeshift brace was already beginning to make it feel better, the movement in his fingers was returning. He redressed in what was left of the black jumpsuit. He grimaced as he pulled on the wet clothes, the wind making it feel as though being naked would be preferable. He shivered almost uncontrollably as the material clung to his body, the damp soaking through his hasty bandages.

He pushed the cold out of his mind and forced himself to focus on his surroundings. In front of him was a half-moon shaped bay, flanked on three sides by tall moss-covered rocks topped with wiry grass that had been flattened by the constant wind, its color deadened to a sickly yellow by the clinging winter. Behind him one of the many offshore islands jutted out of the water. Atlantic Puffins massed on the rocky formation, some diving for fish, others hovering low above the water in search of a meal, the sound of their wings flapping furiously barely audible over the howling wind. He knew he was on the coast of Wales, a lot further west then he had hoped, but he didn't know exactly where along the seven hundred and fifty miles of coastline he was positioned. He'd have to climb out of the bay to get a better look at the landscape, a prospect that made him groan with anticipated pain.

Not wanting to delay the inevitable he scanned the rocks for the easiest way up and found it at his eleven o'clock. He stuffed the contents of the first aid kit into the duffel bag, zipped it up and walked the short distance across the beach to the edge of the cliff. The spot he'd chosen switch-backed several times and the surfaces were covered with heavy moss or course grass, meaning he'd have good traction.

Sometime later the moss had proven slicker than he'd expected, forcing him onto all fours at several points during his climb. He wasn't sure, but he estimated that it took him nearly an hour to reach the top. Breathing heavily, he struggled onto the plateau and looked east. All he could see along the horizon was rolling hills broken occasionally by jagged rocks. No buildings. No roads. Not even an old goat path. Overhead the sun was obscured almost completely by the low clouds, an ivory orb the only evidence of its existence. He guessed by its location that it was nearly five o'clock in the afternoon. At best, he had two hours until dark.

Calling up both his perfect mental map of the British Isles, and of Ireland across the Irish Sea, he decided, based on the location of the airport Fintan's plane had been heading for, that his most likely location was Pembrokeshire and that the large offshore island was Skomer Island. If he was right, he'd eventually meet with the small village of Marloes to the east, if he was wrong he'd meet a sheer cliff leading into the Milford Haven Waterway and be forced to turn north, having wasted a lot of the remaining daylight. There was only one way to find out. Throwing the duffel bag over his shoulder, he walked east.

One hour later the sun was sinking behind the rolling hills, its dying rays hidden by the gathering clouds. A storm was approaching from the east. Declan could see the rainfall many miles ahead of him, the wall of approaching precipitation giving the landscape the appearance of an old oil painting. About a mile from the coastline he'd gotten lucky and found a one lane dirt road heading east. With the injury to his left leg his progress was slow, although he was beginning to think it was due more to sheer exhaustion than the injury. He hadn't slept or eaten since he'd left the United States and with the physical rush that had accompanied his jump from the plane and his fight to survive the landing, his body was feeling the effects. It seemed as though every muscle ached, his head was pounding and his skin was pale, icy to the touch from the onslaught of the Atlantic wind against his wet clothes. He kept his head down in an attempt to keep his face warm, but it made little difference.

Again, for the second time in as many days, he found

himself thankful for the Special Forces training he'd received in Afghanistan and for the lifelong fitness habits it had instilled in him. At the age of forty-one he was in better shape than most twenty-five year olds and it was a good thing, because without it he would not have survived. As he topped a small rise in the dirt road, he glanced up and his eyes settled on a much needed sight.

Directly ahead of him, no more than a mile from his current position, he could see the corrugated steel roofing of several buildings grouped tightly together on the right side of the road. There were no lights visible in the gathering darkness, but at least it was a sign he was heading in the right direction. He quickened his pace as much as possible, invigorated by the thought of a warm place to ride out the coming storm.

Favoring his right leg heavily, he cautiously approached the first of the buildings. A drab sign with white lettering positioned at the three way intersection in the dirt road where the buildings stood announced that they belonged to the Skomer Marine Nature Reserve, confirming his earlier decision that he was on the Marloes Peninsula in southwest Wales. That was good; it meant that the village of Marloes was only about seven or eight miles further to the east, but the thought of walking another seven or eight miles drained his enthusiasm. He decided the hike needed to wait until the morning. He'd take shelter in the Marine Reserve tonight. Perhaps his luck would hold and a worker would have left some food behind; an uneaten lunch or even a pack of wafers would go a long way right now.

He entered the property by walking down a short driveway between two stone buildings that appeared to have been there far longer than the other metal buildings that together made up the complex. Inside the tiny lot enclosed by the buildings there were no lights and the only vehicles were several ATVs in various states of maintenance. Looking over them quickly he realized none of them would be drivable. Standing in the center of what he guessed was a small parking lot he turned three hundred and sixty degrees looking for the building most likely to be the headquarters. There were seven buildings in total, three long and rectangular and four much smaller squares that he surmised were storage buildings. Three foot by four foot hedges were sporadically placed around each building in an effort to bring some life to the cold metal. Like the roofs he'd seen from a distance, the walls of most of the buildings were constructed from grayish corrugated steel, industrial looking windows and doors cut into the sides, a few dark red shutters hanging haphazardly beside some of the windows. He chose the building with the most parking spots and walked to the windowless double doors at the front. The doors were secured with a heavy, padlocked chain. He pulled on the lock in hopes that it was only dummy locked, but it wasn't. He turned and looked to see that the other buildings were all similarly secured. *Damn.*

Reluctantly he bent down and unzipped the duffel bag, withdrawing the Glock 17. With a magazine already loaded, he screwed on the suppressor and chambered a round. Pushing himself tortuously back to his feet he moved to the side of the doors and took aim at the lock. Suddenly a bright light washed over the metal in front of him and he was illuminated by the circular beam. He pulled the Glock close to his body and dived out of the light behind one of the hedges.

Listening carefully, he heard the unmistakable crunch of a gravel road beneath car tires, then the beam of light stopped moving forward. With the roaring wind passing through the joints in the corrugated steel and creating a piercing whistle, he hadn't heard the vehicle approaching. He knew that whoever was driving it had to have seen him. Seconds later he heard a car door open and his suspicions were confirmed.

"Whoever's there, I know you're here. Come out."

The voice was both distinctly Welsh and distinctly female. Declan bent left and right trying to get a look at its owner without revealing his position, but the hedge was too big.

"I know you're here. Come out," the voice repeated. Declan heard a hint of uncertainty, possibly even fear, and he weighed his options. Who was this person, night security? Some sort of caretaker, a camper, or someone else who'd seen him from nearby? He hadn't noticed any houses or campsites and the village was too far away for anyone there to have seen anything.

"Alright, then," the voice sang. "I'll go and tell the police and they'll be round to deal with you shortly. You'd best get back to the moor or wherever you came from. I'd hate to be outdoors on a night like this if I was you."

Declan stashed the Glock in the duffel bag and tugged the zipper closed as he stood and turned towards the vehicle. He couldn't afford to have the police involved and the voice was right, it was bitter cold and only going to get worse as the night progressed. If there was even the slightest chance this person could help him find shelter he had to take it.

"Well, there you are. Finally get done rolling around in the dirt, did you?"

Just beyond the halogen beams, Declan could make out the basic shape of a human. It was obvious from the bulk that she was bundled against the cold. He stepped around the hedge with his empty hands raised to get a better look. Standing behind the open car door as if it might offer her some protection was a young woman, probably in her late twenties, Declan thought. Her cheeks were red from the cold, her hair was covered by a wool stocking cap, and a thick down coat hid the rest of her body from view.

"What the bloody hell are you doing out here anyway?" she asked, eyeing him suspiciously.

"I'm a paraglider," Declan lied. "My rig was blown onto the rocks a few hours ago. I barely made it out alive."

"Well, I expect not in this wind. What kind of bloody trick is that, paragliding in this kind of weather? What're you, mad? You damned extreme sports types. Not an ounce of sense in the lot of you, I'd say."

"Who are you?" Declan asked.

The young woman stepped around the Peugeot she was driving and said, "Hannah Sawyer. I'm the wildlife preservationist here. Just came by to make sure I'd locked up all these doors and they weren't blowin' in the gale. Are you injured?"

Declan was relieved that she seemed to believe his story. "My leg is cut up and my wrist is sprained. Other than that, I'm just exhausted."

"Well, I would expect so, after an ordeal like that," she said, stepping closer. Declan could smell a flowery perfume. "What in the name of Saint David are you doing paragliding in weather like this and in the dark?"

"It was for a new world record. I was attempting to sail around the entire British Isles without stopping. I left from the Firth of Clyde yesterday."

"Wrong time of year for that. Lot of good that record's gonna do you when you're dead. C'mon, let's get you to the village where we can get a better look at your injuries."

Declan breathed easy for the first time in several minutes. "Thank you. That'll be grand. I've some money on me. If you'll just drop me at an inn, I can make my way from there."

"Ah, you'll not find any inns around here that are open this time of year. Tourist season doesn't start for another two months. My dad and I have a place where you can hold up and get some rest. In a day or two I'll give you a ride to Haverfordwest and you can go about getting yourself back home."

"Aye, that's grand. Thank you again."

"Don't thank me yet," she said, with a wry laugh. "You haven't tasted my dad's stew."

Together they climbed into the Peugeot and she shifted through the gears as she turned the car around and drove east towards Marloes. The seven mile drive took about ten minutes over a roughly-maintained road that turned to pavement a few miles outside of the town. Halfway there it had started to rain. Passing a bent metal sign that read *Marloes* in bold, black letters, Declan looked from side to side at the stone cottages that stood barely arm's length from the edge of the one lane road that led into and out of the small village. Through the driving rain he could make out dim lights in some of the homes, but most appeared vacant. He supposed they were vacation homes or rental cottages that saw little use outside of the summer months.

Soon they pulled up to a gray stone house with a rust-colored roof made from what appeared to be clay shingles, and Hannah turned the Peugeot into a narrow gravel parking spot that was just big enough for the compact vehicle. The residence was small; its front yard surrounded by an aging stone wall, Light was visible through two windows beside the wooden front door.

"Well, you'd better give me your name," she said, as she shifted the car into neutral and pulled on the handbrake. "Dad'll want to know what to call you right off."

"Paul Flynn," Declan lied, combining his father's first name and his mother's maiden name. "I really appreciate your hospitality."

"It's nothing. Happens all the time, you lot getting yourselves messed up. The few of us that stay here throughout the year are used to patching people up. Just can't seem to get it through your thick heads that sports are for summertime and daylight."

Declan smiled as they exited the Peugeot. Hannah ran up the gravel path to the front door, the rain horizontal in the wind.

"Well, I found another one, I did," she announced, as she opened the door and walked in, hanging her stocking cap on a peg next to the door. She turned towards Declan and smiled, and he saw she had chestnut brown hair cut just below her ears and huge brown eyes. In the darkness, he'd failed to see how pretty she was.

"You found another wha—? Oh dear," Declan heard an older man's voice say as he stepped into the house. He found himself in the main living area, a brown leather couch in the middle of the floor dividing the living room and the small kitchen where Hannah's father stood with a tea towel in hand. Declan could tell right away that the older man was less enthusiastic about his presence than was his daughter. Drying his hands slowly with the olive green towel, he said roughly, "Rhys Sawyer. And you'd be?"

"Found him at the Reserve, so I did. Says his paraglider crashed," Hannah said, before Declan could respond to her father's question. "His name's Paul Flynn."

Rhys Sawyer stared suspiciously at his guest, his eyes narrowed, and Declan could feel the tension coming from him. He was obviously a great deal older than his daughter, at least sixty, if Declan had to guess. He had dark, narrow eyes bordering on beady, covered by thick white eyebrows. His hairline had receded, and most of his white hair was gone from the top of his head. What was left was thick and unkempt. Unlike his daughter, who was very petite, Rhys was broad-shouldered and carried at least an extra fifty pounds, making him an imposing figure despite his advanced age.

"My daughter has a bad habit of bringing home strays. Unfortunately she refuses to confine the activity to wildlife."

"I'm sorry, sir. I don't mean to impose," Declan said.

"Well, of course you do. You lot with all your fancy gear and immortal attitudes coming down here looking to bounce around and make all kinds of commotion and then when you get yourselves in a mess you look for us regular folk to take you in and patch you up. You got lucky, see, and found the one person out here most likely to do it."

Declan stayed silent, unsure of what to say. He could understand the man's anger. There was a complete stranger standing in his house, someone whose intentions could easily be less than honorable.

"Dad, you're embarrass—"

"Embarrassing you how? You just met him! I've warned you about this, so I have. You cannot bring home every wandering soul you find out there on the moor who just happens to be ruggedly handsome."

Hannah's face flushed a deep red, but Declan couldn't tell if it was anger or embarrassment.

"I apologize for my intrusion, sir. If you could just point me in the direction of an inn or someplace I can wait out the storm, I'll be on my way."

"I've told you already, there's no place open this time of year," Hannah said, as her eyes bored into her father. "I'll drive you back to the Reserve. You can stay there in the office for the night."

"You'll be doing no such thing," Rhys said, his voice a low growl. "My daughter's right, Mr. Flynn, there's no place open. As much as I don't like it, you can stay in our guest cottage out back. Seeing as my daughter insists on ignoring my advice, I may as well keep you in my sight."

Declan was silently grateful. Even though he hadn't seen it, the guest cottage sounded like a slice of heaven. At this point he'd take a barn if it meant he could sleep out of the wind and rain.

"Here, sit down," Hannah said, and she walked into the kitchen and pulled out a chair at the table for him. She kissed her father on the cheek as he stood like a statue, still eyeing Declan. "Were you injured?" Rhys asked, finally exhaling.

"Just a cut on my leg and my wrist is sprained."

"Well, don't you worry a bit," Hannah said. "I'll have you right as rain in no time. Dad's just finished making cawl for supper and afterwards we'll get you all set up out the back."

"We have a small barn out the back that we converted to a cottage a few years back. We rent it out during the tourist season," Rhys said, taking a seat at the table.

"Aye, that sounds grand. Thank you both so much."

The house was warm and the food smelled amazing. The aroma of boiled potatoes, lamb, carrots and bacon filled the air. Declan took a seat at the table across from Rhys and placed his duffel bag at his feet. Looking around at the simple residence, he thought how nice it would be to share such a place with his wife, a simple life, free of the frustrations and complications of his current situation. A fire crackled in the stone fireplace behind him, he could feel the heat on his damp clothes.

"Oh my, your clothes are soaked," Hannah said as she brushed past him.

"I'll get you something dry to wear." Rhys rose from the table and disappeared through a doorway at the far end of the kitchen. Hannah placed a bowl on the table and filled it to the brim with cawl. "Eat, eat," she said, placing a spoon in the bowl. Rhys returned a moment later with a pair of faded blue jeans and a dark red wool shirt.

After he'd eaten three bowls of stew and excused himself for his rudeness, Declan followed as they led him outside to the back of their small lot where a barn with a slanted roof stood. Inside it had been made over into a bedroom, a small bathroom off to the side with just enough room for a sink and a shower. Declan had been right. To a weary traveler, it looked heavenly.

Hannah showed him around the room. "In the summer months it stays rented, always someone from Cardiff or Swansea out here for the hiking or sailing. You know, all that macho stuff you boys are into."

He smiled at her, realizing that she obviously thought he was much younger than he actually was.

"Now, let's see to those injuries," she said.

"Thank you, but it's really not necessary," Declan said. "You've done so much already."

"Oh, don't give me that, you. I'll have none of it. Dad, get my veterinary kit, please."

Rhys sighed audibly and turned back towards the main house.

Her tone of voice was authoritative and, seeing she wasn't going to take no for an answer, Declan gave in. "You'll have to excuse Dad. He's suspicious of everyone."

"He has good reason to be. There are a lot of people out there who aren't very nice."

"Well, I'm a helper. It's what I do. My mum was the same way. Whether it was an injured puffin or a seal, she was always nursing something. She died a few years ago. Dad hasn't been the same since."

Thirty minutes later she had both his wrist and his leg re-bandaged and he already felt better.

"There you go," she said. "Good thing I found you when I did, that leg was pretty bad. Another few hours and you'd have had quite an infection, I expect. You were right about your wrist. It isn't broken at all. A day or two and it'll be fine." She stood up and looked at the shirt and jeans her father had supplied. "Those clothes look like they'll fit you, anyway," she said. "A guy about your age left them here last year. Amazing what people leave behind. We've found everything from cigarettes to foreign money."

"We should leave him be now," Rhys said from his post by the door where he'd been standing guard over his daughter. "I'm sure he needs to rest." Hannah smiled and walked out of the tiny house followed by her father. After they were gone, Declan washed up in the bathroom carefully to avoid his injuries and then, within minutes, he was asleep on the bed, the down comforter pulled up over his head.

CHAPTER FIFTY-TWO

6:42 p.m. Local Time – Thursday
Local Road 1402
Mullaghmore, County Monaghan – Ireland

Constance took a deep breath of damp Celtic air as she stood on one of the many balconies of the seventeenth century mansion owned by the McGuire family. Ivy crept up the sides of the stone house and stretched out along the stone balustrade she was leaning her elbows on, her hands either side of her face. Although she considered herself to be quite well traveled she had never seen any place like this. All of the stone columned buildings of Washington D.C., as awe-inspiring as they could be, couldn't hold a candle to the natural beauty that surrounded her. It was as if nature and man-made things had reached a sort of peace and now lived side by side in harmony.

Upon entering the property, Fintan had explained the layout of the grounds. The mansion stood on over two hundred acres near Mullaghmore, about five miles east of the town of Monaghan. What had once been heavily farmed land now stood empty, home only to the mansion in its northwest corner and to several smaller, but no less atmospheric houses in which the year-round staff lived.

The room Constance had chosen as her own for the duration of her stay was in the mansion's southwest corner and its balcony looked out over the expansive gardens and carefully maintained hedgerows that surrounded the entire house. She'd chosen it because in the distance beyond the gardens a small lake was visible, its water as blue as the ocean they'd crossed just hours before. She imagined the sun glinting off the windswept water and wished Declan could be there with her. She knew that for him, though, this place held many distant memories that he had probably tried to forget. She knew enough about the Troubles to know that many of the IRA's army council had kept homes in places just over the border of the Irish Republic, just far enough to be out of the reach of the British Army or the Royal Ulster Constabulary, the predecessor to Northern Ireland's current police force, the Police Service of Northern Ireland. While the McGuire mansion had obviously been there for many years before the Troubles, and even the war for independence, from what she had garnered from the various conversations she'd heard, Fintan's father had used it as a base of operations for his activities during the thirty year conflict.

She heard a polite knock at the door. "It's open," she said, and listened as someone pushed open the heavy oak door. Moments later Fintan stepped onto the concrete balcony. "Just wanted to see that all your needs had been met, love, and that everything was to your liking."

"It's fine. Thank you."

"There are clean clothes in the closet. I had Mrs. Hogan bring some of her daughter's things that she left behind when she moved to Germany a few years back. They're probably a bit dated, but I think they'll fit."

"I'm sure they'll do fine, thank you. And thank Mrs. Hogan for me if you see her."

Nicola Hogan was one of the staff that lived in the stone houses situated along the narrow gravel lane that led through the grounds to the mansion. When they'd first arrived, the roughly fifty-something woman had seemed delighted at Constance's presence. Now she knew the absence of the woman's daughter was why.

Fintan hovered for just a moment, the silence between them uncomfortable.

"Anything yet?" she finally asked.

He shook his head, knowing what she meant. They had yet to receive word from Declan that he had landed safely and while it hadn't been said yet, they both were beginning to suspect the worst.

"Dinner will be served at seven-thirty in the main dining room directly opposite us and one floor down. I hope you'll join me," he said, as he turned to leave, his movements on the two forearm crutches clumsy.

Constance turned back to the lake as the last rays of the sun fell behind the trees beyond it.

"He'll be grand, you know? He's done this kind of thing before," Fintan said.

Constance turned back to him and forced a smile. "I want to know. I want you to tell me."

"Tell you what, love?"

"About Declan's past. All of it."

Fintan adjusted his crutches and turned back to face her. "I'm sorry to say that I wasn't privy to a lot of it. My role was far more brains than brawn, intelligence gathering and the like. But I'll tell you what I do know."

"Please. I need to understand this. I know a bit about the Troubles, the IRA, their Protestant counterparts. But there seems to be more to this, more to Declan, then the IRA story I'm familiar with."

"Well, love," Fintan said, searching for the correct words. "Things in Ireland during those times were convoluted to say the least. Unless you lived it, it's hard to understand the amount of treachery and double-dealing that was a part of daily life back then. But I suppose there is more to Declan's part than was usual." The words seemed to catch in his throat and she wondered immediately if what he had to say was so bad that it could alter her view of the man she loved. Suddenly she wasn't so sure she wanted to know. But it was too late; he'd already begun to speak.

"For lack of a better analogy, Declan and his mates were like the IRA's version of the Frankenstein monster, and my father, Eamon McGuire, was the mad scientist." Fintan moved back onto the balcony and took a seat on one of the concrete benches that flanked the doorway.

Constance lowered herself onto the balcony floor and sat cross-legged to listen.

"Declan sought out the 'Ra after his parents were killed near their home in Ballygowan by a corrupt constable who was linked to a band of UVF thugs. They'd tried to hide some weapons on his da's farm and had been thrown off. Declan's da' was also a politician deeply opposed to the Troubles and always looking for a way to form a power sharing government between the Catholics and the Protestants. The UVF thought of him as a traitor to his Protestant heritage and his throwing them off his land was the proverbial straw that broke the camel's back. They murdered him and his wife at a fake checkpoint one night.

"I suppose Declan was looking for revenge and a few years later he found it. He was eleven when his folks were murdered, and when he was barely fifteen years old he went looking for their killers. Over the course of the next two years he tracked them down and killed every one of them, with the help of an older boy named Torrance Sands that he'd met in an orphanage in County Down. By seventeen, Declan had taken out eight men that were at least twice his age, most of whom had been killing since the Troubles began in the late sixties."

Constance was in awe as she took in the information. At the age of seventeen she'd been attending governor's school in Savannah, Georgia, and hadn't even been aware that there was a conflict in Northern Ireland.

Fintan continued, "Of course, you don't take out eight paramilitaries and not attract some attention. The attention Declan attracted was that of my father, who took him in as a sort of protégé, if you will; Sands, too. Declan was too young to be an official member of the army, but then so were a lot of the others who were taking part in the conflict. Right away my da' picked him out as something special. He showed an uncanny talent for tactical assaults. He could look at a given situation and within seconds tell you the best avenue of attack and where to strike for the most damage. He could also think on his feet. If an operation went south, and that happened a lot, he reacted fast and adjusted as necessary—most of the time saving the operation and the lives of the men involved in it. For someone of his age and apparent inexperience, it turned some heads. He operated under Da's direction for another year. Then my da' sent him to the Soviets to train. In a lot of ways he was the perfect recruit. He had no living family that could recognize him or worry about him."

"I thought the IRA only used training camps in Libya and such."

"That's mostly true. But Da' had a contact in the Russian special forces, The *Spetsnaz*. A Colonel, some man named Novikov or some such thing. He was in charge of a supposedly top secret unit at the time known as *Vympel*. To the best of my knowledge it was a counter-terrorism unit designed to help the Russian's win their war in Afghanistan, only it didn't operate like a typical counter-terrorism unit. It operated more like the terrorists themselves; bombings, kidnappings, assassinations. Their mission was to significantly destabilize the government of their enemy by attacking its foundation and hopefully causing a collapse from within."

"Why would the Soviets agree to train a foreigner in a top secret unit?"

"Well, you have to remember, by this time it was 1988 and the Soviet Union wasn't in a good way. The collapse had already begun in many parts of the country and there were a lot of military and police units left with absolutely no money or provisions for their soldiers, yet they were expected to carry on in Afghanistan. On top of that, corruption has always been a problem in Russia. I'm told it's even worse now than it used to be. I don't know what Da' paid this Colonel, but I know it was quite a lot. As I'm sure you've noticed, money is one thing my family has in good supply. Da' thought their training would be particularly advantageous in the 'Ra's war with the Brits. He sent twelve men. Only nine returned."

"So Declan fought in Afghanistan for the Russians?"

"I don't know exactly where they trained him for sure. Whatever happened, he came back an entirely different person. Disillusioned, I suppose. By that time there was a full blown power struggle going on in the IRA. Sinn Fein was trying to consolidate power in Belfast and had appointed its incompetent puppets to run the Army units around the North. Da' and several of the other council members didn't like it and were still committed to complete independence from Britain. He used Declan and the other eight to start what he called the Black

Shuck Unit."

"Black Shuck?"

"Aye, it's a legend in southern England about some sort of demon dog that signifies death to any that see it. Da' thought it was funny, a team of Irish freedom fighters dealing out death to their British enemies under a name taken from British folk stories."

Constance nodded her understanding. She'd heard a similar story from Declan about a ghostly dog that was said to guard churches and graveyards in Ireland. The Kirkgrim he'd called it. "So how did all of this end?"

"It ended in 1993 when a member of the unit, Torrance Sands, betrayed my father and his allies to the politicians in Belfast. They subsequently hired Sands to murder the entire Black Shuck Unit. He did, in the basement of this very house nearly twenty years ago. Only Declan, a fellow named Shane O'Reilly, and myself survived."

"That's why you have trouble walking, isn't it?"

"Lower spine was shattered by a bullet from Sands' gun. I spent nearly a year in hospital in Dublin, didn't return here for years until after the peace accords were signed in 2000."

"And Sands, he was a friend of Declan's? You said he'd helped him as a teenager."

Fintan nodded. "Aye, but Sands was never really a friend to anyone other than himself. He was a stone cold killer from the word go. He used my da' to get the training and experience he wanted and then he left."

"What happened to him?"

Fintan shook his head. "Nobody really knows what happened to him. He just disappeared after that night."

"And Declan made his way to America?"

"Aye, Declan went to America and the other survivor, Shane, to England where he continued in a role my father put him in, working as an informer for MI5 to bring down the traitorous bastards in Belfast."

Constance took a deep breath. The holes in the story were almost filled. All except for a few details that she didn't think she wanted to know. She'd heard stories of the Russian atrocities in Afghanistan. At times they'd wiped out entire villages in search of one *Mujahideen.*

She stood up. "Thank you for telling me. I know it wasn't easy."

"Ancient history, love," Fintan said, shrugging off the notion that the story was an emotional one for him. But she could tell he was lying. It was nothing if not a painful memory, a lot of painful memories, actually. She kissed him on the cheek as he stood from the bench.

"I'll get ready for dinner. I'm sure Mrs. Hogan prepares a wonderful meal."

Fintan nodded and said, "Aye, and she'd be most disappointed if you didn't come and enjoy it."

"Then I will."

He nodded again and made his way out of the large room, closing the heavy door behind him.

She stepped inside and closed the balcony door. After locking both doors she stripped from head to toe and turned on the shower in the adjacent bathroom. As steam filled the ornately tiled room and fogged the mirrored surfaces, she thought about Declan. How he'd spent so much of his life completely alone with no one to understand what he'd been through. The thought of him out there alone now dealing with the same type of treachery scared her and brought tears to her eyes. She didn't care about what he'd done in the past. She loved him and that was all that mattered. As she stepped into the streaming water, she hoped she'd see him again, that he'd survive and would return to her so they could get on with their lives.

CHAPTER FIFTY-THREE

6:32 a.m. Local Time – Friday
Gay Lane
Marloes, Pembrokeshire – Wales

Declan awoke to the sound of raised voices. Or was it the wind playing tricks with the clay shingled roof? He couldn't be sure. Maybe he'd even been dreaming. Slowly his vision focused on the low ceiling of the Sawyer's guest cottage. He heard the sound of a man yell, and this time he was sure of it. He swung his legs around and off the edge of the bed, bringing himself to a sitting position. He rubbed his face with his hands trying to clear the clinging extremities of sleep.

How long have I been asleep?

He looked out of the small window near the door. *It's still dark.*

He listened for the sound of the wind and heard none, nor the beating of the rain that had been falling earlier. *The storm's passed,* he thought, as he stood and pulled on the clothes that were draped across the bed's footboard. Thinking quickly through the events of the previous night, he realized that he hadn't used the satellite phone to contact Fintan when he'd landed. Constance had to be worried sick and probably thinking the worst. In his injured state and with his harried attempt to find shelter, he'd forgotten all about the satphone. Hopefully everything had gone smoothly with the landing at Waterford Airport and Fintan had been able to get Constance past the police. Declan scanned the floor for his duffel bag, but couldn't find it. He was certain he'd had it when the Sawyer's had shown him to the cottage. Something was wrong. Images of fully armored police officers surrounding the cottage with their rifles aimed streamed through his imagination. Had the Sawyer's recognized him from television reports? He hadn't noticed a television in the house, but he hadn't seen every room. His recklessness became obvious to him all at once, but he shook it off and forced himself to focus. *What's done is done. There's no going back now.*

Slowly, he turned the doorknob. The wooden door creaked as it opened and he stepped out onto the gravel pathway that led to the main house. The air was damp with lingering moisture from the rain. Overhead the sky was cloudless, the stars bright. He saw no movement along the stone wall that enclosed the backyard and relaxed slightly as he moved to the stone patio. There were no lights on in the house. He gripped the doorknob and turned it, expecting it to be locked. To his surprise it wasn't. He pushed the door inwards, revealing the darkened kitchen and the living area beyond, illuminated only by the faint light from a dying fire. He stepped inside and waited for his eyes to adjust before closing the door behind him.

Sitting alone on the leather sofa, Hannah Sawyer sniffed away tears as he approached. "I'm sorry," she mouthed.

He felt something cold touch the small of his back. He raised his hands slowly, knowing it was the barrel of a gun.

"So do paragliders always carry suppressed weapons?" Rhys Sawyer snapped, as he continued to poke Declan in the back, pushing him forward. "Why don't you try telling me the truth, Mr. Flynn, if that's your real name?"

Declan walked slowly forward and turned to face the old man. Rhys was holding the Glock pistol from the duffel bag in his right hand with the suppressor attached. "I don't mean either of you any harm. I'm one of the good guys. You have to believe that."

"The bloody hell you are. I know your kind, your whole lot in Ulster. You've been trying to restart that damned war for over ten years now," Rhys hissed. "Didn't you waste enough lives last time? How many have to die just so you all can have your damn island all to yourselves?"

Declan considered his options. He wasn't sure what the extent of the old man's experience was, but he knew that Rhys had been trained in the use of firearms just by the way he held the Glock. Declan was reasonably sure he could disarm the old man without much trouble, but if he was able to get off a shot, Hannah could be hurt or worse in the brief struggle. He decided to take Rhys up on the invitation to tell the truth. Maybe it would make a difference, but he had his doubts. The old man's voice had carried a heavy tone of bias and his words had revealed that he was no supporter of the reunification of Ireland.

"My name's Declan McIver and you're right, Mr. Sawyer. I am from Ulster, and I was involved with the conflict there. But that was a long time ago and it has nothing to do with what's happening now." He watched as a flicker of recognition crossed the old man's face.

"You're the one the Yanks are looking for, the one that killed that Jew and those other guys. Police of some sort, weren't they?"

"I didn't kill Dr. Kafni. He was a friend of mine. The others weren't police, at least not anymore. They killed Kafni's assistant and they tried to kill me. I've been set up. You need to believe me. I don't want to hurt anyone, but there are some very dangerous people who are planning something terrible if I don't stop them."

"Hannah, come here now," Rhys ordered. Declan could tell he didn't believe a word of it. Hannah stood up and moved cautiously behind her father, her eyes narrowing as she looked over his shoulder towards Declan. Finally her father had been right about bringing home strays.

"I watched your lot kill too many innocent people. I was in Oman. I served my country and had a lot of good mates there. My time was up, but many of them weren't so favored. They came home from foreign soil only to end up in Belfast getting their arses shot off by their own citizens."

Declan had no interest in arguing the finer points of British expansionism, but he saw it as an opportunity. Rhys had revealed his feelings about the Troubles and Declan thought that if he could use the obviously sore subject to make the old man angry, maybe he'd make a mistake and provide an opening to disarm him without anyone getting hurt.

"The British Government treated Northern Ireland like it was a foreign country, opening fire on civil rights protests and holding entire neighborhoods hostage for nearly three decades, just because they were Catholic instead of Protestant."

"And what were they supposed to do when those neighborhoods openly supported becoming part of another country completely?" Rhys snapped. "There are words for that. At the very least it was sedition, but more likely it was treason."

Declan could see that his words were having the desired effect. Already Rhys had lowered the pistol several inches and now held it at waist level. Declan flashed a purposely smug smile. "So what do you propose we do? Shall we stand here arguing politics all night?"

"I'll be damned before I let another one of you Fenian bastards cross my land in order to get to London and set off more bombs, killing more innocent people! I stood by once before and the letter bombs the bastards mailed cost my brother his sight!"

Declan saw his opportunity as the pistol was lowered even further and he stepped forward suddenly. Rhys quickly brought the gun up to eye level and Declan knocked it aside with a strike to the wrist. Rhys fired two shots from the weapon, but hit only the wall of his house. Throwing his fist forward, Declan caught the old man in the nerve center just above the stomach. As Rhys bent forward in pain, Declan finished his attack with a chop to his neck, compressing his carotid artery and knocking him unconscious. He wrenched the Glock from the old man's hand and slowly lowered him to the tiled floor.

Hannah screamed and stood against the wall near the door, seemingly afraid to move.

Bending down, Declan felt for the old man's pulse.

"Don't touch him!" Hannah screamed, beginning to cry.

"He'll be fine in a while," Declan said, standing up and placing the Glock in the waistband of his jeans. He walked over to where she stood against the wall and looked at her. He wanted to be comforting but he knew nothing he could say would make a difference. The best thing he could do was leave. He bent down and picked up the duffel bag that was beside the back door, unzipping it to make sure the items Lynch had packed were still inside.

"Take care of him," he said, as he walked towards the front door. "When he wakes up tell him he's a brave man. I hope that someday soon you'll both be able to know that I'm not a bad guy. You've done a good thing by helping me. Hopefully you've helped me save a lot of lives."

Taking the keys Hannah had placed in the basket beside the door, he left the house and got into the Peugeot. He didn't like the idea of stealing from them after they'd helped him, but there was no other way that he'd be able to move fast enough to avoid the police, whom Hannah was probably already calling. He started the vehicle and drove away, the thought of having hurt an innocent person already haunting him.

CHAPTER FIFTY-FOUR

Declan zipped the black hooded raincoat up to his neck and pulled the navy blue baseball cap, bearing the logo of the Esso oil company, down over his forehead, hoping to hide as much of his facial features as possible. It went without saying that the Sawyers had called the local police in Marloes and that word would soon spread to the larger towns of Haverfordwest, Swansea, Carmarthen, and then further inland. It would take a few hours, but soon every police force in the United Kingdom would know that he had been spotted and would be keeping a look out for anyone matching his description. For that reason he had left the most obvious evidence, the Sawyers' red Peugeot, parked in the busy lot of the same Tesco supermarket where he'd purchased the coat and hat, along with a pack of cigarettes and a bottle of soda. With any luck it would take several hours or even longer for the police to locate it among the many vehicles of the other shoppers.

Walking around the side of the last building in the plaza containing the supermarket and a host of other smaller retailers, he scanned the parking lot of the Milford Haven Tourist Information Center. His next move would likely be the most important and most critical since he'd arrived on British soil. If he made a mistake here, his capture would be almost certain within a few hours.

Stopping at one of the plaza's several loading docks he jumped up on the edge and took a seat, allowing his legs to dangle over the side as he sat looking across the road at the tourist center. While he would have preferred the parking lot of a busy hotel in the middle of tourist season shortly before nightfall, the tourist center would have to do. The time of year and time of day of his visit just wasn't something he'd been able to control. Hopefully the center would get some visitors despite tourist season still being a few months off. Thumping the pack of cigarettes against his palm, he pulled one loose and lit up. Though he wasn't a smoker he hoped that between the smokes, the soda and the cap with the Esso logo, no one would think of him as anything other than an employee of one of the nearby oil refineries, whose night shift had just ended. Hopefully, he wouldn't have to wait long.

He reached into the duffel bag and withdrew the satphone. Thankfully modern satellite phones looked enough like cell phones to not draw any extra attention. He looked over the black Thuraya XT model device, pressed the red power button and waited as the device came to life. Once the phone had found a signal, a series of beeps and the appearance of a white envelope on the screen indicated a message was waiting. Declan used the phone's circular navigation tab to open it.

Landing complete and guards dealt with. All are safe and en route. Contact the number saved as "Unit #2" in the phone's memory when you're able. – DL

Declan deleted the message and opened the contacts list. On the list were four numbers marked Units #1, #2 and #4. Realizing that the numbers obviously corresponded with the number of parachute rigs aboard Fintan's plane, he knew that he must be holding Unit #3 and that Lynch had taken Unit #2 when they'd exited the aircraft. He hit the send button when he'd highlighted Unit #2 with the navigation tab, and waited. He heard an audible clicking as the call connected and then an electronic ring sounded several times before the line was answered.

"It's about time. Someone's been waiting to hear from you, old son."

Declan smiled. "Ended up trying my sea legs on, but it all worked out in the end."

"Grand. So what's the plan?"

"I need to meet up with Shane, but we have to be careful how we contact him. Thames House is probably the most watched place in Britain."

"Aye, but he's not at Thames House. He's out and about for a few days to go and meet with his informers. He sent word this morning that he'd meet you at your old contingency location at noon today. Do you remember where that is? Because I don't have a clue what he's talking about."

"Aye, I remember."

"Grand. Keep me posted as much as you can. Your missus would like to have a word or two with you now."

"Aye, put her on."

"Phone call for you, love," Declan heard Fintan say with a smile in his voice after he knocked on a door.

An hour and a half later Declan was beginning to think he would have to come up with a backup plan. Having watched and listened as only a few people had entered the Tourist Center, which also contained a museum dedicated to the area, he was encouraged by the fact that none of them had come out again. Whatever was inside was obviously worth taking the time to see, but it wouldn't help him unless someone else visited, and soon. He'd yet to see any police patrols but knew that it was only a matter of time with one of the two main roads from Marloes less than a hundred yards to his left. He turned his head at the sound of a vehicle approaching and watched as a black; four door Nissan Versa turned the corner next to the supermarket and drove towards him. With his hat pulled low over his eyes, he followed the vehicle until it came to a stop in the parking lot of the tourist center. He knew that one way or another, this would be the vehicle he'd been waiting for. He didn't have time to wait any longer.

Extinguishing his fifth cigarette against the concrete dock, he slid off and hurried across the road towards the vehicle. When he was within ten yards an older man stepped out of the driver's side of the car and turned to speak with his female passenger, who was also exiting the vehicle.

"*Sind Sie bereit?*" the man said in German. *Are you ready?*

Declan couldn't believe his luck. As part of his training with *Vympel*, he'd been encouraged to learn three languages in addition to the two he spoke natively, English and Irish. He had learned Russian, French and German from the men in the unit. While he was out of practice having not used any of them much during the last twenty years, the environment he'd learned in was such that it made forgetting impossible.

"Excuse me," he called loudly in English. "Excuse me?"

Both the man and the woman turned to look at him as they left the vehicle and moved towards the front doors of the tourist center, having previously been unaware of his presence. They looked back and forth at each other before responding. Instead of speaking, the man shrugged and made a confused expression.

"*Entschuldigen sie,*" Declan said, causing them to stop in their tracks. *Excuse me, sir.*

"*Ja?*" the man said, as he turned around to look at Declan, his expression clearly indicating that he was surprised to hear his native language.

"I'm so glad I found you," Declan said, continuing to speak in German. "I'm a tourist here, like you, and just had the most horrible thing happen!"

The couple looked at him with worried expressions as he motioned towards the supermarket behind him. "A man just stole my rental car and I need someone to help me call the police. I speak very little English. Can you help me? Do you have a cell phone?"

"*Ja, ja!*" the man said, as he started moving back towards the black Nissan, the woman following.

Declan walked slowly behind them as they both approached the driver's side of the car and unlocked the door. He scanned the area and took a quick look towards the entrance of the tourist center. Satisfied that no one was watching and that there was no line of sight from the building, he pulled his Glock pistol from under his coat; keeping it at waist level as he aimed it.

"*Steigen sie ins auto!*" he yelled. *Get in the car!*

The couple turned their heads and looked at him with horrified expressions.

"Get in the car now! You drive," he said to the man, "and you, in the passenger side!"

The man hurriedly got into the driver's seat and the woman moved quickly around the front of the car and got in next to him. Declan pulled open the back driver's side door and slid onto the seat. "Now drive!"

The man started the car, shifted it into gear and backed out of the parking spot.

Twenty minutes later after ordering them to drive east on the A477 and crossing the Cleddau Bridge over the Milford Haven Waterway, the old man looked over his shoulder at Declan and said, "We are approaching a toll booth."

Declan looked ahead to see that the man was correct. How could he have forgotten the bridge had a toll? He hadn't traveled in the United Kingdom for nearly twenty years, that's how. He cursed under his breath and craned his neck to look behind them. Having already crossed the bridge, there was no way of turning back without passing through the booths.

"Nice and easy," he said, as he moved his pistol from one hand to another so it would be hidden from the toll booth attendant's view by the door panel. "Use the booth furthest to the left, smile and pay the man, but don't say a word."

"*Ja*," the old man said nervously, as he slowed the car and approached the booth.

Declan knew the Germans telling the toll attendant that they'd been carjacked was the least of his worries. His main concern was that the attendants could easily have been told by the police to be on the lookout for anyone matching his description and, by now, may even have been given pictures. In addition, the United Kingdom was infamous for its use of CCTV cameras and the toll booths would surely be equipped with them. That's why he had elected to carjack the couple instead of simply stealing their rental car once they were inside the tourist center. It was much harder to film someone from overhead while they were sitting in the back seat of a vehicle.

Declan pulled his cap as low as he could over his eyes and leaned his head back against the window to pretend he was sleeping. "Keep calm," he ordered as he felt the car stop and heard the old man lowering the window.

"Good day, sir, that's 75p," the toll attendant said. He sounded bored. "Thank you, sir. Enjoy your day."

Declan breathed easy as he felt the car speed up again. Righting himself in the seat as soon as they were past the booth, he froze as he saw a white Ford Focus with a blue light bar on its roof that had been hidden behind the toll booth infrastructure. The yellow and blue logos on the side of the car clearly identified it as a squad car belonging to the Dyfed-Powys police. Declan turned his head to the left and pretended to read the banners attached to the waist high fence that divided the road from the property beyond, hoping the Nissan's tinted rear windows would hide his face as they passed within a few yards of the officer sitting in the vehicle. Sensing the tension in the car, the old man driving placed his hands at the ten and two positions and stared straight ahead.

"Stay on the A477 until it meets the A48 and the M4 motorway," Declan said, his eyes fixed on the passenger side wing mirror as the police car retreated into the distance and finally out of sight, as they entered a roundabout.

Three hours later he ordered the Germans to pull off the M4 onto the A346 towards the village of Marlborough.

"Get out of the car," he said in English, after directing them to pull up in an empty lot a few miles south of the motorway. The couple glanced at each other uncertainly. "Get out of the car," he repeated again in English. "I'm going to shoot you both in the kneecaps."

He watched as the couple exchanged the same confused look, despite the threat. It was clear that they couldn't understand what he was saying. Nearly having to stifle a laugh, he returned to speaking in German. "Leave the vehicle running and get out."

The couple obeyed and Declan climbed out of the back seat. Looking over his shoulder in both directions to be sure no traffic was coming; he patted the man down and then the woman. Satisfied that they had nothing on them that they could use to call for help and that their lack of English would further hamper their efforts to attract police attention, he told them to step away from the car as he got in, shifted it into gear and did a U-turn out of the dirt lot, leaving them standing alone in a cloud of dust and surrounded by nothing but miles of countryside.

Returning to the M4 and driving east for another twenty-nine miles, he exited onto the A34 and drove south towards the town of Newbury, knowing he was nearly an hour late. Hopefully Shane was still waiting.

CHAPTER FIFTY-FIVE

12:53 p.m. Local Time – Friday
West Mills
Newbury, County Berkshire – England

Pulling the Nissan into an empty parking spot in front of a terrace of Tudor-era houses next to the River Kennet, Declan shifted the vehicle into neautral, applied the handbrake, and got out. He tossed the keys onto the dashboard and left the doors unlocked. With any luck some opportunist thug would happen by and take the car for a ride. With the amount of CCTV cameras in the United Kingdom he knew he'd been picked up by at least a dozen cameras as he'd driven the vehicle the short distance between where he'd left the Germans and the town of Newbury. When the police finally figured out what had happened and connected him with the Germans' carjacking, a thug riding around in their rental car could be a great distraction.

Walking a few blocks through the seventeenth century town center, he kept his hands in his pockets and his head down, the chill in the air aiding him in trying to make himself as inconspicuous as possible. Like all British towns of this age, the streets made odd turns and dead ended suddenly, creating a crowded feeling and demonstrating the lack of planning that had accompanied the growth of the area. People walked briskly along each side of the narrow streets. Declan made several lefts and rights, doubling back occasionally to be sure that no one was following him. While he knew the police probably hadn't caught on yet, in the U.K. there were other more dangerous agencies to worry about, starting with the infamous Security Service, and since he was there to meet a man who worked for them, it wasn't impossible to imagine that agents of the service could be present as well.

Shane's connections to the IRA were known to his superiors, but Declan didn't think that their connection to each other was. Shane had seen to that, he was sure. But the more he thought about it as he walked around the area, the more he realized how wrong he could be. Rumors abounded that the intelligence agencies of Great Britain watched their own people as much or more than they watched everyone else. While he and Shane hadn't had any significant contact in a number of years, the little bit they had had could have easily been documented by his employers.

As he neared the meeting site, he nearly turned around and headed back to the Nissan. There was still time for him to make it further inland and possibly find a good place to hide out while he considered his next move. But that was the problem. His next move was finding the person within the British Government who had agreed to pass highly classified information to the people who had conspired to kill Abaddon Kafni and aid Ruslan Baktayev in committing an atrocity, and Declan couldn't think of anyone more suited to help him with that than Shane O'Reilly. He walked on towards their meeting spot.

The spire of Saint Nicholas' Church stood stories above any other building in the center of Newbury and in 1991, as the leader of a four man Active Service Unit of Black Shuck; Declan had chosen it as the third of their four meeting spots in case their primary and alternate sites were compromised. The plan the site had been a part of wasn't something that made him proud and as he approached the church, memories of what could have been flooded his mind. The plot had been the entire reason Eamon McGuire had created and trained Black Shuck, an audacious operation against the capital of Great Britain that involved a multi-level attack on the city's leaders, infrastructure, and military and police installations. If completed, the attack would easily have cost thousands of lives in the city of London.

Thankfully the plan hadn't come to fruition but had instead faded away with the deaths of Eamon McGuire and the other members of Black Shuck.

Reaching the north side of the churchyard where a large grove of trees was planted, Declan stopped and entered a telephone box at the corner of Bartholomew and West Mills streets. Inserting several coins he'd picked up from the ashtray of the Nissan, he dialed some random numbers and held the receiver to his ear as he inspected the side of the base unit and saw a single line about three inches long that had been made with a blue dry erase marker. He rubbed the mark off with his thumb and looked towards the grove of trees, knowing that Shane was waiting for him.

It had been nearly two decades since he'd made contact with anyone this way, but the process hadn't changed. With the phone to his ear he pretended to have an animated conversation and turned casually in several directions looking for anyone that appeared to be watching. In the cold and often wet atmosphere of early spring in the United Kingdom, anyone watching should have been relatively easy to spot. While most people would be hurrying from one place to another to avoid the wind and light rain, someone watching would dally here and there and never really leave sight of him. He saw no one exhibiting that behavior. The few people that were out did exactly as he expected, they darted from one building to another. Next he looked for patterns of people leaving and going in case the people watching were part of a team with a more elaborate surveillance routine. Again, he saw no one.

Satisfied that he was on his own, he hung up the phone and exited the telephone box. He walked to the four foot high wrought iron gate that joined two sections of the nearly six hundred year old rock wall that surrounded the gothic church and pulled. As it squealed open, he casually turned into the churchyard clearing his three, six and nine o'clock positions again as he closed the gate behind him. Stepping briskly over the cracked pavers that formed a walkway around the entire half-acre churchyard, he entered the grove of tall oak trees that shaded the north wall of the church.

"It's about time," a voice sang from within one of the many

stone alcoves.

Declan turned to see Shane O'Reilly leaning up against the church, wearing a tan overcoat and a brown long island cap, tufts of his curly red hair sticking out above his ears. A broad smile formed on the man's face as he stepped forward.

"It's good to see ya, ya Fenian bastard," he said.

Declan felt his own mouth curl into a wide grin. "Aye, good to see ya."

"I was afraid you wouldn't make it," Shane said, his face turning serious. "They've got you jammed up pretty bad."

Shane withdrew a copy of the *Daily Telegraph* from inside his coat and unfolded it, handing it over. Declan took the newspaper and inspected the bottom of the front page, where the headline talked about the nationwide search going on for him in the United States.

"We've got only one advantage at this point," Shane said, "they don't know you're here, yet."

"Aye, but it's not going to stay that way for long."

Shane chuckled. "I don't want to know how you got yourself here, do I?"

"Are you sure there's no one following you? Nobody from the spook house knows we're connected?"

Shane shook his head. "Nah, I don't think they know. If they do they're not too fussed about it, because I'm certain I wasn't followed. I've booked myself out for the next two days to meet with informers around the country. To everyone back at Thames House you're simply agent 3210, one of the twenty or so agents I'm in charge of handling."

Declan nodded. "Aye, sounds like a grand cover, but what're they gonna do once they learn I'm here?"

Shane grimaced. "Same thing any government does, I suppose. Send alerts out to every police station in the country with a picture and instructions on what to do and who to call if you're spotted."

"That's not what I mean. I mean what're they going to do about *you* when they find out I'm here? They may not be worried about our connection now, but if they know about it, I guarantee they will be when that little fact reaches their ears."

Shane placed his hands in the pockets of his overcoat. "I

don't think they know. But that's all the more reason why we need to get moving and make this as short a visit as possible."

"Aye. Have you had any luck with finding out who we're looking for?"

Shane shook his head. "I'm afraid all I can tell you is that it came straight from the top through the Deputy Director himself. Very rare for my department these days, so whoever's after you is well-connected."

"Where does the Deputy Director get his orders from?"

"From the Director-General and the Joint Intelligence Committee, a weekly meeting of the minds for all the intelligence-related services in Great Britain."

"Who attends?"

"I don't know for sure. It's real hush hush kind of stuff and unfortunately I'm just not at that level. I know it's chaired by a permanent chairman from Whitehall and that the committee itself is made up of the heads of the three intelligence agencies; Five, Six and GCHQ, as well as advisors, staffers and representatives from various ministries, all related to defense. Honestly, I really can't tell you any more about it than Wikipedia probably can."

"Does anyone from foreign governments attend or is this strictly a British affair?"

"Supposedly the London station chiefs of certain intelligence agencies from around the world attend when matters concerning their nations are being discussed, but I don't have any idea who they are or how often they attend."

"Well, it would only be nations that are allied with Great Britain, right? That would certainly include the United States. The CIA has a presence in London, don't they?"

"Aye, it's unofficial, but they have an office at the American Embassy in Grosvenor Square. Five works with them sometimes when interests coincide, but most of that is on Islamic terrorism these days. I haven't seen the CIA in my department in a good while."

"But there is a CIA boss in London and that could very well be the person we're looking for. Do you have any idea who it is?"

Shane shook his head. "No. They don't exactly broadcast

their people's names. I can't say for sure, but I'd venture a guess that they're all undercover to some degree. Even if you walked down the hallways of Grosvenor Square and read the nameplates on the doors you'd probably only come up with a bunch of fake job titles."

Declan shook his head.

"Look," Shane said, as if he was trying to defend himself, "I'm a Grade 5 salaried intelligence officer, Dec. I can't exactly ring the members of the Joint Intelligence Committee for tea."

"It's okay. It's grand. We just need to think this through. These people are bureaucrats. They're like mating garter snakes, all in a big ball seeing who can screw the one lone female the fastest."

Shane's face twisted in mock disgust. "Jesus, Dec—"

"I mean they're all connected in ways that would make the average person's head swim. Now think who and what from the intelligence community has been in the news lately, for any reason."

Shane thought for a moment and then took back the newspaper he'd handed Declan. Opening it to a page about three quarters of the way through he said, "Here," then handed it back. He stabbed a finger at a lengthy article containing a picture of an older gentleman with graying blonde hair who was standing next to two Irish wolfhounds alongside an aging rock wall. "That's all I can think of."

"Lord Dennis Allardyce," Declan said aloud, as he scanned the article, the *acting* director-general of the Security Service. I remember him. He used to be friends with my father."

Shane looked up suddenly. "He was what?"

"A friend of my da's."

"Do you think he remembers you?"

"I doubt it. That was a long time ago. I wasn't but nine or ten. Why's he the *acting* director-general?"

"Because the bleedin' sod that was in charge couldn't keep his willie in his Y-fronts and damn near caused an international incident, bloodied the poor bird up a bit as well. Allardyce has been appointed temporarily, but is expected to be confirmed as the permanent replacement within a matter of weeks. As such, he sits in the weekly meeting of the Joint Intelligence

Committee."

"So he was there when the request was made?"

Shane nodded. "Aye, should've been."

"Then that's who we need to talk to."

Shane glared in disbelief. "Dec, we can't just walk up and knock on his door. He's the head of the Security Service. Going to him would be like turning yourself in."

"He's the only person we know of that was in that room. So unless you have any other ideas, he's all we've got."

"Alright, alright," Shane said, putting his hands up in submission and looking around the churchyard. "But what if he made the request himself? What if they're all connected, like you said, and whoever's after you put the request directly to Allardyce?"

"No, I don't think so," Declan said, continuing to scan the article. "If they had access to someone like Allardyce, the orders given to you yesterday probably would have come much earlier. Instead they had to wait until the meeting, which likely means that it was someone *not* connected to the British Government."

"Someone like the CIA Station Chief."

"Exactly."

"Alright, grand, let's just say you're right and Allardyce can point you in the right direction. What makes you think he will? What makes you think he'll help?"

"I don't know if you remember or not, but Allardyce once held another position before his rise to the level of the Lords Temporal or whatever he is now. He's been in the British Civil Service a long time; he used to be the Secretary of State for Northern Ireland in the early 1980s, which is how he knew my father."

Shane thought for a moment and finally nodded. "Yeah, we were barely old enough to be out of nappies, but I think I remember."

Declan smiled in amusement. "Well, you might've been late to toilet training, Shane, but in seventy-nine I was campaigning with my da' for parliament and I remember Allardyce. He was the closest thing the IRA had to a friend in the British government during those years. He honestly thought the

Catholic population had been done wrong by and at least tried to be understanding of the IRA's position, a fact that didn't exactly win him a lot of friends after events like the Mountbatten assassination and the Warrenpoint ambush. The bombing of the Grand Hotel in Brighton in eighty-four ended his tenure. By then Da' and Mum had been murdered and I'd been in and out of orphanages and was flirting with the 'Ra. I never saw him again after my parents' funeral."

"And you're thinking that if we can get to him, talk to him and tell him the truth of your situation, then maybe he can help us find out who made that request and that may lead us to the person who's behind all of this? It's a bit of a long shot, but I suppose it's the best we've got."

"Aye, it's the best we've got," Declan said, pointing to the picture in the article. "Where is this?"

"Greumach Manor is in Scotland. About two hours west of Aberdeen in the Cairngorm Mountains."

"That's a long way, but the article says he's spent every weekend there since he was a boy. Let's hope that's a tradition he's continued now that he's the nation's top spook."

CHAPTER FIFTY-SIX

9:14 a.m. Eastern Time – Friday
Constitutional Condominiums
6th St. & Maryland Avenue – Washington D.C.

The few hours of rest he'd managed to get hadn't helped his state of mind any. As he poured another cup of coffee from the brewer on his desk, David Kemiss sighed and leaned back in his chair again, sipping from the cup. He'd been up for most of the night again and had been staring for hours at every piece of paper intelligence they'd managed to gather on Declan McIver. He was convinced that somewhere in the documents was a clue to where the man was heading. If they could figure that out and get ahead of him, then it would be game over. Wherever he lived, Colin Bellanger was doing the same thing. Two brains were better than one, Kemiss reasoned, and Bellanger was much more used to paperwork than he was.

He sat up as his phone rang. "What?"

"Senator, it's Robert Evers."

"Oh. Mr. Evers. Good. Thank you for calling. What have you got?"

"Some good news and some bad news, sir. The good news is that we've had what we're pretty sure is a confirmed sighting."

"And the bad news?" Kemiss felt his face flush.

"The news came in the form of a phone call from the Dyfed-Powys police."

"The *what* police?"

"He's in Wales, or at least he was a few hours ago."

"In Wales? How the hell did he get to Wales?" Kemiss slammed down the coffee mug, slopping hot liquid onto his mahogany desk.

"I'm not sure, sir. I'm as surprised as anyone."

"I mean, you've got the airports sealed up, right? His name's on the 'no fly' list. How could he have possibly gotten out of the country and all the way to Wales?"

"Sir, with the information you've helped to uncover about McIver I really wouldn't be surprised to learn that he has a fake identity, maybe even more than one. Being as he's from the United Kingdom originally, that identity could very well have been that of a British citizen. With a minor change in appearance and what appeared to be legal documents, he could've slipped through the TSA pretty easily."

"And they're sure it's him?"

"Apparently he convinced some kind of wildlife worker in a place called Pembrokeshire to take him in. He stayed there the night and took off in their car when they recognized him. That was early this morning. The Chief Constable there called me as a courtesy. He's already notified his superiors and they're preparing a Task Force of some kind to track McIver down and apprehend him. While it's surprising news, it's really good news all around. The Brits have a much tougher system of policing than we do here in the States. With the amount of CCTV in that country I'd lay down a wager that they'll have him by the end of the day. They've been tracking his kind for over forty years."

Kemiss willed himself to calm down. While he considered the news to be anything but good, he couldn't let Evers know that. "Fine, then, let me know if there's any updates."

"You'll be my first call, sir."

Kemiss listened as Evers hung up and then tossed the phone across the desk, where it flew off the other side and pulled the STE's base unit off the desk with it, the two landing on the carpeted floor with a soft thud.

He took a moment to compose himself. Slowly, he stood and walked around the desk to pick up the phone. Returning it to the desk and straightening some other items, he considered the new development in the situation. He felt like he was losing control. He had lost control. If Declan McIver was in Great Britain then any influence he had over the direction of the manhunt was at an end. Evers would keep him up to date, but he was no longer in charge and the information would be just that; information, not intelligence. Not the kind of thing that Kemiss needed to insure that instead of being arrested, McIver was eliminated.

Maybe it doesn't matter anymore, he thought, as he ran a hand through his thinning hair and retook his seat behind his desk, closing his eyes. McIver's name had been so bloodied that maybe it didn't matter what he said when he was caught. Nobody would believe a word of it. But then if he was proved eventually to be correct, which Kemiss knew he would, then these things had a way of coming back. There was always some investigative reporter or some lawyer hungry for a book deal that would believe it and try to piece together exactly what had happened. The American public loved a conspiracy theory, and while nothing came of most of them, many of the government's secrets had been outed in just such a way. Whether it was the existence of the Navy SEALs, the lack of WMDs in Iraq, or the blow by blow details of the Osama Bin Laden raid, the media had a way of exposing things that nobody wanted exposed. While he couldn't be sure that an exposé would link back to him, he wasn't willing to risk it either. He had been careful, but the web that had been created was even beginning to confuse him. Had he made a mistake somewhere that might leave him exposed? It was possible and for that reason things would be far better off if Declan McIver were dead.

He leaned back in his chair and tried, for a moment, to put himself in the shoes of a man fleeing the law, a man fleeing a conspiracy. Where would he go? What would he be trying to accomplish? If McIver had wanted to disappear, then he would have done it. He never would have come back to the security company and put himself in harm's way, nearly getting himself caught. No, everything he had done had either been an overt move to try and expose the forces against him or a reaction to those forces' continued pressure. Now, in a different country, he had to believe that he had more room to breathe, to search for whatever it was that he was looking for. But what or who was he looking for?

Simard. The name hung on the edge of Kemiss' mind for a moment. He opened his eyes. Lane Simard was in London. But how could McIver know about Simard? He couldn't. The Agency didn't publish the names of its employees, but that was the only connection that he could think of in Great Britain. He shook his head. Maybe McIver was just a desperate man on the run. He had a past in the British Isles. Maybe he was just running hard and fast, hoping that he wouldn't be found. Still, Kemiss had a nagging feeling that that wasn't the case. If McIver had somehow learned of Simard then there was a definite connection back to him. He had met with Simard personally and tasked the man with finding out everything the Brits had. He knew that Simard wouldn't break easily; the man was a trained spy. But that didn't matter. If he broke at all, then Kemiss was finished...but not if Simard was finished first.

He reached into his pocket for his cell phone and dialed a number.

"Lukas," he said, as the line was answered. "I have a problem that I need you to help me with."

CHAPTER FIFTY-SEVEN

9:26 p.m. Local Time – Friday
Cairngorms National Park
Six Miles Northwest of Ballater, Aberdeenshire – Scotland

"Aye, that's it, the B976." Shane said as he turned on the overhead light in the late '80s model Range Rover and looked at the map he had unfolded in his lap. "Middle of nowhere, innit?"

"Aye," Declan said looking at the signs on the side of the three way fork in the road. The SUV's headlights shone over a weathered metal sign with a brown background and white lettering that pointed west and gave directions to Balmoral and Braemar Castles, tourist attractions that wouldn't begin their open seasons for nearly a month. "Are you sure about this?"

"Aye, that's Gairnshiel Lodge," Shane said pointing to a smallish, Gothic era castle that sat a short distance off the road behind an ancient looking rock wall. "According to my source the drive's just another few miles down this road on the right."

"According to your source? You mean you've never been here before?"

"Like I said, Dec, I'm not exactly on the guest list when it comes to your lordships and ladies. I have an informer in Falkirk that's rather decent with a computer. He found the location and provided the directions."

"Grand. We've hacked our way to the secret location of the MI5 director's weekend home."

"Looks like a single track road. It's gonna be hard to spot the drive in the dark."

"Oh, what do ya mean?" Declan said, in a mocking tone. "I'm sure there's a bright neon sign."

"This was your idea," Shane said, as he shifted the Range Rover back into gear and the engine made a whining sound as he piloted the vehicle down the roughly paved, one lane road. From the passenger side, Declan watched as the ancient rock wall surrounding Gairnshiel Lodge passed by. In the distance he could make out the barren looking peaks of the Cairngorm mountains up ahead. In a matter of minutes they'd not only be in an extremely remote and forbidding wilderness, they'd be there in the pitch black of night.

After a mile, the rock wall ceased and a quickly flowing river joined the road on its right hand side, a metal guardrail preventing what little traffic probably traveled the road from accidentally taking a swim. The road continued on over small hills and valleys until the river retreated away into the distant fields on the right and finally the headlights of the SUV fell over a hollowed out stone building that looked like it had been standing since the days of Robert The Bruce, if not longer.

"There," Shane said, pointing to the building. "The drive's gotta be right here somewhere."

As soon as he said it, they passed a rough dirt road. Shane braked hard and shifted the SUV into reverse. Backing up, he turned right onto the road and slowly proceeded past the old stone building. Declan noted two knee high metal poles on each side of the drive as they entered.

The vehicle's shocks squeaked loudly as the Range Rover bounced through deep potholes filled with water that sloshed audibly as the tires passed through. The road wound down a hill between two fields, a waist high barbed wire fence on either side, before entering a cluster of trees. Declan looked left and right, but couldn't see anything through the tree cover; what little bit of light there was, was blocked by the thick forest. He could see his breath on the cold glass of the window as he strained his eyes. This place was dangerous, he could feel it.

"Supposedly Greumach Manor was originally built in the fourteenth century after the end of the First War of Scottish Independence," Shane said as the forest ended and the vehicle moved again into open terrain. "Robert The Bruce deeded the lands to his supporters in the Clan Graham and they've held them ever since."

Declan looked left at two more ruined stone buildings. "Aye, looks old enough."

"Rumor has it that the RAF built a base nearby that included a bunker for the Royals during World War II. It was supposedly an evacuation point for Balmoral Castle if the Queen happened to be in residence when the Germans attacked. The existence of the bunker has never been verified, but the possibility is enough to keep every chattering conspiracy monkey frothing at the mouth at what goes on there now that it's no longer needed. Just like Rudloe Manor in the south with all the rumors of aliens and such. Blarney, if you ask me."

The SUV bounced and groaned as it passed over a rickety bridge spanning a ten foot gap in the terrain where a small creek flowed. "Looks like the end of the road," Declan said, as the headlights fell over a metal gate that blocked the way, about twenty yards ahead of them.

Shane stopped the SUV. "I guess we knew it wouldn't be that easy."

Declan opened the passenger's side door and stepped out.

"Where're you going?"

"We passed several security sensors along the drive in. They know we're coming."

Shane's expression changed to one of concern. "What do we do?"

"Stay here and hope they don't shoot you on sight," Declan said, flashing a smile. "I'm going to make my way out and about a bit. See if I can't get a look at what's coming at us."

He quietly closed the door and moved away from the vehicle, the damp cold of the Scottish evening attacking him suddenly now that he was away from the heater inside the SUV. Having been in the car for over eight hours as they made the journey north, his joints popped and his muscles stretched now that he was moving. He ran into some tall grass beside the road and crept along a narrow ditch towards the metal gate. It wasn't a security gate, but rather the kind of gate you'd see on a cattle ranch or horse farm. What could be either a storage shed or guard house stood on the right hand side of the driveway, its wood blackened by the moist weather and harsh temperatures. Along both sides of the gate was a rock wall that amounted to a pile of stones about eight feet high, held in place by wooden posts and mesh fencing. It was clear that whoever lived here wasn't expecting any visitors, nor were they prepared for any kind of security needs. Had he not seen the hastily placed sensor poles when they'd pulled onto the drive, there wouldn't have been any sign of security at all.

He exited the ditch and crossed quickly to the storage shed. The building had only one window, but he couldn't see through it in the dark. He ducked again and moved around the back of the building to the base of the rock wall. Grabbing onto one of the fence posts, he pulled himself up and over the wall. He landed on the uneven ground on the other side and caught himself with an outstretched hand as he nearly fell. Keeping low, he moved along the wall towards the gate.

At the gate he noticed a narrow path that cut off to the left from the main drive. Even from his position on the opposite side he could clearly see the tracks of a vehicle that had passed over the muddy road in recent days. He looked ahead and kept moving, the terrain inclining more as he moved along the wall. As he neared a grove of thick trees he came to a place where the rock wall turned ninety degrees and continued up and over a hill. He stood upright and again grabbed onto one of fence posts to lift himself over the wall. Instead of going all the way over this time, he lifted himself onto the top of it so he could see over the hill. As he did, he was hit with the smell of burning wood.

Looking down towards the base of the hill he could see the source of the smoke. A two story stone house sat just out of view from the main drive. Surrounded by a smaller rock wall and with a heavily overgrown garden in the back, he knew he couldn't be looking at Greumach Manor. For a lord's house he expected something far grander. He looked back towards where he'd left Shane parked. The SUV's headlights had been turned off but he could tell the vehicle was still running by the cloud of exhaust rising from its tail pipe. He was about to pull himself the rest of the way over the wall when the unmistakable sound of an engine starting came from somewhere near the house.

His turned his attention to a small barn when a pair of headlights were turned on and pierced the holes between the barn's wooden slat construction. Suddenly the doors were thrown open and a black Range Rover pulled forward, stopping briefly so the man who had opened the doors could get in.

"Anything?" he heard a British voice yell.

"No," came the response. "It's not moved away yet."

The man getting in slammed the door and the SUV took off. Declan ducked from view as the vehicle passed, making a quick right and then a quick left around the ninety degree turn in the rock wall. As soon as it was around the wall and its headlights shone over Shane's SUV, the driver floored the accelerator. Thirty yards later, the driver turned the vehicle suddenly and skidded to a stop in front of Shane, the passenger side door opening.

"Get out of the car!" Declan heard someone yell as he jumped down off the wall and began making his way back towards the gate, using the wall as cover to prevent his approach from being seen by what he could only assume were some kind of security guards. As he neared the gate he removed the Glock pistol he was carrying from his jacket and chambered a round. Securing the suppressor he'd been carrying in his pocket, he stopped at the edge of the gate and peered around. Two men stood behind the open doors of the black Range Rover, each aiming a sidearm in Shane's direction.

"Get out of the car now!" one of them yelled.

Declan watched as the driver's door of Shane's olive green 1986 Range Rover opened.

"Alright, alright," Shane said, his arms raised above his head as stepped out of the car. "I'm obviously in the wrong place."

"Keep your hands up and come around the front of the vehicle!"

Declan watched as Shane did as he was told. "I'm just a lost motorist," Shane said loudly. "Don't shoot. Don't shoot."

Looking through the windows of the black Range Rover, Declan could tell by the illumination from the headlights that the two guards were the only people in the vehicle. As Shane stepped slowly towards the front of his SUV, Declan pulled himself up and over the gate by placing his hands on its top rail and hopping over. He silently absorbed the impact of his landing by bending his knees and quickly withdrew the pistol from his belt again as he stood upright. The guards' attention was focused on Shane and neither saw him approaching as he moved slowly towards the rear of the vehicle. Whether Shane saw him, he wasn't sure. He just hoped that he was ready to act when the time came. He stopped at the back of the SUV and waited as Shane reached the front of his own Range Rover with his hands raised.

"Right then," the driver of the black Range Rover said, "Cuff him."

The passenger guard slowly moved out from around the door with his weapon still aimed.

"Easy, easy," Shane said. "I'm not looking for any trouble."

"Shut up," the guard replied, as he looked quickly over his shoulder at his partner. The partner nodded, indicating that he had the scene covered so his counterpart could holster his weapon and retrieve his handcuffs. Slowly the guard did just that, withdrawing a pair of white flexi-cuffs from the pocket of his black cargo pants after holstering his sidearm. Declan watched as he stepped towards Shane. Over the rumble of the two Range Rovers' engines, neither guard heard a sound as he stepped towards the right side of the black Range Rover and crept towards the driver, his pistol held by his side.

For a moment, Declan locked eyes with Shane who kept his hands in the air as he held his friend's gaze.

"He's not lookin' at me!" the driver suddenly shouted and he started to turn, but it was too late.

As the passenger guard dropped the flexi-cuffs and went for his sidearm, Shane stepped in and grabbed his gun hand before he could draw the weapon and threw a punch across the bridge of the man's nose. Declan blocked the driver's turning motion by grabbing his wrist as he struck him in the temple with the butt of his pistol. The man collapsed against the inside of the driver's door and slowly, Declan allowed him to fall to the ground still holding onto his gun hand. He wrenched the pistol away as the guard stared at him, bleary-eyed from the powerful strike.

"Jesus, Dec," Shane said from a few yards away. "I've still got it. Even after all these years."

Declan stood to see Shane wrench the passenger guard's pistol away, his hand under Shane's boot and pinned to the ground at the wrist. Shane stood with a smile, rubbing his knuckles.

"C'mon. Up with you," Declan said, as he grabbed the driver and pulled him to his feet, pushing him against the side of the black Range Rover with a hollow thunk.

A loud static filled the air. "Celt 2, this is Celt 1, over? Is everything clear down there?"

The voice came from a radio unit located on the dashboard of the guard's Range Rover. Declan and Shane locked eyes, each of them thinking the same thing.

CHAPTER FIFTY-EIGHT

"I repeat, Celt 2. This is Celt 1. Do we have an all clear?"

"Give 'em the all clear!" Shane said, as he leveled the passenger guard's sidearm at the man Declan had shoved against the side of the SUV.

"No," Declan said, raising his hands between Shane and the guard. "We can't risk it. He could give them an emergency code and we'd never know. You do it."

"Are you having a laugh?" Shane asked.

"Do it, in your best London accent. You've lived there long enough, haven't you?"

Shane lowered the weapon and stepped towards the driver's door of the SUV. "We could just as easily give them the wrong code," he said, as he lifted an eyebrow and looked at Declan.

"Well we've gotta give them something. From the way these guys have operated so far I'm guessing the security isn't exactly top of the line. I'm rather surprised, really."

Shane nodded with a slight grimace and slid into the driver's seat, picking up the mic on the front of the radio unit. "Celt 1, this is Celt 2. All's clear down here, just a lost tourist. We've got him sorted and on his way, his encounter with the famed British SAS coming soon to an American travel blog near you." He spoke the last sentence with more than a bit of sarcasm in his voice.

Several seconds passed after Shane clicked off the mic. He sat still in the driver's seat, waiting. Declan watched the eyes of the guard against the Range Rover for even the smallest sign of delight. Instead the man's eyes darted between him and Shane with worry.

"Roger that, Celt 2," the radio crackled. The voice sounded almost elderly now that it had relaxed. "God only knows what that poor bugger will think is over these hills."

Shane smiled broadly. "Werewolves or something, no doubt, Celt 2 over."

Silence followed and Shane hung the mic back on the front of the unit.

"Well, that's that," he said with a nod as he stepped out of the vehicle. "Now we just need to find the manor. I'm sure his lordship has a fire on in the hearth for us."

After Declan had cleared the stone house around the bend of any other inhabitants, he and Shane secured the guards in the barn with their own flexi-cuffs and took their keys. Locking the black Range Rover's keys inside it and leaving it parked outside the house, they drove back to the gate and unlocked it, pulling through onto the worn dirt road beyond.

As the SUV bounced over more potholes, Declan kept an eye out for more security measures, especially roadside sensors that might give away their approach. Twenty minutes and seven rough miles later he hadn't seen any. "Where in the bloody hell is this place?"

"Just over this next hill if the map my agent provided is correct."

"Then let's stop here. From the looks of the inside of that farmhouse down there, his lordship isn't expecting those two guards to come and visit him."

Shane nodded and stopped the SUV just before the base of a steep hill. "So what's our approach?"

"Let's get a look at this place first. Then I'll figure something out."

They exited the vehicle and climbed the hill, the inky black of the Scottish night and the low cloud cover making it nearly impossible to see more than twenty yards in any direction.

"Supposedly this place sits at the southern end of Loch Builg," Shane said, as they crested the hill and looked over into the valley below. Through the fog it was hard to see anything very clearly, but there was definitely a loch judging from the mist settled over it. Declan scanned the area and through the mist could just make out the dim lights in the windows of a building. "There," he said pointing.

"Aye, I see it."

Partially buried in a thick fog was a stone building with a round spire on its front right corner, its roof invisible in a white wisp of frozen air. Declan started down the hill and Shane followed. More of the building became visible as they came closer. Greumach Manor appeared to be three stories tall and was small by castle standards. It was clear from the style of the architecture that the castle had been built during the Perpendicular Gothic period, and in places its outer walls were covered in thick ivy. A small motor court stood on the left directly opposite the spire they'd seen from the hill above, a stone archway stretching over it to allow a vehicle to drop its passengers without them getting wet from the frequent rainfall. A black late-model Bentley was parked under the archway along with another black Range Rover, a twin of the vehicle the security guards had been driving.

"Jesus, Dec. We could have a full team of night vision wearing snipers looking at us from the roof and we wouldn't know it in this fog."

"If they're wearing night vision in this weather they're in more trouble than we are."

"Oh, right," Shane said, as he remembered that night vision goggles were useless in the fog. "Well, we still can't walk up and ring the bell. What're you planning?"

Declan noticed a flickering light in a large second floor window and watched as a shadow moved past. "There," he said pointing to the window. "It looks like you were right. His lordship has a fire on for us."

Shane followed his hand to the arched picture window.

"The windows in this place are rather old," Declan said. "I bet with the right motivation they'll open right up."

"Yeah, but we have to get to them first."

Declan ignored the objection and walked quickly towards the archway over the motor court where a rusted metal pipe ran down the side to drain water away from the roof. Grabbing ahold of it, he shook it to see if it was secure. It would hold. He grabbed onto the metal bracket that secured it to the stone archway and pulled himself up, using his feet to push from the bottom. His boots slid slightly against the pipe, but the rust gave him all the traction he needed. Water began to immediately soak through his clothes as he pulled himself up onto the archway's roof and leaned over the edge. "Here," he said sticking out his hand for Shane.

He looked up towards the windows making sure, as best he could through the fog, that no one was watching them. Feeling Shane grip his hand, he braced his arm and pulled upwards. He could hear Shane's shoes slide against the rusted metal and reached out with his other hand to help him along. He didn't want anyone inside to hear them. The element of surprise was critical to gaining entrance. He pulled Shane onto the roof and stood, doing his best to brush the water off his clothes, though it had already soaked through in multiple spots. He could feel the cold air sharply against the wet material and wished for a moment that he was back in the United States where the temperatures were far milder.

"Now what?" Shane asked.

Declan didn't respond. Instead he pushed the thoughts of his adopted home away and moved towards the end of the archway that was attached to the building. A few feet above the end of the archway an architectural ledge was built into the side between the first and second floors.

"Ah," said Shane, as he spotted it, "now I'm with you."

The sound of a door squealing on its hinges as it was pulled open came from below them. Declan placed his back against the wall and waved his hand at Shane, who responded by crouching down out of view. They waited silently as the sound of heavy boots descending a set of stone steps followed the closing of the door. Soon a heavy sigh and the unmistakable sound of a cigarette lighter came from below and Declan smiled. He moved forward, taking care not to make any noise as he did so. Shane flashed him a panicked look and mouthed the words, "What're you doing?"

Declan held a finger to his lips and moved towards the other end of the archway. Crouching down at the end of it, he looked over the side as a puff of bluish smoke rose into the air from below him. He waited for several minutes as puff after puff of smoke rose from the same spot. When he saw a cigarette butt fly out from under the archway and disappear into the dark, he prepared to make his move. He placed his hands against the edge of the archway and as he heard the sound of boots walking back towards the door, he leapt over the side and twisted as he landed onto the gravel drive, absorbing the impact. The sound of his landing was enough to draw the attention of the man who had been smoking and, as he started to turn around, Declan rushed forward and delivered a knife-edged chop to the side of his neck where the carotid artery was located. It was a gutsy move and it paid off, as the man collapsed onto the pea gravel drive underneath the archway, the blood flow to his brain temporarily interrupted by the forceful strike.

"Change of plans," Declan whispered upwards to Shane. "Get down from there. We're going in the front door." He pulled the downed security guard out of the line of sight of the front door and ran up a set of stone steps that led to a porch and an oak door. He depressed the thumb latch on the door as he heard Shane land on the gravel drive with a thud. Looking over his shoulder to be sure Shane was on his way, he pushed the door open.

A rush of warm air flowed through the open doorway and Declan cautiously stepped inside, his eyes moving around the castle's large foyer. The floor was black and white parquet and directly ahead of him, along the left side of the mahogany-paneled walls, was a grand staircase leading to a second floor balcony that overlooked both the foyer and whatever room was beyond the closed wooden door on the right side of the staircase. The lighting was dim, but he could see an open-arched doorway to his right and a dining room beyond it containing a long wooden dining table. To his left, a small parlor with a writing desk and a chair stood surrounded by floor to ceiling windows.

Shane stepped in behind him and gently pushed the door closed. Declan started to reach for the pistol in his belt, but thought better of it. He had no desire to shoot anyone inside and if someone shot at him, he'd just have to duck away. Killing innocent people simply wasn't an option.

"Wait here," he whispered to Shane, as he pointed to the

small parlor.

Shane nodded and walked into the room, taking a position just inside the door where he couldn't be seen if someone were to approach from inside the house.

Declan cleared the dining room with a few quick glances and moved onto the red carpeted stairway. Looking up towards the balcony, he climbed the stairs, watching carefully for any signs of more security guards. The flickering light he had seen through the second story window had to be from a fireplace. Hopefully it was some kind of den or study where Lord Allardyce was located. He had no desire to traipse throughout the entire castle trying to find the man, even if the castle was on the smallish side.

Declan reached the top of the stairs and turned right after clearing the hallway to his left. It contained only another closed wooden door, no sign of any lights on inside the room beyond showing around the edges. He approached the other side of the balcony where another staircase lead to the third floor and looked over into the room below. It was a large den with a fireplace along the right wall and a set of circular picture windows that presumably looked out over the loch when the weather was clear enough to see it. Knowing he was exposed on top of the balcony, he moved past the staircase, where a long hallway led to a closed wooden door. Four other doors stood closed along the hallway. With his back pressed to the wall, he moved past each of the doors.

From underneath a doorway halfway down the hall he saw what he was looking for; a faint flicker of light from a fireplace. He moved across the hallway towards the door and listened. From inside the room beyond, he could hear a low key conversation. He reached out and gripped the wrought iron door handle and depressed the latch, pushing the door open and bathing the hallway in orange light.

CHAPTER FIFTY-NINE

Declan waited momentarily for his eyes to adjust. Slowly, when no noise or motion came from inside the room, he stepped around the edge of the doorframe and revealed himself. Two men looked in his direction from a billiard table, surprise evident on their faces.

"Who are you?" the man on the opposite side of the table from the door said. Declan recognized him from vague, childhood memories and from the *Daily Telegraph* article he had read earlier.

Lord Dennis Allardyce was a lanky man with thinning blonde hair and touches of gray over his ears, wearing a dark red wool sweater and brown trousers. He stared blankly at Declan, his face momentarily registering uncertainty, before turning emotionless again.

"I don't mean you any harm," Declan said, raising his hands to show that they were empty.

"Well, I should say you do if you've gone to the trouble of breaking in here. I suppose you're the lost tourist and that the all clear we just received was from my men who were afraid for their lives."

Declan nodded. "They're fine. A few bumps and bruises, but fine."

Allardyce grimaced and the man standing opposite him with the pool cue in his hand turned slowly around. He was an elderly man, gray haired, with a receding hairline and a wrinkled face. His brown eyes darted between the door and Declan as he tried to register the situation.

"Well, get on with it if you must," Allardyce said, straightening himself as if he was preparing to take a bullet. "I'd hoped we were free of your lot trying to assassinate us, but I guess that'll never be so."

Declan lowered his hands. "I haven't come here to assassinate you. The minor harm done to your security was regrettable, but necessary."

"Do you know how many crimes you've committed by breaking in here?"

"Nothing compared to what I've committed trying to get here. In the last four days I've committed more violent acts than in the previous forty-one years combined, and that's saying something because I've got quite a story. My name is Declan McIver and I've only come here to talk to you."

"Declan McIver?" Allardyce asked, as he looked Declan up and down. "If that's true, there's a good many people looking for you."

"That's why I need your help."

"My *help*," Allardyce said, with a quick smile that bordered on a sneer. "Oh, you'd have better luck assassinating me."

"Just hear me out. If you don't believe what I tell you, you can hold me here until the police come." Declan withdrew the Glock pistol from inside his coat and stepped forward, placing it on the billiard table before backing away. Allardyce tensed as he saw the weapon, but relaxed again as it was laid down.

From outside of the room came a violent thud as the door opened and a black-clad man was shoved through, his face bearing a red swelling near the eye and cheek. "Found this sorry bastard outside plotting some violence," Shane said, as he appeared in the doorway behind the man and holding what Declan presumed was the security guard's pistol.

Allardyce cleared his throat as he looked at his vanquished security. The room quickly returned to the way it was before the interruption. "That's a nice gesture," he said, nodding at Declan's surrendered pistol, "but since you didn't come here alone, that pistol won't do me much good, will it?"

"My list of friends has become extremely short in the last few days, but thankfully I still have one or two."

"Well then, since I'm being press-ganged into playing your

host, why don't you get on with it?"

Declan did. He reviewed briefly his life, his movements before the bombing at the university, and everything he'd done since. When he was finished, Allardyce let it all sink in for a moment before he spoke. "I don't suppose there's anyone who can verify any of this, is there?"

Declan grimaced and shook his head. "No. They've cut me off from everyone and everything. If not for the help of a few old friends I'd probably be dead by now, my wife, too."

"I'm sure that I don't need to tell you the percentage of people in our prisons that claim they are innocent of the charges against them."

"Why would I risk everything to come here if what I'm saying is a lie? Why would I have the audacity to come to you, a lifetime civil servant of Great Britain, for help if I didn't really need it? You knew my father and he regarded you as an honorable man. He told me once, shortly before he died, that if I ever needed help that I should contact you. I'm about thirty years late, but I'm here, hoping against hope that he wasn't wrong."

"Your father?"

"Paul McIver, elected Member of Parliament for the North Down constituency in the elections of 1979. You campaigned with him while you were Secretary of State for Northern Ireland. He was murdered along with his wife, Lorna, the very next year. His son, Declan, witnessed the deaths of his parents from the backseat of their newly purchased 1981 Mercedes Benz."

Allardyce looked down, examining the crimson carpet for a moment as he mulled over the names. When he looked up he said, "You're the son of Paul and Lorna McIver?"

Declan nodded as Allardyce stared in his direction.

"Where did they live?" the aged aristocrat charged.

"In the town of Ballygowan, in a two-story stone house on the Tullygarvan Road near the intersection with Springmount Road."

"What was the name of the house?"

"The Brae Bridge House, but you'd only know that if you pulled back the ivy on the right stone column near the entrance, where the black iron shingle was placed."

"You've done your research."

"My father carried a black, leather-bound journal with him in his briefcase," Declan said. "My da' woke up at sunrise every morning and spent a few hours in his study before the rest of the family awakened. The last entry in his journal was on June 16th, 1980, the morning before my parents were murdered at a fake UDR roadblock while driving home along the Ravara Road. The journal was given to me in 1987 by Father Liam Donnelly. Today it sits in an armoire inside my house in Roanoke, Virginia, in the United States. The inscription on the inside cover is a quote from Thomas Jefferson and reads, 'Nothing can stop the man with the right mental attitude from achieving his goal.' Writing in that journal is something he learned from you. You gave those journals to all of the candidates for Parliament who supported the idea of a power-sharing government in Northern Ireland in the 1979 election."

Allardyce looked at Declan for several moments, his stare unblinking. "My God," he said, "the little blonde-haired boy who campaigned with his father all those years ago. I never made the connection. And what of all this talk about an IRA hit squad targeting London? Also a made up lie, I suppose?"

Declan shook his head. "No. That part's true. As I said, I'm about thirty years late and I'm afraid the circumstances of my existence in Northern Ireland after the deaths of my parents found me in the company of some rather violent men."

Allardyce nodded slowly, his face softening a bit. "That's a sad story which has been repeated many times in Northern Ireland, so many there were caught up in the Troubles despite not being political hardliners of one persuasion or another."

"You can't seriously be considering helping this man," the older man who had been standing silently in the room all along said. "He's a wanted terrorist. You're the director-general of the Security Service. It would be political suicide."

"I've served my country for a long time, Tom. Don't lecture me on politics. If I've been used, and my country as a result, by someone with less than honorable intentions then I want to know about it and set it right."

"Then you'll help me expose this conspiracy?" Declan said. "You'll tell me who requested the information on me and where it went?"

"No," Allardyce said, as he set down his pool cue and withdrew a Walther PP from the pocket of his trousers. He aimed it at Shane. "Drop the weapon, son."

The older man whom Allardyce had just called Tom reached over and picked up the Glock that Declan had surrendered.

Shane stayed where he was, his pistol still aimed at the security guard standing in front of him. He looked between Allardyce and Declan.

"Drop it, Shane," Declan said. "We're not here to hurt anyone. That's not going to help us."

Slowly, Shane allowed the pistol to fall out of his grip and hang by his index finger. He held it up as the security guard in front of him relaxed and turned, taking his pistol back.

"Now what?" Declan asked.

"Now you're both officially in the custody of the Security Service," Allardyce said, "and until I get this matter straightened out, that's where you're going to stay."

CHAPTER SIXTY

David Kemiss walked over to the door, opening it in response to the sharp knock. "Come in, Colin. Come in."

Colin Bellanger stepped into the apartment. In the button-down shirts and ties required at the Senate office building, Kemiss thought the young man looked awkward and lanky. But tonight, in his off hours, wearing a black twill zip-up jacket that fitted his lean figure perfectly, with his hair wet from the rain outside and his glasses exchanged for a pair of contacts, he looked athletic and maybe even sophisticated.

"Dinner's just been delivered. I hope Chinese from City Lights is okay."

"Great. City Lights delivered all the way to Stanton Park? Impressive. Thank you, Senator."

"Perk of the job and its David tonight, I get tired of all the titles."

Bellanger smiled and unzipped his coat, pulling out a thick file from underneath that he had been shielding from the rain. "I can understand that, I guess."

The young man seemed nervous.

"So, I hate to bring you out on a night like this, but you said you'd found something?" Kemiss asked.

While he was trying very hard to be polite and to come

off as cool and collected, inside Kemiss was feeling almost panicked. Earlier in the day he had learned that Declan McIver had been spotted in Wales and news since then had seemed to confirm Kemiss' worst fears; McIver appeared to be heading inland towards London. Police in the U.K. had discovered that he had carjacked a couple of tourists not far from where he had spent the night with a wildlife worker and her elderly father. The tourists' stolen car had turned up only an hour outside of London, but McIver had yet to be located. In response to the developments, Kemiss had charged Lukas Kreft with hiring assassins to kill Lane Simard, the only person in London that could positively tie Kemiss to McIver and so to the attacks on Liberty University and Abaddon Kafni. The question burning in his mind was could Kreft find the kind of men they needed to do the job in time? Having never hired professional killers, Kemiss would have had no idea where to start. Hopefully, Kreft was more experienced and better prepared.

"So what is it, what have you got?"

"Well, I think I've finally found something. I hope it will be useful."

"Well, don't keep me in suspense," Kemiss said with a smile, as they moved into the apartment's main living area and took a seat on the sofa. Two large bags filled with various Chinese entrées were on the table, but Kemiss pushed them aside as Bellanger placed the folder on the table and opened it.

"Yes, sir." Bellanger began removing some of the papers inside the file. "I've been going over the documents you asked me to and I've made what I think is an important connection. Do you remember the plane that the FBI had boarded when it landed in Ireland?"

"Yes."

"Well, I think it was connected to Declan McIver after all."

"Do tell."

"A lot of the names in the file have been redacted and the connection isn't an easy one to make without them, but by process of elimination I believe I've figured out the man who was running the show in the Black Shuck Unit of the IRA. I believe it's a man named Eamon McGuire."

Kemiss bristled for a moment. How could Irish law

enforcement have allowed an international fugitive to get off an airplane without seeing him? And what about McIver's presence in the U.K.? He hoped Bellanger wasn't wasting his time. "As in McGuire & Lyons Industries?"

"Yes, sir, the company that owned the plane. Eamon McGuire never played an active role in the company. I guess he was far too busy with his IRA activities, so he left the running of the family business to his brother. Both of them are dead now, but the company is run by Eamon's son, Fintan, who's one of the names on the list of suspects in the Black Shuck Unit."

"And you're betting that *Fintan* is a chip off of the old block and is helping his old childhood friend, Declan McIver, hide out?"

"Yes, sir. Now, I know what you're thinking, that this can't be connected because McIver's in England, not Ireland, but hear me out?"

Kemiss nodded.

"Fintan McGuire was one of the people on that plane when it landed in Ireland, which means he was in the United States. Now, I've gone over everything I can find about him on Google and all over the Internet and I can't find any reason why he would be in West Virginia. I can't even find any reason why he would be in the United States, especially for such a short time. McGuire & Lyons Industries is focused primarily on emerging economies across Europe, Southern Asia and South America. Now, is it possible that he was in town for a meeting at the Greenbrier? Sure it is. But that's an awfully big coincidence, if you ask me, and I don't believe in coincidences."

"He was here to get his old friend out of the country," Kemiss said, though he thought the young man was reaching, possibly out of a desire to make a name for himself in the powerful company he found himself in. Careers in Washington had been made on less. Still, Bellanger was onto something and though he couldn't have known this, the airport McGuire's plane had landed and taken off from was a small, out of the way place not normally connected with the Greenbrier Resort, and that lent itself to the idea that McGuire had been trying to hide something. "Well, I'll admit there are a lot of factors in play and your theory has at best a fifty-fifty shot, but it's worth checking into further."

And it was worth checking into further. Though Declan McIver had been seen in the U.K., all of the eyewitness accounts had said that he was alone. There had been no sign of his wife which meant that he had to have hidden her again, and property associated with McGuire & Lyons Industries was as good a place to start as any. Even if McIver himself wasn't there, the presence of his wife would mean that he would eventually show up. Kemiss picked up his cell phone and dialed a number. "Allan, it's David. I have something I want you to look into."

Kemiss quickly caught Allan Ayers up to speed and set the NSA analyst to work. When he hung up the phone, he turned back to Bellanger and said, "Let's eat."

He had invited the young man to his home not because he had said he'd found something, Kemiss could have learned that over the phone, but to ensure that he had the young man's confidence. The job he'd been charged with was highly sensitive and while he had been told that at the time Kemiss had given it to him, he needed to be told again and made to realize the consequences of betraying that trust.

CHAPTER SIXTY-ONE

8:19 a.m. Local Time – Saturday
Greumach Manor
Loch Builg, Aberdeenshire – Scotland

"Well, if nothing else," Shane said, as he looked around at their surroundings, "we've established that there is, in fact, a bunker underneath Greumach Manor. I can make a small fortune writing books about it from my jail cell. My kids will appreciate it, I'm sure."

Lying on one of the eight sets of barracks-style bunk beds that occupied the stone walled cellar they were in, Declan opened one eye and flashed a smile. "You don't have any kids."

After their failed attempt to win the aid of Lord Dennis Allardyce, they had been taken beneath the castle and locked in what appeared to be the barracks part of whatever there was underneath the small fortress. As they'd been led below, they'd passed through several oak doors that appeared to be as old as the castle itself, and that had been reinforced with iron beams. With each of the doors undoubtedly locked as Allardyce and his security guards had returned to the upper floors, escape was impossible. The only other entrance stood at the far end of the room and was secured with three iron crossbars that had been riveted to the stone walls. Whatever was beyond had obviously not been used in a very long time.

"Right," Shane said, standing from his own bunk and causing a cloud of dust to rise from the thin mattress. "Well, I'll find one of those old birds that have a thing for inmates, you know? We'll get married, have conjugal visits and adopt a whole cadre of orphans from around the world. Just like Brangelica."

"Brangelina."

"Right, whatever."

Shane was never beyond a joke, but Declan knew the seriousness of their situation wasn't lost on him. Without the help of Allardyce, not only would they both be arrested and tried for their various crimes, but the only hope of learning the identity of the person who'd passed Declan's information from Great Britain to America was gone and with it, the last chance he had of exposing the conspiracy he'd become the center of. While Allardyce had said he would "get the matter straightened out," Declan couldn't think of anyone that the aristocrat would have contact with that would possibly know the truth of what was going on. Short of an undercover sting operation being run by the governments of both Great Britain and America to entrap the conspirators, Allardyce would only get the official version of the events which, as far as Declan knew, had been designed and directed by the people who had been controlling the investigation through Seth Castellano. Despite the gravity of his own situation, Declan rested easy knowing that Constance was in good hands. Fintan would protect her, help her change her identity, and while her life might not be what she'd hoped for, she'd be alive and in time could possibly find happiness again.

A loud sound echoed from outside the room and Declan knew immediately that it was the sound of the doors being opened along the hallway that led to their current location. But why? Had the authorities finally arrived to take him into proper custody? By his best estimation, it had been just over eight hours since he'd broken into Greumach Manor and confronted the MI5 director, and eight hours was almost exactly how long it had taken them to drive from London the previous day.

With another loud slam as one of the iron deadbolts was released, the door to the barracks room opened and two of the black-clad security guards slowly stepped in, each aiming a pistol. Neither Declan nor Shane moved as the two guards regarded them coolly for several moments. Finally, they stepped aside and Lord Dennis Allardyce appeared in the doorway, wearing the same clothes he had the previous night.

"Leave," Allardyce said, waving his two security guards out, "now."

The two men exchanged surprised looks and then slowly turned and left the room. Allardyce pushed the heavy wooden door closed behind them and took a deep breath. "I've spent the last several hours going over this," he said, as he tossed a thick file onto one of the two rectangular, wooden tables that separated the two rows of bunks. Dust shot into the stale air as the file landed with a thud. "It's very interesting reading, but it leaves a lot to be desired. Starting with the confirmed guilt of any of the one hundred or so men mentioned as possible suspects."

Declan looked at the legal-sized manila folder, its edges worn with age and its contents held inside by a thick rubber band. Faded red letters stamped on top of the folder read *CLASSIFIED* over the official seal of the United Kingdom's Cabinet Office. On the folder's tab the words *PIRA – BLACK SHUCK* were clearly visible in blue ink.

"Your name appears thirty-eight times in this file," Allardyce continued. "Every single mention of you is pure hearsay and speculation on the part of the informer, in fact every single mention of anyone in this file is hearsay and speculation, yet the American, and now the international, media seem to be under the impression that you've already been tried and found guilty of every possible crime listed."

"The radio show hosts don't call them the Drive-By media for nothing," Declan said, "guilty until proven innocent."

"Yes, well, your statements to me last night would, in fact, indicate your guilt, but I'm getting the feeling this isn't something you're interested in hiding anymore. Am I correct?"

"I'm sure every man listed in that file is guilty of something," Declan continued. "For my part, I was a member of the South Armagh Brigade of the Provisional IRA from 1986 until 1993. During that time I trained with a secret unit codenamed Black Shuck. But to answer your question, no one is guilty of Black Shuck, because the entire operation never made it past the intelligence-gathering phase. The attack the unit was created for never happened. The media believes I'm guilty because the people controlling the release of that information aren't interested in the truth. They're interested in burying my credibility, along with my lifeless body."

"And that's your saving grace," Allardyce said. "This information was provided on the condition that it would only be used to affect an arrest of the chief suspect, *you*, in both the bombing and subsequent assassination. However, the release of this information, in any form, to the media was not part of that deal. I may look like an aging politician, but I assure you I'm a military man with a long career in the world of espionage. I know a black bag job when I see one. My phone has been ringing off the hook since this hit the airwaves on Thursday afternoon and, despite having just taken this position over less than a month ago, it's been made clear to me that my leadership of the Security Service will be extremely short if I don't get a handle on this and keep it from becoming a very embarrassing episode for the government of the United Kingdom."

"You and I both know there's only one way that information was mishandled," Declan said. "On purpose. The person or people you released it to weren't working for who they said they were."

Allardyce nodded slowly. "Yes, well, they're not the only ones with contacts abroad. Before this file was delivered to me a few hours ago I spent time gathering information on the two of you. I was quite shocked at your identity, Mr. O'Reilly. Imagine my surprise when I learned that the legendary IRA informer, *Homeless Viper,* was a low ranking intelligence officer in my own Irish & Domestic Terrorism Department. One of our own aiding an international fugitive is a serious offense."

Shane grimaced and his eyes darted between Declan and Allardyce. "Declan's no fugitive. He's the best friend I've ever had and if you want to get to the bottom of this, he's the best friend you have."

"Yes. That would seem to be true. As far as I can tell there's only one person who's told me the truth since this entire thing began in the briefing room on Wednesday morning, and that's you, Mr. McIver. Try as I might, I cannot come up with any reason why you'd be involved in either the bombing or the assassination. You certainly have the experience to commit such an attack, your apparent friendship with Abaddon Kafni gave you the necessary access to commit such an attack, but as far as I can tell, you have absolutely no motivation to commit such an attack. The idea being passed around in the media that your motive is financial is ridiculous. You're sitting on nearly two million dollars in assets and your wife is heiress to another small fortune. If there's one thing you have in good supply, it's money."

"You've done your research," Declan said, flashing a brief smile.

"The man who requested that the Committee release its information on you is the London Station Chief of the American CIA."

Declan and Shane exchanged a knowing glance. "Just like we thought," Shane muttered.

"Where can I find him?" Declan asked.

"I'll take you to him."

CHAPTER SIXTY-TWO

4:06 p.m. Local Time – Saturday
Ashford Road
Two miles south of Faversham, County of Kent – England

Lane Simard sat alone in the backseat of the black, late model Range Rover that the United States Government provided him in his duties as the Central Intelligence Agency's London station chief. He watched through the tinted windows as the four man team of youthful agents that were in charge of his security and transportation entered the two story Tudor-style farmhouse he was preparing to spend a rare vacation in.

The house sat at the end of a mile long lane called Baggins Road, an undoubted reference to the author, Tolkien. The house belonged to the family of an English couple whom he and his wife had made friends with during their four year stay in London and who had graciously offered the country estate for his use on several occasions. The rigors of his work often kept him away for several weeks at a time and he was looking forward to spending a relaxing few days with his family when they joined him later in the evening.

"All set, sir," one of the young agents said, as he opened the rear passenger side door for Simard. "We've scanned the entire house. It's clean."

Simard knew the man meant that the home had been found to be free of any kind of listening devices and even though he wasn't planning on making or receiving any sensitive phone calls, such conversations were always a possibility in his line of work.

"Thank you," he said, as he stepped from the car and walked towards the arched front door. "I want two of you posted at the end of the lane with one of the SUVs and waiting for my family to arrive. They're being driven down from London in a few hours."

"Yes, sir," the man said, as he opened the home's front door and stood aside. "Myself and Agent Fuller will handle it."

Simard nodded and entered the house. He felt his cell phone vibrate in his pocket as he entered the spacious, stone walled kitchen and withdrew it as he stepped through an archway and into the home's living area.

"Hello?"

"Mr. Simard, David Kemiss," the voice on the other end said. "You're a hard man to surprise."

"Good evening, Senator," Simard said, feeling slightly uncomfortable with the level of friendliness in Kemiss' voice. The seasoned politician had, to date, never been anything other than abrupt, sometimes bordering on insulting. "How can I help you?"

"Oh, you've already helped me a great deal and I wanted to express my gratitude. I sent a gift to your London residence, but the delivery company was told you had left for a few days."

"Well, thank you, Senator. That's a great gesture. I'm away from London for a vacation with my family. I'll look forward to receiving your gift when I return."

"I'm afraid by then it won't be much good. Perhaps I could have the delivery company bring it to your getaway? You and your wife could enjoy it during your well-deserved vacation."

Simard didn't like the thought of someone coming to the farmhouse but, as his mind raced to think of a good excuse to refuse the offer, he settled on the notion that saying "no" to the senator would be a bad idea. "That would be great, thank you. I don't know the exact address, but I'm at a farmhouse in Kent, it's two miles south of the M2 motorway near Faversham. It's the only house on Baggins Road and it's at the very end. They can't miss it. I'll have one of my men meet them out front."

"Beautiful area, my wife and I visited there some years back.

I hope you enjoy your stay. I'll notify the delivery company immediately. Thank you again for everything you've done for me, and for your country."

Simard nodded, though he knew Kemiss couldn't see him. "My pleasure, sir."

He felt a swell of pride at being personally thanked by such a high-ranking member of his country's government, even though all he had done was his job. He listened as Kemiss hung up before he closed the phone and returned it to his pocket. Climbing the home's narrow wooden staircase, he entered a hallway and made an immediate left into the study, which overlooked the gravel driveway leading into the property. He removed some papers from his briefcase along with a copy of a book by one of his favorite authors. Setting the papers down on the desk before loosening his tie and removing his shoes, he took a seat in the leather chair next to the room's picture window. Without meaning to be, he was asleep within a few minutes.

He awakened suddenly as he heard the front door of the farmhouse slam closed. Glancing at his watch, he stood and looked through the window. Judging from the faint orange glow to the west that illuminated the green shrubbery along the driveway, the sun was just about to set for the day. He leaned over and placed his hands on the window sill, admiring for a moment the majestic evening that was just beginning. His thoughts were interrupted as he noticed a pair of headlights coming down the drive. Was it time for his family to arrive already? He smiled and thumped his closed fist against the sill victoriously before turning to exit the room.

CHAPTER SIXTY-THREE

6:02 p.m. Local Time – Saturday
Intersection of Ashford Road & the M2 Motorway
Half a mile south of Faversham, County of Kent – England

"How is it that you came to work in Her Majesty's Security Service, Mr. O'Reilly?" Lord Dennis Allardyce asked, as the Range Rover they were riding in cruised smoothly off the M2 motorway onto Ashford Road. Declan tried to hide a smile as Shane shifted uncomfortably in the front passenger seat. Like their involvement in both the IRA and Black Shuck, their dealings with the intelligence agencies of Great Britain were a long story.

Shane cleared his throat. "I became an informer for the FRU in the late eighties. That's where the codename *Homeless Viper* came from. When things went bad and the IRA tried to execute me, my handler, Harold Thom, brought me to London. I've worked there ever since. Who better to run Irish informers than an Irish informer, right? I made a deal with Her Majesty's Government to provide high-value intelligence in exchange for immunity, and employment."

"But you didn't fulfill that agreement completely, did you? You made sure that Her Majesty's Government didn't find out the true identities of the Black Shuck Unit, including that of your friend, Declan McIver."

Shane nodded.

"And you've kept in touch with him over the years and were

able to warn him that someone was trying to leak his past in an effort to frame him for Abaddon Kafni's assassination?"

"Something like that, sir. I've known Declan since we were teenagers. He's saved my life a number of times. I would never have protected anyone that I wasn't sure of. Declan turned his back on violence, even before I did."

"I believe you. Here is something that I still don't know the answer to," Allardyce said, as he looked over at Declan. "How is it that an Irish paramilitary and a conservative Israeli celebrity became friends in the first place? That can't be a common thing."

Declan thought about the question for a moment. Allardyce had been peppering both him and Shane with questions most of the journey and it was starting to annoy him. Talking about his past wasn't something he enjoyed doing, but he felt, with Allardyce, like he had no choice. Thankfully, in what Declan considered to be typical aristocratic behavior, Allardyce had made it clear that he had no intention of making the ten hour drive to where the CIA chief was located. Instead, Allardyce had chartered a small private aircraft and the journey had been completed in less than half that time.

"There's more to Abaddon Kafni than a lot of people realize," Declan said. "I first met him in Belfast in 1990."

Allardyce smiled as if the answer to the question had suddenly become clear to him. "He was undercover for Israel, wasn't he?"

Declan nodded. "Aye, he was the leader of a small contingent of Mossad operatives in Belfast who were keeping watch on the Provos' connections with the PLO."

"Thatcher made it illegal for Mossad to operate in Northern Ireland, but I'm not at all surprised to learn that they ignored her. They've never been an organization that's particularly good at following rules. What was their cover?"

"Bookstore, they ran a secondhand bookstore called Salinger's on the A6, a few blocks northwest of the Belfast Synagogue."

"Amazing," Allardyce said, shaking his head with a laugh.

"Here we are, sir," Tom Gordon said from the driver's seat. "Baggins Road."

Gordon slowed the Range Rover and turned onto a one lane gravel road with thick overgrowth on either side of it providing a natural fence between it and the fields beyond.

Declan looked forward through the windshield from his seat on the rear passenger side next to Allardyce. They had left Greumach Manor at noon for the county of Kent, where Lord Allardyce had located Lane Simard, the CIA's London Station Chief and the man who had requested the U.K.'s files regarding Declan. He didn't know how exactly Allardyce had located him, but he had a strong suspicion that the Security Service kept a watchful eye on the diplomats and embassy personnel of other countries. He wasn't surprised.

The fact that the CIA had been the agency that had requested his records shouldn't have surprised him, and yet it did. It was the first official evidence he had that the people who had conspired to kill Kafni and were trying to kill him were part of the American government. He had built his dreams in America and he believed wholeheartedly that it was very much the land of opportunity, that anyone from anywhere with any background could come and, if he was willing to put in the time, build a better life for himself and his family. The whole idea that the government of the United States was involved in covering up the presence of a Chechen terrorist who had a lengthy record of terrorist attacks and more blood on his hands than a butcher during cookout season, seemed farfetched, despite the events of the last five days, but apparently that was the case. Someone, somewhere within the bloated bureaucracy in Washington D.C., had a reason to kill and hopefully the man they were going to see could shed some light on exactly who, and perhaps why.

"What's this?" Gordon said as the Range Rover's headlights fell over a parked vehicle. He slowed the SUV to a stop and craned his neck to look at the others in the car with him. "Some tosspot's gone and left his car here with the doors wide open."

"No, I don't think so," Declan said from the back seat, his face mirroring the same concern as Shane and Lord Allardyce. "What do those license plates mean? They're not the same as the other cars we've passed."

"They're diplomatic plates," Shane said. "It means the

vehicle's been set aside for use by a foreign organization. The 274 means it belongs to the United States and the X means it's for non-diplomatic staff. The CIA station chief would have such a vehicle, maybe more than one."

Declan pushed open the door and stepped out.

"Here," Allardyce said, "you might need this." He handed over the Glock pistol Declan had surrendered the night before.

"I'll turn the lights out," Gordon said as he reached for the knob beside the steering wheel.

"No," Declan said as he took the pistol. "If someone's watching and they see the lights go out they'll know something's up. Once I'm out, back the car up to the end of the road and make like you're leaving. Drive a short distance and turn around, this time entering with the lights already off. And stay off the brakes. Use the clutch." He closed the door slowly, quietly allowing it to latch. He had a bad feeling that he wasn't going to like what he was about to find and if someone was watching or listening, he wanted to avoid tipping them off if he could. He released the magazine from the pistol and checked it before pushing it back in and chambering a round.

He heard Gordon shift the car into reverse and begin backing away as he approached the black Range Rover, his pistol aimed at the passenger side door that was standing open. Rounding the door as he reached the vehicle, he saw exactly what he was expecting. Two bodies, each clad in a black suit and hunched over in the front seats. It was clear from the blood covering the upholstery and the driver's side window that they'd been shot from about the same place he was standing, and recently.

"What have we got?" Shane asked from the passenger side window as Allardyce's vehicle returned, now shrouded in darkness.

"Whoever they are, they're dead, shot from the looks of it and not very long ago."

"Good heavens," Allardyce said, from the backseat. "What do you think is happening?"

"If you ask me, someone's tying up loose ends and Mr. Simard is one. We need to get to the house, now!"

Declan reentered the vehicle and Gordon shifted through the gears, shooting the Range Rover forward as Declan closed the door.

"Stop here," Declan said, as a graveled motor court came into view fifty yards ahead, a Tudor farmhouse beyond it. "I don't want you all out in the open. We don't know what we're running into."

"We've been doing this kind of thing for a long time, Mr. McIver," Allardyce said. "Go on, Tom, pull to the right of the house under that overhang. It'll provide some cover."

Gordon obeyed and skidded to a stop beside the house, the vehicle covered from the left by the structure and only exposed on the right. Declan didn't like it, but he wasn't in a position to argue. He opened the door and stepped out, breaking into a run as his feet hit the gravel. He ran to the arched front door, his eyes darting around looking for assailants, his pistol aimed in front of him. On the other side of the motor court sat a tan Land Rover, its front doors wide open.

The front door to the farmhouse was ajar and he entered, finding himself inside a stone walled kitchen. Next to an oak island in the middle of the kitchen was another body dressed in a black suit. Clearing the doorways, he reached down and checked the young man for a pulse. He was dead.

"That's not Simard," a voice said from behind.

Declan sprang upwards and around aiming his weapon. Lord Allardyce threw his hands up. "It's me, Dennis!"

Declan let out a deep breath.

"Sorry," Allardyce said. "I guess it's been longer than I realized."

"Go back to the truck. I can't protect you in here."

"I didn't ask you to," Allardyce said, producing his Walther PP from his inside coat pocket, "and you have no idea what Simard looks like. You'll need me."

"Stay behind me and cover my back." Declan relented, unwilling to argue about whether an aged member of the British aristocracy should be inside a house with the likelihood of armed gunmen present. Should Allardyce be injured or worse, killed, then the only lifeline that was keeping him out of the hands of the British police and consequently the hands of the men trying to kill him would be severed.

"Lead the way."

Declan moved through the kitchen and into the home's living area. The house was completely dark without even a faint glow from a digital clock. Clearly the power had been cut and the assault had come quickly, as there were no signs of a struggle. The furniture was upright and with the exception of the three dead men, the house was in perfect order. He cleared a dining room off the main living area and moved to a staircase. Listening as he moved up, he swept right and left as he arrived at the top of the stairs.

He cleared two small bedrooms and then moved left, entering a study. On the floor near a picture window that overlooked the motor court was another body, this one holding a gun. Declan kicked the gun loose from his hand and reached down to check for a pulse, though he knew the man was a goner.

"That's not him, either," Allardyce said. "From the looks of it, I would say these men are his transportation team. They drive him around London and provide security. He arrives at Downing Street every Wednesday morning with them."

Declan stood, but before he could form a coherent thought, several gunshots from outside interrupted it. Followed by Allardyce, he moved out of the room and down the stairs two at a time, blazing through the kitchen to the front door.

"Where's Shane and Gordon?" he asked as he arrived at the Range Rover and found it empty.

"I sent them to cover the back."

He ran quickly around the house, where he found an empty deck surrounded by a knee high rock wall. As he approached, he saw Shane stand up from behind the wall with a gun aimed towards a row of trees lining the back of the house.

"What happened?" he asked, as he arrived next to Shane. Tom Gordon stood up from beside the rock wall.

"We moved around the house as Lord Allardyce suggested and saw someone run out," Shane said. "Two men came out after him and opened fire on us."

"Simard," Allardyce said. "He must be trying to get away from the attackers."

"Stay here and cover the house to make sure they don't double back," Declan said to Gordon. "Shane, go around that side of the hedge. Dennis, come with me."

The three of them fanned out with Shane soon breaking off to the left as they approached the six foot wall of shrubbery twenty yards from the back doors of the farmhouse.

"What's this building for?" Declan whispered, as he and Allardyce reached the right side of the hedge and began making their way down the side of the square barrier it formed.

"Stables, I'm sure. The hedge creates a naturally fenced in riding arena. There's probably a gate not far ahead."

He was right. Declan spotted a break twenty feet ahead of them and approached cautiously. The green metal gate was closed, but with the increased visibility it gave him, Declan could tell the stable door was wide open. Which way had Simard gone? Had he jumped the gate and ran for the stables or had he continued on into the dark fields? It was a fifty-fifty shot and the outcome could mean Simard's death at the hands of whoever was after him. Declan rolled the dice that the property owners wouldn't have just left the stable door open when no one was home. Aiming his pistol around the clearing inside the hedge, he hopped over the gate using one hand as a brace.

Allardyce was slow to follow, but made it over the gate as Declan reached the stables and rounded into the doorway. Empty horse stalls were all he could see. He turned back to Allardyce as he arrived. "He must've run into the fields, dammit!"

As the words came out of his mouth a gunshot sounded from behind the building followed by a painful cry. Declan ran for the side of the building as fast as he could, audibly crushing clumps of grass as his feet pounded over the ground. He rounded the building in a wide circle with his pistol raised. As he reached the back of the building he made out the shadows of two men holding assault rifles standing over a third . One turned as he approached and he responded with two shots center mass, knocking the man backwards onto the ground before firing again and dropping the second man with a head shot. The man quickly collapsed and lay still. Declan reengaged the first man who he could still see moving on the ground and fired a fourth round into the man's head, snapping it back with a crunch as the back of his skull hit the ground.

Keeping his gun aimed, he leveled it at the man on the ground between them.

"Thought I was a goner, mate," Shane said from the ground as he gripped his knee, blood oozing between his fingers.

"Where's Simard?" Declan said, looking over the black-clad men he'd just killed. They were dressed in fatigues and wore bulletproof vests. It was clear from their weapons and appearance that they were professionals and had shot Shane in exactly the right spot to bring him to the ground without killing him, probably believing him to be Lane Simard.

"Didn't see him," Shane said, as he grimaced in pain. "These two rounded the building just ahead of you."

"Help him up and get him back to the house," Declan said to Allardyce. "Simard must've run into the fields or doubled back. He can't have gotten too far."

As he scanned the area in a circular motion for a good direction in which to start his search, a bright light shot out from around the side of the house and a mechanical grinding sound followed.

"The other Land Rover!" Declan yelled, breaking into a run as he made for the house. Simard must've doubled back and was trying to escape in the tan Land Rover that had been parked in the motor court. With the two assailants down, Declan ran furiously for the gate and jumped it, landing in a run on the other side. He ran the fifty yards between the stables and the house, feeling like his feet were barely touching the ground as he moved. He cleared the side of the house and moved into the motor court where Tom Gordon was standing by the driver's door of the black Range Rover they'd arrived in.

"Here," the older man said tossing him the keys. "He's getting away!"

Declan looked towards the edge of the motor court where the tan Land Rover had just pulled onto the one lane driveway and was moving towards the road, its driver grinding the gears as he attempted to shift the manual transmission. Sliding into the driver's seat of Allardyce's Range Rover, he started it up and shifted it into reverse as he stomped on the accelerator. The vehicle shot backwards and Declan turned the wheel sharply as he shifted the vehicle into gear and moved after the tan military-style SUV.

Shifting the gears smoothly as the vehicle picked up speed,

he gained quickly on the other driver who was clearly unfamiliar with a manual transmission. The tan Land Rover lurched over the gravel drive ahead of him and just before he nearly rear ended it, he pulled to the right, driving around it and stomping on his brakes as he cut in front, bringing the SUV to a dead stop as it collided with his left fender.

Leaving the cab, he rounded the front end of the Range Rover and aimed his gun at the driver of the tan SUV.

"Don't shoot," the man said slowly raising his hands from the steering wheel. "Don't shoot."

CHAPTER SIXTY-FOUR

"Please don't kill me," the man said, as Declan motioned for him to exit the Land Rover. Beads of sweat rolled down his narrow face and his hands shook as he held them up, palms open. "I haven't done anything to you."

Declan could tell by the way Lane Simard's eyes were locked on him as he pushed open the door that the man recognized him. He lowered the pistol as Simard exited the vehicle and it became evident that he was unarmed.

"I'm not going to kill you," Declan said, "but that's more than I can say for those commandos that were chasing you."

He quickly patted Simard down for any weapons he might have hidden and then pushed the man forward along the gravel driveway towards the farmhouse, staying several feet behind him in case the veteran CIA man decided to try an attack. While the man's fear seemed to be genuine, Declan was sure that the agency training in deception was top notch.

"I need to get to London," Simard said, turning partially around as he pleaded. "My family was supposed to be here by now and they haven't shown up. I need to know they're alright."

Declan didn't respond. He wanted to but he didn't know exactly what to say. He knew all about concern for his family and Simard's role in threatening them would determine whether or not he had any sympathy for the man's plight. He waved Simard on and they got to the front of the house as Allardyce and Gordon were helping Shane around towards the front door.

"Lord Allardyce?" Simard said, as he took note of the three

men.

"Mr. Simard," Allardyce said, with a grimace.

Simard stopped walking and turned, looking between Declan and Allardyce. "What's going on here?"

"We'll be the ones asking the questions, Mr. Simard," Allardyce said. "Now get inside."

"I'm not going anywhere until someone—"

Declan grabbed the CIA man by the shoulders and shoved him through the front door. As the man recoiled and attempted to throw a right-handed hook, Declan effortlessly blocked the punch and drove his fist into the man's stomach. "That's for helping to set me up," he said, as Simard collapsed to the floor and struggled to draw breath. "Your answers to my questions will determine just how much more pain I inflict on you."

"Setting you up?" coughed Simard. "You murdered dozens!"

Declan jerked him upwards by the collar and shoved him through the kitchen and into the farmhouse's living area where he pushed him into an armchair. "We both know I've never murdered anyone. Now I suggest you start talking or what those goons lying dead out the back had planned for you is going to look like a walk in the park!"

"Steady, now," Allardyce said, as he and Gordon helped Shane onto a sofa. "He may not have had anything to do with setting you up. Requests made to the Committee follow a strict procedure, which he adhered to. I'm not sure how things work on the other side of the Atlantic, but I'm sure Mr. Simard will tell us all about it."

"I'm not telling anyone anything until I know my family's safe! I have a wife and two boys en route from London!"

"And my wife and I have been on the run from assassins and the police agencies on two continents for a week!" Declan said. "So far you're not tripping my sympathy meter."

"Please, everyone, calm down," Allardyce said, as he stepped between Declan and Simard, his eyes moving between both men. "Now, Mr. Simard, we have as much interest in your family's safety as you do. We haven't done anything to harm them and we never would. Why don't you take a deep breath and then tell us what's happened here tonight versus what was supposed to happen."

Simard's eyes bored into Declan for a moment. "I'm here for a vacation with my family. I arrived early, as I always do, for security reasons and all. My family was supposed to arrive after my boys were done with their weekend football games. They've never shown up."

"And who were the men chasing you?" Allardyce asked.

"I don't know. I saw a pair of headlights coming down the drive, assumed it was my family, and the next thing I know the agent that was positioned outside came running through the door followed by those men, who then shot him. Another agent and I ran upstairs but they followed too quickly for us to get away. They killed him and moved me to the back room there," Simard said, nodding his head towards the dining room. "They said they'd called in London for me and had been told I wasn't home. They were about to kill me when another vehicle came to a stop outside. They were distracted so I took the opportunity to run."

"That would have been us arriving," Allardyce said, looking at Declan. "Sounds like we arrived in the nick of time. What happened then?"

"I ran out the back door and they chased me. I lost them when I doubled back around the hedge surrounding the horse barn. That's when I tried to leave and this damn terrorist caught me."

"He's not a terrorist, at least not anymore," Allardyce said. "From the sound of it, you two have a lot in common. Assassins have come several times for him in the last few days, too. Luckily his experiences in life have helped him stay alive. Now you're telling me that you have no idea who those men were or who could have sent them after you? They simply showed up here, in a house that you don't own and where no one should have known to look for you, to kill you?"

Simard stayed silent for a moment, his eyes darting around the floor as he apparently thought over the entire situation. "Kemiss," he finally said, "that son of a bitch."

"Who's Kemiss?" Declan asked.

Simard looked up. "Senator David Kemiss, a member of the Senate Intelligence Committee in the United States."

"Jesus," Shane said from the sofa, where Gordon was helping him keep pressure on the gunshot wound near the top of his knee, "a bloody politician?"

"He called me earlier this afternoon and said he had sent a gift to my London residence to thank me for helping him get information on you. He asked to forward it here and a few hours later those men showed up. That son of a bitch, he tried to have me killed."

"So he sent those men to kill you because you knew who he was, because he'd asked you directly to get information from Her Majesty's government?" Allardyce asked. "Information that he then released to the press."

Simard nodded. "Yes. I met with him at his request earlier this week while I was in Washington for some meetings. In my position you don't say no to someone who sits on the Intelligence Committee without a damn good reason. He said he'd been asked to help by someone in the Richmond Field Office of the FBI."

"Castellano worked in the Richmond Field Office," Declan said. "He's the lead investigator that led me into the ambush by Baktayev's men while he was supposedly transporting me to jail."

"The same one they accused you of killing?" Allardyce asked.

Declan nodded. "He was shot during the initial ambush. I tried to save him, but I couldn't. He died behind a dumpster where we were both ducking for cover."

"Why would a sitting politician in the United States want to help a Russian terrorist commit an atrocity against his own country?" Allardyce asked, though it was apparent from the look on his face that the question wasn't directed at anyone in particular.

"I think we need to ask him," Declan said.

"Please," Simard said loudly. "I need to find out if my family has been harmed!"

"Get the man a phone," Allardyce said. "He's earned it."

CHAPTER SIXTY-FIVE

"They're okay," Simard said, as he hung up the phone. His voice cracked as he spoke. "They never left London. My youngest boy had an asthma attack during ball practice. My wife's been at the doctor with him and they've been trying to reach me. But they're okay."

Declan, Allardyce, Gordon and Shane were now seated around the dining table and nodded their approval.

"I thought for sure those men had shown up at my house and that my family was dead," Simard said, as he took a seat at the table and handed Shane's phone back to him. "I don't ever want to feel like that again."

"The feeling like you'd do anything to have them back. To undo all the wrong you'd done in your life and suffer the worst fate imaginable just so they could go on living. I know all about it," Declan said.

Simard looked down and nodded, examining his hands which were now folded in front of him on the table. "I uhh...I don't know anything about what's happened to you. I'm sorry."

Declan nodded though the words were of little comfort.

"I don't wish the feelings I was having moments ago on anyone," Simard said, "but I don't understand. I was told that you were a terrorist and that you had set up the entire attack against Kafni using your influence as a member of his security detail. Now you all are telling me that all of it was a lie?"

Everyone at the table nodded. Allardyce was first to speak. "A damned lie, apparently, and I'm sorry for the role I played in allowing it to be perpetuated. Had Mr. McIver not had the courage to come to me and explain the situation, despite the intense danger he faced, I'm afraid he'd be dead by now and our American cousins would never know about the horror that was about to befall them."

"They still don't know," Declan said.

"That's true," Allardyce said, with a grimace.

Simard looked from person to person as if he was expecting someone to elaborate. When no one did, he said, "I'm sorry, but how do you all know any of this is true? I saw the files the Security Service has on this man. He has a list of terrorist offenses as long as my arm!"

"If you'd bothered to read that file," Shane charged, "then you'd know that Declan was never actually convicted or even arrested for anything! Was he involved with the Troubles? Aye, just as me and a significant part of the population in Northern Ireland were. Those were terrible times that you can't even begin to understand unless you lived through it."

"Shane, it's grand, it's grand," Declan said holding up his hands. "He's asking the same question that you or I would have if we'd just met me in this current situation."

Shane ceded the point with a wave of his hand, but finished with, "Declan's never turned his gun on anyone that wasn't a thieving, raping, murdering, madman!"

"And what of this Black Shuck thing?" Simard continued. "An attack on London designed to bring down the city's infrastructure, assassinate and kidnap its leaders and throw the entire British society into disaster?"

"Black Shuck," Shane said, "was a planned operation that never materialized, in large part because Declan McIver had a change of heart and helped to stop it before we all took a nose dive into a very dark abyss that would have plunged Northern Ireland into a cycle of violence that it never would have returned from!"

"Enough!" Allardyce said, pounding his fist on the table. "While Mr. McIver's past certainly holds things that we may all, understandably, take issue with, the point is that it was a very long time ago under extremely dubious circumstances. As part of the British government in Northern Ireland during those days I can honestly say that we weren't always the upstanding men we claimed to be either. Today, right now, is what we are concerned with. My country has been used to obtain information on this man under false pretenses so that this Senator Kemiss could vilify him in the media and frame him for murder. The very fact that Kemiss sent assassins to kill you, Mr. Simard, should be evidence enough for you that what Declan McIver is saying is true. He has been framed for crimes he didn't commit to cover up the real intentions of Kemiss and whoever is working with him. Am I correct?"

Simard nodded slowly.

"Good. Then let's dispense with this argument and get on with what we're going to do about this. Somehow the Americans have to be warned that Kemiss, for whatever reason, is using this Chechen, this Ruslan Baktayev, to accomplish a heinous terror attack that would make September 11th and July 7th look like a dress rehearsal."

"With all due respect, Lord Allardyce," Simard said, "David Kemiss is an experienced and calculating professional politician. I guarantee that he's covered his tracks extremely well. Even with the political clout you have as a member of the House of Lords, no one in the American government is going to believe the word of someone who has been tried and convicted as a terrorist, even if it's only in the court of public opinion, without a lengthy investigation. And from what you're all telling me, there isn't time for that."

"No, there's not," Declan said. "Baktayev could be unleashed at any moment. In fact I suspect the only reason he hasn't already been is because Kemiss has been trying to make sure he has all the loose ends tied up beforehand." He pointed his thumb at himself and then at Simard.

"Then we have to do this ourselves," Shane said, with a nod towards Declan. "Just like *Vympel* taught us all those years ago, find a weakness and apply pressure. Get him to confess what he's done. Get him to tout on everyone else involved and stop this thing before it happens."

"I don't want to be the naysayer here," Simard said, "but even if you can get to him and force him to confess, it still won't prevent the need for an investigation before anyone in the U.S. will act. A confession made under any kind of duress is not admissible in our courts and will not convince the government to act, especially when it's a seasoned member of their own exclusive club that they'd be acting against."

"Aye," Declan said, "but politicians fear scandal more than anything else."

"Exactly. We'll have to use the court of public opinion, the power of which you just pointed out, Mr. Simard," Allardyce said. "Tape the confession, release it to the media and anyone else that will air it, and hope that it rocks those involved back on their heels enough to cause them to call off the entire thing. If the very thing they are being accused of organizing comes to pass, then it will be all that much harder for them to defend themselves against it. There's no chance they'd go forward if such a confession came to light."

"That may not stop Baktayev," Declan said. "We're making the assumption that these people have him under lock and key, but I doubt that. He's an animal. I'm surprised they've been able to control him this long."

"It's the best we've got," Allardyce said. "And even if, God forbid, the attack does happen then at least those who are actually responsible will be identified, investigated and brought to justice instead of being allowed to accomplish whatever their goals are in committing the attack in the first place. I guarantee that an American senator isn't killing innocent people for the glory of Allah or the freedom of Chechnya."

Everyone around the table nodded their agreement.

"Good," Allardyce continued. "Now, what do we know about David Kemiss?"

CHAPTER SIXTY-SIX

"Looks like I won't be with you on this one," Shane said, as he and Declan were left alone in the dining room while everyone else fanned out around the house. Shane gripped his leg just above the knee where a bullet had passed through the flesh, narrowly missing the kneecap, but bringing him to the ground as the shooter had intended. Declan had cut his pants leg off at the thigh and had cleaned and dressed the wound with bandages from the farmhouse's bathroom.

Declan nodded. "No, not this time, but you'll be up and at 'em again before long."

"I want to see this bastard bleed, Dec. I want to be there when his face wrenches up in pain and he spills his deepest secrets. It's his type that's wrong with the world, ya know? It's his type that's the reason we have conflicts, the reason why innocent people have to die, so."

"I'll take a photo for you, but first we have to get to him," Declan said. He could relate to what Shane was thinking and feeling, that same notion was why he had decided to take a stand against those conspiring against him rather than run and hide. Together, they'd seen a lot of people die because of corruption and political agendas. "It'd be hard enough if we had weeks to plan and gather intelligence. It's going to be even harder in the short amount of time we're talking about."

"Aye, but you're up for it. You always have been. You remember that bloody bog you pulled me out of near the Amu Darya River after the Russians dumped us in the middle of nowhere? You found that shack, dragged me to it and managed to hold off a dozen heavily armed *Mujahideen* with a Makarov you nicked from one of the soldiers as they tossed us out of the troop carrier. I wouldn't have made it back to Ireland if not for you. You can handle this."

Declan smiled. "Aye, you always get emotional and reminiscent when you've been shot."

"Ah, screw you," Shane said, as his face turned red. "I wasn't shot that time."

"No, you tripped in a hole and—"

"Pardon me," Lane Simard interrupted, "but I've found something I think you'd like to have a look at."

Declan nodded, the smile disappearing from his face as he stood. Shane stayed seated, his face turning an even brighter shade of red as he realized that Simard had likely overheard their conversation.

"Hey, Dec," Shane said, just before Declan left the room. "Thanks, man."

"Aye," Declan said with a half-smile as he walked out. "What is it you've found?" he asked, as he followed Simard up the narrow stairs to the study.

"Kemiss seems to have been pretty careful about revealing too much about his personal life, so I wasn't able to come up with much until I found this," Simard said, as he took a seat in front of a computer on an oak desk and moved the mouse, causing the screensaver to clear and a website to appear.

"It's a recent article on Kemiss. Before this there's not much information on him outside of his political career, but it seems this last election cycle was particularly nasty and forced him to reveal more in an effort to hold onto his seat. He was probably trying to humanize himself or something. I found it on a site called blueridgeparents.com. It's a reprint of an article that appeared in *Fatherhood Magazine* in August of 2010."

Declan looked at the picture near the head of the article. A gray-haired man with a receding hairline and thin-rimmed glasses sat on a fence in front of a large Georgian mansion wearing a dark red sweater vest over a light blue button-down shirt, trying his best to look friendly. Declan couldn't be sure if it was because of what he'd recently learned about Kemiss or if it was real, but there seemed to be a regal chill in the politician's eyes that refused to be hidden, despite the man's obvious effort.

"It says his family has lived for two generations on an old vineyard in the Graemont area of Virginia, just north of Charlottesville. That's the property behind him in the photo and here it is on Google Earth," Simard said, as he clicked away from the magazine site and brought up a satellite image. "It's close to a hundred acres and surrounded on three sides by trees. The nearest neighbor's a mile away. It's really the only spot to hit him. Trying to get him in D.C. would be impossible."

"Aye," Declan said, as he scanned the image.

"There's one more thing and I'm hoping it's not an election year lie. The article says Kemiss has a traditional family night once a week that he never misses. It says the family tries to do it every Sunday night. It's not a guarantee, but if that's true, then he'll be at the house tomorrow night."

"That doesn't give us much time," Declan said, looking at the clock in the bottom corner of the computer screen.

"What doesn't give us much time?" Allardyce asked, as he appeared in the doorway of the study.

Simard quickly brought him up to speed.

"Hopefully it's all the time we're going to need, because it's all the time we've got," Allardyce said. "But there's no way you can do this alone. If you're going to have any chance of pulling this off, you're going to need help. For obvious reasons I can't be involved in this as any more than a background player. Neither can Tom, and Shane's going to be off that leg for a good long while. What about the men your wife is with? Could they help?"

Declan shook his head. "No. I'm not getting them involved and exposing Constance in the process. She's safe where she is and I want it to stay that way."

"I hope you've still got a few friends out there somewhere, then. I have contacts throughout the military and intelligence world, but few that would be able to help us with something like this at such short notice and without a lot of questions being asked."

"I've only got one idea and at this point I'd say it's a long shot. I've already been trying to get ahold of them most of the week without any success. I need a phone."

Declan took the phone that Allardyce withdrew from his pocket. This would be his fifth attempt at reaching Okan Osman and Altair Nazari, the only two men he could think of that would be up to the task before him. Allardyce was right. He needed help. He couldn't charge into the home of an elected politician, who likely had at least some kind of physical security, all by himself; at least not if he wanted to preserve the lives of the people he found inside. While he wasn't sure that he believed in divine providence, now would be the time to ask for it.

He dialed Osman's number and waited as the call connected.

"Hello?"

Declan's words caught in his throat for a moment at the sound of Osman's voice.

"Who's calling?" Osman said forcefully.

"Osman, it's Declan."

"Declan! Where are you? We've been trying to reach you for two days now!"

"I've been little busy."

"Yes, I'd say. What is going on? Where are you?"

"I'm in England and I'd rather not say anymore at the moment."

"I understand. Are you safe? Constance?"

"We're fine. Where are you?"

"In Roanoke. As I said, we've been trying to find you for two days. Nazari and I boarded a plane as soon as the reports reached us."

"I need your help."

"Name it."

Without going into any more detail than he had to, he caught Osman up on everything that had happened since he'd left the messages for him earlier in the week.

"And you're certain Kemiss is behind it? I've met the man in passing. Abe knew him. This is an unimaginable betrayal."

"I know," Declan said. "He just sent assassins to kill the CIA chief who helped him locate the United Kingdom's files on my past activities. We got here just in time."

"Then he has to be stopped. What are you planning?"

"A forced confession. We're going to need weapons and equipment for a raid. Some kind of surveillance would be great, if we can get it. Once this is done we're going to need someone with a lot of political connections to get it into the right hands. We need Asher Harel."

"Done," Osman said. "Harel already knows. We left Israel under his orders. He's had a team of men from the Israeli embassy helping us locate you. He doesn't believe you're guilty of this anymore than I do."

Declan felt his mouth curl into an involuntary grin. He didn't know whether it was the divine providence he had thought of moments before or sheer dumb luck, but David Kemiss was about to go down, hard.

CHAPTER SIXTY-SEVEN

11:19 a.m. Eastern Time – Sunday
Charlottesville-Albemarle Airport
Charlottesville, Virginia

The two Honeywell turbofan engines howled loudly as the rented Hawker 800XPR bounced onto the runway at Charlottesville-Albemarle Airport. The howl slowed to a consistent drone as the midsize aircraft made its way north on the airport's single runway towards the private hangar that had been arranged for the arrival of Lord Dennis Allardyce. Once the plane was inside, the double doors of the hangar were closed so the plane's occupants could disembark in complete privacy.

"It was an honor having you aboard, sir," the captain said, as he exited the cockpit. He extended his hand toward Allardyce. "I hope you'll consider Jet Plus for all of your future flying needs."

The fascination British subjects had with the aristocracy never ceased to amaze Declan. He stood behind Allardyce, dressed as one of his two security guards. Clad in black from head to toe and covering his facial features with a low-drawn cap, he nodded to each of the pilots in turn. He had been very skeptical of the idea of renting a private jet to return to the United States, but accepted Allardyce's assertion that there really was no other option and that no one was looking for him in the company of a British lord.

"Rest assured, Captain," Allardyce said, as he shook the

man's hand quickly and stepped onto the staircase. The crew members beamed as Allardyce and his two man detail descended the stairs and entered the black limousine that was waiting for them.

"There now," Allardyce said, as Declan closed the door behind them and he and Tom Gordon removed their caps. "That went off without a hitch."

Declan nodded. "Aye, now we just have to keep our presence quiet long enough to get Kemiss where we want him."

"That'll be the trick, I'm afraid," Gordon said. "What exactly is our plan?"

Allardyce held up a hand. "We don't want to know, Tom."

Gordon nodded as the limousine was driven out through a smaller set of doors at the rear of the hangar and onto a two lane driveway leading off the airport's property. At a rotary in front of the airport's main terminal the car turned east. Declan watched through the tinted windows as the vehicle passed twenty-four hour pharmacies, fast food restaurants and car dealerships; a view that was uniquely American.

Turning south onto the main road leading into the town of Charlottesville, the limousine's driver spoke to them over the intercom.

"We're approaching the address you provided, sir. It's a self-storage. Are you sure this is where you want to go?"

"Yes," Allardyce answered. "We'll be dropping one of my security team there and then we'll continue to the second address listed."

"Yes, sir," the driver said, as he turned onto a concrete driveway and made his way to the top of a hill where an old house sat in front of a high chain-link fence, a metal callbox situated in front of an automatic gate next to the house. Beyond the fence Declan could make out rows of metal storage buildings. He pulled the black cap he'd removed back on and lowered it over his brow as he opened the car door. "Thank you," he said over his shoulder to Allardyce.

"Just bring this villain to his knees and stop this madness."

"Where will you go from here?"

"I've always admired Thomas Jefferson and I understand he has quite a history in this area. We'll be nearby if you need us."

Declan closed the door and walked up to the callbox as the limousine reversed and began turning around. Withdrawing a piece of paper from his pocket, he punched in the sequence of numbers he'd been given and waited as the gate slid open. He walked past the rows of rectangular storage buildings to the end of the property, where he saw what he was looking for. A black Ford Explorer sat in front of the corner unit at the very end of the last row.

Opening the smaller of the units two doors, he stepped inside.

"It's about time you got here," Okan Osman announced with a crooked grin, as he ran a cloth over an AR-15 rifle. "We thought maybe you'd just decided to turn yourself in and cancel our fun."

Osman and Altair Nazari were standing at a workbench along the right hand wall of the eight hundred square foot, dimly lit unit. On the workbench in front of them was a collection of handguns and rifles, along with high capacity magazines and ammunition for them all.

"It's all here," Nazari said, as he picked up an H&K MP5 machine pistol and ran a cloth over it to remove any dust. "Do we really need all of this stuff just to take one house?"

"No," Declan answered, as he stepped up to the table and looked over the equipment. "This stuff isn't for the house. It's for what may come after the house."

Osman and Nazari looked at each other and raised their eyebrows. "I thought that this Senator Kemiss was behind the whole thing? We stop him; we stop the entire thing and shed light on those who actually killed Abe, right?"

"Aye, but unfortunately we can't rely on the Americans to take down Baktayev without first proving that Kemiss is guilty in a lengthy investigation. Once Kemiss has confessed to the operation he's set up, someone still has to make sure that Baktayev and his men don't continue on uninterrupted. They didn't need Kemiss or anyone else when they planned the attack in Beslan so they won't need him here. I'm not planning on getting in any gunfights, but we need to be prepared for anything. How far away is the house?"

"Not far," Nazari said. "We've made a couple of passes

already. You can't see much from the road, but it's there. We placed three men in the forest near the house to keep a watch on it and we have two more men watching Kemiss."

"And we can trust these men?"

"Of course," Osman said. "They're Mossad, stationed here in America to collect and disperse intelligence and to connect with our worldwide network of *sayanim*."

"And the American government doesn't know they're here?"

"I wouldn't say that. I'm sure the Americans are aware at some level that these men likely work for Mossad, but it's just one of those things that no one talks about. The same for American agents in Israel, of which there are quite a few. What really matters is that no one knows they are currently sitting in the trees a hundred yards from the Senator's back door watching every move on the property and reporting to us."

Declan flashed a smile. He'd been happy to learn that Asher Harel had made sure that Osman and Nazari were joined by half a dozen men that Abaddon Kafni had known personally, meaning that each person they'd be working with had a personal stake in making sure the operation was a success and that David Kemiss wouldn't know what hit him.

"So, exactly how are you planning on getting this guy to talk?" Osman asked.

"Did you get the other things I asked for?"

Nazari pointed to a nylon tool bag and some other items near the door. "Fresh off the hardware store shelf."

"Grand. Make sure all of this is in the vehicle and ready to go by nightfall. I've got some calls to make," Declan said, as he walked towards the door and opened it. "If this guy wants to threaten innocent children, let's see how he likes it when someone threatens his."

CHAPTER SIXTY-EIGHT

6:42 p.m. Eastern Time – Sunday
Van Deman Industrial Park
Dundalk, Maryland

"You can't just keep me here!" Sharpuddin shouted. "Albek! He's going to kill me! You can't just keep me here!"

The door to the grubby bathroom opened a few inches and a vertical shaft of light came from the room beyond. A shadow passed in front of it as a bearded face appeared. "Quiet, boy." The door closed again returning the room to complete darkness.

Sharpuddin pulled against his restraints, but his wrists were too bruised from previous attempts to keep pressure on them for long. He gave up, wincing. He didn't know what time it was, or even what day. The only people he had seen in what seemed like days were the men who came in to use the toilet that stood next to him, many of them turning towards him as they urinated. He'd attempted to leave the building as soon as Abu Tabak and his chief deputy had gone, but had only found what he had already suspected, that they had no intention of letting him leave.

"Albek! Help me! He's going to ki—"

The door to the bathroom opened wide with a bang and Sharpuddin squinted as bright light flooded in. "Shut up boy!" he heard someone say, as a hand was placed around his throat, forcing his head back against the porcelain sink he was chained to.

"Easy, Anzor," a voice said from outside of the bathroom. Sharpuddin opened his eyes and blinked as Abu Tabak wandered into the doorway, casually holding a serrated bowie knife.

"Don't kill me, Abu! Don't kill me, General! I'm not going to cause any trouble. I swear!" Sharpuddin was pleading for his life, even though he didn't think it would do much good. He had watched Tabak kill several times during their days in Chechnya. On one occasion, Tabak had even taken the time to decapitate slain Russian soldiers so that he could place the men's heads near their own crotches as a final insult and as a warning to those who would discover the grisly scene. At the time, Sharpuddin had cheered the deed; the soldiers were foreigners trying to dominate Chechen land. But looking back, he wished he had done differently. He wished he hadn't been there at all.

"Vakha is already dead. Let me go. Let me bury him with honor. Put his body in the trunk of his car and I will take him home. By the time anyone discovers I was here, your plans will be completed. I won't get in the way. I swear."

"We should kill this traitorous dog!" Anzor said, spitting at Sharpuddin as he stood alongside Baktayev.

"No," Baktayev said. "I have other plans for him." He bent down and placed the serrated edge of the bowie knife at Sharpuddin's throat. "You're going to bring news to the world of the brave servants of Allah who are about to lay down their lives in service to our God and our country." He turned his head to look over his shoulder and called, "Albek?"

The thick-bearded man who had been keeping watch over Sharpuddin appeared in the doorway.

"Make sure everything is in the vans and ready to go. We're leaving, now."

"Yes, General," Albek said, as he turned and moved hurriedly into the workshop outside the grungy bathroom that had become Sharpuddin's prison.

"We cannot rely on this dog to tell anyone anything! He will lie with his forked American-loving tongue!" Kasparov protested.

Baktayev smiled as he smelled the air. The sound of engines

starting came from the workshop, the smell of exhaust fumes filling the cramped building. He looked up at Kasparov. "Well, I wasn't going to fork it, and who said anything about him speaking?"

Sharpuddin's eyes went wide and his feet scrabbled against the concrete floor as if there was somewhere he could escape to. "No, Abu—No—anything but that! Please! Anything but that!"

CHAPTER SIXTY-NINE

7:53 p.m. Eastern Time – Sunday
Graemont Lane
Charlottesville, Virginia

David Kemiss turned off Reas Ford Road onto Graemont Lane, the gravel drive his home shared with three others, though they were spread widely apart. The headlights of his navy blue Cadillac illuminated the thick pine forest on the side of the road as he steered the vehicle around the street's turns and into the cul-de-sac his driveway ran off. As soon as the brick columns that marked his driveway came into view he heard his cell phone ring and brought the vehicle to a stop as he reached for the device.

"Dammit," he breathed, as it rang for a third time and he struggled to remove it from the pocket of his coat, which was draped over the passenger seat. "Kemiss?" he said abruptly as he flipped open the phone and brought it to his ear. Hopefully this was the call he'd been waiting for.

"Sir, it's Allan Ayers."

Kemiss sighed loudly. The caller wasn't who he'd hoped. He was waiting to hear from Lukas Kreft, who was supposed to be helping him eliminate a potential witness. It had taken nearly twenty-four hours for Kreft to get men in place who could do the job and when they had finally arrived at Lane Simard's residence, they'd found only the man's hired nanny. In a last ditch effort, Kemiss himself had placed a call to Simard to learn the man's location. By now Simard should have been dead for twenty-four hours, but still no word had come from Kreft.

"I think I've found them, sir," Ayers said, after several seconds of silence from Kemiss.

"You think? I'm not interested in what you think you've found."

Ayers was silent for a moment, only the sound of his breathing coming over the line.

"Well, get on with it!" Kemiss ordered.

"The information is nearly a sure bet. I've tracked down all the properties in Ireland that are or ever have been owned by McGuire & Lyons Industries or any of their executives. There's an old manor house in an out of the way place called Mullaghmore, just over the border from Northern Ireland."

"And you're positive that they're there?"

"I entered all of the properties into the ToRuS program, so I'm as positive as I can be without actually seeing them."

"What the hell is Torus?"

"The ToRuS program is—"

"The shorthand version."

"It tracks the usage of utilities such as water and electricity. It's designed to tell when there's been a rise in usage, which normally means the presence of guests. In this particular property that's very significant because as near as I can tell the place has been vacant for quite some time."

"And it's your working theory that Fintan Maguire has taken Declan McIver and his wife to this house?"

"The program has found a large spike in utility usage at the property, so yes, that's what I'm thinking."

Kemiss smiled and breathed out a short laugh. Declan McIver seemed to have nine lives, but sooner or later he'd run out, and by Kemiss's reckoning, it was about that time. No matter how good he was, the man couldn't dodge every bullet that was fired at him indefinitely and his friends had to be running out of places to hide him. "Send me the information on the property. I'll make sure there's no way they can get out of there this time."

He ended the call and tossed the phone onto the passenger seat. This cat and mouse game was getting tiring. While he enjoyed rising to a challenge, this kind of stuff had never been his forte. His idea of a challenge was racing a rowboat on the Potomac or now, in his later years, a spirited game of racquetball, not facilitating teams of assassins. That kind of stuff was for someone far below his pay grade. Hopefully the men Kreft had found to take care of Lane Simard had been successful and were up for another job in Ireland. Only this time, if Kemiss had anything to say about it, there'd be a lot more men involved. Taking out a simpering bureaucrat like Simard was one thing, but taking out Declan McIver would be far more difficult if the events of the last week were any indication of what to expect.

Kemiss took his foot off the brake and allowed the Cadillac to move forward onto the drive. Hitting the accelerator as the driveway ahead of him began to incline towards his house, he swore to himself as he noticed all the lights in the three story mansion were off. Wasn't anyone home? They'd better be. He hadn't wasted all of this time driving just to find an empty house. He turned towards the home's garage and pushed the button on his overhead console to open the garage door. The door shifted and raised a few inches before returning to the closed position.

"Now what the hell?" he said, raising his voice though no one else was in the car to hear. "Can't even leave the garage door unlocked when you know I'm coming home?"

The frustration he constantly felt with his wife was mutual, he was sure. Theirs had become a marriage of convenience and had ceased to have anything to do with love a long time ago. At times he wasn't sure if it had ever had anything to do with love, but he guessed at some point they had at least liked each other enough to have had two children together. Now it was all about mutual benefits. He was the Senator with the beautiful stay-at-home wife and well-mannered children and she got to play rich socialite in venues around the country, and sometimes around the world.

He slammed the Cadillac into park and pushed open the door as he grabbed his coat and took his keys from the ignition. Walking around the house to the front porch, he inserted the key into the door and pushed it open. Just as it had appeared from the driveway below, the house was completely dark.

"Hello?" he called, as he stepped inside and pushed the door closed with his foot. The house was big, but not big enough for the sound of his voice to echo, though he imagined it doing so in the obviously empty first floor. "You know, I don't ask for much but a little respect would be great. If you're not going to be here you could at least call and let me know. It's not like I had any work that I could be doing or anything."

He set down his coat and keys on the oak table in the foyer and turned on a lamp. He knew that the regularly scheduled family night they had been observing for years really got on his wife's nerves and that she would rather be elsewhere. So would he, but their two boys loved it and, aside from using it as a political check mark during election years, that was why he insisted that the tradition be kept alive. The boys were the only good thing that had come of their union, in his mind, and they were still too young to realize that their parents' relationship had disintegrated. Maybe that time had come and his wife, who spent more time with the kids than he did, had realized it and finally found the excuse she needed to end their weekly pow-wow.

"Well, screw you, too," he said, as he started towards the stairs that would lead him to his third floor study. He could still do all of the work he needed to do from home, but he preferred the distractions that came with the Washington D.C. lifestyle. As he placed a foot on the first step, he looked into the darkened living room beside the stairs and stopped. Rolling his eyes and letting out an audible sigh, he said, "Don't tell me. It's time for one of our talks, right? Jesus Christ, Mary Ellen. How many times do we have to go over the same stuff? You'd better want a divorce this time."

He stepped off the stairway and down into the sunken living room where the figure of his wife was seated on their leather sofa. "You know, you could at least answer me. You could at least tell me the boys are asleep before I go cussing through the house." He stepped further into the living room and as he did, a glint of light caught his eye. He narrowed his eyes and looked closer at the shadowy figure sitting on the couch.

"Oh!" he said, as he stumbled back, realizing the woman's mouth was duct taped and her hands and feet were bound. He turned quickly towards the doorway. As he stepped back up into the foyer with a hand out for his car keys on the table, he felt something cold press against the back of his head from inside the living room. Raising his hands and turning around slowly, he saw the barrel of a suppressed handgun.

CHAPTER SEVENTY

"Who the hell are you?" David Kemiss said, as he squinted into the darkness towards the darkly-clad figure holding the pistol to his head.

"By now, Senator, I would've thought we were good enough friends for you to recognize me," Declan said, as he stepped out of the shadows, a black balaclava rolled up onto his forehead in order to reveal his face. "My name's Declan McIver and we've been doing a little dance of sorts. It's my turn to lead."

"I don't know what you're talking about."

Declan could tell by the slight narrowing of Kemiss' eyes as he spoke that the man knew exactly who he was and why he was there. He was prepared for all of the standard denials and the attempts at convincing him that he had the wrong man, but he knew otherwise. Everything about Kemiss set bells ringing through his subconscious like fire alarms in a public library. Finally, after numerous attempts on his life, he had found the man who had conspired with Ruslan Baktayev to murder Abaddon Kafni and commit an act of terror against his own country. Now all he had to do was get him to admit it.

"Save it, Senator," Declan said, as he stepped closer and grabbed Kemiss by the shoulder, pushing him towards the door. "It's time for a bit of schooling in how to tell the truth."

"You won't get anything—"

Okan Osman, dressed in the same black attire as Declan and with his balaclava pulled over his face, stepped in front of Kemiss as he stumbled forward from Declan's push. Catching the man in the stomach with his closed fist Osman said, "That's for the children of Abaddon Kafni," as the senator doubled over and gasped for air.

"Everything is set up," Osman said, as he kept Kemiss from falling to the floor in pain.

Declan nodded. "Let's show Mr. And Mrs. Kemiss a bit of Irish hospitality, shall we?"

Osman stood Kemiss up and led him away as Declan returned to the living room and lifted Mary Ellen Kemiss from the sofa by the bindings around her wrists. The woman made muffled pleas through the duct tape covering her mouth as he pushed her into the foyer and past the stairwell after Osman and her husband.

Osman stopped briefly and pulled open a door at the back of the mansion's luxurious kitchen. As the door swung open, Declan felt a blast of heat hit his face and heard a monstrous roar. A dim orange glow came from the darkened room beyond and he swallowed hard, the idea of what he was about to do piercing through his conscience like a splinter of glass.

Osman marched Kemiss into the garage as Declan followed with his wife, pushing her down into a lawn chair positioned just inside the room before closing the kitchen door behind them and locking it. The temperature inside the three car garage was sweltering and immediately sweat formed on Declan's forehead. He turned away from Mary Ellen Kemiss towards her husband, whom Osman had placed in another lawn chair in front of a makeshift spotlight that shone brightly against the garage door. Seated on his hands, which Osman had secured behind his back, David Kemiss wriggled uncomfortably in the chair as he looked around his unrecognizable garage, clam shell sweat stains forming under his arms. Standing at the man's left shoulder, Declan followed his gaze as he laid eyes on the third masked man in the room who was bent down and holding a fireplace poker in front of a roaring 30,000 BTU propane tank heater that was the source of the room's temperature and of the nearly deafening noise. The end of the poker was beginning to glow red as Altair Nazari turned it slowly in his hands, ensuring the surface was evenly heated.

Next Kemiss moved his head slightly towards a large black tarp hanging from the ceiling and concealing part of the garage from view. "So you're going to torture me?" he breathed, as sweat rolled down his forehead. "I can cope with torture."

Declan stepped into his line of sight shaking his head and said, "No, Senator. I don't think you can. I've done a bit of research on you and I'm pretty sure the closest thing you've ever experienced compared to what you're about to is burning your mouth on your morning cappuccino, and while that hurts, it's nothing compared to a red hot poker pushed against the inside of your leg. Do you know what happens to human flesh at 1500 degrees?"

Kemiss swallowed hard and tried to wet his dry lips with his tongue. "The American government doesn't negotiate with terrorists."

The idea that Kemiss would invoke the name of America and attempt to align himself with the United States filled Declan with rage. Was there no end to the kind of depravity that men like him were capable of? Could they not just realize they were caught and admit their guilt? It wasn't like the man could claim ignorance. Hurting innocent people, especially children, was wrong no matter what country you were from and what language you spoke.

"Oh, I know," Declan said, doing his best to keep his temper in check. "But I'm not interested in negotiating and you're not the American government. We both know who's been doing the terrorizing in this case. Why did you kill Abaddon Kafni?"

"I didn't. You did. After the bomb you planted at the Barton Center failed to do the job."

"That's a very well-rehearsed story, Senator. I have to admit, I'm a little impressed with the way you've gone about constructing it," Declan said, as he turned around and pulled a tarp-covered steel service cart over to where Kemiss was seated. "Unfortunately you picked the wrong person to set up. Do you know what happens when you strike the top of the human kneecap with a claw hammer?" He pulled back the tarp to reveal a variety of tools, including a hickory handled claw hammer. "If you strike just the right spot at just the right speed, the claw breaks the skin and lodges behind the kneecap. Then you just push up on the handle and pry the patella out like a crooked nail. It works even better if you make a small incision first."

Declan popped open the blade on a folding knife he withdrew from his pocket.

Sweat rolled off Kemiss' forehead and although he did his best to blink it away, it stung his eyes, causing tears to form in the corners. He opened and closed his mouth several times, licking his lips, his discomfort obvious.

Declan continued as he picked up a bottle of water from the service cart and took a sip, "You and Castellano seemed so interested in my past activities with the IRA that I thought I'd give you a little demonstration of what the Provos did to people who'd turned on their own team, like you've done." He slowly poured the water on the ground at Kemiss' feet and picked up a small extension cord from the service cart, holding its end up and twisting it around in his hand before slicing one end off with the folding knife.

"You see, the IRA didn't take kindly to touts. Informers, if you'd prefer. They got really grumpy when they found out someone was consorting with the enemy. They would schedule a session with an internal security unit called 'the Nutting Squad' and, if you were smart, you'd present yourself at the right place and time, answer their questions honestly and put the matter behind you. That's if you weren't guilty. If you were guilty, well, the quicker you told the truth, the better, because these men liked to inflict pain. They really got off on it and you don't want to know the outcome of a long, drawn out interrogation, Senator."

Declan stopped talking and let his words sink in. He didn't like talking about the kinds of things the IRA did to people that were thought to have been informers. The IRA's brand of justice was anything but evenly applied and often times the torture began before a word was even spoken. He didn't have any direct knowledge of how the Internal Security Unit operated, but word got around. Many times the victims had turned out to be completely innocent and even with the ones who made confessions, their guilt was questionable. Under such appalling circumstances people would admit to anything just to stop the pain. In the case of the Nutting Squad, the hostility ceased with a visit from a priest and a bullet in the head.

Declan did his best to push the thoughts of dumped bodies

and grief-stricken wives and children from his head. They were memories from a chapter in his life that he would do anything to rewrite and while he had never directly caused such pain or been involved with the men who had, he was guilty by association. The act of torturing another human being was atrocious to him and certainly not something he condoned or thought could ever be useful. It was the psychological effect of the possibility that did the trick most often and that was the linchpin of his plan tonight. If he allowed Kemiss to see through it, then the game they were playing would be at an end and Declan would lose.

"Why did you kill Abaddon Kafni and why are you conspiring with Baktayev to attack your own country?"

"You're insane," Kemiss said, as he closed his eyes tightly and screwed up his face. "You're an animal."

Declan could tell Kemiss was just about at the point where the grand finale he had planned would have the desired effect. "An insane animal? Good thought, Senator. I'm sure you know all about insane animals and what they do to the kind of innocent people you've conspired with them to attack. The Chechen militants like Baktayev? They're insane animals and he's the leader of the pack."

"I don't know any Ruslan Baktayev!" Kemiss spat, as he mustered what seemed like his last scrap of intestinal fortitude.

The temperature in the room had to be nearing combustion levels and the consistent roar of the propane heater was clearly having the effect Declan had intended. The entire environment had been designed to be as stressful as possible and Kemiss was proving to be every bit the pansy Declan had thought he would be. "I never said his name was Ruslan, Senator. Checkmate."

Kemiss' eyes opened and darted around the room between Declan, the two masked men and his wife, who was again making muffled pleas.

"I think your wife has something to say to you," Declan said, as he walked over and pulled back the tape on her mouth.

"You son of a bitch!" Mary Ellen Kemiss screamed. "You've been sitting here all this time and you never even thought to ask about your children!"

Kemiss' eyes darted to his wife as Declan placed the tape back over her mouth.

"Oh, I'm sorry, Senator," he said. "Did you think I was going to do all of these things to you?"

Across the room, Nazari ripped down the tarp that had been concealing the far side of the garage. Keniss watched in horror as two small people sitting on metal chairs were revealed, their wrists bound behind their backs and black hoods covering their heads. Each wore only a pair of white underpants that were clearly soaked with sweat that ran from their pale skin.

Kemiss drew in a labored breath and his eyes went wide as he saw his two sons seated at the other end of the garage. Declan reached for the claw hammer.

"I'll tell you what I know!" the senator screamed. "I know who Ruslan Baktayev is and I know that he killed Abaddon Kafni. I know you're innocent, I swear! Seth Castellano and I set you up after you witnessed Baktayev leaving the scene of Kafni's death. We had to keep anyone from finding out he was in the country."

"Why kill Kafni?"

"Because that was the price Baktayev wanted for doing business. He had a personal vendetta for something, I don't know what, and he would only do what was wanted of him if we helped him kill Kafni."

"Why Baktayev?"

"Because he had a history in committing the kind of terror that was planned, he was behind the Beslan School crisis and nobody would think twice about him doing it again. It was a suicide mission, a martyrdom for Allah, so he wouldn't be around for interrogation. He planned the entire thing himself in 2004 before he was arrested in Russia. We only got him out of jail and asked him to pick up where he left off."

"And who set up the bomb at the Barton Center?"

"We did. The bomb was a distraction to get Kafni evacuated, but we were hoping he would be killed and that Baktayev wouldn't get the opportunity to murder him the way he was planning. It didn't work. Kafni escaped and you followed him to where he was staying."

"Who were the men who set up the bomb? Were they the

same men that came after me?"

"Castellano hired them. He knew them from somewhere, I don't know where. He hired them to set up the bomb in the trunk of the security car and to distract Kafni's men. After he interviewed you and realized you knew who Baktayev was, he sent them to kill you and your wife."

"Why did you do all of this?"

"It wasn't my idea. Someone else came to me with it months ago."

"Who?"

Kemiss shook his head as if he wasn't going to tell.

"Who?" Declan yelled, picking up the claw hammer.

Kemiss licked his lips. "A man named Kreft. Lukas Kreft. He planned and financed the entire thing. He came to me for help in getting Baktayev into the country undetected and getting the documents he needed to plan the assault."

Declan had thought about the possibility of Kemiss not being the only one involved. Was what he was saying true or just an attempt to shift blame by a corrupt old man trying desperately to separate himself from the evil he was involved in? At this point in time it didn't really matter. All of that could be ironed out once the plot was stopped and being officially investigated.

"I only have one more question for you, Senator, and your answer will determine the end of our time together. Is it going to end quietly or with the tortured screams of your young boys? It's up to you. Where is Ruslan Baktayev?"

Kemiss did his best to spit at Declan, but little in the way of moisture came out. "What makes you think I know that? Kreft's not an idiot. He kept that a secret, even from me. He knows who the weak links in the chain are. He blackmailed us. Castellano was gay. We were lovers, have been for years. If people knew, they'd think he got his position in the FBI by sleeping with me. Kreft used him to control the investigation and he used me to gain unrestricted access to the U.S. He set up illegal donations to my last campaign and threatened to reveal them. I'd have been ruined."

"You're lying, Senator. The stigma of being gay went out with the last century. And would you really choose your career over the lives of hundreds of innocent American children? I don't believe there is a chain, so how can there be any weak links? You're attempting to distance yourself from this whole thing and I'm getting very impatient."

Nazari made a loud exhibit of removing the now cherry-red fire poker from the grill of the propane heater as he stood, turning towards the seated boys.

"One last chance, Senator," Declan said. "Where is Ruslan Baktayev?"

Kemiss writhed in his seat and closed his eyes. "In a vacant warehouse in Dundalk, Maryland. The sign on the door says Broughman's Welding Service, but you're too late. He's already been activated. He and his men are on their way to a junior high school in Victoria, Virginia. Those people are going to die and if you try to stop him, you will too!"

Declan exploded. Unable to contain his hatred for the man seated in front of him he grabbed Kemiss by the shoulders of his shirt and jerked him out of the chair, shoving him hard across the garage. Kemiss stumbled uncontrollably over a trash bin full of garden tools. Declan advanced on him again, but was stopped suddenly.

"Enough!" Okan Osman shouted as he tried to hold Declan back, his feet sliding against the smooth concrete floor. "We still need him!"

The fire poker clattered to the floor as Altair Nazari joined Osman, taking hold of Declan around the neck and locking his arm in place with his hand. Declan's nostrils flared and his eyes bored into Kemiss as the politician looked up from the ground, his nose bleeding. Slowly Declan relaxed. "Get him out of here, now."

Nazari kept his hold as Osman let go and jerked Kemiss to his feet, pushing him quickly past Declan to the kitchen door, which he unlocked with a key before dragging the senator through and disappearing into the house.

"Alright," Nazari said. "Alright?"

Declan nodded and Nazari let go. They each took a deep breath and Nazari moved to the propane tank heater, turning a black knob on top of it until it popped loudly and the roaring stopped. Next he moved to one of the garage doors and pressed a button next to it, allowing the door to open about twelve inches before stopping it. Immediately a cold rush of air flooded in and it seemed like the temperature dropped dramatically.

Declan looked around as Nazari continued moving around the room turning off the makeshift spotlights that had been used on Kemiss. In seconds the room began to look again like the suburbanite three car garage they had found earlier in the evening when they had arrived at the Kemiss property. A muffled protest drew his attention as Nazari flipped on the halogen lights in the garage ceiling. Mary Ellen Kemiss struggled against her restraints, but stopped as Declan locked eyes with her.

"I would never hurt you or your children, Mrs. Kemiss," Declan said, as he walked around the two boys and pulled off their hoods. Her eyes went wide and became tearful as she saw the sweaty faces that blinked rapidly in the sudden light.

"Is that it?" one of them asked, as Declan removed a set of large headphones from his head that had been concealed under the hood. "Are we done filming?"

"Aye," Declan said, as he pulled the other boy's headphones off.

"Good thing, man. I was really getting tired of that music."

"Go out this door here and the men outside will make sure you get paid. Great work, lads." Declan cut the loose restraints that were barely holding them and they stood, pulling on two bathrobes that had been folded and stored near the door as they walked through it.

Declan closed the door. He didn't think he'd ever allow his own children, should he ever have any, to act in the kind of movie he'd said he was filming when he'd called the entertainment agency earlier in the day, but thankfully there were some parents who didn't seem bothered by it.

"Your two boys have been in the upstairs guest room watching a movie this entire time," he said, as he turned back to Mary Ellen Kemiss and walked over. He cut her restraints and slowly peeled back the tape on her mouth. "I'm sure they'd like to see their mother now."

"You son of a bitch!" the woman said, as she stood and slapped him across the face. "How could you do this, to anyone?"

He pushed her gently towards the door and Nazari guided

her into the house, shutting the door behind them. When they were gone, Declan walked over to the spotlight that had been positioned in front of Kemiss and pushed the *off* button on a small digital camcorder that had been secured to the bottom of the light. Walking back towards the kitchen door, he stopped and slumped down into the chair Kemiss' wife had been sitting in and put his head in his hands, breathing heavily. Had Kemiss called his bluff, he would have lost, and America would have lost with him.

CHAPTER SEVENTY-ONE

"Alright, boyos," Declan said, as he entered the kitchen from the garage, having finally been able to calm himself down after the events of the last few hours. "What do we have?"

Osman and Nazari had spread a map across the granite countertop of the center island and had turned on a laptop computer, which Nazari was typing away at.

"Victoria, Virginia is here," Nazari said, as he reached over and circled a town with a red sharpie. "Dundalk, Maryland is here, and we are here." He circled two more towns and Declan looked at each of them in turn.

"That could give us some advantage," Osman said, looking at the location of Dundalk on the map, just southwest of Baltimore. The three circles formed an obtuse triangle with the location of Baktayev's base being the furthest away.

"Yeah," Nazari said, "but if it's as the senator said, than Baktayev's already gone from there. For all we know he's already set up in the school and waiting for tomorrow morning when everyone arrives."

"I can make a call," Osman said. "There's a few 'diplomats' from our Washington embassy that could go and have a look at this Broughman's Welding Service. That way we'll know whether there's anyone there and if there ever was. I don't trust this scumbag upstairs to have been telling us the truth."

"He was," Declan said. "The only thing he fears worse than losing his power, is losing his two boys."

"Then you think that bit about it not being his idea was the truth?"

Declan nodded. "He got extremely stressed at that point in our conversation so either he really believes it or else it was a poorly prepared attempt at shifting the blame. Hard to tell which, but it's irrelevant. What we have to focus on is stopping Baktayev."

"Still, it won't hurt for someone to take a look at Dundalk. Maybe they can give us some kind of an idea what kind of preparation these guys were doing."

"Aye, that could be useful. We need information on the town of Victoria. There has to be some reason they've chosen that as their target."

"The Wikipedia entry for it basically indicates that it's a pretty impoverished town," Nazari said, as he turned back to the laptop computer. "Not much in the way of employment and I found several news articles about some serious drug issues in the area."

"That explains a lot," Declan said.

"The school itself, W.N. Page Junior High, is the oldest of three schools in the area. Here's a picture." Nazari turned the computer around so that Declan and Osman could see it.

"That explains even more," Declan said, as he looked at the picture of the single story, industrial-era building, with its rectangular architecture and narrow, metal rimmed windows. "They're using the same basic plan they did at Beslan in 2004. That school was the oldest in the area as well. Can you bring up an aerial view from Google Maps?"

Nazari turned the computer around and went to work. "Here," he said, turning it back around.

"Just like I thought. Look at the way the building is spread out in all of those weird angles," Declan said, pointing at several locations on the image. "Just like Beslan, the building's a tactical nightmare. Only two driveway entrances, both easily covered from the building. It's on a large open lot surrounded by trees, all of which is easily covered from multiple points in the building. Even the places across the street are mostly forest and wouldn't provide any kind of a decent operations point. The police would have to set up somewhere a good distance from the school and wouldn't have any line of sight."

"Looks like some residences there," Osman said, pointing

to a few small buildings across the street that had some open ground around them. "There's some tree cover, too, the police could set up SWAT teams there in case of an emergency raid."

"I don't think so," Declan said. "Get me a street view."

Nazari reached over and punched a few buttons.

"See there?" Declan continued, as the screen changed to the street view. "With the building on that kind of an incline and all of those windows facing the road anyone crossing that street would be doing so under heavy fire. It'd be a massacre."

"So he's planned this well in advance," Nazari said.

"Aye, this isn't just about killing innocent people. It's about making a statement while killing innocent people. Baktayev learned some lessons from Beslan. The poverty and drug problems in the area likely mean low parental involvement. There'll be a lot of children arriving on the buses and few being dropped off by a parent who might notice something out of the ordinary. That, coupled with the likelihood that there's very little police presence in such a small, out of the way town, means Baktayev won't have any trouble gaining control of the building and its occupants. Once he's inside and he has his hostages he doesn't have any intention of anyone leaving alive. He'll take as many emergency responders with him as possible, too."

"So how do we stop this guy?" Osman asked. "There's just the three of us. The other men who have helped us this far are spies, not warriors. They won't be much good to us in a fight. We have Kemiss's confession. That's what we came here for. Why do we need to go any further?"

Declan glanced between Osman and Nazari. He could see doubt on both men's faces and he understood it. What they were about to do could get them all killed.

"Look, Os," he said, "I know how you feel. Taking on a team of heavily armed terrorists isn't my idea of fun, either, but there's no one else to do it. What would Abe want us to do? He wouldn't stand by and let this happen. He'd do everything in his power to stop it, and you know that."

Osman ceded the point with a nod. "No argument there, but why does this have to involve us marching up to these guys and calling them sissies? Call in a bomb threat. Get school cancelled for the day and it's finished."

"I wish it was that simple. Although in the end it may be. We're not planning on any lengthy assaults here," Declan said. "Baktayev's entire plan rests on the element of surprise. Without it he's got nothing. He can't afford a long, protracted gunfight to take control of the school. Once attention is brought to his presence, he'll be forced to run. But we can't risk him having a backup target either, another school within driving distance or even a church daycare center or something, so we've got one chance at stopping him and it's got to count."

Osman nodded slowly. "Alright, alright, I'm in."

"Grand. Let's look at the big picture. We've got to try and figure out where they're going to be coming from."

Nazari moved around to the other side of the kitchen island and used the wireless mouse to zoom the satellite image out. "The main highway leading through the town goes right past the school."

"Aye, but I don't think they'll use that. The presence of any vehicles on the property overnight could attract a police patrol and in the morning the administration would know something wasn't right. Baktayev will be looking for a way to enter the property without anyone knowing."

"There," Osman said, pointing at a dead end road northwest of the school. "Zoom in on that."

Nazari clicked the mouse several times and the screen zoomed in on a road that ended in a parking lot and a cluster of buildings.

"Looks like some kind of apartments or townhouses," Declan said, shaking his head. "Too risky."

Nazari moved the view out again.

"What's that there?" Declan said, as he noticed a thin gray line that ran through the forest behind the school's property.

"Tobacco Heritage Trail," Nazari said, as he read the label that became visible as he zoomed in on the location.

"Is it a road?"

"I don't think so," Nazari said. "It looks too narrow to me." He clicked over to a different tab on the internet browser and typed the name into Wikipedia. "Nothing here." He clicked over to another tab and typed the name into the Google search engine. An official website came up at the top of the search results.

"The Tobacco Heritage Trail is a system of long distance, multi-use, non-motorized trails following abandoned rail corridors throughout Southside Virginia," he read.

Declan looked over the pictures on the website as Nazari scrolled through it. The so-called trail was nearly as wide as a road and covered with gravel. "That's it," he said. "It's gotta be. And that road there, just east of the school, that's how they'll enter the trail. Look at it, no nearby houses and completely wooded. They'll pull their vehicles far enough down the trail to keep them hidden and they'll enter the school from the back. No one will even know they're there until it's too late. They could go back and forth from the vehicles all night carrying in whatever they want and no one would notice. By morning they'll have the entire place wired and booby trapped. They'll take control one person at a time as they enter."

"Twin Cemetery Road," Osman said, as he leaned in for a closer look at the road Declan was pointing at. "Let's go get 'em."

CHAPTER SEVENTY-TWO

10:54 p.m. Eastern Time – Sunday
Eleven miles outside of Victoria
Lunenburg County, Virginia

"They're out of there and aren't planning on coming back from the looks of it," Osman said, as he ended a call on his cell phone. "Looks like they've been living there, according to the guys I asked to have a look. They found sleeping arrangements in the building for at least twenty, and evidence of homemade explosives."

The black Ford Explorer bounced over a set of dormant railroad tracks as Nazari guided it over the antiquated pavement of a two lane country road, passing tall trees and flat, empty fields on either side. The view was occasionally broken up by the sudden appearance of dilapidated residences that looked as though they had been there longer than the road itself. Even in the darkness of night, the poverty of the area they were heading into was evident.

"They found three bodies in the rear lot of the building, too, stacked up in a storage container."

"That might explain why the police haven't found any bodies to back up my experiences. Baktayev's been taking his dead home with him," Declan said from the back seat. "Any clue as to what kind of arms they're carrying?"

Osman shook his head. "They found spent rounds in a few different calibers, but no weapons. Whatever was there, they've got it all with them."

"Could they tell how long they've been gone?" Nazari asked.

"It can't have been that long," Osman said with a grimace. "They found a young man chained up in a bathroom with his tongue cut out. He was still alive so they can't have been gone very long. It looked from the tire tracks in the muddy lot like they left in two fairly large vehicles, possibly vans or SUVs of some kind. There were multiple sets of tracks laid down over the last few days, so it was impossible to tell when they left for sure."

"They were driving dark red Suburbans when they attacked Kafni and Levitt and they had a white cargo van when they attacked Castellano and me," Declan said. "It could be the same vehicles."

Nazari slowed the vehicle as they rounded a bend in the road and came to a stop sign. Without coming to a complete stop, he looked left and continued driving to the right.

"What's that?" Osman asked, as he craned his neck and looked at a collection of green-roofed, concrete buildings behind several tall fences. Search lights passed over the property from tall towers along the fence.

"A prison," Declan said, as the compound passed out of sight. "It's one of the only major employers in the area."

"Remind me not to put Victoria down as a retirement destination," Osman quipped.

A mile down the road the dark fields began to blend into the lots of more impoverished residences. Stately brick homes that looked to have once belonged to wealthier families in the town's industry-oriented past were cramped between mobile homes and hastily constructed single story dwellings, all with overgrown lawns and vandalized automobiles.

"Charming place," Declan said, as they moved onto the town's main street, where businesses sat boarded up on the bottom floor of two and three story brick storefronts. Outside of one small place a street light flickered and people gathered under it, smoking, in front of what appeared to be a bar.

"We're getting close," Nazari said, looking at the GPS suction-cupped to the windshield. "I call the H&K."

Declan turned and reached over the back seat, grabbing the H&K MP-7 machine pistol from underneath a blanket. "The AR's mine," he said, as he pushed a forty-round magazine into the H&K and handed it forward to Osman, who placed it in Nazari's lap.

"That leaves me on shotgun," Osman said.

"We need to take everything we can with us," Declan said. "Once we're in this there isn't going to be any running to the truck for more ammo. If we're out, we're dead." He handed a Mossberg 590 tactical shotgun with a pistol grip and a box of sabot slugs over the seat to Osman.

"Move past it to the second entrance," he continued, as Nazari began to slow down, the school approaching on their right hand side as they cleared the town. "Nice and casual, if they're in there waiting, I want them to think we're just some wee chancers out for a kiss and a cuddle."

Nazari drove the SUV slowly past the first pitted concrete driveway, a darkened single story building looming above them on the steep incline. Clumps of uncut grass stuck up throughout the sloped front yard giving the place an unkempt appearance. Dingy streetlights illuminated broken glass and barred windows, more evidence of the area's intense poverty, on the front of the building as they reached the second entrance and continued on.

"From the looks of that place you'd think it was abandoned," Osman said.

"Aye, rough place to be a kid, I'm betting."

Declan hadn't seen any evidence outside that anyone was in the building or even nearby. Several of the doors that had been visible looked like they might have been pried opened at some point, but it was hard to tell for sure with the amount of vandalism. "Let's find this Twin Cemetery Road," he said. "If we're the first ones here, I don't want any evidence of it. I want Baktayev to think it's smooth sailing."

Nazari drove three quarters of a mile and made a right. The road looped around past several neighborhoods, empty fields and thick patches of trees. After nearly a mile the residences were gone and only field and forest surrounded them. As the road curved back towards the school, the headlights washed over a roughly maintained cemetery that sat on both sides of the two lane road, a narrow dirt lane just past a rusted wrought iron fence on the right. Nazari slowed the vehicle to a stop. "Twin Cemetery Road," he said, looking at the crooked sign on the corner of the street.

"Right then," Declan said, as Nazari pulled the SUV to the side of the road under some overhanging tree limbs and cut the lights off. He pushed a thirty-round magazine into an AR-15, charged the rifle and extended the stock. "I'm on point," he said, as he pushed open the door and stepped out. "Nazari, you're behind me and Osman, on the rear. Ten paces apart until we know we're alone."

CHAPTER SEVENTY-THREE

11:06 p.m. Eastern Time – Sunday
W.N. Pace Junior High School
Victoria, Virginia

Ruslan Baktayev held up a hand signaling the sixteen men behind and around him to stop. He held his head high in the light breeze for a moment as the trees rustled slightly around them. Battle was coming. He could feel it in the air and it energized every fiber of his being. He had lived for this moment and only this moment for a week now. His enemies were dead and even the last attempt, the last gasp of the Americans, had fallen before him with the defeat of the punk kid who had dared to challenge him. *Sharpuddin*, he thought as he scowled and spat.

With their vehicles well hidden along an old railroad bed, now a hiking trail, that ran through the woods behind the school, everything had gone as planned. They had arrived in Victoria with plenty of time to spare and would be firmly entrenched by the time the faculty began to arrive shortly after dawn. First, they would take each of the teachers and administrators as they arrived, forcing them to conduct business as usual while unloading the school buses that were scheduled to begin arriving at exactly 8:15 a.m. None of the few parents who dropped their children off at the front doors would think anything was out of place as Anzor Kasparov greeted them and ushered the children into the building. He had been doing that same thing as the facility's custodian for years.

Headlights washed over the trees momentarily and Baktayev turned around, focusing as his men each sank to one knee. Three car doors closed quickly but quietly as they watched, Kalashnikov rifles held across their chests and at the ready. Dressed in jungle fatigues and military boots, the men blended into the dense green forest at the edges of the school's property. Even their heads were covered in camouflage dew rags, with the exception of the few, including Baktayev, who had chosen instead to wear their black Islamic *taqiyahs*. After all, this was a mission of God and they were his soldiers.

Slowly, Baktayev wrapped the shoulder strap of his AK-47 around his hand and brought the rifle up into position as three men approached, each of them obviously armed. Waiting until the men were in the midst of his squad, he stood suddenly and barked an order in his native tongue, his men following his lead and standing with him.

Triumphant growls sounded as the three newcomers dropped their guns and held their hands up high in the air. Baktayev smiled as he looked at the blood on their clothes. "It is done, then?"

The nearest of the three men smiled and nodded. "It is done."

The three men had left separately from the rest of the group in a smaller vehicle and had been dispatched to the home of the town's school resource officer who would be the quickest link the school would have to the local police. Now the man, and his family as well, were in no condition to respond to anything. They were dead. With the officer not expected at his post until the start of the school day, it would be hours before anyone noticed he was missing and by then it would be too late.

Baktayev waved a hand motioning his men forward. Slowly they cleared the trees and moved out into the overgrown field a hundred yards from the back of the school's gymnasium. Keeping low and moving fast, they reached the building and lined up against the high brick wall. Though Baktayev thought they had little to fear from any of the townspeople, he wanted precision and stealth from his men. This was the most critical phase of their plan. If they were spotted here by anyone with enough sense to pick up a telephone then all of their planning, all of their preparation, would be for nothing. They would be forced to flee and the glorious death each of them had been praying well into the night for would be a fleeting dream.

Taking position ahead of his men at the corner of the building, he leaned over and looked down the row of them. He motioned to Anzor Kasparov to join him at the lead. Kasparov was the man with the keys and their ticket inside the building. "Are you ready?" Baktayev said, as the man arrived at his position. Kasparov jangled the keys in one of his pockets and smiled, resting his rifle on his shoulder. Baktayev turned back to the corner of the building and readied his rifle. He waved his hand and rounded the corner, staying low and creeping up the side of the building towards a courtyard twenty yards ahead of them. He held up his hand in a stop command as he reached the corner of the courtyard and looked out into the enclosed breezeway that connected the school's gymnasium with the rest of the building. In the center of the breezeway was a door, their planned entry point. Kasparov would have two minutes to make his way to the front of the building and disarm the building's security system as the rest of them fanned out around the building. Having cleared the courtyard of any surprises, Baktayev moved back behind the building and pressed his back against the wall.

"When you hear the door open, General," Kasparov said, "wait thirty seconds and then move into the courtyard. I will prop the door open with a rock, as the teachers do in the warmer months, before I go in."

The night seemed to grow quiet around them as if nature itself was waiting breathlessly for their victory. Baktayev tightened his grip on his rifle as he nodded his understanding. Kasparov withdrew a bulging set of keys from his pocket, picking through them quickly until he found the correct one. He pumped his fist in a victorious gesture and turned the corner into courtyard.

A loud crack echoed across the school yard and Kasparov's head exploded, covering Baktayev and the two men closest to him in rufescent gore. Baktayev furiously blinked the blood away as the remaining four and a half feet of Anzor Kasparov collapsed onto the ground, the keys in his dead hand jangling as they fell loose. Slowly registering what was happening, Baktayev dropped to his knees and then to his stomach as a deafening clatter filled the air around him.

CHAPTER SEVENTY-FOUR

"Surprise, old son," Declan said, as the brass was ejected from the side of his AR-15 and he watched the body of the man he'd been aiming for fall to the ground. Had it been Baktayev in the lead? He couldn't tell in the low light. He flicked the selector switch on the side of the converted rifle to automatic and pulled the trigger again. With the amount of men he was facing he needed to do as much damage as he could, and fast. The weapon bucked in his grip and methodically he inched the barrel to the right, moving down the line of Chechens against the brick wall of the school sixty yards in front of him. Several men close to the front of the line were thrown against the wall as the bullets impacted, their bodies falling onto one another. Declan knew the accuracy of the weapon at this range wasn't great, especially in the dark, and within a few seconds of pulling the trigger, the rifle was empty.

Okan Osman stood from behind the downed tree where he'd taken cover and aimed his shotgun. Even as he pulled the trigger rapidly and the rifled slugs exploded from the barrel, it was clear that the weapon wasn't accurate enough to have much effect from where he and Declan stood in the tree line at the edge of the property.

"Down!" Declan yelled, as several of the Chechens rose up and aimed their AK-47s in the direction they'd seen the muzzle flashes coming from. Osman took cover behind the fallen tree again and Declan stepped behind a thick pine, removing the magazine from his rifle and sliding in a new one as the clatter of the Kalashnikovs began. As chunks of wood were torn off the trees around him and bullets whizzed through the leaves, causing bits of greenery to fall to the ground, he flung himself forward onto his stomach for better cover.

"They're leapfrogging!" Osman yelled, as several of the Chechens moved forward while their comrades continued firing. "We've got to move, now!"

"Go! Go! Go!" Declan yelled, as he leveled his rifle from his prone position and pulled the trigger. Rounds burst from the weapon and the Chechens dropped to the ground, taking cover in the uneven terrain of the schoolyard. In his peripheral vision Declan watched as Osman took off running, keeping his head low as he passed behind Declan and back towards the trail they'd entered from. As the weapon again ran empty, Declan knew it was his turn to run and hoped that Osman had made it far enough to provide some cover fire. He jumped to his feet and ran, listening to the foreign yells of the Chechens as they realized they were in the clear. Looking to his left as he dodged through the thick trees, he saw someone stand from behind the row of camouflaged thugs. Even in the dim moonlight, he recognized Ruslan Baktayev as the man ran to the corner of the building and disappeared around the side. Declan turned his attention back to what was in front of him as the sound of machine gun fire started again. He kept his head low, but it quickly became obvious that the Chechens hadn't been able to see him running and were still focusing their fire on the spot where he and Osman had launched their initial assault. He pushed on until he heard gunfire in front of him and saw the muzzle flash ahead in the trees. Realizing the fire was directed towards the Chechens, he made his way towards it and soon joined Osman who was now standing near Altair Nazari as he fired his H&K MP-7 from behind a burned out metal barrel that stood a few yards into the tree line. Declan turned and looked as several of Baktayev's men were hit and fell to the ground. Taking the opportunity provided by Nazari's fire, he reloaded his rifle.

"How many did you count on their way in?" he yelled.

"Nineteen, and it looks like there's twelve left standing!" Osman yelled.

Declan tossed his rifle to Osman who caught it. "I'll trade

you," he said. "Baktayev ran. I'm going after him!"

Osman nodded and withdrew the shotgun that was secured to his back by its shoulder strap. "There's only four rounds in it, but there's still fifteen in the strap!" he yelled, as he tossed it to Declan. Declan caught it as Nazari's fire stopped and Osman raised the AR-15 to continue the assault. Declan dropped the olive green satchel he was carrying his extra magazines in at Osman's feet and looked at Nazari who was reloading. "Did you disable their vehicles?"

Nazari nodded.

"Good. Finish as many of these guys off as you can and get outta here! The police can't be far off!"

"Where are you going?" Nazari asked, having not been privy to Declan's conversation with Osman.

Declan pumped a round into the shotgun. "After a coward!"

CHAPTER SEVENTY-FIVE

Gradually Declan made his way from the forest onto the Tobacco Heritage Trail, aiming the shotgun in front of him. The trail was nearly as wide as a two lane road and covered with finely crushed aggregate to make it ideal for bikes or horses, though from the overgrowth it looked scarcely used. He'd seen Ruslan Baktayev flee from the schoolyard and run east away from the building. In order to make it to the vehicles he would have had to double back once he reached the forest, but Declan couldn't imagine him going anywhere else if he wanted to escape the area.

Carefully, he surveyed the two white cargo vans and worn Honda SUV that Baktayev and his men had arrived in and that were now parked in a line along the edge of the trail, about a thousand feet from the nearest road. The engine compartment of each vehicle was open, evidence of Nazari's sabotage, and if Declan had to guess, he was sure that Nazari had either pulled the fuses, removed the distributor caps and disabled the rotors, or blocked the air intake to keep the vehicles from starting. Either way, no one was going anywhere with any of them.

He sank to one knee and listened intently. Sirens had started in the distance and were growing closer, and the occasional burst of gunfire came from the school, but it was clear that the fight was winding down. Having been caught on open ground, Baktayev's crew had been cut to pieces by the surprise attack. Declan focused his attention in front of him, listening for anyone approaching, but he heard nothing. Had Baktayev continued east on foot? Had he hidden another vehicle near the school? A stick snapped in the forest to his left and Declan turned, aiming the shotgun into the darkened trees as he took cover behind one of the vans. Suddenly the commotion increased and continued toward him, leaves crushing and twigs snapping under the weight of the approaching figure. In the darkness, Declan didn't see it until it was nearly on top of him. A slender doe bounded out of the tree line, stopped suddenly and looked at Declan before bolting to the right and continuing across the trail into the forest beyond.

Slowly Declan turned and redirected his attention to the east. The trail ahead of him was still empty, with no sign of the terrorist leader. A dim red light shone suddenly through one of the cargo van's tinted windows and a sputtering sound came from the forest. Declan moved fast to the front of the vehicle and aimed his weapon into the trees east of his location. Through the thick overgrowth he could still see the square red light, brighter now that he wasn't looking through the darkened windows of the cargo van, and the sputtering continued. Realizing what it was, Declan shouldered the shotgun and ran forward along the trail as the sound of a twin cycle engine roared to life and the little red square of light began advancing through the forest.

Declan ran furiously trying to intercept the dirt bike. Thirty yards from the cargo van, its rider jumped the slight incline at the edge of the trail and landed the bike on the road a few feet away. Declan jumped forward as the rear tire slid on the fine gravel and wrapped his arms around the rider's waist, bringing him and the bike to the ground, the shotgun sliding off his shoulder as they landed.

With a bellow of surprise, the man struggled to free himself from Declan's grip, throwing his elbow behind him and connecting twice with the side of Declan's head. Declan rolled away from the man and stood, the rider of the bike doing the same and turning to face his attacker with a threatening growl.

In the low light, Declan easily recognized the man in front of him as the same man he'd seen a week earlier when Abaddon Kafni had been murdered at the Briton-Adams Mansion. "Hello, Ruslan," he said, breathing heavily and assuming a fighting stance as he looked at the Chechen.

The Chechen narrowed his eyes as he pulled a long, serrated

knife from inside his camouflage coat. "Who the hell are you?"

"Crossing guard," Declan quipped. "No motorbikes allowed in school zones."

The Chechen growled and launched forward with the knife. Declan blocked the attack with a sweep of his arm and thrust his fist into the side of Baktayev's jaw as the man stumbled past him. Baktayev absorbed the impact by turning with the strike and again attacked, this time stabbing downward. Declan grabbed the hand that held the knife as it came down and propelled the heel of his boot into the Chechen's stomach, rolling onto his back and allowing the man's momentum to carry him over. Baktayev landed on his back and the air rushed from his lungs in a painful gasp.

Declan raised himself to his feet and watched as the Chechen did the same, but with more difficulty. The man's crude fighting skills were clearly no match for him. "C'mon, Ruslan, I was expecting so much more from you."

"Arghh!" yelled the Chechen, advancing again, swinging the knife wildly from side to side. Declan stepped backwards methodically, allowing the blade to narrowly miss him each time. On the Chechen's fifth attempt, he blocked the attack and drove his heel into the man's side, causing him to double over and stumble backwards at the same time. As Baktayev tripped on the loose gravel and fell onto his back, Declan heard the sound of another twin cycle motor.

A single headlight washed over the area and Declan dived out of the way as another rider on a dirt bike sped past, attempting to run him down. The rider braked hard and spun the bike around. Declan stood as the rider revved the engine and sped forward, pulling a pistol. Shots sounded and he ducked low, running into the trees for cover as the rider stopped at the fallen Baktayev and continued firing. From a prone position out of the rider's line of fire, Declan watched as Baktayev got slowly to his feet and mounted the bike behind its rider, who continued to aim the pistol into the trees and fire the occasional shot. The rider revved the engine again, stowed the pistol and the bike shot forward, churning gravel behind it as it tore down the trail.

Declan jumped to his feet and ran for the dirt bike that he'd knocked Baktayev from and that was still lying on the ground, its engine idling. He quickly scooped up the shotgun and slung it over his shoulder as he stood the bike up, mounted it and gripped the accelerator. The bike shot forward, its front wheel lifting off the ground momentarily. Declan stood from the seat and shifted his weight forward to bring the bike back onto two wheels. Ahead he could see a tiny flicker of red light and knew it was the fleeing terrorist several hundred yards down the trail. Where was the man going and who was the other rider who had appeared from nowhere? Was it part of a backup team with a second target in mind? Declan couldn't risk that, he knew he had to catch them. He pulled the accelerator tighter and leaned forward, the air slapping him in the face and bringing tears to his eyes as the bike sped up.

With the bike ahead of him carrying two, Declan was lighter and able to travel faster. He gained ground steadily as he crossed underneath an overpass and rounded a curve. Ahead he could see that the trail was beginning to open up, the forest on one side coming to an end. Baktayev's bike was a hundred yards from him when the trail opened into a vast field containing three large metal buildings and a long, flat stretch of pavement. From the flashing lights near the buildings and along the pavement, Declan knew it was an airport. Quickly, he scanned the runway and saw a single engine plane near the far end, the lights on its wings blinking. Was this Baktayev's destination?

A gunshot sounded ahead of him and he swerved the bike to the noticing that Baktayev had turned in the seat and had a gun aimed. Declan pulled the accelerator as far in as it would go and the bike shot forward closing the distance between him and Baktayev to fifty yards. Baktayev fired several more times, but couldn't get a decent shot. The terrorist leader turned forward, giving up as the rider of the bike slowed and pulled off of the trail, riding down an embankment towards the airport's runway and the waiting plane.

Knowing that he was taking a big risk and could be riding into an ambush, Declan steered his bike to the right and jumped the incline at the edge of the trail, landing on the rough terrain thirty yards from the runway. Gunning the engine, he bumped hard over the ground, racing towards the other bike and attempting to intercept it. As he crossed onto the smoother grass twenty yards from the runway, he reached up and drew the shotgun from around his back.

Fifteen—ten—five. He held the end of the shotgun out, striking Baktayev in the head as he raced past and skidded to a stop, the back wheel of the bike sliding around. He leapt off it and brought the shotgun up, aiming it towards the plane and anyone that might be standing near it. He could see through the windows of the small craft that there was only one person inside. The pilot stared out the window at the scene.

Ten yards in front of Declan, between him and the plane, the bike Baktayev had been riding was lying on the ground, both rider and pillion struggling to get out from underneath it and off the ground. The rider was the first to find his feet. The man stumbled for a second and finally rested his eyes on Declan, reaching hastily into his camouflage coat. Declan fired once, pumped in another round and fired again. Two large holes opened up in the man's chest and he flew backwards, tripping over the downed motorbike and landing on his back, where he lay still.

Baktayev struggled upright as Declan pumped a third round into the shotgun. Blood ran down the side of the Chechen's face as he stared at Declan with beady, coal black eyes and slowly raised his hands in surrender.

"Your ride's leaving without you, Ruslan!"

The Chechen glanced over his shoulder as the plane taxied forward, heading away from the scene.

"This was your plan all along, wasn't it? Get your men entrenched in the school and then make a run for it just before the siege started! That's why this plane is here, isn't it? An escape route. Is this how you survived Beslan? What would your damn Allah say to such cowardice?"

The plane's engine grew louder and its speed increased. As it passed the last of the metal buildings, it lifted into the air and cleared the tree line at the end of the airport, the two blinking lights on its wings the only evidence left of its presence as it faded into the distance.

Baktayev turned his head back towards Declan and spat on the ground. "You know nothing about the greatness of Allah!

His vengeance is patient and his actions are—"

Declan pulled the trigger of the shotgun. A jagged hole appeared in Baktayev's stomach as his eyes opened wide. Declan pumped the weapon and fired again. The second round struck the Chechen in the left temple as he stood doubled over, blood spilling from the first wound. The impact of the slug with his head drove him backwards. He landed on his back next to the rider of the motorbike, his arms spread wide. Declan lowered the shotgun and walked over. Standing at Baktayev's feet and looking at the man's blank stare he said, "That's for Abaddon Kafni."

This was one set of dead eyes that wouldn't haunt him when he lay down at night.

CHAPTER SEVENTY-SIX

Two Days Later
Lee Highway
Gainesville, Virginia

David Kemiss sat down on the edge of the bed inside the room he had rented the night before and lit a cigarette. He had quit smoking years ago, but with the events of the last forty-eight hours anyone who begrudged him a smoke could go straight to hell. A tentative knock sounded on the door and he stood. After adjusting his tie and collar, he walked over the badly worn carpet and opened the door.

"She's here, Senator," Colin Bellanger said.

"Show her in, show her in."

Bellanger stood aside.

"Senator Kemiss," a blonde haired woman in a dark red skirt suit said.

Kemiss nodded. "Ms. Courtney. Come in, please."

The woman stepped into the small room, followed by a camera man who set up a tripod in the corner. Both looked around with an expression of amazement bordering on disgust. Bellanger closed the door behind them and moved to the opposite side of the room, where he took a seat on the bed.

"Sorry about the accommodations," Kemiss said, "but I'm sure you can understand my need to be discreet."

The Manassas Gap Motor Lodge was a far cry from the kind of place he would normally stay in, but the anonymity it provided in a time like this was a necessity. Twenty four hours ago, after finally being let out of his own house, which he had been held in for over twelve hours by some masked men linked to Declan McIver, he had emerged back into the world to learn that a gunfight had occurred at a school in Victoria, Virginia and that twenty dead Chechens had been found at or near the scene.

At first the media had showed only a passing interest as the town and its surrounding areas were common sites of drug related violence, but hours later, when the police had finally cleared the building, it became evident that something far more sinister had gone on. In the possession of one of the dead men had been letters making demands for the release of hostages, as well as maps and blueprints of the school. The police, and soon after the media, quickly and rightly surmised that what had been planned was nothing short of a hostage situation by terrorists linked to Islamic jihadists. Who had stopped the attack and killed the men found around the school was a mystery and rumors were already beginning to spread that the United States Army or some highly trained unit of the FBI had been involved, and that things had gone very wrong. Now every major television network from across the globe was descending on the town which was normally home to less than two thousand people.

"I appreciate you inviting me, Senator, and being willing to sit down for an exclusive. I must say, I'm a bit shocked that such a small affiliate as WSET was your first call."

"In times like this, Ms. Courtney, it can be hard even for someone in my position to rise above the noise. I've found in the past that smaller outlets can be the best bet. I understand that you have a working relationship with both a local radio station and a newspaper as well?"

"Yes, sir."

"And my comments will be featured in all three venues?"

"Yes, sir."

"Then let's get started."

The reporter took out a spiral notebook and a digital tape recorder and set them on a table near the room's picture window. She straightened her skirt and took a seat in one of the mismatched chairs as Kemiss took a drag from his cigarette and sat down in the opposite chair.

"Don't tell my wife," he said with a smile, as he exhaled and crushed the cigarette out in an ashtray.

The reporter gave a courtesy laugh and quickly flipped open her notebook and pressed a button on the tape recorder. "Go ahead, Kenny," she said, giving a slight wave to the cameraman.

"This is WSET's Stacey Courtney," she said, as the red light on the front of the camera came on, "and I'm seated here in an undisclosed location with United States Senator David Kemiss, who has agreed to answer questions about the troubling events in Victoria, Virginia that were discovered thirty-six hours ago. Senator, the comments you made to me last week in Lynchburg after the death of Dr. Kafni, which you have repeated to the press gathered in Washington, were that you were deeply saddened by the death of Dr. Kafni and that you were being assured by federal law enforcement authorities that everything was being done to find his killers. Now, in light of the alleged terror attack in Victoria, a town that is located in your former congressional district before you were elected to the senate, you claim that you have information that links the two events, is that correct?"

Kemiss cleared his throat and straightened up in his seat. At first he hadn't known exactly how to react to the news that Declan McIver had managed to stop Ruslan Baktayev and in so doing had stopped the plans he and Lukas Kreft had put in motion, but he'd quickly shocked himself into campaign mode and decided that going on the offensive was his best shot. If he was honest, he was relieved that the attack had been stopped and, as a bonus, if he spun things the right way, he could actually come out of the entire situation better off. Kreft's vague promises of being able to spin the deaths of so many innocent Americans into a political victory could be damned. By the time this interview was over and the subsequent ones that Kemiss was sure would follow, he'd be a hero with the story that he'd cooked up.

"That's correct," he said. "Abaddon Kafni was a personal friend of mine and he was murdered by a mad terrorist bent on revenge."

The reporter nodded slowly. "Forgive me for saying, Senator, but that's not new information. It's been the working theory since Dr. Kafni's murder that he was killed by Islamic fundamentalists whom he'd run afoul of many times during his career."

"Let me finish, please. Thank you. The revenge exacted on Dr. Kafni that I was speaking of wasn't due to his career, but rather due to the fact that he was my friend. He was murdered because I rejected an attempt by his killer to blackmail both me and my office into aiding in the attack in Lunenburg County."

"Senator, you're saying that the same people who attempted to take school-aged children hostage early yesterday morning had contact with your office and that they killed Dr. Abaddon Kafni?"

Kemiss nodded. "That's correct. Dr. Kafni's murder and the associated bombing of Liberty University were intended as a warning shot to me and my staff. I was scheduled to be in attendance at the gala unveiling of the C.H. Barton Center for International Relations and Politics, but was called away by what was later revealed to be a ruse. I would have likely been killed and that was the message the terrorists wished to send."

"And how did you react to this 'warning shot', Senator?"

"Well, Ms. Courtney, the terrorists made a grave error in their calculations when they decided to try and blackmail me. Perhaps someone with less experience in Washington might have been a better target, but I have many contacts and was able to get word to counterterrorism experts in both our military and our federal law enforcement agencies."

"And together you came up with a plan that resulted in the Victoria attack being stopped?"

The question was asked in an almost giddy tone of voice and Kemiss knew that Stacey Courtney was eating every word he said right out of his hand. He fought back a smile as he answered.

"That is correct. Through a joint effort by the Federal Bureau of Investigation, the Central Intelligence Agency and the National Security Agency, we were able to find and identify the offenders before they could commit their planned attack. Due to the efforts of this country's fine men and women in uniform many lives were saved yesterday morning."

"There are rumors, sir, that something went wrong yesterday morning which resulted in a gunfight at the school. Can you comment on that for us?"

"No, I can't. That is simply information that I do not have. Obviously I wasn't on the ground in Victoria when our brave officers attempted to arrest the offenders and clearly something did not go as planned."

"Are the officers okay? Were any of them injured in the assault?"

"I don't know, but if they were then my prayers are with them and their families."

Courtney looked over the notes that she had been making as Kemiss spoke and nodded several times. This was the kind of story that made careers in the journalism world and he could tell she was nearly beside herself.

"One last question, Senator. I almost forgot in light of your revelations, but what of the ongoing manhunt for former IRA terrorist Declan McIver? Is he the man who tried to blackmail you? Is he the terrorist who is responsible for all of this?"

"No," Kemiss said. "Declan McIver's involvement in this matter is still very much an unknown. We do know that he is involved at some level, but we do not believe that he was acting alone or that he was in charge of anything. I'm sure when he is apprehended, and he will be apprehended, that his full role in this will come to light."

"Thank you for all of this information, Senator. I know the world will be waiting breathlessly for the outcome of the official investigation. This is WSET and I'm Stacey Courtney."

"Thank you again for calling me, Senator," Courtney said, as she clicked off the tape recorder and the red light on the camera winked out.

"Thank you, Ms. Courtney. Please call my assistant, Mr. Bellanger, with any further questions. I'm sure there will be a lengthy investigation and more questions will come up. I will be happy to answer them all."

Colin Bellanger stood from his perch on the bed and walked to the door. He opened it and held it as Stacey Courtney and her cameraman gathered their things and left the room.

"I think that went well, don't you?" Kemiss asked, as Bellanger closed the door again.

"Yes, sir, very well."

Kemiss nodded and stood up. "I hope so. Get the car ready. This place isn't going to stay a secret for long with that news van outside."

"Yes, sir." Bellanger opened the door and left the room.

Kemiss walked towards the bathroom, but stopped half way when his cell phone rang. After pulling it out of his pocket, he looked at the caller ID and answered. "Where the hell have you been? I've been trying to reach you since Saturday night!"

"Apologies, David," Lukas Kreft said. "It's been a busy couple of days."

"No kidding! I've been dealing with this entire situation alone!"

"I trust you've got a handle on it. You're an experienced man."

"That's not the point. The point is, I could have used your help in spinning this to the press. Your man Baktayev screwed up, again. Thankfully, McIver shot him full of holes or else we'd have a real nightmare on our hands."

"*Our* hands? You mean *your* hands, David. Your attempt to spin this story in your favor will not work. All you've done is speed your own demise by directly involving yourself. When the investigation begins, all the authorities will find is that the entire operation leads directly to your front door."

Kemiss turned and looked frantically around the room. "What are you talking about? I didn't have anything to do with this. All I've done is what I was told to do by you!"

"Let's examine that for a moment," Kreft said. "It was your influence that allowed Ruslan Baktayev to enter the country as an asylum-seeking refugee. It was your influence that obtained the blueprints and maps found in the school. The school was located in your former congressional district, an area where you have maintained relationships that enabled you to get said documents. The vehicles and building Baktayev used are owned by a shell company in the Grand Caymans bearing your name, and payments made to various people involved will all lead nicely and neatly back to paperwork you signed and accounts that you are responsible for. Even your latest action, the attempted hit on CIA chief Simard, was paid for through those accounts. Now, what do you think the authorities are going to say when they learn all of this?"

"You son-of-a-bitch, you've been planning this all along," Kemiss said in a hoarse whisper. "I was never going to make it out of this, was I?"

"Correct, David. Your relationship with Castellano will show how you tried to influence and control the investigation, and even your latest move in talking to the press, while bizarre, will only look like motivation in light of everything else. This whole thing will look like an attempt to revive your sagging political brand. The American government will be embroiled in controversy for months and the voting public will have even less confidence in their elected representatives than they already do. The divide between American politicians and American voters will grow even wider and even more attention will be paid to what's going on inside the country, where it should be focused, instead of on the affairs of other nations."

"You didn't care if Baktayev was successful or not, did you, as long as the whole thing could be pinned on me? You were setting me up from the beginning!"

"Yes, David. And you made it far too easy."

"Well, I've got news for you, Lukas, McIver got a taped confession from me Sunday night and I gave him your name! As soon as he releases that tape, you're going to have some serious people asking a lot of serious questions and it will be you who's calling me for help!"

"Nice try, David, another desperate attempt to make yourself look innocent."

"Just wait! I may be going down, but I'm taking you with me!"

The phone line went silent and Kemiss brought the device away from his ear to look at the LED. The call timer was flashing. Lukas Kreft had hung up. Kemiss set the phone down on the dresser, next to the television. Slowly, he sank down onto the bed and put his head in his hands. He could feel the heat coming off his skin.

"Senator?" a voice said from outside the room as a hurried knock came on the door. "Is everything okay in there? Senator? I heard someone yelling. Are you okay in there?"

Kemiss could hear his heart beating in his chest and the world around him sounded like it was underwater. Had he really been yelling? He hadn't realized it, but maybe he had been.

The knocks on the door grew louder. "Senator? Are you in there?"

Kemiss reached over to the dresser and unzipped the front pocket of the suitcase he'd brought in. Pulling out a .38 revolver, he caressed the shiny, nickel-plated weapon. He didn't want to be around for the storm that was coming. He couldn't face his children with something like this hanging around his shoulders.

CHAPTER SEVENTY-SEVEN

Sligo Airport
Strandhill, County Sligo – Ireland

After going to ground for two days, Declan had finally been able to make his way out of the United States with the help of Fintan McGuire. With both the media and the law enforcement communities completely occupied by the foiled hostage crisis and the fear of other attempts around the country, Declan had been able to slip away undetected. Now as Fintan's Embraer Legacy 500 banked sharply to the left, he looked down on the mid-sized Irish town of Sligo, the crisp, navy blue waters of Ballysadare Bay and the North Atlantic Ocean beyond as the plane began its final approach from the east. Once the plane straightened out and descended, it bounced forcefully onto the runway and the engines screamed as they reversed to slow the corporate jet. Declan could see a line of four black Range Rovers waiting just off the runway, and as the craft taxied to a stop, the vehicles moved forward.

The cockpit door opened and the captain walked out. Declan stood as the man smiled and nodded at him and continued on towards the plane's rear exit. When the captain had opened the door and lowered the plane's wheelchair ramp, Declan thanked him, and descended to the pavement where the grouping of Range Rovers was now waiting.

"There's my old son," Fintan said with a huge smile, as Dean Lynch opened the rear door of one of the Range Rovers and the mop-haired entrepreneur exited the vehicle on his forearm crutches.

"What's all this?" Declan asked, as Fintan arrived at the edge of the ramp.

"You can't do everything you've done in the last week and a half and not expect a bit of a fanfare, mate," Fintan said, as the doors to several of the Range Rovers opened and people began to step out. Declan scanned the gathering group with a smile as Lord Dennis Allardyce, Tom Gordon and Shane O'Reilly arrived at the ramp. Declan smiled the biggest at the sight of Shane hobbling along on a set of crutches. "Now you two can have a race," he said, nodding towards Fintan.

"The hell with that, and these things, too," Shane said, in mock anger.

"Well done, Mr. McIver, very well done indeed," Lord Allardyce said, as he extended his hand and slapped Declan on the shoulder like a father would a son. "A lot of people are going to be very grateful when the dust settles and everything that's happened is revealed in its entirety."

Declan smiled. "I'll settle for a glass of iced tea and no one shooting at me for a while."

He looked past the small group at the sound of more doors opening and closing. Altair Nazari and Okan Osman exited the third Range Rover in the row of four.

"Now, here's two guys I didn't think I would see again for quite a while," he said, as the two approached and they all shook hands. "I thought you'd both be laid up on a beach in Eilat soaking up the sun and drinking martinis."

"And we will be, very soon," Osman said with a laugh. "We just had to make a brief pit stop first." He nodded in the direction of the Range Rover they'd just gotten out of. A tall man with thinning gray hair and a chubby face had left the SUV and was walking towards them.

"Prime Minister," Declan said as Asher Harel arrived and they shook hands firmly.

"Our meeting at airports is becoming a habit, Mr. McIver. I'm glad this time it's under better circumstances," the aged Israeli said.

"Yes sir. So am I."

"I don't want to bring your reunion to a halt, but there's a lot that needs to be discussed. Have you heard the latest news out of the United States?"

Declan shook his head. "No, sir. I've been in the air until just a little while ago. We made a two hour stop in Reykjavik, but I never left the plane."

Harel nodded. "The story developing out of the United States is quite frankly bizarre, to say the least. Senator David Kemiss has apparently committed suicide after meeting with a television reporter." Harel continued to catch Declan up on all of the claims Kemiss had made in the interview that was now being played throughout the world's major media.

"That lyin' bogtrotter," Shane said, when Harel had finished. "He actually took credit for what Declan and your men did?"

Declan grimaced as the Senator's statements from two nights prior flashed through his mind. Had Kemiss really had a partner? If so, was the man Kemiss had identified a further danger or had the events in Virginia been the culmination of his threats? At the time Declan had thought it was all just another desperate attempt by Kemiss to keep people from learning the truth, but now he wasn't so sure.

"I guess my point is," Harel continued, when no one else spoke, "that while your actions certainly saved a lot of lives, it doesn't seem to have done much to end the manhunt for you. You're still very much a wanted man."

Declan nodded. "Maybe this will help," he said, as he withdrew a red flash drive from his coat pocket. "It's the confession Kemiss gave us at his house the other night, the confession that led us to Baktayev. That should help the authorities piece everything together if we can get it into the right hands."

Harel took the drive and turned it over in his hand for a moment. "I'm sure it will. I'll make some calls to my contacts in Washington right away and a copy of this will be in the President's hands by tomorrow morning."

"That will certainly help in the long term," Allardyce said, "but we need to worry about the short term."

"Lynch and I are returning to Dublin as soon as we're done here," Fintan said. "Mullaghmore is your home for as long as you need. I would think you and the missus will be plenty safe there."

"Aye, that's grand," Declan said, "but what we'd really like is to go home, back to our old lives before all of this happened."

"I'm afraid," Lord Allardyce said, "that that is the one thing nobody can give you."

Everyone looked up at the aged aristocrat.

"The cat is out of the bag, as the Americans say," he continued. "Even if, God willing, the truth is discovered among all of the obfuscation Kemiss has put out, the media will not soon forget what they've learned about you. There's a new ripple in their reality and I don't think their fascination with it will go away for quite some time."

"You're saying that even when I'm proven innocent, the stigma of my past isn't going to leave us alone, that we can't return to the way things were, no matter what?"

Allardyce nodded. "I'm afraid that's exactly what I'm saying. While I believe your heroic actions in having brought this terrible plan to a happy ending will play very well for us all in the eyes of the government, I don't think the same can be said for your friends and business associates. Even if you're completely exonerated, and I'm certain you will be, what's their reaction going to be to all of this, to the news that you're a Russian trained terrorist that can probably kill them in more ways with a plastic fork than they can ever imagine?"

Declan shook his head and smiled. "I don't know. When you put it like that, I guess I don't see us getting many trick-or-treaters for the next few years."

The group of men laughed. In all honesty, Declan really didn't care how other people looked at him right now. There was no going back to undo past mistakes and if he'd learned one thing throughout the last week and a half, it was that every cloud had a silver lining. His training had saved both his and Constance's lives, in addition to hundreds of others, and he was confident that they would move on, together, and rebuild their lives.

He looked around the group towards the SUVs.

"We didn't tell her you were coming in, old son," Fintan said. "With the covert nature of your movements, we thought it wouldn't be very nice to get her hopes up in case we had to stash you away again or something."

Declan nodded.

"That's Mr. Hogan," Fintan said pointing to an older gentleman in the driver's seat of the fourth Range Rover. "He's the head of the staff at the estate and he'll take you home or to anywhere else you want to go. I'm sure your missus will be pleasantly surprised when you roll up to the front door."

As the black Range Rover made a sharp turn onto a roughly paved driveway and waited for a set of wrought iron gates supported by two stone columns to open, Declan finally felt as though he could stop running. In decades past the two-hundred year old estate he was entering had been a safe haven and he hoped it could remain that way for a while longer.

The SUV pulled through the gates and rumbled up the driveway past three large cottages until it arrived in the motor court of a three story stone house, its walls covered in dark green ivy. "All set then, Mr. McIver?" Alan Hogan said, as he left the driver's side and opened the rear door.

"Grand," Declan said, as he took hold of a small duffel bag and exited the vehicle.

The heavy wooden door of the house opened with a thunk and Constance startled both of them as she rushed out of the doorway. Declan dropped the duffel bag as she threw herself at him in a wide embrace, her long auburn hair spilling over his head as he lifted her off the ground. After rubbing his face and kissing him several times she said, "Hi," with a sheepish grin.

"Hi," he said, as he put her down and beamed at her. "Did you miss me much?"

She gave a small, nervous laugh and stood beside him as a portly woman in a white apron appeared in the doorway.

"Good evening, dear," Alan Hogan said, as he picked up Declan's duffel bag and moved to where his wife stood in the doorway. He gave the rosy faced woman a quick peck on the cheek and said, "It'll be grand to have a family around again, won't it?"

Inside, Declan and Constance followed the Hogans through the home's elegant foyer and into a large den where three brown leather sofas stood around a fireplace. A green area rug with multiple colors and designs woven into it covered the stone floor and it was obvious that the home had been unoccupied for quite some time. The surfaces near the fireplace and the window sills had been recently cleaned but the haste of the job was evident in the streaks made by the cleaners as they'd done the best they could in short notice.

Declan looked around the room as memories came rushing back at him. This house had once belonged to Eamon McGuire and he had used it as a base of operations for the Black Shuck team. Though it had at one time been the closest thing Declan had to a home as a young adult, he hadn't returned in many years. The last time he had seen the house was the night that he and Shane had discovered the murdered bodies of their teammates and officer commanding.

Declan walked to one of the wide windows beside the fireplace. He looked out over the expansive Irish countryside for a moment before turning back. Constance held her hand out and as he reached out and took hold of it, she pulled him into a tight embrace.

"Dinner's at eight, sir," Alan Hogan said, as he and his wife left the room, closing the door behind them.

"There are still a lot of things coming down the pipe at us," Declan said, returning Constance's embrace. "I wish I could say that it's all one hundred percent over and done with, but there's still going to be a lot of questions that need answering."

"I don't care about any of that right now. I only care about the fact that you're here with me and that we're both safe. Tomorrow we'll do whatever we have to, but tonight, right now, I just want to enjoy a few moments with you, alone."

Declan smiled. "Aye, that sounds grand. You know," he said, as he motioned out the window to the east where the last rays of the sun were shining on the rolling hills Ireland was so famous for, "I was born in a farmhouse just sixty miles from here."

"Funny you should mention being born," Constance said.

He looked back at her suddenly, suspicion rising in him and giving way to excitement as he saw her small smile get wider.

"I'm pregnant," she said. "You're going to be a father."

THE END

If you've enjoyed reading this book please consider leaving a review on Amazon.com, BN.com, or the website associated with your purchase. Reviews are a great help to authors and readers alike. Thank you!

Also by **Ian Graham**:

PATRIOTS & TYRANTS

A FEW WORDS
OF APPRECIATION...

This book has evolved over several years from a simple idea into the completed project it is now. During the long researching and writing process there have been many people who have supported and encouraged me and I would like to thank them here.

The Troubles is a conflict that has no modern equal in my opinion. In addition to the often shocking violence; the amount of spying, treachery and double dealing that became a part of daily life in Northern Ireland are difficult for an outsider such as myself to understand. **Joe McCoubrey** and **Harvey Black** were kind enough to offer me their expertise and have both helped me immensely.

Paul O'Brien, Andrew Scorah and **Rebecca Erickson** shared with me their knowledge of the political parties and inner workings of both the Irish, British and United States governments respectively and without them this book wouldn't be what it is.

There are several scenes throughout the book that feature characters who speak languages other than English. I would like to thank **Ian Kharitonov, Mark Greaney** and **Marcos Ramirez** for their help in understanding the languages and customs of Russia, Germany and Mexico. In addition to the altogether foreign languages, many of the characters live in or have backgrounds in Great Britain, Northern Ireland or the Irish Republic and while their langauges are technically English, they're still quite unique to an American like me. Thanks to **Andrew Scorah, Andrew Peters, Matt Hilton, Ian McAdam, Graham Smith, Stephen Cheshire** and **Col Bury** for helping me not to embarrass myself (too badly.)

Any book worth the pages (or screen) it's printed on cannot have become so without the help of a superb graphic designer, formatter and editor. Thanks to **Jane Dixon-Smith** for her excellent artwork, **Lucinda Campbell** for formatting the ebook version and to **Julie Lewthwaite** for her eagle eyed editing! Any mistakes that have wormed their way into this book are mine (due to my constant tweaking) and not hers.

And for all things flight related...**Colin Graham**, congratulations on earning your fixed wing pilots license, bro-ham.

In addition, to my family (**Cristina**, **Hannah**, **Kinley**, **Dennis**, **Karla** and **Brittany**) for their support and encouragement and for putting up with what started as a nagging idea and became a complete obsession. You'll be happy to know that I only have about 8 – 10 more books planned.

Lastly, to the people who lived through and continue to live with The Troubles, the first and second Chechen Wars, the Beslan school crisis, September the 11th, July the 7th and the other acts of terror referenced in this book; **God be with you, you are the real heroes.**

ABOUT THE AUTHOR

Ian Graham was born in New Hampshire on July 4th, the third generation of his family to share a birthday with the United States of America. His three main interests have always been politics, religion and history. The stories and characters he writes about are centered on the explosive conflicts created when the three intersect.

His writing has previously appeared in Action Pulse Pounding Tales alongside best selling thriller authors Matt Hilton, Stephen Leather, Adrian Magson, Zoe Sharpe and Joe McCoubrey.

He lives in the Blue Ridge Mountains of the eastern United States with his wife and two daughters.

VISIT WWW.IANGRAHAMTHRILLERS.COM FOR MORE

www.ingramcontent.com/pod-product-compliance
Lightning Source LLC
Chambersburg PA
CBHW070825260626
47170CB00007B/2268